The Twist

The Twist

James E. Causey

Copyright © 2011 by James E. Causey.

Library of Congress Control Number: 2011914781
ISBN: Hardcover 978-1-4653-5350-4
Softcover 978-1-4653-5349-8
Ebook 978-1-4653-5351-1

All rights reserved. No part of this book may be reproduced or transmitted in any form or by any means, electronic or mechanical, including photocopying, recording, or by any information storage and retrieval system, without permission in writing from the copyright owner.

This is a work of fiction. Names, characters, places and incidents either are the product of the author's imagination or are used fictitiously, and any resemblance to any actual persons, living or dead, events, or locales is entirely coincidental.

This book was printed in the United States of America.

To order additional copies of this book, contact:
Xlibris Corporation
1-888-795-4274
www.Xlibris.com
Orders@Xlibris.com

The world is a dangerous place, not because of those who do evil, but because of those who look on and do nothing.
—Albert Einstein

CHAPTER 1

"MOM, I KNOW we talked about you moving in with me about a year ago and you said no, but this is the third shooting near your house in the past three weeks."

"I'm going to be all right, Tray. I'm not going to let these gang bangers drive me outta my house," Thelma Brown says, a little upset from being awakened at the crack of dawn by her only child. "This could've waited 'til in the morning, baby."

When mom didn't want to discuss something, she had a way of changing the conversation, a trait that always irritated me.

"I saw your Uncle Willie this morning. He stopped by and dropped off some groceries."

"Mom, how many times do I have to tell you to stop taking stuff from him? I was going to take you to the grocery store this morning."

"Don't be like that, Tray," my mother says. "Willie said he had some business to take care of over here anyway."

"I bet he did," I say under my breath.

"He just dropped off some eggs, bread, greens . . ." my mother keeps talking.

"Mom, don't you know that Fat Willie is the main reason that the block changed? I don't want him coming to the house. I really wish you would think about moving in with me. You know I have plenty of room."

"Tray, I don't know anyone where you live. All my friends are over here. I'm going to be all right."

"I only live twenty-five minutes away."

"I know how far you live. You think gang bangers don't have cars? You can be shot anywhere. What time is it?" she asks.

"Mom, listen to me. You're all I got and I don't know what I'll do if something happened to you," I say, looking over at her picture on my dresser.

"I love you too, the big-time columnist. I always knew that you would make it, baby. Even when your father left us, I knew that I wouldn't have to worry about you. You always did the right thing."

"Well, let me do the right thing now and take you out of here."

"Tray, don't you realize that besides you, this house is the only thing that me and your father ever had together? I can't leave."

Knowing that it was a battle I could not win, I concede.

"OK, Mama. You know my door is open to you. I'm going to let you get some sleep." I glanced over at my blue neon alarm clock: 4:45 a.m.

I hang up the phone and struggle to pull my grandmother's huge quilt over my head, trying to drown out the sound of the television that I let play all night.

I can't believe it. Here it is March 20th, the first day of spring, and we're still getting that wet, break-your-back snow. I'm growing tired of this brew city weather. I guess the only good to come from this is that I don't have to shovel, one of the benefits of living in a condo on the city's lower east side.

As I clear my head from a night of writing, drinking, and flirting, I realize this is the first Saturday I've been able to sleep in for a long time and not worry about my annoying alarm clock startling me. I took the day off for my frat brother's bachelor party.

Glancing over at my laptop, I see at least a dozen new messages. I know one is from my frat brother Darnell, who is worried about his party tonight. I sit up on the bed and wipe the sleep from my eyes; I stretch toward the dusty black ceiling fan.

What a night! After writing a column on how the Bucks' defense was about as strong as a wet paper towel, I went to the grand opening of a new hot spot, Club Swank, with an atmosphere geared toward the "buppie" crowd–young black professionals, with plenty of disposable income–which really means they have yet to max out three credit cards.

After about an hour and a half of socializing with people pretending that their jobs are better than what they really are, Janet Russell, a Filipino woman I dated about six months earlier, came up from behind and gently grabbed my hand. "Hello, Travon," she says seductively as I turned around, quickly recognizing her voice.

"Hey, Janet, how are you?" I ask, glancing at her beautiful olive-colored skin and slanted sexy eyes.

"I'm surprised to see you here," Janet says. "Shouldn't you *still* be at work?"

"Nice low blow." Janet loved to tease me about being a workaholic and often complained that I was an all-work-and-no-play kind of guy. But I knew working hard kept me out of trouble.

Although Janet and I dated about eight months, our hectic schedules got in the way. I was either on the road, traveling with the Bucks, or going to Vegas to cover a fight. She was working as a middle school teacher, pursuing her MBA.

Our relationship mainly consisted of us sitting down and trying to pencil each other into a workable schedule.

Our week went something like this:

"How about dinner Monday?" I would ask, checking my schedule.

"I can't. I have a test first thing Tuesday in statistics," she would respond, flipping through her planner.

"How about Wednesday, baby?" she would ask.

"That won't work. I'm following the Bucks out on their West Coast swing for a column. That takes us to Saturday . . ."

It got to the point that we were seeing each other once or twice every three weeks, if we were lucky. And when we did get together, we tried to fit everything into that day, from sex to catching up on the latest movies.

When I told her that our relationship was not what I envisioned and that I thought about seriously dating someone else, she thought I was spoilt and didn't want to work hard at staying together.

Now we were standing in front of each other with alcohol in our hands, wondering if being apart for the last six months was worth it. As acid jazz drowned out idle conversation by other couples in the dimly lit nightclub, Janet and I attempted to catch up on old times.

After ten minutes of awkward chitchat, Janet asked if I'm seeing someone.

"Never mind, I don't want to know," she says quickly as she nervously took another sip of her green apple martini.

"No, I'm not seeing anyone—exclusively," is my response.

She looked up with her brown eyes and smiled. "Let's toast to single life," she says as we clinked our glasses.

After a few more drinks, Janet snuggles her five-foot-five frame a little closer to me at the bar as the wannabe playboy bartender replenished her drink and complimented her on her gorgeous eyes.

"Easy, Casanova," I warn the bartender, giving him the evil eye.

After Janet repeatedly brushed her leg against mine, we leave and end up at my place.

From the moment we enter my bedroom, I could sense Janet's apprehension. We stand in front of the bed, staring into each other's eyes and holding hands as if we didn't know what was going to happen next.

As I touch the thin shoulder straps of Janet's figure-hugging black dress, her breathing becomes ragged and her face becomes flushed.

Without taking my eyes off hers, I gently slide the dress down her body and let it fall to the floor. She slowly steps out of it and kicks it to the side.

"What?" she asks.

She was standing before me in a peach-colored bra and thong and black knee-high boots with three-inch heels.

"You're beautiful," I reply, placing my hands on her hourglass hips and pulling her close to the tent already set up in my pants.

"Travon," she starts to say. I place my lips upon her soft wet mouth and kiss her with a passion I hadn't felt in quite some time.

She moans.

I scoop her into my arms and lay her on my mink comforter. After tasting her lips, I slowly work my way down to her neck, planting kisses as I go.

"Travon, please don't stop," Janet begs as I continue to move slowly, hoping that she would not change her mind.

Not wanting her beautiful breasts to feel neglected, I cup each one in my hands and begin to suck hungrily until the nipples are standing at full attention. As I caress her erect nipples with my thumb and index finger, I continue kissing down her body until I reach her perfectly manicured mound of pleasure.

"Please don't tease me."

I deeply inhale her hot female scent and taste her slowly leaking nectar.

When she grabs my head, forcing me to taste more, I pull away, making her hotter.

"Make love to me like you used to," she whispers as I stand up and remove my pants, freeing my member from its prison.

I am still unbuttoning my shirt when Janet takes me into her mouth.

I make love to her tongue, as she entertains herself with her free hand. As I leak, she takes her wet hand and rubs my shaft faster before tasting the mixture of us.

I climb up on the bed and lie on top of her, slowly resting my weight upon my elbows as I slide into her moist place. The ten pounds she had gained since our breakup had gone straight to her hips, and I loved it.

"Oh, TraVon! Mmmmmmmh!" she moans, wrapping her arms and legs around me tighter. Her muscular legs squeeze me like a python, and I am her prey.

I wrap my hands around her ass, and as I thrust deeper, Janet's eyes widen and when her mouth open, I insert my tongue, which she eagerly accepts, sucking on it as I stroke her faster. With every stroke, she gets wetter and the scent of our lovemaking fills the room.

When I feel myself starting to lose control, I pause so that she can feel my throbs.

"One, two, three, four," she counts as my member jerks inside her.

As more blood rushes to my shaft, she can feel me swelling up inside her.

"Travon, you are so big," she whispers into my ear as she squeezes me tighter.

When she senses that I am losing the battle of keeping my juices contained, she orders me to release them.

"Cum in me, Travon!" she says, moving her hips in a circular motion to make her demand come true.

When I explode, my hips jerk forward, propelling my fluid deep into her womb. With every shot she screams, "Yes! Baby! Yes! Give me every drop."

We make love three times, in every position imaginable.

It felt like old times, comfortable sexually, but neither one of us willing to fully give our souls even as our bodies moved in perfect rhythm. Our escapade takes us to new heights. As Janet begins to climax, she enters an altered state of consciousness. Her eyes close, her muscles tense, and tears roll down her face and onto my arms as I hold her. I pull her closer into my chest. She weeps quietly until she falls asleep.

As I watch the rhythmic rise and fall of Janet's chest, I wonder what she is dreaming about. Propped up on one elbow, I gaze down at her and lightly stroke her hair so as not to disturb the sleeping beauty.

My mind begins to drift off into its own dream.

* * *

"Hey little man," Fat Willie says, walking up to me as I sit on the porch, eagerly awaiting my father's arrival to take me to the car show for my tenth birthday. "Hey, Uncle Willie," I say standing up and embracing my play uncle. "Where's my dad?" I asked. "I thought both of you were taking me to the car show today?"

Fat Willie sits on the stoop in front of my mother's house and pulls me down beside him.

"Tray, I've got some bad news for you and your mother, son," he says.

"What is it, Uncle Willie?" I ask impatiently. "Did something happen to my dad? Is he hurt?"

"Calm down, Tray," Willie says.

"Nothing bad happened to your father, but he's not coming," Willie says, pausing to look down at the chalk outline I made on the sidewalk of my father, him, and me going to the car show.

"Oh," I respond, disappointed. "Well, at least we can still go, Uncle Willie," I say.

"You don't understand, Tray," Willie says, as if to brace me for the blow of his next words. "Tray, your pops ain't gonna be 'round here no more."

"He wanted me to tell you that he thinks you will be better off without him being around. He said he needs to get his career going as a saxophonist before he can be a good dad to you and a husband to your mother."

The more Willie talked, the less I heard him speak. I stopped hearing him after he said my pops wasn't coming around anymore. The reasons why pops didn't want to be around didn't matter. I felt like I was in a dream; more like a nightmare, and I could not wake up.

"Tray," Willie said as I continue to stare off into space. "Travon, say something, son."

"Huh," was the only word I could muster.

Willie continues, "Look, Tray, I know you're hurting right now and this is a lot for you to take in, but know this, son, I'm always here for you—no matter what, Tray."

"Your father wasn't man enough to tell you all this to your face, so maybe it's best he isn't around anyway."

"It's gonna be a bit rough, Tray, but you gotta man up now! You don't have a choice, but I'll be there to guide you along the way. I'll do whatever I can, son."

"Tray, do you hear me? Tray! Boy, do you hear me!"

* * *

When I wake up reaching for Janet at about four o'clock in the morning, she is gone.

She leaves me a note written in bronze lipstick on my dresser mirror, saying that she still loves me. The message is brief. She wants to know if we could ever be one again, in and outside the bedroom.

For too long, I went to bed with women before I ever got to know anything about them, or even knew their last name. Unfortunately, when I did get to know them, they were never the type of woman I would want to take home to my mother.

Janet and I still have a strong connection. I believe it was that magnetism that drew us to the club last night and brought us back to my place early this morning. But if Janet and I were going to make it this time, I knew we would have to start with a clean slate.

CHAPTER 2

I HAVE TO MAKE sure everything is going to be perfect for my frat brother's bachelor party tonight. I also need to tell my adopted uncle that although I appreciate him doing stuff for my mother, his going over to my mother's house could bring unwanted drama to her.

Even though I went to the Twist—a dark, seedy, hole-in-the-wall strip club—a month ago to make the arrangements with the club's owner, Willie, on the number of girls and the price, I don't trust him. As long as I've known my uncle, he has usually been up to no good, shady, just like his business.

I decide to give Willie a call to make sure everything is still on for eleven o'clock tonight. As I search my wallet for Willie's signature business card, depicting the silhouette of two women kissing with the words "Cum to the Twist to get off" encircling them, my phone rings.

"Hello."

"Yeah, is this the nappy-headed kid?" a guttural voice on the other end asks, joking about my dusty brown dreadlocks, which are now down to my shoulders.

"This is Travon," I respond. "Is this Fat Will . . ." I ask before I'm cut off by the man I've known as far back as I can remember.

"This is Big Willie. So I got you five girls coming over tonight. I did right by you this time, Tray," he boasts.

"Willie, my mother told me that you stopped by the house yesterday."

"Yeah, I did. I dropped off a few groceries," Willie says, over the thumping music playing in the background of his club.

"The block is hot, Willie, and I know that a lot of people would like to see some bad things happen to you," I say.

"Wait a second, young blood. I raised you like you were a son, and I've known your mother before your ass was even born. Do you think I would put her or you in harm's way?"

Around Willie I always felt safe, even though a lot of people around him always ended up dead. He was always a magnet for violence, but he's right, as long as I can remember, nothing bad ever happened to us.

"You ain't got nothing to worry about, young blood. Now are you ready to talk business?"

Willie, a sixty-something, pot-bellied, ex-street pimp, doesn't let anyone get away with calling him "Fat" except me.

When I was a kid boxing at the King Center, I remember a much thinner Willie driving around town in his Big Bird colored '78 Coupe de Ville with bone-white interior and fat, white walled tires. Willie always traveled with three or more scantily clad women. He was a gorilla pimp–the big, high-yellow fly guy who would backhand his women in a heartbeat, if his money wasn't right. Willie maintains a menacing look, even for an old-timer. He was loved by few and feared by most; just the way he wanted it.

One thing Willie loved just as much as pimping was boxing. While I was a teenager, he was involved in my amateur boxing career. He always made sure that I had all the proper equipment, training, and money in my pocket because he said he didn't want me to end up like him, surrounded by leeches.

When he would come to amateur boxing shows at the Eagle's Club, with its painted murals of boxing legends Joe Louis, Muhammad Ali, and Floyd Patterson, Willie would tell anyone within earshot that I was his boy, oftentimes working up a sweat by cheering for me before the first bell even sounded. After three rounds, Willie was usually hoarse from screaming: "Stick and move, Tray!" "Hit him, Tray!" And I didn't disappoint Willie either, winning my first twenty-five fights. When I first lost a bout, in a controversial decision, he was the first person there to console me. When I won the Golden Gloves in Rockford, Illinois, Willie surprised me with one of his best girls–Rose.

I lost my virginity to Rose that night. I was fourteen, Rose was thirty-three. Although I lost my innocence to Rose, she showed me how to find a G-spot. Rose was a great teacher and I was a more-than-willing student. Best of all, she took her time. Sex education with Rose was my favorite subject, and I put in extra effort so as not to disappoint her.

From Willie, I learned a lot by observing how he treated women. He loved his mother and supplied her with expensive furniture, jewelry, money, and cars. He visited her every Sunday and took her to Metropolitan Baptist Church, a chapel just a few blocks from where most of his women got down on their knees to make money late into the night. Although he never went inside the church, he gave his mother a hundred dollars to put in the offering for him every week. When the church needed something, Willie had it done, from a new roof to new robes for the choir. All Willie's mother had to do was mention that the church needed something, and Willie did it. His mother was the only person who could make the big teddy bear cry.

Although he treated his mother like a queen, he treated his hos like dogs. When Rose wanted to quit the ho game after a john raped her, Willie broke her arm and sent her back onto the streets the next day in a white cast signed by him. "You are my property," Willie told her. "You stop when I tell you to stop! Until then you keep making that money!"

The john who beat Rose was found shot dead a couple of weeks later in an alley, about a block from where Rose was attacked. He was a married banker from the suburbs with three children. The story was all over the news. Some people speculated that he was the victim of a gang initiation. Others said he was being blackmailed and got himself into trouble.

Willie went to the guy's funeral with Rose, which raised eyebrows. Both Willie and Rose were dressed in matching money-green outfits and didn't blend in among the sea of black suits and dresses. Some suspected that Willie had something to do with it, but without any proof, what was anyone going to do?

Some speculated that Willie went to the funeral to prove that he was untouchable. Others said he just wanted to send a message: "Cross me and you will end up in a pine box." Willie would hurt anyone who caused pain to his girls.

Willie never talked about his business. A lot of what you heard came from the streets, where he was a living legend. When he was shot five times in the back by a rival pimp during a bar fight and survived, his legend grew. Willie always had problems with other pimps because he was usually moving in on their territory and stealing their women. He said the other pimps were just jealous because his stable grew to more than twenty-five girls.

As a kid, I knew I didn't want to be like him, living above a strip club and always looking over my shoulder.

"Travon! Tray!" bellows the voice on the other end, snapping me out of my daydream. "That's going to be $200 dollars when they show up. By the way, these girls are better than the ones you picked out. I got these girls from an old friend in Chicago who owed me a favor. You know I'm cutting you a deal, right?"

"Wait a second Willie, I already gave you eight hundred dollars and now you going to hustle me out of another two? And how are you changing the girls on me at the last minute?" But I know he has me in a bind, regardless.

"Well, that was before you got that promotion, Travon," Willie says matter-of-factly, smacking his gum loudly.

I received a hefty raise and my *own* column after the National Press Foundation named me sportswriter of the year for my in-depth look at the corrupt promoters of boxing. The series caused the Nevada State Boxing Commission to do its own investigation that landed seven promoters before a federal grand jury. I'm sort of shocked that Willie still keeps up with my affairs. I have not talked to him about my personal business in years. However, the freckle-faced entrepreneur–who still has a flair for brightly-colored suits and expensive cars decked out to the point of gaudiness–has a knack for knowing the business of people he has vested interest in.

To be honest, I owe a lot to Fat Willie; he kept me out of trouble when I was a kid. After my pops left, I started running the streets with a gang called the Tray-Nine Boys. Willie approached me with an alternative to the street life. I will never forget how he approached me after my posse robbed a corner liquor store.

"I know you're a tough kid and all, Travon, but you don't know these streets like I do," he said when he stopped me in the neighborhood one day. "You're going to end up dead or locked up." Willie's honest reality is something my father should have shared with me, but he split when I was ten.

Willie got me interested in amateur boxing, which was his passion and soon became my obsession. I became a gym rat, living and breathing boxing, seven days a week.

I remember watching old boxing tapes at Willie's house and him telling me I could be just as good as Sugar Ray Leonard or Tommy "The Hitman" Hearns.

"You see, Tray, Ray is a killer. He smiles on those commercials and interviews, but that boy is a killer. I want you to be just like that in the ring. A killer," he said never taking his eyes off his huge floor-model Zenith television set, covered with boxing memorabilia.

When I started to box and win awards, they ended up on top of the Zenith as well.

Willie not only studied boxers, he knew them. Mixed among the awards were pictures of Willie and Leonard, Hearns, John "The Beast," Mugabi, and Julian "The Hawk" Jackson.

I'll never forget how he took me to this smoky little corner bar to see the first Leonard vs. "Marvelous" Marvin Hagler fight. The owner of the bar didn't want to let me in out of fear of being busted by the police. Willie asked him if he was more worried about getting busted for having a kid in the bar or for stealing cable. Needless to say, the bar owner let us in.

I got my first buzz that night in the basement of the bar by sneaking a taste of Korbel from Willie's glass, when he went to the bathroom. Willie didn't even notice because he was so caught up in the fight. I didn't remember much; I fell asleep on Willie's shoulder.

The next day, Willie held a Ray Leonard party at his house and invited the entire block. Everybody showed up. Willie, always the showman, had three grills going with burgers, chicken, ribs, hotdogs, corn, and more alcohol than an Arab liquor store. Later that night, his backyard was filled with women dancing to all sorts of booty-shaking music and men getting lap dances–and some even more.

When everyone under the age of eighteen was told to leave, Willie let me stay to see how "the grown folks get down." "Getting down" consisted of heavy drinking, heavy petting, heavy gambling, getting high, and a whole lot of cursing.

"Nigga, I told you I would give you your money when I get it!" yelled the neighborhood fiend, cross-eyed Nate, who was talking jive.

Nathaniel "Nate" Briggs loved to get high and gamble, but he never had the money to pay off his debts. Briggs, a Vietnam vet, had the kinkiest, big-tooth comb breaking naps you ever wanted to see, but that was offset by his clear dark skin that always seemed to glow, even in the winter.

Standing about five-foot-eight, Briggs was strong for his size and still had the muscles to prove it. He always walked around with his shirt off or pulled behind his neck to show off his abs and broad chest, which made him appear taller than he was. He did odd jobs in the neighborhood—cleaning up yards, fixing lawnmowers. You just had to keep an eye on him because your lawnmower could end up in the hands of the dope man. People loved Nate, though, because he could fix anything for $10 and he never complained about anything you asked him to do.

When Briggs was clean, which was rare, he was the nicest guy you would ever want to meet. But when he was high or seeking that next fix, forget about it.

He got the nickname Cross-eyed Nate because of a wandering right eye. He was injured when a tank he was riding in ran over a mine in 'Nam. The explosion caused major nerve damage to the right side of his face.

I preferred to call him Dr. Jekyll and Mr. Hyde because of his split personality. When he was high, Mr. Hyde came out.

"Shut up, Nate, talking crazy before I send you home with all that yelling and shit," Willie said to Briggs, who was arguing with a bunch of guys he was trying to cheat at blackjack.

When he needed a quick fix and nobody gave him the money to do it, Nate always talked about killing somebody. His famous line was "I killed about forty men in 'Nam so nobody's gonna miss a nigga in the ghetto."

Although most people couldn't stand Briggs when he was high, those were the times when he served as Willie's personal clown. Willie never laughed much, but Nate was his regular court jester. But Nate, like everyone else knew the one thing that was never joked about: Willie's family.

Willie had two sons and both were locked up. One was doing life in prison for a homicide; the other was doing time for armed robbery of a liquor store while high on heroin. Willie never talked about them, visited them, or accepted their collect calls. When I asked him why, he said he had to worry about people that he could help, like me.

I guess he did have an interest in keeping me on the straight and narrow, although that won't stop him from stiffing me for another $200 tonight.

"OK, Willie, whatever," I say.

"It's just business, Tray. Just business," Willie says with a chuckle before hanging up.

* * *

I had been at the liquor store earlier in the day and the trunk of my Lexus IS 300 is filled with Jim Beam, Bacardi rum, Korbel, several two-liters of Coca-Cola, and four, 30-packs of MGD. Now all I have to do is make sure the man of the hour, Darnell Jackson, is ready for tonight.

Just as I'm about to call Darnell, he calls me.

"What's up frat?" I answer the phone.

"Hey frat," Darnell replies.

"So, you ready for tonight?" I ask, hoping I can get Darnell through tonight and down the aisle in less than twenty-four hours.

"I don't know about this marriage thing, frat. You know I love Taylor with all my heart, but I don't know if I'm ready to take that leap." As Darnell talks, I search through my iPod for the right jam to put him at ease, at least for the moment.

Darnell stands six-foot-three and weighs about 215 pounds. His head is clean-shaven; his way of hiding a receding hairline. His skin is the color of sand and I don't think he has ever had a pimple in his life, though he does have dimples. Lucky bastard! Even with his athletic build and chiseled good looks, Darnell is still extremely shy when it comes to the opposite sex.

A lot of people think we're biological brothers because Darnell is only an inch taller and we have the same build. The differences in our mentalities, however, are great when it comes to dealing with women. While I have never had a problem meeting or talking to women, Darnell is the true definition of a "shy brother." Before he met his soon-to-be bride, Darnell dated women through his job as a welfare counselor. Although it was against his company's policy to date clients or coworkers, Darnell often broke those rules in the female-dominated field.

He only stopped after his friend and fellow counselor, Todd, got one of his clients pregnant—a woman who already had five kids. After Darnell's only means of dating dried up, he moved on to the Internet for help.

Frat was an Internet pimp. The Internet offered Darnell a safe haven to come out of his shell and say all the things he could not say to a woman, face-to-face. He had women in every major city, not that it did him any good since he never went anywhere. He also honed his skills to know what weaknesses to look for in a woman's profile. If someone said they were "seeking for a long-term commitment," Darnell was the guy.

If a woman said she was looking for "friends first," Darnell knew how to play that role as well. He was a chameleon, changing into whatever a woman was hoping to find. If she was "of ample size," guess what? He loved a woman with a few extra pounds. "More cushion for the pushing," he told a woman in Dallas. After a couple weeks of chatting and exchanging numbers, she flew the 1,100 miles to Milwaukee to visit him.

One so-called "regular girl" he met from Jackson, Mississippi, took the twenty-three hour train ride to visit and didn't want to go home after sleeping with him. She was a little crazy.

Everything was a big game to him until he came across Taylor Kincade's page.

Taylor had no pictures on her page, no fancy background, only a simple description of herself: "SBF looking to meet interesting people. I love books, intellectuals, and travel. I'm not going to describe myself because I'm looking for more than relationships based solely on the physical. If you're a playboy, cheater, or someone who is into playing games, don't even bother to drop me a line. I don't have the time."

From their first e-mails, Taylor challenged his mind. She wanted to know who he was and not what he had. She refused to fall for the cliché lines and quickly told him that he had to come at her much better than that. The banter between them went on for weeks.

When he told me that this woman was the one for him, I thought she was out of his league, considering that frat's reading consisted of the jokes in his monthly Playboy magazine, and the extent of his traveling was flying to Las Vegas with me to gamble and catch a heavyweight title fight.

After two months of chatting with Taylor, he finally snagged a date. They spent all of their free time together. I hardly ever saw Darnell anymore. When he introduced me to Taylor, I quickly understood why all of Darnell's free time was consumed. Taylor had it going on: honey-brown skin, gray eyes, long brown hair to the middle of her back and a body that would make Jake proud. In addition, this woman was both book and street smart.

The daughter of a lieutenant general, Taylor was used to being treated like a princess, but she didn't let that go to her head, which made her even more beautiful. Now, I knew that I shouldn't be lusting after my best friend's woman, but this natural beauty was definitely a jaw-dropper.

Taylor turned out to be a great fit for Darnell. The two traveled together, and she even got him to join a book club. Darnell was truly whipped. But like Willie told me when I was a kid, there's nothing wrong with being whipped if you both are in love.

Taylor taught Darnell how to love again after the rough relationship he had with his daughter's mother. Angie Horton hurt Darnell and wouldn't let him see his daughter. She ultimately moved to California to be with a man she met on the Internet.

When Angie left, Darnell turned into a Rottweiler, something completely out of his nature. When he wasn't picking up random women weekly at clubs, he was searching for easy pickings on the Internet.

When Taylor popped up into Darnell's life, she taught him not to go through women like you would the daily newspaper. Ultimately, she saved his life.

Soon I find the right song and I plug it into my Bose speakers.

"Frat listen," I say as Darnell continues to babble. "Frat listen!"

> Just one look at you
> And I know it's gonna be
> A lovely daaaay
> .... lovely day, lovely day, lovely day ...
> .... lovely day, lovely day, lovely day ...

"Oh snaps," Darnell says. "That song takes me back."

When Darnell and I were on line, Big Brother Wavy G. made us sing Bill Withers' "Lovely Day" while doing odd things like cleaning toilets with toothbrushes and painting his apartment to build brotherhood.

"Remember when we were supposed to be learning our chapter history and we crept out to that AKA party to see that fine-ass girl. What was her name?" Darnell asks.

"Yeah, we thought Wavy was out of town but he was at the party and he saw us," I say cracking up with laughter. "I thought he was going to kill us."

"He damn near did," Darnell replies. "We both took so much wood that night."

"Yeah, hell week came a month early for us," I say, reminiscing over how far we both had come.

But through it all, I always had Darnell's back covered and he mine. Our friendship was much deeper than that of frat brothers. We could really be honest with each other and tell the other one when he was doing wrong, something most friends can't do because of fear of losing their friendship.

One thing I know for sure is that the woman Darnell plans to marry is a good woman for him.

CHAPTER 3

MY FRATERNITY PUT me in charge of all the arrangements, because most of the men had wives who would kill them if they knew their husbands were going to be spending their grocery money on strippers.

When I picked out the girls at the Twist a month earlier, I tried to give my brothers a sampling of everything: a chunky girl with several rolls; a girl so skinny that you could see her ribs; a milky–white girl, a dark and lovely girl; and a girl so sweet and nice that she could be your sister. I picked a caramel-colored sister with long hair and a pear shape; a small Asian girl with a flat ass; a thin sister who was the spitting image of Whitley Gilbert from *A Different World*; a stacked sister for all the tittie men; and Jackie, a woman with so much ass that after she walked in her left and right cheek followed about three minutes later. Everything was going to be on and cracking.

But now that Fat Willie was throwing a monkey wrench into the plans, we could very well end up with female impersonators. Although I wanted everything to be perfect, it wasn't worth stressing over too much because I knew the mixture of alcohol, thumping beats, and weed could make Suge Knight look like a G-string diva. Quite honestly, my frat wouldn't care as long as there was plenty of ass shaking and the women were not stuck up.

But before I pick up Darnell, I need to get some sleep. As I start to doze off, my landline rings. After a couple of clicks and no sound on the answering machine, my cell phone chimes in with that silly "Laffy Taffy" song. Damn, I'm going to strangle my little cousin for downloading that ringtone into my phone.

"Hello!" I yell into the phone, without checking the number.

"What's wrong with you?" is the terse response from Nicole on the other end.

Nicole Branton is a woman I met about a year ago while buying a couple of suits for my job interview in Orlando, Florida. Although there was no immediate chemistry between us, I thought we could easily be friends. Nicole is a dark-brown honey. She stands five-foot-seven, with small perky breasts and muscular, well-toned thighs that would give KFC a run for its money. Nicole always wears a jet-black weave about midway down her back. She keeps her hair done on the regular; I didn't know it wasn't her hair until the first time I ran my fingers through it during sex and became caught on one of her tracks. She was a good sport about it though.

After hanging out for a couple of months, I realized that we had some things in common but not enough on my part to build a relationship.

Although Nicole is educated, child-free and attractive, sexually she doesn't hold my interest.

For a long time, I juggled many women, a behavior stemming from being introduced to mature women at such an early age. Willie definitely didn't do me any favors by setting me up with many of his women during a time when I wasn't even old enough to drive.

Sexually, I was never one to experience moving to first or second base with a young woman—rites of passage for an adolescent boy. When most young men were talking about their first kiss, dry humping or finger fucking, I was having sex with some of the hottest women in town, all dimepieces. So whenever I met a woman who failed to pique my interest sexually right away, I really didn't want anything to do with her. This pattern carried on throughout the years.

As I got older, my relationships with women grew to the point of not just cheating but having two or more women in the same bed, at the same time. It was surprisingly easy to find women willing to break this ultimate taboo. Multiple sexual relationships helped me avoid commitment, because I didn't want to risk being hurt.

Although I didn't realize it at the time, this lifestyle was killing my soul. For too long, I was allowing my soul to connect with women I had no interest in other than on a sexual level. A wise woman once told me to be careful about who you sleep with because when you do you share souls, and one day you may come across a woman whose soul may not want to let go easily.

My grandfather, who helped raise me, had a better philosophy. He said: "Boy, don't ever sleep with anyone that you wouldn't want to be the mother of your child."

I was hardheaded though, besides I thought "safe" women were boring or not as fine or experienced in bed.

Darnell told me I was his idol because of my sexual prowess, but to be honest, I idolized him and his relationship with Taylor, who was definitely wifey material. She taught Darnell that a real man does not prove his masculinity by sleeping around. And that no matter how bad he felt from his relationship with Angie, sleeping around would not ease his pain.

When I met Nicole, I didn't want a sexual relationship with her, because I was scared that I was going to hurt her like I did with so many women before. I also did not see a future with her.

"So are you going to be good tonight?" Nicole asks, trying to read into my every word over the phone.

"I'm always good," I say. "You know that."

"That's what I'm afraid of," Nicole snaps back. "That's exactly what I'm afraid of."

Nicole is extremely jealous, something I've never gotten used to. She doesn't think any man can be friends with someone of the opposite sex, which may explain why she doesn't have any male friends.

"Nicole, I was about to lie down and get some sleep for tonight, OK?"

"Why do they always put you in charge of stuff like that?" she asks.

"Because, Nicole, I'm the only one who's still single. Darnell is my best friend and I know how to negotiate prices."

"I just hope you aren't negotiating anything else on the side," she says under her breath after a short pause.

I know Nicole's pattern so well. First, she'll start an argument, and then she'll want to come by and see me to make me late. I really don't want to play that game tonight because I want to focus on my brothers.

"I was going to drop something off for you that I picked up from the mall today," Nicole says, hoping that I will invite her over. "And don't you need me to twist your locks tonight?" Man, does she know how to lay it on.

She is right about one thing. My locks do need a fresh twist, but I'm not going to make it that easy for her.

"That would be cool, but you know I have to pick up Darnell."

"I wasn't planning on staying long," she says.

To avoid any conflict, I invite her over with hopes that I can at least get in about two hours of sleep before she shows up.

With Nicole, I always fall for the same thing over and over again, sort of like when Lucy pulls the football away from Charlie Brown every time he gets ready to kick it.

* * *

Buzzzzzz! Buzzzzzzzzzzzzzzz!

What tha! Who is that ringing my doorbell like a maniac? I glance over at the alarm clock; the neon blue light reads 7:49 p.m. I put on my slippers and head toward the intercom system to buzz in Nicole. Soon, I hear the clicking of heels coming down the hallway. "Remember to stay cool, Tray," I think as I open the door.

"Hey, sleepyhead," Nicole says giving me a kiss on the lips as I open the door.

"How are you?" I ask, greeting her with a hug as she crosses the threshold of my condo.

"Did you go out last night, Travon? I called up until five o'clock in the morning and didn't get an answer," she asks in her probing style that just irritates me.

Before I can answer, she hands me a garment bag.

"This is a little present I got you for your promotion."

Women have spoiled me throughout my life and Nicole is no exception. She buys me gifts for any occasion, but my favorites are the "just because" gifts.

As I take the black garment bag, I feel like a kid in a candy store. She often spoils me with clothes to the point that I literally have no closet space left in my two-bedroom condo. I never ask her how she pays for $700 suits, $200 shoes or $100 shirts. I don't want to know. When it comes to gifts and Nicole, we follow the "don't ask, don't tell" policy.

As I unzip the bag, Nicole can hardly control herself. "Do you like it?" she yells before I can get the blue and white, athletic cut pinstripe suit out of the bag.

"It's gorgeous," I reply, as she holds the jacket up for me to slip my right arm in and slide it on. Nicole is a great saleswoman and she's equally good at selling herself to others about how good a woman she is.

"When I saw it, I had to get it for you," she says. "You know your promotion came on our one-year anniversary of when we first met. Don't you remember?"

"I guess it slipped my mind," I reply not knowing if she's telling the truth or not.

Nicole and I only had sex a couple of times early in the relationship and then she got all religious on me. It didn't bother me that much because quite frankly she wasn't that experienced in bed anyway. Because I valued her more as a friend, it was an easy transition for me. However, for Nicole, going against her beliefs just to sleep with me those two times meant that we were a couple.

"Thank you Nicole, but you shouldn't have," I say as I slip the pants on. Although I know every expensive gift I take from her links us closer, I just cannot stop myself from taking them.

"So let's talk about tonight," Nicole says as she saunters over to my couch, pulling me by the hand.

"What do you want to talk about? I need to get ready soon and pick up Darnell."

"I wish you didn't hang around those nasty women all the time," Nicole says, looking at me with those deep, chocolate-brown eyes of hers. "You know I love you, and I would do anything for you, Travon. Why don't you love me in that way?" Her eyes start to water up.

Why does she have to get all deep on me now?

"I don't know if this is the time to talk about this right now. You know I like you Nicole, and I value our friendship, but I told you in the very beginning that I was not looking for a relationship." I know this will open up a conversation that I do not want to have. Not here. Not now.

"Well, why did you sleep with me, Travon?" she asks, brokenhearted. "What are you scared of? I don't understand. I'm a good woman. I do things for you that

I have never, and I mean *never*, done for any other man, and now you tell me that I'm wasting my time."

For the first time in my life I'm being completely honest with a woman, and I'm still the bad guy.

"Nicole, I realize that sleeping with you ten months ago was a mistake. I consider you a very close friend. But I told you months ago that we should just be friends."

"So what is it, Travon? Is it that my ass ain't big enough for you? My breasts ain't big enough for you? Is it that I'm not as nasty as all the women you had before you met me?"

As the conversation turns to anger, the phone rings.

"*Girl shake your Laffy Taffy. Your Laffy Taffy. Your Laffy Taffy. Hey, Missus Bubble Gum, I'm Mr. Chico Stick. I wanna duh-na-na, oh, cause you so thick . . .*"

Man, I never thought I would be glad to hear that song. I rush to grab my cell phone in my bedroom.

"Hello," I say, but the call has gone to voicemail. "Damn, who is this calling me with a restricted number."

Nicole has followed me into the bedroom, and taken her tone down a couple of notches.

"Baby, I just get so jealous because I love you so much," she says. Tears start to roll down her chubby cheeks.

"Well, I love you too, Nicole–as a friend," I say, staring into her eyes. "Nicole, what we have is special and I don't want to mess that up."

When I first met Nicole, my own mother told me not to hurt her.

"She's so sweet," my mother told me. "Now don't do her like you did all those other girls."

It's funny how my own mother knew that I was bad in relationships.

Actually, as I think back on it, I haven't ever been that good of a boyfriend. I was always into the conquest.

At twenty-eight, this is really the first time in my life that I have been honest with a woman I really have feelings for–but they are not the feelings that you have when you know you are truly in love. You see, while I do love Nicole, I am not *in* love with her, and she can't understand why.

Besides, something is just not right about Nicole and I can't put my finger on it. It's like she has a secret life that I never could become a part of. Sort of like Martin Lawrence's friend Tommy from *Martin*–I've never quite known what she does for a living.

I know Nicole wants to be married; in fact, I think she is more in love with falling in love, than love itself.

An article in *Essence* magazine said "Blacks are the most un-partnered society in America. Only 34 percent of blacks are married, compared to 57 percent of whites."

Nicole does not want to remain in the unmarried category.

"We can be good together, baby, why you don't see that?" she asks.

To be honest, I have been with enough women to know what I want and what I don't. Unfortunately for both of us, being with Nicole is not where I want to be.

"I can't keep doing this," she says. "I can't keep waiting for you to see that I'm the one for you."

Nicole walks out of my bedroom, a room she hoped to one day share with me, grabs her purse off the coffee table and walks out the door and out of my life.

Honesty is a bitch!

CHAPTER 4

AFTER HITTING THE shower, shaving, and picking out my outfit, I douse myself in Eternity for Men and use two of my locks to tie my hair up in the back. Most of my friends describe me as a muscular, clean-shaven, Bob Marley. I don't mind the comparison, considering that I was the first person to bring dreadlocks into the newsroom.

When I first walked into the newsroom with newly-twisted hair, I didn't know what to expect from my editor, a loudmouth from Philadelphia who was hired to shake up the sports department. He was caught up in his own hype, and everybody knew it. Although he was married, this forty something, charcoal-black man with chapped lips, and an always-cracking voice due to his two-pack-a-day smoking habit, loved to ogle the interns hired every fall and summer.

"Did you see the ass on that girl with the black hair that started Friday?" Marcus Hicks asked me, seeking some sort of affirmation that he was still cool.

I did little to give him the satisfaction. "I didn't notice," I said laughing inside, while typing up my column.

"You must be blind or I'm working you too hard if you missed that. I'd leave my wife for her, but she'd end up taking half and I worked too hard for this."

I knew that my career would never take off with him as the alpha male of the pack, or shall I say the department. I knew he didn't like me much, but he loved my talent of getting athletes to open up. However, Marcus only kissed my ass when the managing editor was within earshot.

Although he had a hard time giving compliments to others, he was very good at bragging about how great he was.

Once, when I asked him to write me a letter of recommendation for a journalism fellowship, Marcus penned this:

To whom it may concern:

I don't know Travon very well but what I do know of him, I think my mother would have liked.

You see my mother raised me and my two sisters by herself and fought to keep me off the streets so that I could succeed. My mother continues to be my strength and she remains a pillar in the community.

When I graduated from a tough public school in Philly, my mother told me that this was just the beginning, and she was right.

After graduating from Syracuse University in upstate New York with a journalism degree, my mother was also there.

Now as the leader of the sports department, my mother is still there encouraging me to do more.

You see, I really don't know Travon that well, but what I can tell you is that my mother would have liked him because he's under my wing.

If you choose Travon for this fellowship, you will not be disappointed. You will have someone that has learned from the best. Me.

Sincerely,
Marcus Hicks
Managing Sports Editor
Milwaukee Guardian

Of course I could not use this letter for the fellowship, but after reading it, I knew I had to choose. I could either wait until Marcus caught a sexual assault charge for trying to cop a feel on one of the interns or try to move to a larger market to see how good I could really be.

I wasn't eager to leave Milwaukee, but the city was really starting to wear on me with the escalating racial tensions, high taxes, high minority unemployment, and the longer-than-ever winters.

It's the middle of March and the temperatures are still hovering around twenty degrees. With the forecast calling for five to eight inches of the fluffy, white stuff this week, my patience is running a little thin.

I guess the straw that broke the camel's back came after I asked Marcus if he had enough money in the department's budget to send me to a sports journalism convention in Atlanta, and he said the budget wouldn't allow it. Several months later however, he went, and took his fine-ass receptionist. I would not have cared, but he spent three of the five days on some swank golf course, and she came back two shades darker from tanning all day.

I remember asking Marcus how the conference went and his response was simply, "You missed it, Tray . . . the honeys came out to this one."

While Marcus was golfing on some posh green in suburban ATL, I was busy keeping the department together by breaking three big stories for the front page.

It was actually quite refreshing to have the loud yuck mouth gone for an entire week. You could tell that the department was more relaxed without Marcus around. Marcus was such a good bull shitter that he found ways to make it look as if his influence kept the department running like a well-oiled machine, even when he wasn't around. The higher-ups bought into it, but not the rank and file.

CHAPTER 5

"WHAT ARE YOU wearing tonight, Angel?" Desiree asks from the bedroom as her lover gets ready in the small bathroom.

"I don't know, Desiree, I really don't want to do this tonight," Angel says. She applies foundation and then eyeliner while looking in the bathroom mirror in their small one-bedroom apartment on Chicago's South Side.

"You know I would be there for you, baby, if I could, but this flu has me down," says the bald, nearly six-foot tall Desiree as she watches Angel carefully apply makeup on her face. "This should be some easy money tonight. It's just a couple of black frat boys, and Memphis said you should be able to make an easy $400 or $500 in tips."

"I know," Angel says, tugging on the hem of her silver micro-miniskirt that keeps riding up in the back. With Angel's meaty thighs and perfectly round ass, the skirt seems even shorter.

As Angel gives herself another look in the mirror, Desiree gently places her arms around her lover's hips and kisses her on the neck.

"I love you so much, baby," she says softly into Angel's ear as she starts to kiss the back of her neck and down to the middle of her shoulder blades, stopping just short of a tattoo with the name Dexter.

As Desiree continues to shower her lover with kisses, Angel stares blankly into the toothpaste-splattered mirror, wondering how she went from pursuing a nursing degree five years ago to being in the arms of a woman who talked her into a life of stripping, and ultimately into sharing a bed.

"Stop, Desiree. I have to go." Angel pulls Desiree's hands out of the back of her silver thong.

"Come on, baby, we have some time." Desiree tugs Angel's arm, pulling her toward their dimly lit bedroom that is cluttered with shoes, stockings, and clothing everywhere.

"No, baby. I have to finish getting ready. I will be back soon."

"I just want to take care of you before those fools start groping you," Desiree says.

"It's OK, Ree. I don't want to get sick, baby . . . Go lie down now."

Desiree continues to pull on Angel but is interrupted by the faintest voice from the living-room couch.

"Mama, where are you?"

It's Angel's little angel–Kane.

"I'm coming, baby," Angel says, making her escape.

"What's wrong, baby?" Angel rubs her three-year-old's head.

"I thought you were gone, Mama," Kane says.

"Mama does have to leave, but I will be back before you know it," Angel tells her son as he clings to her with his Spiderman pajamas on. "Where are you going, Mama?" the chestnut-colored boy asks.

"Mommy has to go to Milwaukee tonight for work," Angel says, looking into the teary eyes of her only child.

"Miwelkee?" Kane attempts to say through his sleep.

"Yes, darling." Angel nods in a motherly fashion as Desiree looks on from the hallway, wiping her nose and coughing. "Milwaukee is about ninety miles away from here, but I will be back before you wake up to take you to see Grandma."

Desiree steps over. "Me and Kane will be good tonight," she says, taking the little web slinger from his mother's lap. "You can sleep with your no. 2 mommy tonight."

"Goodnight, mommy," Kane says, waving to his mother as he and Desiree disappear in the darkness toward the bedroom.

Angel hates it when Desiree tells Kane she is his second mommy.

As a matter of fact, Angel is not even close to accepting the fact that she is sleeping with a woman. Before she started sleeping with Desiree about a year ago, she despised lesbians.

Angel met Desiree about a year after Kane's father got arrested for selling cocaine about two miles away from her parents' home.

After she got pregnant with Kane and Dexter proposed to her, Angel's parents had allowed Dexter to move in. Dexter kept two secrets from Angel and her family. Not only was he selling drugs, but he was also using, eventually exhausting, the money they had saved up to get married.

Angel met Dexter at the Northbrook Mall while out shopping for a present her mother could buy her for her seventeenth birthday. The slick-talking 21-year-old approached her while she was looking at some gold hoop earrings.

"I can buy those for you, shortie," Dexter said. "You ain't got no man to buy you no earrings?"

Angel had never been approached in that way. She nervously bit her lip and absentmindedly twirled a strand of her hair while trying to think of something sophisticated to say.

"Hey, shortie," Dexter said, waving his hand in front of Angel's dazed face. "Cat got your tongue or what?"

"Nah," Angel replied. "I don't need you to buy me those earrings, but I sure could use something to eat."

"That's cool, ma," Dexter said as he took Angel's hand and they walked toward the food court.

In a few hours, Dexter molested her mind with dirty talk and compliments. He told her that she was mature and not like other girls. And she believed every word that came out of his mouth. When he asked her how old she was, Angel said nineteen, but he knew from her conversation and her lack of experience that she was much younger. That didn't deter him from pressuring Angel to give up her most valuable asset–her virginity.

Although Angel was not quite ready to have sex with Dexter after only a few weeks of knowing him, she didn't want him to look at her like some young little girl not ready to experience adult pleasure. Angel really liked Dexter, and during that time of her life she felt that she needed him.

Against her better judgment, she allowed Dexter to deflower her on her seventeenth birthday. He said it was the best present he could ever give her. It was not what Angel expected. Dexter was clumsy, rough and rushed, trying to finish before his mother arrived home from work.

'Forgettable' was the word that came to mind when Angel relived the episode. From Dexter's struggling to put on a condom, to him helping her out of her panties, nothing was romantic.

"He didn't even pull his pants all the way down," she remembered.

But as long as it kept Dexter from leaving her, the six minutes of pain spent on a raggedy orange couch in his mother's basement was worth it.

* * *

When Dexter was set to be sentenced, he begged Angel not to show up. He told her he didn't want that to be the last memory his family had of him. The real reason was because three other baby's mamas that she never knew existed showed up at the sentencing crying over Dexter.

After the judge sentenced Dexter to eighteen years of prison, one of his baby's mamas fainted.

Another woman with his child tried to help her up. And the third baby mama with a child about the same age as Kane, wanted to fight her outside the courtroom.

Shortly after Dexter went to prison, Angel's father moved out, her mother took ill, and the bank threatened to foreclose on the house. Angel knew that she had to drop out of nursing school and make money fast. It was when she was riding the El train to a job interview for a secretarial position at a downtown law firm that she met Desiree, who told her she could make money using her body, a body that Desiree secretly desired for herself.

When Angel didn't get the secretarial job, she decided to give the seasoned Desiree a call. Desiree invited her to a show at the Illusions nightclub on Chicago's west side. Illusions sits on a one-way street across from a vacant salvage yard. Although there weren't any houses on the block, parked cars took up both sides of the street. As Angel pulled onto the street in her mother's rusted-out 1986 Cutlass Calais, she noticed there weren't any parking spaces within two blocks of the club.

When she finally found a parking space, she checked herself in the rearview mirror before mustering up the courage to exit the car and make her way toward the club's entrance. Walking, Angel felt vulnerable, as if her only form of protection was the flickering street lights on this cold Chicago night. She avoided several broken bottles and beer cans strewn about her path. As she neared the doors, Angel noticed the line of a dozen or so men eagerly waiting to enter this fantasy playground, their $10 cover in hand.

As she waited in line, men continuously flirted with her and one was even crass enough to offer her $50 to go to the car with him "just to talk." She immediately refused.

"Well, fuck you then, bitch," the man replied, glaring at Angel. "You ain't all that anyway. Damn trick."

Angel's wait in line was short-lived thanks to the club's bouncer spotting her and calling her to the front of the line.

"Are you waiting on someone, miss?" the burly man, decked out in the black Illusions' shirt, inquired.

"No, I was invited by Desiree," Angel replied.

"Oh, snap!" the bouncer said. "Desiree is one fine Amazon. What would your name be, pretty miss?"

"My name is Angel, Angel Houston."

"Well, Ms. Houston, I'm pleased to make your acquaintance. You go on in and have yourself a good time. Cover charge is on me tonight," he said, smiling at her and looking her up and down.

"Thank you," Angel replied smiling as she made her way inside.

The first thing Angel noticed while making her way down the club's three flights of stairs were several pictures of half-naked women posing in compromising positions, while smiling for the camera. As she looked at the club's "Wall of Fame," she found a framed photograph of Desiree.

When she approached the cashier—a sixty-something black woman with a lot of makeup—she almost forgot what to say when the woman said "$10."

"Uhmm," Angel replied dumbfounded. "The nice man at the door said it was on him tonight."

"Shit, Terry ain't running nothing," the older woman said, looking around for help. "Somebody tell Memphis to take $10 out of that nigga's check," she says to no one in particular as three men start to line up behind Angel.

"Step to the side, miss," the woman gestured toward Angel with her long pink fingernails. As the three men paid their cover, Angel started to look in her purse for money.

"Maybe I should leave," Angel said, realizing she had only $5 and loose change.

"Can you leave a message for Desiree and tell her that the girl she saw on the El the other day stopped by," Angel said before turning to leave.

"Wait a second," the woman said coming off her padded stool. "You didn't tell me you were Desiree's guest. I thought you said Terry had you covered," the woman said apologetically.

"Take this card and tell the bartender to give you a drink on the house." The woman handed Angel a club business card with "VIP" stamped on the back.

As Angel walked past the turnstile, she was hit with sensory overload. From the neon lights to the loud music to the stale smoke, she was experiencing something she never had before.

As 2 Live Crew's "Pop That Coochie" blasted from the speakers, two women on stage were moving their hips as fast as they could, while several men slapped their asses with dollar bills. In the corner, an older white dancer was sitting on a customer's lap, facing him and rubbing the bulge through his jeans.

As Angel made her way to an open seat at the bar, men grabbed her arm and some offered money to her for her services.

"I'm not a dancer," she said politely to a young-looking mahogany-colored man who didn't look old enough to be in the club in the first place.

"I've got $25," the man insisted.

"I don't dance," she repeated.

"Well, you should, with all that ass," he said rudely, stuffing his money back into his front pants pocket. "That's a waste to have all of that and don't make no money off it."

When Angel settled onto a wooden stool at the bar, the bartender—a light-brown woman with full lips, a bald head, and a number of biker tattoos—asked if she could get Angel something.

"Yes," Angel spoke up over the thumping Miami bass. "I have a drink card someplace but I misplaced it," she said, looking through her purse.

"Don't worry about it, sweetheart," the bartender said. "What do you want?"

After a brief hesitation, the bartender blurts out, "You must be a virgin."

With eyes as big as saucers, Angel replied, "I beg your pardon. I have a three-year-old at home."

"No, sweetheart," the bartender said, smiling. "Is this your first time in a strip club?"

Embarrassed, Angel innocently nodded.

"Don't worry about it, fresh meat, we'll break you in, nice and easy," the bartender said.

"How about a sloe gin and juice?"

"I don't know. Is it good?" Angel asked.

"If you don't like it, I'll drink it and bring you something else."

As Angel waited for her drink, she noticed that the two dancers on stage were now grinding on each other, with the men in the club around them chanting for the chocolates and the champagne bottle trick.

When the bartender placed the drink in front of her, Angel jumped.

"Don't worry, baby, I told you I won't hurt you. That is, unless you want me to," the bartender said, revealing a huge silver stud in her tongue.

Angel looked down in her glass and asked if the dancers were always so wild.

"Roxie and Lexus are always wild. That's just the way they are," the bartender said wiping down the bar.

After about thirty minutes, Angel felt more comfortable in the smoked-filled atmosphere. She didn't know if it was because of the drink or the sexual tension in the air. At that moment, she realized she had not had sex in more than ten months. It had been ten months since Dexter was locked away. During that time, he had not called or written once.

"I guess he has been busy with his other three babies' mamas," she said to herself. For a second, a frown masked Angel's face.

When a table opened near the jukebox, Angel moved over to take a seat.

While the music played, Angel watched the strippers work the crowd, take drink orders and give grinding lap dances to customers.

When a customer offered her a cigarette and bought her a drink, Angel felt more relaxed. When Desiree came on stage to wipe down the silver pole in the middle of the ten by ten foot space, Angel felt embarrassed and excited at the same time.

As Desiree strolled over to the jukebox to play Sade's "No Ordinary Love," customers started to take their seats in anticipation of the show.

Desiree did not disappoint.

> I gave you all the love I got
> I gave you more than I could give
> I gave you love
> I gave you all that I have inside
> and you took my love
> you took my love . . .

As Sade's crooning voice came out of the old lighted jukebox, Desiree London moved as seductively as an artist's paintbrush across a clean canvas. When she grabbed the pole and pulled her body all the way to the top, wrapping her legs around it and sliding down ever so slowly, men and women walked up and dropped $10 and $20 bills on the stage as though it was an offering pot.

Desiree made love to the audience, staring customers in the eye and looking into their souls. She made everyone in the audience feel special–men and women. She became your fantasy fulfilled.

"Damn, I love that bitch," were the words that came from a table a couple of feet away from Angel. "She takes about a third of my fuckin' paycheck every week."

When Desiree pulled off her bra to reveal the most beautiful natural breasts that were the size of two perfectly ripe cantaloupes, more men walked up to the stage.

When Desiree spotted Angel toward the back, she whispered Sade's song at her.

The hot performance was punctuated by Desiree lying on her back, legs spread apart, moving in a way that simulated someone tasting her honey and then making love to her. As she rubbed her hands over every inch of her perfectly toned, pecan-colored body and moaned, an older white woman sitting at a table in front of Angel secretly pleasured herself hiding her hand with her purse in her lap.

When the song ended, Desiree rolled up on her knees and collected her money as many in the crowd started to clap over the announcer's voice: "Let's give a hand to Desiree, people! She is here every Thursday, Friday, and Saturday night!"

Before Angel could pull herself up from the table, Desiree approached.

"So how did you like my show?" she asked.

"Ummm, it was great," Angel said, going into her purse for money to give to Desiree.

"Girl, what are you doing? You know you ain't got no money to be giving me," Desiree said. She put her hand on top of Angel's and pushed it back into the purse.

"The question is, do you think you can do this?" Desiree asked of the overwhelmed 21-year-old single mother. Before Angel could digest the question, Desiree said, "I want you to meet the owner. His name is Memphis, and although he acts like a grizzly, he's really just a big old huggie bear."

That was how it all started, Angel thought to herself as she slipped into her silver catsuit for the evening. Although dancing and grinding on men helped Angel save her parents' three-bedroom brick house that she grew up in, it did little to help build Angel's personal foundation.

After countless lap dances, degrading comments from customers, and lies from her days with Dexter, Angel hated men and didn't know if she could ever love another man again.

CHAPTER 6

"DARNELL, ARE YOU ready? I'm only about fifteen minutes away," I ask of my always fashionably late frat brother.

"I'll be ready when you get here, Tray. I'm just trying to decide on a sweater," says a bit more upbeat Darnell.

"Hey Tray, by the way, I don't want to do anything tonight that would get me in trouble, OK? You know how the brothers can get sometimes. You remember Robert's bachelor party?" Darnell asks, reminding me of a party a couple of years ago when one of our frat ended up eating out a stripper and catching gonorrhea of the mouth.

"Don't worry, frat, I won't let anything get out of hand," I say, laughing. "We can't have you walking down the aisle smelling like another woman's ass. Besides, Taylor has the nose of a bloodhound. If she smells another woman on you, she will kill us both."

As I hang up, I quickly search for the right music to get me hyped and to help get me through what stands to be an unpredictable night.

As I cruise down a surprisingly crowded Interstate 94, I come across the right song, The Time's "Gigolos Get Lonely Too."

"Go ahead, Morris Day!" I yell in the car, bobbing my head and trying my best to sing like Day. This promises to be a good night, I say to myself as I hear the alcohol bottles rattling in my trunk when I switch lanes.

One thing I know I have to do tonight is to protect Darnell from doing something that he could regret. Our last party got pretty wild, with guys getting blow jobs, eating out strippers, and even lining up for $50 quickies.

As I start to second-guess everything for tonight, my cell phone rings again with *Laffy Taffy*.

"I'm sorry, Tray," Nicole says. "Do you still love me?"

"Nicole, it's not a question of love," I say after a brief pause. "It's a question of compatibility. Nicole, I really need to get out of here."

"Fine, Tray!" Nicole is hysterical. "Have fun with your little bitches tonight!"

"Whatever, Nicole," I hang up on her.

I guess what that lady told me a long time ago about being careful with whom you sleep is catching up with me.

As I arrive in front of Darnell's place, I'm not surprised that he's not ready.

"Come on, Darnell," I say as I hit the horn. It's already 10:50 p.m.

It's another ten minutes before Darnell races out of his house, dressed in a pair of tan cords and a black turtleneck with his Greek jacket. I must say, he's always preppy.

"Sorry, man, I was talking on the phone with Taylor," Darnell says before slamming the car door shut. "Man, it's cold as hell out here."

"I know, and now it's starting to snow," I say, turning on my wipers.

We catch up on small talk on the way to the condo guesthouse, where the party is set to begin.

"So have you heard anything back from Miami yet?" Darnell asks about the job interview with the Miami Herald that I had nearly two months ago.

Although I am past anxious to hear something from Florida's largest newspaper, I'm not about to let Darnell know it.

"If they call, they call," I say nonchalantly.

Quickly changing the topic, I tell Darnell that I ran into Janet last night.

"You don't run into anyone of the opposite sex, Tray. You run in them," he says, laughing. "I just hope that Nicole doesn't kill you."

"How many times do I have to tell you that I'm not with Nicole?" The snow starts to come down a little harder.

"She called yesterday, wanting to know what time my wedding starts. She thinks she's going with you," Darnell says.

"What did you tell her?" I ask, almost spinning out.

"I told her it was at noon. I just assumed you were bringing her."

"Damn, Darnell, I wish you would have said something sooner."

"My bad frat," Darnell responds. "She's hooked on a Sigma. There's nothing wrong with that."

We pull up in front of the guesthouse and I can see several of my frat brothers inside. Bachelor parties bring out brothers who have not been seen in years and a lot of old heads as well.

One of the old heads, Big Bother Bo Bo, is in the house, still goofy as hell and drinking like there is no tomorrow. His claim to fame is having hazed a kid so hard that he broke his leg in three places.

"Hey, Tray, where are the girls?" one of my frat members asks. "I hope you didn't bring us a bunch of hos with bullet holes and cigarette burns."

As more frats arrive, they quickly consume a majority of the alcohol that I brought.

"Damn, frat, when are the bitches gonna show? It's almost midnight and I've got to be home before my old lady starts acting a fool," one of my frat brothers who crossed at Howard University says.

Fat Willie has never stood me up for anything. For him, his word is his bond. Even though he is a con man, he is still a man of his word. But that doesn't stop me from sneaking off to the bathroom to give him a call.

"Willie, where are the girls?" I ask in a panic.

"Calm down, son. I just got a call from Memphis; they ran into some bad weather but they should be there in forty-five minutes. By the way you still got that $400 don't you?" Willie asks.

"Four? You said two."

"That was before this bad weather, Tray."

"Don't do this to me now, Willie. I can't believe you asking for more money and the girls are not even here yet!"

"I told you they are on their way. Now you just have the money ready, all right. Tell your so-called brothers to keep their dicks in their pants. Everything is going to be all right."

Now, Willie is upset at me for questioning him, but my reputation is on the line, and he has to understand that.

If the girls are not here soon, some of my frat brothers are going to be too drunk to enjoy themselves.

* * *

"Damn, these roads are bad and they never throw down enough salt," Memphis Wright says as he attempts to keep his big, black Cadillac Escalade ESV on the highway, in what is quickly turning into a mini-blizzard.

"It's been years since I've been to Milwaukee. They don't have enough black folks for me," Memphis says, trying to make small talk with the five different personalities in his SUV. "It's not like Tennessee. We got towns in Tennessee where it ain't nothing but black folks."

Angel, who is sitting in the front passenger seat, appears to be the only one remotely interested in carrying on a conversation with the often volatile Memphis. She learned to watch herself around him, because he felt he had a right to fuck his strippers, and she did not want to become another notch on his headboard.

Memphis only stands about five foot seven and his stocky build, midnight complexion, and wino eyes made him look like the late African American comedian Robin Harris. But when one deals with Memphis there are very few laughs. Memphis often shorts the girls' checks, and he blows his top if one of them points it out.

"You sweating me over six fucking hours!" he'll say. Oftentimes, it isn't even worth talking to him about, because the girls can make up the differences by doing bachelor and house parties.

Memphis tries to live the life of the rich and famous like some of Chicago's most successful pimps, with his clothes, cars, and money. Memphis says he buys Cadillacs, because the women he messes with have too much ass to fit into a Honda.

When Angel pulls down the visor to check her makeup, she glances in the mirror at the competition the four other women in the back rows will bring her tonight. While Angel considers herself more of a dancer or a performer, she considers her competition your everyday strippers or hookers.

"I should not have agreed to this," she says under her breath as she tries to calm herself down.

"So Memphis, this party isn't going to get too wild is it? Because you know I don't get down like that," Angel asks.

"Shit, I hope it does," Memphis says, looking at Angel and licking his chapped lips. "If you trying to get paid like the rest of these hos in here, you'd better hope it gets wild. If you play your cards right, all of us should make our money."

After a brief pause, Memphis turns down the radio and yells out, "Are you hos trying to make some money tonight? If you ain't trying to make no money, let me know now, and we can turn around and go back to Chi."

The other girls start giving each other fives and talking about how they are going to get their money, their baby daddy drama and the games girls play on their dumb boyfriends.

Directly behind Memphis is this thick, white girl name Stallion, who looks like the porn star Nina Hartley. Stallion is the gossip and Queen B of the club. She loves to run back to tell Memphis everything to earn a few brownie points. Next to her is this newbie named Jade, who will surely burn herself out by this time next year. Jade, nineteen, has a build like the porn star Heather Hunter. Jade dances six days a week and does private shows on the seventh day. She never rests.

Memphis loves Jade's naiveté and has made a lot of empty promises to her about turning her into a star.

The other two strippers, Lexus, thirty-one, and Roxie, thirty-three, make it hard on all the girls at the club, because they are the ones willing to do anything for a dollar. They simply have no morals or tact. They often perform together, and they hang out all the time. The heavier-set, Roxie, drinks a lot and cannot perform without Jim Beam flowing through her system. Lexus is a country girl who can be talked into anything for the right price.

These two get wild with toys, fruit, and an outrageous Champagne bottle trick. They do hot lesbian performances at bachelor parties, but both claim they are not gay.

"I think I exit right up here," Memphis says, looking at a piece of paper on his lap while trying to control the steering wheel at the same time.

"Memphis, let me see the directions," Angel insists.

"I got it!" he says. "You just worry about making that money."

"Don't be ridiculous, I can read off the directions," Angel says, taking the crumbled paper from his lap.

When she looks at the scribbling on the paper, Memphis' secret becomes clear to Angel. He doesn't say a word, but just stares at her helplessly.

Memphis is functionally illiterate.

His notes are a series of squiggly lines and letters.

"I think I make a right up here," Memphis says, gently taking the paper from Angel's hand and turning his attention back to the road. About ten minutes later, they pull up in front of the guesthouse.

"Let's make this money, bitches!" Lexus yells out in her country twang as the girls start spraying perfume on their thighs, arms, and chest before they begin to file out of the vehicle and into the snow.

Before Angel can exit the warm vehicle, Memphis grabs her arm. But before he can say anything, she tells him, "Don't worry, it's our little secret."

* * *

Ding dong!

As I go to the door I feel like a crazed contestant on "The Price is Right," and Bob Barker is revealing my prize.

I open the door and the five women quickly walk past me one-by-one. But before I can get a good look at them, a short, red-eyed man extends his hand.

"Are you Tray?" he asks, revealing a dozen or so gold teeth.

"Yes, I am," I respond, as I'm quickly drowned out by the chorus of catcalls for the strippers. "You must be Memphis."

When I reach to shake his hand, the troll dressed in a lime-green suit with green gator boots looks me in the eye and sternly tells me the obvious. "I believe we have some financial matters to discuss before any ass shakin' jumps off."

"OK, step outside for a few minutes," I say, leading the way back out into the cold.

"Big Willie said you were a good kid, so this is how it's going to go down. Don't do anything stupid to my girls, you understand me. 'Cause if you do something stupid to my girls, I'll do something stupid to you."

He lights up a pungent cigar.

"I'll be back in about four hours and I believe you owe me $400," he says, coughing into his hand.

After I pay off the Green Goblin, he scurries away to his oversized truck and drives off into the night.

"I believe I was just checked by a man old enough to be my grandfather," I say to myself. It makes me chuckle.

"Let's get this party started!" Bo Bo yells. "I want to see some asses shaking and booties wiggling! For real!"

"OK, ladies, please follow me and I will show you where you can change," I tell the women to a chorus of boos from more than forty horny men, including the man of the hour, Darnell.

As the women follow me to a bedroom, men are grabbing at their arms, flicking their tongues out and one is already going into his pockets for money for a private lap dance.

Once inside the bedroom, I get my first real glimpse of the performers.

"Hey, ladies, thanks first of all for coming out in this bad weather," I say, looking over each woman. "Do any of you need anything to drink, or are you OK?"

"Shit, since you asked, can I get your number and some J&B?" the flirtatious Roxie asks.

"How about if I start you out with the Jim Beam first. Would anyone else like anything?"

"I would like some water," Angel timidly speaks up.

"Sure, sweetheart," I respond to the most naturally beautiful woman in the room.

"What is your name, beautiful?" I ask.

"Angel," she says holding back an all-tooth smile.

Before I can exit, some of the brothers are starting to bang on the door.

"Stop hogging up all the pussy for yourself, Tray! You get enough pussy as it is!" Bang! Bang! Bang!

"So let me go get your Jim Beam," I say, looking at Roxie. "Angel, I'll bring you bottled water, but let me calm these fools down first."

Before I can leave, Roxie walks up to rub her long, hot-pink acrylic fingernails down my stomach, asking, "So, what kinda party is this going to be? I mean, can we get wild, or what?"

"We wanna know if we gonna make some money up in here tonight," says Lexus, popping her gum and revealing a prominent gap in her teeth.

"I will put it to you this way. You can do whatever you want, but keep in mind that most of these men have been drinking nonstop for about three hours, so if you get wild, I guarantee they will get wilder."

I slide out the door as five guys try to sneak a peep inside.

"Damn, Tray, was you helping them out of their panties?" one asks.

"Can ya'll calm down? Ya'll acting like you ain't never seen women before," I snap back.

In the kitchen, a few brothers are gathered around a small television watching a *Black Tail* porno tape.

"The party will get started as soon as I take them their drinks, so everybody into the front room," I instruct, like a teacher to a bunch of bratty kindergartners.

As I herd the animals to the front of the guesthouse, I stop at the bedroom to drop off the drinks.

"Knock. Knock. It's me, Tray, with the refreshments."

The door slowly opens. Angel takes the alcohol and passes it to the other girls and then takes her water.

I can hear Roxie saying, "Tell that fine-ass brother to come on in here" to a bunch of giggles from the other girls.

"Thank you," Angel says, stepping out into the hallway. "Hey," she says shyly. "I just wanted to tell you that I like your dreadlocks . . . Oh god, how corny did that sound?"

"Thank you," I respond proudly. "You have fun tonight, OK, and I will talk to you later."

In the largest room of the guesthouse, men are toasting the soon-to-be married Darnell, who is now showing the effects of drinking spirits on an empty stomach.

"Yo, Tray! I like that thick white girl. Tell her to come here," Darnell says, slurring his words.

Within minutes, the murmur of chatter turns into cheers as Roxie, Lexus, and Jade come out all together to Apollonia 6's "Sex Shooter."

> I need you to get me off
> I'm your bomb getting ready to explode . . .

As Jade simulates going down on Darnell, who is seated in a metal chair encircled by cheering men urging him to get a blow job, a group of men watch as Lexus and Roxie lay down plastic for their soon to be messy performance, which includes chocolate, whipped cream, strawberries, and champagne.

After forty minutes, Stallion comes out stomping hard in her clear stilettos and black micro-mini skirt. While Stallion does the splits and shows off her assets to another group, Lexus and Roxie are spreading chocolate on each other in the 69 position. Soon the two girls are pulling each other's panties off as brothers throw down money and shout instructions like video-on-demand.

"Put your tongue in her pussy," yells one from the crowd as money comes raining down on them. "Open that shit up so I can see," yells another.

The brothers are truly enjoying themselves.

As I keep an eye on Darnell, who has Stallion sitting in his lap and kissing his ear and neck, my buck-toothed frat brother Chris is wondering where the other stripper is. "I thought it was supposed to be five of them," he says.

"I'll go check on the other girl, frat," I say, trying to get away from Jaws. "Now don't spend all your money in one place."

"Knock, knock," I say, slightly tapping on the door. "Some of the fellas are wondering when you're coming out."

When the door opens, the twenty-something dancer has mascara running down her face.

"Oh, shit, what's wrong?" I ask, stepping inside. "Did someone do something to you?"

She shook her head no and tried to conceal her emotions.

"I'm fine," she says, lying. "I just can't do this anymore. I'm done," she says trying to wipe her face.

"You're not fine," I say to her. "You want to talk about it? I've been told that I'm a pretty good listener."

I sit down on the bed.

"You have a party to host. I will be fine," she says, turning toward me and revealing the most perfectly proportioned body I have ever laid eyes upon.

"Angel, the party is for my frat brothers. I could care less about all the other stuff. Now sit down and talk to me."

"This is not what I wanted out of my life. I wanted to be a nurse and everyone around me doesn't seem to care," Angel says burying her head in my chest and sobbing.

"You can still be a nurse," I say, gently wiping away Angel's tears.

Angel goes on to tell me what it's like to raise a little prince while being ashamed of what she's doing.

"I have to leave him alone while I have men touch me and drool over me, and then I come home and tell him that he can be anything he wants to be, while his mother can't even get on her feet. Worst yet, his father is in prison, and he won't be out until my son graduates from college," she says. "He doesn't even know his dad."

Angel continues to talk, as I listen. She tells me it's the first time that she's talked to anyone in years without them being judgmental. I try to help her see the upside to her challenging situation.

As the hours passed, Angel's crying stops. I tell her how my father left me early in life, and that my male role model is a street pimp named Fat Willie who has looked out for me and ultimately paid my way through college.

I lie back on the bed and Angel snuggles up to me like metal to a magnet. She plays with my locks, as I stroke her cheek. When I look into her eyes, I knew there was something deeper that I needed to know about Angel. I become lost in her gaze, and before I know it we are involved in a passionate kiss. It feels too good to be right. I hug Angel so hard that you would have thought that she was my life preserver, and I was stranded out at sea.

As I caress Angel's soft skin, she jumps like she hadn't ever been touched by a man before and for a fleeting moment her mind drifts.

"What are you thinking about?" I whisper into her ear.

She squeezes my hand and softly kisses my fingertips.

"I don't remember being touched like this," she says.

I continue to stroke Angel's soft sepia-colored skin. It feels like a dream. She was the starlet, and I was her leading man. I take my time, as I kiss her perfectly rounded C-cup breasts while stroking her arms and neck. The breathing increase as I suck on her engorged nipples.

She rolls from beneath me and stands up, as I lie on the bed eyeing her longingly as she slowly starts to peel out of her catsuit. Soon, she is completely naked and vulnerable, standing in front of me.

As I stare at her body, she covers up her breast with her arms.

"Why are you looking at me like that?"

I stand up in front of her and strip for her.

Her mouth opens as she catches a peak in between my thighs.

"You can touch me," I tell her.

She runs her hands over my arms and stomach and then she slowly kisses my Greek tattoos and brands on my arms.

"Did this hurt?" she asks as she traces the Greek letter with her fingernail.

"Only for a second."

I don't try to hide my excitement. I sit back on the bed and pull her on top of me. I slide right in and she immediately starts to ride.

"We should stop," she squeals.

She keeps riding, and soon I began to feel myself throb feverishly within her warm, love walls, and the sensation sends us over the edge.

I gently roll Angel over onto her stomach and enter her from behind. We interlock fingers as my locks cover her face. As I stroke her deeply, she locks her legs onto mine. Being trapped makes me explode with the energy of a phoenix. My eruption causes Angel to scream.

"My god, Tray. I'm cumming!"

I collapse on top of her as she gently kisses my arms.

"That was the best experience I've ever had," I say softly.

She moaned.

"Me, too."

Our bliss was soon interrupted by a knock at the door. We both jump up quickly and rush to put on our clothes.

"Who is it?" I scream.

"It's Chris. Frat, you better come out here quick. Darnell is fucking this white girl," he says laughing. "You've got to see this."

"What? Oh, shit."

Before leaving, I turn to Angel and give her a kiss that leaves me intoxicated.

She falls back onto the bed as I run out of the room, slamming the door behind me.

As I make a beeline to Chris, I can still smell Angel on me and on my hands.

I think to myself that I made love to this girl, and she doesn't even know my last name.

CHAPTER 7

AS I RUSH into the main room, the first thing I see is a group of men in a circle around a flurry of activity. In the middle of it all is Darnell prone with Jade sitting on his face and Stallion riding him like he's a horse. The other brothers are shouting encouragement to this live porno performance.

"Oh, shit," I say, pushing past the group. "Darnell, what are you doing? Get up."

Darnell doesn't hear me. The others tell me to calm down.

"What's wrong, Tray?" Bo Bo says. "Let the boy have some fun. He's going to be stuck with the same pussy for the rest of his life. Until then, he can sneak a little bit on the side. He's not married yet."

"And he won't get married doing this," I say, walking away from Bo Bo and snatching Stallion off Darnell.

"Damn, T," Stallion snaps back while grabbing dollars off the floor. "A bitch is just trying to get paid." She rolls her eyes at me.

I help a drunken Darnell up and take him to the kitchen to a chorus of boos.

Bo Bo pipes up, "Hey Stallion, why don't you let me ride that phat ass like Seabiscuit?"

"You got $50?" she asks.

"Shit, I've got thirty-five, I've been tippin' your ass all night," Bo Bo says, taking a sip of Grey Goose and grapefruit juice.

After looking at her knock-off Movado watch, Stallion agrees.

"OK, I can work with that," she says as she motions for Bo Bo to get prepared for a penetrating lap dance.

"Wait a second, ho!" Bo Bo yells, reaching in his coat pocket. "A nigga's got to get a rubber."

Chris tells Bo Bo, "I hope you didn't buy that from the Arab store because I got an e-mail saying that they put holes in their rubbers so more women would get pregnant."

"Nigga get out of here with that shit," Bo Bo says. "I go doubled strapped anyway," he says pulling out another Ruff Rider.

"Come on ho," Bo Bo tells Stallion. "A nigga ain't got all night."

* * *

"Darnell, you fucked up, and I fucked up for not watching your back." I sit him in a wooden chair in the kitchen.

"I don't feel so good, Tray," Darnell leans to the side and holds his stomach as he pukes his guts out.

"Chris! Chris!" I yell to my frat with the overbite. "Can you go get me Darnell's pants out the front room? I'm going to get him out of here."

"What does his pants look like?"

"You're drunk, too?" I ask. "It should be the only pants on the floor where everybody is. And hurry up!"

"Darnell, let me get you to the bathroom because you look like you need to throw up again," I say.

On our way to the bathroom, Angel sticks her head out the door and asks what happened.

"They're getting buck wild in the front room, that's what's happening, and I have to get him ready for his wedding in a few hours.

"I'll get the door for you," she says.

I push Darnell inside to pray to the porcelain god. Angel and I have a brief moment before Chris stumbles back with Darnell's pants.

"These them?" he asks, holding up a pair of wrinkled tan cords with sex stains on the front placket.

"Yeah, I'll take them. Thanks." I take the pants and catch Chris staring at Angel.

"So are you going to come and dance for us? I've been saving my money for you all night," Chris says with his bucktooth grin.

I push him down the hallway and back to where the party is. "I like her though, Tray, she's got class!" he yells on the way.

"Tray, I want you to know that I'm not like them. I don't do," Angel starts to explain, before I take my finger and put it to her lips.

"Listen to me, Angel. I don't do this type of thing either. What we shared was explosive, and I don't want to take that away, but I would like to get to know you better. I mean a lot better."

"You know, when you first walked through that door I knew there was something about you. I want you to take my number, and I want you to call me as soon as you make it home tonight, OK?" I tear off a piece of a brown paper bag and write down my cell phone and home numbers. "I really want to hear from you."

"Thank you Tray," she says kissing me before heading back to the room.

* * *

As the dancing turns to straight sex and some men line up to get blow jobs from Jade, Angel starts to pack up her stuff and wonders what she will tell Memphis, who will probably be here soon.

When the money dries up and the men want something for nothing, the women slowly head back to the bedroom to count their small fortunes.

"Girrrrrl, we got paid tonight!" an excited Roxie says to Lexus, who is already up to $455.

"None of you bitches made as much as I made," a sassy Stallion answers counting her wrinkled bills on the floor. "My pussy is like crack. These niggas keep coming back for another hit."

"Somebody better go out there and get Jade," Stallion says. "That bitch is like the Energizer bunny, she just keeps sucking, and sucking, and sucking." Roxie and Lexus crack up.

"Why you so quiet over there, girl?" Stallion asks Angel. "I didn't see your ass all night."

"That's because she was in here fucking that fine ass nigga with those dreadlocks," Roxie says.

"If she did, I hope she got paid, because if she didn't, Memphis is going to kick her ass," Stallion says.

"None of you bitches need to worry about me, because none of you will ever be anything but what you are right now," Angel erupts.

"That's right, rich bitches!" Roxie shoots back. "We're going to see how tough you are when Memphis shows up."

"From what I hear, Memphis is the last thing she needs to worry about. She got a six-foot Amazon at home that I know will kick her ass when she hears about this," Stallion says.

CHAPTER 8

"WHERE'S MY MOMMY?" Kane asks Desiree after waking up out of a sound sleep.

"I'm right here," Desiree says, pointing at her chest.

"Not you mommy, my real mommy."

Desiree pulls a long string hanging above her bed to turn on the overhead light.

She composes herself and then sits up in the middle of the bed.

"Kane, sit up and talk to Mommy for a second." She pulls the cover off the doe-eyed three-year-old.

"I want to explain something to you that may be difficult for you to understand," Desiree says, looking into Kane's brown eyes.

"Do you know who your father is?"

Kane shrugs his little shoulders and yawns.

"You're too young to remember your father, but he has gone to a place where he won't be coming back until you are really big," she says gently.

"As big as you?" Kane asks.

"Yes, darling, as big as me." Desiree's eyes start to fill up with tears.

"You see, Kane, I took the place of your father." Desiree takes a picture off the nightstand, of her, Angel, and Kane. "I'm your father and your mother," she says as Kane cuddles up next to her.

As she hugs the exhausted little boy, she tells him that they will always be together.

"I love your mommy," Desiree says.

"You love mommy," Kane repeats, giggling.

"And I love you, too," Desiree says, scooping Kane up into a playful helicopter spin and then blowing a zerbert into his stomach.

As the little boy laughs, Desiree playfully tickles him until his stomach hurts.

"Don't you want to be with me and your mommy forever, Kane?" she asks.

Kane is confused by the question. "I'm sleepy," he says, wiping his eyes.

"You can go to sleep now," she says. "I've already fixed it so that we will always be together." She lays the sleepy child down and pulls the covers over him.

"No one will ever leave me again. I've made sure of that," she says as she pulls the string to turn off the light.

CHAPTER 9

"YOU ALL RIGHT in there, Darnell?" I ask over the coughing and vomiting on the other side of the bathroom door.

"Can you pass me my pants, Tray?" Darnell asks before he pukes more into the toilet.

As some of my frats start to pour out of the door into the cold, I am wondering how I'm going to get my boy ready for his wedding at noon.

"See you in the morning, Tray," several of the men say as we exchange secret handshakes before they leave.

"It's a lot of snow out there," Chris comes back to tell me.

"Tell me something I don't already know, frat," I say.

"Is he going to be all right?" Chris asks. "He's marrying a fine girl in the morning."

"To be honest, Tray, I picture you with someone like Taylor. That's your speed."

After exchanging frat goodbyes, Chris hands me one of his business cards.

"Can you give that to the stripper that didn't dance?" he asks sincerely. "Maybe she can give me a private show or something sometime."

"Get your ass out of here," I say jokingly to Chris, balling up his card and tossing it in the plastic garbage can as he turns to leave.

As the last of my frats file out the door, Memphis walks in past them like he owns the place and right up to me.

"So where are the girls?" he asks impatiently. "I hope everything was to your liking."

Before I can answer, he quickly turns and walks toward the bedroom where he can hear Stallion's and Roxie's loud mouths.

Memphis knocks on the door and barks, "Come on, bitches, let's go 'cause it's snowing hard out there!"

When the door opens, Lexus, Jade, Roxie, and Angel quickly file out and down the hallway. As Memphis mean mugs, Angel and I are able to make eye contact before Stallion stumbles out of the room.

Angel whispers that she will call, as she walks out the door.

As Memphis and Stallion walk out, Stallion whispers to Memphis, "I've got something to tell you."

When they're outside, I rush over to lock the door. No need having this pimp come back in here and try to punk me out again.

"*Girl shake your Laffy Taffy. Your Laffy Taffy. Your Laffy Taffy . . .*" my cell phone goes off, causing me to jump with nervousness.

"Hello," I say.

"Travon, is this you?" Nicole asks.

"Nicole, what do you want?" I ask in a weary tone.

"It's obvious that I want to talk. I want to know how you feel that you can use a person's body and think you can just walk away from them like you're a john or something," she says.

Damn, she knows about Angel, I think to myself.

"What are you talking about?" I ask.

"We made love, and now you are walking away from me like I'm nothing. Travon, I love you, and I'm not going to let you walk away from me like that. I know you love me, too."

"Nicole, are you finished?" I ask.

"Just answer this for me, Travon. Did you have sex with any of those tramps at the party?"

"If you did, I swear it's over between us."

After a pause, I tell Nicole, "Yes, I did."

"Why are you lying?" she cries.

Darnell stumbles out of the bathroom with one leg up on his pants and the other leg around his ankle.

"I know you're lying. You would not do this to us. You would not destroy what we have like that!"

"I'm sorry, Nicole, I have to go." I hit the "END" button on my phone.

Darnell collapses into a wooden chair in the kitchen and rubs his bald head. He looks much older than his twenty-eight years.

"I fucked up, Tray," he says rubbing his head. "I fucked up bad. And I was fucking that broad raw dog. Taylor is going to kill me."

"Don't worry about it, Darnell," I say, trying to calm his nerves.

"Maybe I'm not ready to get married," Darnell says, looking up at me. "If I get myself into a situation like this, I can't be ready to get married. I've got to tell Taylor."

"What! No, frat, you don't have to tell her nothing. Look, you fucked up and I fucked up for not watching your back, but you have to get married."

"I've got to tell her the truth," he says. "She needs to know."

I pull up a chair and sit in front of Darnell. I explain to him that telling Taylor what happened has to be the worst thing that he could do.

"You have to deal with it, Darnell, and never let it happen again."

My phone starts to ring.

Damn, it's Nicole again.

"You can answer it, Tray," Darnell says looking like a beaten man.

"To be honest, frat, I'd rather be talking to Memphis right now instead of her."

This gets a laugh out of Darnell.

"What was he, the Kermit the Frog pimp?" Darnell says.

"So, Tray, where were you when I was . . . you know?" Darnell asks, getting serious on me all of a sudden.

"I was, umm, in the back," I say, searching for something believable.

I didn't have the heart to tell Darnell that I was making love to Angel. Somehow it just didn't seem right to tell him the truth when he's getting married in the house of the Lord in about six hours.

CHAPTER 10

"THIS DON'T MAKE any sense! It's about eight inches of snow on the ground," Memphis says as he cleans off his windshield and lights for the drive back to Chicago.

In the two years that Angel has danced at Illusions, she's seen Memphis raise his voice and throw things around when he's mad, but she's never seen him get violent with any of the girls. That's why Desiree thought he was just a softy. Angel is not in the mood to find out tonight.

As Memphis walks around the truck cleaning off the windows, Angel can hear Stallion whisper something under her breath that must be directed at her because Roxie and Lexus are cracking up.

"Is something funny?" Angel asks, looking directly into the face of that sloppy, white slut.

"I suggest you turn your ass around in that seat before I snatch your stuck-up ass baldheaded," Stallion says rolling her head and pointing her finger like a stereotypical black girl.

"Make me!" retorts Angel.

The next thirty seconds are filled with swinging, yelling, cursing and scratching. Angel comes out of her seat and into the back with a fury. As she wails away on Stallion, Roxie grabs her hair from behind.

The fight is interrupted only when Memphis opens his door.

"What the fuck is you bitches doing!" he yells, snatching Angel off his snitch. "Y'all must be crazier than a mutherfucka, fighting in my truck like this."

Once out of the truck, Memphis stands between Angel and Stallion, and like two fighting cocks they still cannot be completely separated. When Stallion attempts to kick Angel's leg, she slips in the snow bringing Memphis down with her. Before she can get up on her knees, Angel hits her as hard as she can on the side of the head. She tries to strike Stallion again, but Memphis pushes her so hard that she falls backward, landing on a mound of dirty snow.

Just when Angel thinks it is over, Memphis stands over her, balling up his fist like he is going to hit her. As she covers and braces for the inevitable, a voice screams at Memphis to stop.

* * *

"I know you don't think you're about to hit her?" I yell at Memphis as I step between him and Angel.

I help Angel up and brush the snow off her.

"Now this don't even concern you, partna'," Memphis says going chest to chest with mine, being much larger. Although Memphis tries to prove that he is no punk, when I offer him the first punch, the so-called "Chitown Player" looks down at his feet.

"Hit him Memphis!" Stallion screams from behind. "He was fucking Angel, that's why she didn't make any money tonight."

"He did what?" Memphis yells.

"You fucking my bitches for free is like you fucking me for free, and I ain't yah ho."

Memphis swings at me as hard as he can but misses by a mile, stumbling off-balance like a drunken skater. When he regains his balance and swings at me again, he falls, splitting his pants in the back revealing orange boxers with a reindeer print.

The girls laugh.

Memphis yells for Stallion and Angel to get in the truck.

"I'm gonna deal with you bitches later," Memphis says as he stomps off to his truck nearly falling again as he gets in.

As Angel walks away, she knows that she has put her foot in Memphis' nasty-ass club for the last time.

On the way home, Stallion tries to start some more shit in the truck, but Memphis tells her to shut up. The silent drive back is broken only by Memphis mumbling about revenge. He looks in the glove compartment, revealing a silver semiautomatic pistol.

"Yeah, that nigga's got something coming for him," he says, slamming the glove compartment shut. "He ain't even gonna see it coming."

As tears roll down Angel's face, Memphis puts in James Brown's "The Payback" and curses at everyone in the truck.

CHAPTER 11

"YOU'VE GOT TO get up, man," I say to Darnell, who is still visibly sick from the party. "You've been lying there for about two hours."

"Give me another thirty minutes, Tray," Darnell begs from the bed where Angel and I made love earlier. "Just thirty more minutes."

As Darnell recovers, I reflect back on the last twenty-four hours, starting with me running into Janet and reigniting our flame and ending with me in the arms of a dancer. Although being with Janet reminded me of old times, being with Angel brought out feelings in me that I thought were long gone. To be honest, I have not been in love in a long time.

I stopped believing in love after I had my heart ripped out by a woman named Evette Hall when I was nineteen. Evette was a boxing groupie, but I didn't realize it at the time. Five foot nine, stunning good looks, and the darkest eyes I'd ever seen. She always hung around the gym. Boxers never complained though, because she was the perfect eye candy. Boxing gyms are cruddy places. They're dark, filled with mold, sweat, and thousands of broken dreams. Dried blood is splattered everywhere, but the sweat melts it away.

From the sounds of jump ropes, to the thuds of someone hitting the heavy bags, to the beautiful sounds of perfection on a speed bag, a gym was no place for a woman as sexy as Evette. But she was there looking for the right one.

When we first met, I was ranked among the top American amateur fighters in the 165-pound weight class. She came to Baby Joe Gans' Boxing Club five days a week to watch my coach work me to exhaustion. And just when I didn't think I had anything left to give, she would give me a kiss or a smile and get just that much more out of me. She was the first woman I thought I could build a future with.

I loved her and I thought she loved me, but all of that changed after I suffered a right cross that tore my retina in the Olympic trials. Although I went on to win the fight, my 78th as an amateur, I lost the war.

My career ended after that fight and Evette left me three months later for another up-and-comer. She told me that she could not be with a regular guy; she needed an athlete. She craved the adrenaline rush boxers gave her, and I could no longer provide it. I never fought again. I finished my career with a record of seventy-two wins, four losses, and two draws.

I cried for days. Willie cried for weeks.

He videotaped every one of my fights. He studied them. He thought I had the heart of Leonard with the boxing ability of "Sugar" Ray Robinson. He thought I could have been a world champion.

While I was recovering, Willie had a championship belt made for me to go along with all the other trophies and medals I had accumulated over the years. I never kept any of the awards; I always gave them to Willie. I figured I would always win more.

When I got back on my feet, Willie helped me to pay for college. I ended up giving him something better than a championship belt; I presented him with my journalism degree.

I lied when I said Willie's mother was the only person who could make him cry. He cried many times over me.

* * *

"Time to get up, Darnell! It's 8:15 and I know your wifey is wondering where you are."

Darnell rolls off the bed, slips into his shoes, and walks slightly ahead of me out the door and to my car like he was being led to the gas chamber.

"Man, it's not that bad," I tell Darnell as we sit inside the idling vehicle. "I'm sorry I wasn't there to watch your back, man, but you've got to pick your head up."

"It's not your fault, Tray. You can't watch my back forever." Darnell uses his thumb to scrape away the dried white substance on the front of his trousers.

"Well, Darnell, if we live long enough there's going to be a lot of things that we wish we could take back."

I ease the car out of the driveway of the guesthouse.

The sun starts to peak through the clouds, helping to warm both of us up. I glance over at Darnell and tell him that I can think of only one thing he would regret from today, and that is not marrying Taylor.

"It looks like it's going to be a great day for a wedding," I say, making small talk. "Now you have to take that dark cloud from over your head before Taylor kills you and then me."

The spring blizzard severely increased my drive time, and Darnell and I didn't make it to my condo until 9:45 in the morning.

"Darnell, we've got to hustle." I've adopted the voice of a drill sergeant. As Darnell runs to hit the shower, I pull out the black, long-tailed tuxedos. When I look over at my answering machine, the flashing number shows me that I have twenty messages.

I push the "PLAY" button, and sit down on the edge of my bed, hoping that one of the calls is from Angel. Unfortunately, it's a series of calls from Nicole.

"First message: 10:55 p.m.," the automated voice says.

"I can't believe you hung up on me like that, Travon! I thought I meant something to you, and you treat me like a dog. I hate you."

Quickly, I hit the "SKIP" button, "Second message, 10:59 p.m.: I love you so much, Tray, and you do this to me." Nicole is crying.

"SKIP"

"Third message, 11:03 p.m.: You need to call me back right now, Tray! We need to talk this out and I mean it Tray . . ."

"SKIP"

"Fourth message, 11:10 p.m.: You are a dog, Tray, and I don't want your ass anyway! If you keep fucking around with those nasty-ass girls out there you're going to catch something the doctors can't . . ."

"SKIP"

"Fourteenth message, 1:04 a.m.: Hello. Hello. Tray, if you are there, pick up . . ."

"SKIP"

"Fifteenth message, 1:18 a.m.: Just tell me what did I do to you that was that bad. I gave you everything, Travon. I tried to love you. I tried to love a man who was incapable of being loved. Is that what you're saying to me, Tray? Is it?"

"STOP" button.

"Come on Best Man, get off the edge of the bed and hit the shower so we can get out of here," Darnell says with renewed energy. "I've got a good woman to marry."

I tell Darnell about the twenty psychotic messages Nicole left me overnight.

"I told you that she was just in love. Now get ready. Look man," Darnell says, "even when a relationship is finished, the typical black woman has so much separation anxiety that she finds it difficult to move on and let go of her feelings."

"It has a lot to do with our history of slavery. We start out our lives programmed to feel overwhelmingly anxious at the idea of losing someone who is close to us," Darnell explains.

"Wow! That's pretty profound."

"That's not me, Tray, that's from Dr. Gwendolyn Goldsby Grant's *The Best Kind of Loving: A Black Woman's Guide to Finding Intimacy*. You know Taylor has me in that damn book club. Now hit the shower man," Darnell says, putting his hand on my shoulder. "So we can get out of here."

As the warm water runs down my body, I keep thinking that it's time for me to really make a change so that I can someday be in Darnell's shoes-confessing my love to the woman of my dreams.

Maybe the woman of my dreams is Angel.

As I reflect a little about last night, Darnell pounds on the bathroom door.

"Meet me in the car," he yells. "We've got about twenty minutes to get there and about fifteen minutes before Taylor's father has me sent to Abu Ghraib. Now hurry up!"

I jump out of the shower and give myself a two-minute shave with my trusty straight-edge razor. I slide on my pants and shirt, grab my tuxedo coat, and head out the door to Darnell pressing the horn on my car.

Earlier this morning, he was thinking that he couldn't go through with it, and now he's rushing me.

* * *

"Man how late *are* we," Darnell says, glancing at the clock radio in my car. It reads 11:32.

"It's thirty minutes fast, frat, now calm down, we're here now." We drive past a number of Greek license plates. "You ready to do this?" I ask one last time.

"As ready as I'm ever going to be," he says staring at the people still walking into the church.

"If you're ready, then why are you still sitting here?" I ask, reaching across him to open the passenger-side door.

"OK, I will see you in there as soon as I park."

As he steps out into the snow and into the church, I spin off to park in the crowded church parking lot.

I guess I can park in the assistant pastor's spot.

As I walk into the back of the church and head to the prep room, Darnell is pinned up by Taylor's father, who thought he was standing his daughter up.

"Hey . . . Hey . . . Hey! What's going on," I say.

"What took you so long to get here?" Taylor's father yells. "If you are thinking about standing my daughter up at the altar, I'll kick your . . ." He's choking Darnell as people scurry out of the way.

As I pull the lieutenant general off Darnell, I quickly tell him it's my fault that we're late.

"Sir, Darnell wanted to walk here after my car put us down on the highway and we tried to call but my cell phone was dead," I say, easing his tension just a bit. "He's more than ready to marry your daughter."

"Girl shake your Laffy Taffy. Your Laffy Taffy. Your Laffy Taffy . . ." My cell phone goes off at the most inopportune time.

"I thought you said your cell phone was dead."

"It is," I lied. "This is my younger cousin's cell phone. You didn't think I would have a phone with a ring tone on it like that, did you?" I smile.

As the lieutenant general walks out the door, eyeing both of us suspiciously, I quickly answer the phone.

"Travon Brown?"

"Yes, this is Travon," I reply puzzled.

"This is Jonathan Burnett, managing editor with the Miami Herald. I just wanted to tell you that our parent company has lifted our hiring freeze and you are on the top of my list."

"So what are you saying, Mr. Burnett?" I ask, sort of irritated that he's beating around the bush.

"Travon, I would love for you to be a part of our staff. I've been watching your progress and I loved what you did with your boxing promoters' series."

"I'm willing to make you a great offer," he says.

"I'm listening." I sit down next to Darnell, who is looking in the mirror straightening his black bow tie and talking about how he should have struck his soon-to-be bride's father.

"I'm offering you a sports columnist position here covering the Heat and anything else you want to write about. You will be the official voice of the biggest sports team here."

After a brief pause, he adds, "Did I tell you we are also giving you a $35,000 raise?"

"Do we have a deal?"

"I really don't know what to say. Can I call you back after I think it over?" I say with surprising calm.

"OK, Travon. But before I hang up, can you tell me what will it take for me to get you down here?"

"Right now, I just need some time to think about it."

"Can I give you a call back in a couple of days?" Burnett inquires.

"That would be fine," I say and hang up.

"Who was that, Tray?" Darnell asks.

"The Miami Herald offered me the job," I say, trying to suppress my excitement.

"That's great, man, what are you going to do? Or should I ask, when are we leaving?"

"I told them I would think about it." I check my nose and mustache in the mirror.

"Tray, can you fix my tie?" Darnell stands before me rocking, like a kid who has to pee.

"Dude, are you going to be still?" I say scolding him.

"Man, what are you going to do? I know you're going to take that job. What are they offering you? Will you be able to write about whatever you want?" He fires off the questions in rapid succession without waiting for a response from me.

"You know that old man wanted to kill you, don't you?" I change the subject while tugging at his tie.

I already know that I am going to take the job, and I really don't need Darnell or anyone else influencing my decision one way or another.

Just as I get his tie perfect, there's a knock at the door.

"Who is it?" Darnell yells.

Our frat Chris pokes his head in and says, "They said the music is going to start in two minutes. Maaaan, that's a sharp tux!" Chris says.

"You should see the girls out there. Tray, I don't think you can have all of them to yourself, so I think I'm going to help you out." When he laughs, he shows all those crooked teeth.

"How do I look, Tray?" Darnell asks.

"You look almost as good as me, now let's go."

"OK, Morris Day," Darnell mocks me.

"What about me, Tray?" Chris asks, flicking lint off the light brown off-the-rack suit he's wearing with a pair of too casual for the occasion tan Hush Puppy loafers.

"Well, Chris," I say to my five foot five frat with oversized glasses, "you go out there and do your thang."

"Thanks, Tray," he says, walking out the door with new pep in his step. "I'll go tell them to start the music."

When Stevie Wonder's "Ribbon in the Sky" starts, I'm standing up front and Darnell is standing next to me shaking like he's going to fall over.

As Taylor makes her way down the aisle with her father, camera flashes light up the room. It helps you to see why this becomes a woman's best day.

After the vows and the I dos, one of my frat passes some peppermint breath spray to the front of the line. Darnell opens his mouth and I give him three squirts before he plants a big, long kiss on his bride.

The church erupts with laughter and a bunch of "Awwwwwhhhhhs."

A small broom is placed in front of the newlyweds. They interlock arms and make the leap together.

As everyone files out the church, Nicole approaches.

"So, did you have fun last night?" she asks with her lip poked out. "I don't want to think about all the stuff you may have done last night, Tray."

As I start to walk away, she says she's sorry.

"I just get so jealous, Tray. You know that."

Talking with Nicole, I realize that she has a lot in common with cross-eyed Nate.

Both are crazy as hell, but right now both offered some form of comic relief.

Right now, I don't know if Nicole's type of crazy is dangerous or not.

"Tray, are we going to the reception?" Nicole asks. "I've got new film for my camera."

"Wait a second, Tray!" Nicole stops me as I continue to follow the crowd out of the church.

"Excuse me. Can you take a picture of me and my boyfriend?" Nicole says to a woman leaving the church.

"Sure, baby," the silver-haired lady says, reaching for the Nikon.

Nicole places her arm around my waist and smiles for the camera.

"Which button do I push, baby," the photographer asks, making my pose just that much more agonizing.

"It's the red button on the top," Nicole says.

After a few more flashes, I agree to drive to the reception with Nicole in her car.

On the twenty-five minute ride, Nicole never mentions the twenty messages she left on my answering machine or the argument that prompted her to storm out of my condo.

She doesn't even mention the fact that I hung up on her.

What she does want to talk about is her biological clock, and how she does not want to be forty years old having a baby.

"Well, I'm sure when you find the right man, you two will not have a problem having a bunch of pretty babies," I tell Nicole.

"What are you talking about, Tray?" she looks over at me. "If I have any babies, it will be by you."

"I don't want any children, Nicole," I say, staring out of the passenger-side window.

Trying to keep things pleasant, she talks about how pretty the bride looked and how my frat Chris tried to talk to her.

"What is his problem?" she asks me, laughing. "I swear, members of your frat act like they don't even know that we are together."

As we pull up to the crowded reception hall, I perk up at the sight of other brothers who "crossed" me and several other sorors. Inside, young and old are already doing the electric slide, and pictures are being snapped of the huge, five-layer chocolate cake.

When it is time to eat, I make the first toast, and it comes from the heart.

"To Darnell and Taylor: I don't feel like I'm losing a brother, but I'm gaining a family.

Taylor, I have known Darnell for ten years and he has been my best friend the entire time. I have always looked out for him, like he has for me.

From the first time I met you Taylor, I knew you were the one.

You fixed his heart and taught Darnell how to love again and through that you saved his life. You made him a better person and because of that, I love you as well.

When he told me that he was going to ask for your hand in marriage, I asked him what took so long.

When he cried at my house when you went away to visit your mother for a week–yes, he cried–I told him to call you and tell you how he was feeling; he ran my phone bill up that night. When I woke up in the morning and saw that he was asleep, snoring, with the receiver in his hand, I thought, what is he doing? When I took the phone from him to hang it up, he said, "She's still on the line. She misses me too and wanted to go to sleep next to me so this was the next best thing."

You both have shown me how to believe in true love, and I will never forget that.
I love you, Taylor, and I love you, Darnell.
May you both continue to live your lives as newlyweds."

As I hold my glass up, Darnell and Taylor hug and kiss me.

CHAPTER 12

"I DON'T KNOW WHEN I'm coming home," Faith London tells her mother while pacing back and forth on the phone in her newly renovated 1930s Cape Cod just south of Atlanta.

Faith moved to Atlanta more than fourteen years ago to attend Spelman College, where she majored in business administration. Although her college years were difficult, living under the same roof as a molester was even more difficult. She had not been back to Chicago since setting her heels on the campus of the private, historically black college for women—not for holidays, birthdays, or even summer vacations. Although being nearly a thousand miles away from everybody she knew was hard, being around black women empowering themselves gave her the strength she needed to survive after the years of sexual abuse she endured at the hands of her stepfather.

Instead of visiting family back home during college breaks, Faith found campus jobs and a post office gig to keep money in her pocket. During one Christmas break, her roommate, Sandra Mills, invited her to go home with her to Chicago and Faith jumped at the opportunity. The two became fast friends from the moment they met on campus, and Faith quickly adopted Sandra's family as her own, even calling Sandra's parents Mom and Dad.

During the visits to Chicago with Sandra, Faith never once thought about visiting her family, even though she was only an hour train ride away. There were too many bad memories left in the house she grew up in, to ever go back.

"I know you're sick mama but I really can't get away because it's really busy for me at work," Faith says, reaching for excuses.

"I know I run my own business mom, but that doesn't mean that I can drop everything at once." Faith takes the receiver away from her ear and stares at the ceiling.

"Mom, you are not dying." Faith says this with care, but she refuses to fall for her mother's self pity.

"Hold on, mama." Faith is barely able to get a word in over her mother's persistence. "I have someone calling me on the other line."

As her mother continues to talk, Faith clicks over.

"Hello!" Faith yells into the phone, hoping she didn't miss the call.

"Faith London?" the startled caller asks.

"This is," Faith says in a professional tone, not knowing if the call is business-related or coming from an annoying telemarketer.

"My name is Jonathan Moore and I'm calling in regard to the brick, five-bedroom, three-and-a-half-bath ranch in Morningside County."

"Oh yes," Faith responds, rushing upstairs to her home office.

Before she sits down at her desk, Faith remembers that her impatient mother is still holding on the other line.

"Mr. Moore, can I put you on hold for just thirty seconds please?"

She clicks over to tell her mother good-bye.

"Mom, are you there?" She hears the sounds of muffled crying.

"Yes, I'm here," says the fifty-seven-year-old Mary Houston.

"Mom, are you crying?"

"I'm fine, dear," Mary Houston says. "Go handle your business; I know it's important to you. But you don't have to work yourself so hard."

In a way, Mary Houston is right about Faith; getting lost in her work as a real estate broker keeps her outside of reality. Instead of dealing with people, she mainly deals with numbers. Dealing with people, especially men, is often difficult for Faith because of her abusive childhood.

When she started to date men in college, Faith had no idea what to do when a man made a pass at her. So instead of telling a guy no or to stop, she simply gave in because she felt that it gave her some sort of power. Before the end of her sophomore year, she realized that she had slept with more than thirty men, none of whom had ever called her girlfriend.

As a matter of fact, few called back for anything else but sex.

It wasn't until Sandra informed her of the reputation that she was developing that Faith realized she had a problem. When she told Sandra about how her stepfather abused her, it was the first time in a long time that someone hugged her and didn't want sex in return.

Sandra persuaded Faith to get counseling to talk about her problems. After two months of therapy, her counselor informed her that it was time for her to confront her abuser.

The day she called Robert to tell him how he made her feel when he took advantage of her, he hung up. When she wrote him a letter, she got no response from him, but she got an earful from her mother.

The message was loud and clear: "Don't say anything like that to my husband again."

* * *

"Mom, I'm not going anywhere until you tell me why you are crying." Faith's eyes start to water as she senses her mother's pain.

Mary rarely revealed her emotions; it was only the third time Faith had heard her cry. The other times were when Faith's granddad passed away and when Faith's father left them when she was five.

"What is it, Mom?" Faith asks frantically. "You're starting to scare me. What did the doctor say? Is it your lupus?"

"It's not that, Faith. It's," Mary pauses, then blurts out something Faith has been waiting to hear for years—an apology.

"I'm sorry I didn't believe you," she says.

"What?" Faith asks, incredulous.

"I said I'm sorry that I didn't believe you when you told me about Robert." Mary repeats this time clearing her throat so that every word comes out clearly.

The words feel like cold water rushing down Faith's spine. Goose bumps rise on her arms and legs, even though it is already in the mid-90s outside.

"Wait a second, I don't believe this," Faith shoots back. "Are you saying that *now* you believe me, after all these years?"

"I've always believed you, Faith," her mother says, crying. "I just never wanted to believe *it*. I just didn't want to believe that Robert would do something like that to you."

"Why didn't you help me, mama?" Faith asks in a voice weakened from the shock. "I told you over and over again that he was touching me, and you did nothing to stop it. You called me a liarrr," Faith strains to get the words out.

"I love you, Faith. You are my firstborn, but I did not want to lose my family again. Faith, do you remember how your father beat me? Did you forget about that? Then he left us. You don't think I hurt, Faith? You don't think it was hard for me? When I met Robert, he was so different than your father. He was the man of my dreams, the man *your* father should have been! Robert was kind. He worked hard, and he never laid a hand on me!"

"But he raped me, Mother! He raped me!"

Mary ignores Faith's pain.

"Robert loved me and he loved us, Faith. Now he's gone too. I don't know how I'm going to make it without him. I'm struggling to keep this house."

"I can't believe you're worried about saving that house after what happened to me there. Mama, why do you think I never came back?

"I can't set foot in that house because it was a prison for me. I could not escape Robert. I felt trapped. When you're thirteen, and you have nowhere to turn, and the person who is supposed to be protecting you is molesting you, where do you go?"

Faith begins to hyperventilate.

"I can't do this right now. I can't believe that you are sitting up here taking up for him, after what he did to me."

"What was I supposed to do, Faith? Ask my husband why he was fucking my oldest daughter instead of me?"

"I have to go, Mama." Faith slams the phone down.

About twenty minutes later, the phone rings again.

"Hello, is this Faith London?"

"I'm so sorry, Mr. Moore," Faith apologizes, still trying to recoup from the conversation with her mother.

After a moment, Faith is able to focus her attention on Mr. Moore.

"Is this a bad time?" Mr. Moore asks.

"I'm fine, Mr. Moore." Faith straightens up her blouse as if Mr. Moore can see her.

"Let's see here, I'm looking up the home right now," she says.

As Faith's computer begins downloading the information, Mr. Moore tells her that she came highly recommended.

"You remember Dr. Steven Lancer?" he asks.

"Yes, I do," Faith says. "I sold him a five-bedroom Tudor in Lawrenceville. When you talk to him again, tell him I said hello."

"You should tell him that yourself," Mr. Moore says. "You know, he's divorced now. I hope I'm not being pushy, but I was playing golf with him last weekend and your name came up and he was telling me how attractive you were."

Faith is not flattered by the invitation, considering that every time she saw Dr. Lancer, he was with his wife and children, and now his golf buddy is telling her that he was checking her out at the same time. How disrespectful is that?

"That's too bad," Faith says. "They seemed like such a happy family."

"Well, he's single now," Mr. Moore says.

Quickly moving the conversation back to the matter at hand, Faith informs Mr. Moore that the property he's interested in is going for $1.25 million.

"I can get you in to see it as early as Tuesday," Faith offers, typing a 5 percent commission into her calculator. It would give her $150,000 on the deal if she sells the house.

"It's a gorgeous property in a gated community and a perfect place to raise a family," she adds. "What time works out best for you, mornings or evenings?"

"About three o'clock would be good for me, Faith," Mr. Moore responds.

After exchanging other information, Mr. Moore makes one last attempt to play matchmaker.

"Remember what I said about Steven," Mr. Moore says. "Would you like his number?"

"I think I already have it," Faith says, hoping that he will drop the subject, while at the same time trying not to sound rude. "I'm flattered that Steven would say that he finds me attractive but I'm seeing someone," she lies.

"Well, I hope he's someone special," Mr. Moore says.

"He is," Faith responds. "He's someone very dependable, strong, and he never lets me down."

"Well, you be sure to tell him he's one lucky man. I will see you Tuesday, Faith."

After she hangs up the phone, Faith suddenly feels lightheaded. She walks into her bedroom and collapses into a heap on the bed.

"I can't believe after all these years she has the nerve to tell me this now," Faith thinks about her mother. And then she begins to cry again.

Hugging a body pillow and staring at the ceiling, Faith feels just as vulnerable today as an adult, as she did when Robert first crept into her bedroom.

Faith had stayed home sick that day from school. Her mother had dropped her little sister off at school and gone to work.

Robert called his job and told them he would be late.

He brought the television and chicken soup into Faith's room. She thought that everything was fine until he asked her if she loved him as much as her real dad. Faith shrugged her shoulders and then smiled and told him yes.

The day Faith stayed home sick from school changed her relationship with Robert forever.

When he took a cup of orange juice to Faith's room later that day, he had on only a pair of loose gray boxers.

Embarrassed, Faith looked away, but he told her that it was OK to look.

"It's fine to look and touch," he said as he sat down at the foot of her twin-sized bed and rubbed himself. She wanted him to go away, but he didn't.

When he stood up on the side of the bed and faced her, he rubbed himself faster. Even though her eyes were closed, she could hear him moaning and his hands moving. When he called her by name, she did not look. Soon his rubbing stopped, and his breathing slowed down. When he finished, he said, "Thank you, Lord," and kissed her on the side of the face. He cleaned himself off with Faith's pink housecoat that hung on the back of the door.

Before he left her room, he made Faith promise that this was their secret.

She cried after he left and wondered what she did to provoke him to do this. She thought it was because she started to develop fast. Although Faith was only thirteen, she was more developed than any girl in her seventh-grade class, and she hated it because high school boys often tried to talk to her.

When Robert came home from work that night, he brought her a pair of $80 Nike Air Max that she'd wanted for her birthday but her mother had said were too expensive.

Faith tried to block out what happened that day and pretend that it was a bad dream, but he wouldn't let that happen.

The frequency of his encounters increased, along with his boldness. He even began assaulting Faith when her mother was home. Each episode ended with him telling her not to tell, because her mother would get mad and make him leave like Faith's father did.

The first time Robert actually touched Faith was a day before her fourteenth birthday. It was a Saturday. Her sister had dance lessons. Although he usually took her sister, he asked Faith's mother to take her on this particular day.

He took Faith to a puppy store and let her pick out whatever dog she wanted.

She chose the cutest chocolate Lab in the store, and named him Coco. When they got home, Robert looked at his watch and told her to take a shower while he put Coco away.

Faith was in the shower when she heard the bathroom door creak open. "Hello?" She called out, but there was no response.

When she shut the water off and pulled the curtain back, Robert was standing in front of her, naked. She grabbed a towel to cover up. He told her it was OK. He asked Faith to wash his back.

He turned on the water, grabbed Faith's hand and pulled her back in.

When she told him that she felt uncomfortable and that this was wrong, he told her that the Bible said that children should obey their parents.

She washed his back with one hand, still clutching the towel to herself with the other. He turned around, revealing his excitement, took Faith's hand and forced her to wash his private parts.

When rubbing no longer satisfied him, he carried Faith to her bedroom.

Her mind went blank, as the man she had looked up to like a father had his way with her.

When he was finished, he got her a dry towel and told her he was going to have to get her on birth control, because he didn't want her to get pregnant.

That was the first of more than a hundred encounters with Robert.

When Faith finally told her mother while they were shopping one day, Mary called her a liar and slapped her face. When Faith tried to tell her mom again at fifteen and said she thought she might be pregnant, Mary threw her out of the house.

Mary let her back in the house a week later but told Faith that if she was pregnant, she would have to move out because Mary wasn't raising someone else's kid.

Faith never told anyone that she miscarried on the toilet.

Even though Robert knew that Mary knew what he was doing, it barely slowed him.

Faith allowed it to continue because she feared what he would do to her baby sister.

Although her sister was his daughter, Faith didn't really know what he was capable of.

She never told her sister what he did.

Robert killed a part of Faith every time he touched her. When she left the house for college, she was nearly dead.

Her mother's lame-ass apology did little to resuscitate her.

CHAPTER 13

"YOU KNOW YOUR boyfriend's days are numbered," Memphis says to Angel as he pulls his truck up in front of her apartment. The spring storm had dropped about five-and-a-half inches of snow, and as Angel opens the door, a gust of Chicago's brisk wind harshly greets her.

"And another thing," Memphis says, grabbing Angel's wrist before she can get out. "You owe me $400. Figured the pussy you gave that nigga for free is at least worth that. Now get your ass outta my truck!"

Angel slams the truck door so hard it wakes the sleeping tramps in the back.

"Ugly bastard!" Angel yells as Memphis turns the corner of the block.

The short trek to the small brownstone is like walking in white quicksand.

"What am I going to tell Desiree?" Angel wonders as she makes her way up the stairs and to the front door.

The lights are still out in the apartment. As Angel makes her way to the bedroom, she hears the gentle snores of Kane and Desiree soundly sleeping.

"Thank goodness," she says under her breath as she sneaks into the kitchen to find something to eat. The fridge is all but bare, but the freezer is packed with microwaveable meals.

Minutes later, Angel is at the kitchen table, looking through an old *Vogue* magazine, sipping green tea, and eating a sausage biscuit.

Memphis is taking the other girls out to breakfast to collect his share of *their* money and to probe them for information on Angel, which they would be more than willing to share.

Memphis liked the girls to be at odds with each other because the backstabbing kept them from forming a united front against him. If one lied about her earnings and another hipped Memphis about it, it often resulted in Memphis taking a larger percentage of the liar's purse, or worse yet, giving some of her hard-earned money to the girl who snitched.

How much money Memphis would take for his share depended solely on your loyalty to him and his so-called empire. Since Stallion was his personal watchdog, she usually kept 90 percent of what she earned, and ratting on Angel, like she did tonight, surely gave her an opportunity to keep all of her cash.

* * *

"I never trusted that bitch anyway," Stallion says as the group sits in a booth at a greasy diner on Fifth Place, just east of downtown Chicago. "She better be glad you pulled me off her ass. Don't let her come back to the club, Memphis, 'cause she can't be trusted."

"You did good, Stallion," Memphis says, kissing Stallion lightly on the cheek.

"What you havin', baby?" Memphis asks Stallion as the impatient waitress stares at the loud group.

"Gimme the cheese omelet, wheat toast, and a large coffee," Stallion orders, smacking on the same stale gum she's been chewing since the party. As Jade attempts to order grits and a small orange juice, Stallion interrupts, "Is the coffee fresh? Last time that shit was stale, and it gave me the runs."

Memphis frowns and lights up a cigarette. "That's why I can't take yo crazy ass nowhere. You always say some old silly shit," Memphis says.

"Just bring me a cup of black coffee," he tells the waitress.

"I'm sorry, baby," Stallion apologizes. "You need to eat something or else your face is gonna look all sucked in like skinny-ass Jade," Stallion takes a jab at her main competition, drawing chuckles from Roxie and Lexus.

Jade ignores Stallion and excuses herself to the bathroom.

"I thought you scarf and then barf," Stallion whispers to Roxie, so as not to attract Memphis's attention.

Roxie orders a Denver omelet, toast, and three buttermilk pancakes. Lexus orders the same and pulls a small bottle of hot sauce out of her purse.

"Girrrrl, you country as hell!" Roxie yells out, causing a few customers to glance over at the boisterous booth.

"You know I can't eat no greasy-ass eggs without my Red Dot," Lexus says.

When Jade returns to the table, Memphis has her start off the session.

"I made $625," Jade says, taking the money from her small purse and handing it to Memphis.

"Damn, you did good," a delighted Memphis says. "I'm going to have to make you employee of the month."

Stallion rolls her eyes at Jade, calling her a "dick zombie" under her breath.

"Hold on to it, baby girl," Memphis says, pushing Jade's hand back toward her purse.

"So how did you two do?" he asks Roxie and Lexus.

"We made $618," Roxie speaks up.

Memphis bats his eyes and takes a long drag on his cigarette.

"So let me get this straight," he says. "Baby girl made more than both of you bitches? You mean to tell me she made more than both of you!" Memphis's voice is rising.

"You two used to be my best moneymakers."

Roxie starts to speak, but Memphis gives her an evil glare, which quickly shuts her up.

"Don't say shit to me unless it has something to do with you makin' more paper!" Memphis points his finger at Roxie. His fingernails are long and dark.

He turns to Stallion.

"Tell me something good."

"I only made $450, baby, 'cause them niggas wasn't trying to see no thick white girl," Stallion lies, popping her gum between words.

"You telling me that's all you made?"

"Them niggas just wasn't feeling me," Stallion says. "Plus I had to check on Angel fucking you over on your money."

As Memphis is about to get loud, the waitress shows up with several plates.

Soon the loudest table in the diner becomes the quietest—just the sounds of metal forks scraping across porcelain plates that were made in Taiwan.

Memphis scribbles in a green pocket-sized memo book and then tells the girls he wants to see all of them in his office at six o'clock the next evening, where he will tell them what percentage they owe him.

Memphis likes the mystery of keeping the girls in the dark about how much he will take, but it also covers up the fact that he really doesn't know what percentage he will pocket. One thing he knows is that he is disappointed in what Roxie, Lexus, and Stallion have made.

He is also perturbed that he has lost money on Angel.

* * *

While Jade was his best moneymaker, he ended up taking the largest percentage from her, more than $400. He believed it kept a youngster like her hungry and itching to earn more. For Jade, partying, dancing, and tricking was still fun. When she had stumbled into his club about six months prior, Memphis went to his office, dropped down to his knees on his stain-ridden imitation Persian rug and thanked his almighty creator for her.

Not only was Jade impressionable, she was willing to do whatever she was told without any backtalk, unlike Roxie and Lexus, who were both getting a bit too comfortable for their own good. They thought they were running things and were becoming too hard to control.

The relationship between a stripper and a club owner is similar to that of a prostitute to a pimp. The only difference between the two is that a stripper feels as though she can walk away at any time. Although she feels this way, she really can't. The lifestyle drains all your energy and eventually affects other parts of your life.

Many strippers find it impossible to maintain healthy relationships with anyone not in the lifestyle. How many people are proud of the fact that their wife, girlfriend, or sister strips? To be honest, many strippers are embarrassed by their profession. When they meet someone outside the lifestyle that they believe they can develop a relationship with, they hate to say what they do for a living.

It usually comes out, "I'm a dancer" or "I'm a performer." Or the classic line, "I'm in the entertainment business."

For many strippers, the club becomes their safe haven because their coworkers are usually in the same boat as them or will soon be experiencing the same thing at home. This is the main reason strippers are drawn to the club like zombies even on their days off. The club is the only place where they have some control.

Even the strongest-minded strippers can become absorbed by the addictive behavior associated with the lifestyle, from the stares and adoration from men to the fast money and local celebrity status. Other than a stripper or a prostitute, how many other professions end up with you taking all your clothes off for a person for money within the first five minutes of knowing them?

Although strippers love the attention, at least in the beginning, many of them hate men, which is why a majority of them either become bisexual or even lesbian. If you are uncomfortable with your sexuality, stripping could be the worst job for you. You could very well end up between the legs of a woman who shows you any kind of attention.

Some of the strippers have rules when it comes to their sexuality and what they will do for money. For example, Roxie and Lexus have sex with each other during "working hours," but when they are off the clock they consider themselves heterosexual. Others like Jade will have sex with anyone, if the money is right. Jade did a small lesbian party last month and ended up eating out the birthday girl. She said it was her first time with a woman, but the other girls believe that's debatable.

However, in the stripping game, things aren't always what they seem.

CHAPTER 14

"WHY DIDN'T YOU wake me up?" Desiree asks walking into the kitchen wearing only ultra-sheer black panties. "I didn't hear you come in."

"Tell me you didn't sleep next to my baby like that," Angel says staring at the gazelle-like Desiree, who now has her head in the refrigerator, sniffing an open container of milk.

Turning around slowly, Desiree models the low-rise underwear, which from the rear looks as though she isn't wearing anything because the back has crept up between her butt cheeks.

"You like?" Desiree asks, pulling on the underwear from the side. "They're Dolce and Gabbana Lulu panties. They cost a grip, but when I tried them on, I knew I had to have them." She grabs a bowl out of the sink for her Honey-Nut Cheerios. "Don't worry, baby, I got you a green pair," she says, oblivious to Angel's growing agitation.

Angel gets up from the kitchen and folds her arms across her chest. "I thought I told you I didn't want you dressing like a tramp around my son!"

"Why are you trippin?" Desiree fires back. "You act like I'm fucking *our* son."

"He's not *your*...!" Angel stops, throws her hands up in frustration and walks out of the room. She goes into the front room to get Kane's things together for their weekly visit to Grandma's house.

"Where are you storming off to?" Desiree slams her cereal bowl on the table. "I hate it when you do that!"

Desiree follows Angel into the cluttered living room.

It's the biggest room in their apartment and it does double-duty as Desiree's walk-in closet. Clothes, shoes, boxes of outfits, and hangers are everywhere. A lot of the outfits scattered about the room haven't ever been worn, and some still have price tags on them.

"Why do you walk away from me like that?" Desiree grabs Angel by the arm. "What's your problem?"

"My problem is how you dress around my son."

"You mean *our* son," Desiree corrects her.

"No, I mean *my* son. You are going to have to respect that."

Desiree reaches for her hand, but Angel turns away and searches for Kane's shoes under the pullout sofa bed.

Every little shoe she pulls from under the bed is different. Soon she has seven shoes next to her and none of them match.

"Why are you buying him so many shoes?" Angel scoffs.

"Because his daddy ain't doing shit for him," Desiree says, reaching for a black silk robe that's lying across several boxes.

"What are you looking for?" Desiree asks.

"I'm looking for Kane's other shoe."

"You know that's not what I'm talking about," Desiree says.

After two minutes of silence, and Angel pretending that finding Kane's shoe is the most important thing in her life, Desiree realizes that the conversation is dead.

"You are really trippin," she says, breaking the silence. "By the way, the match to his blue and white Jordan is next to the TV," she says on her way out of the living room.

Seconds later, the bedroom door slams.

With Desiree in the other room, Angel can finally exhale.

As she gathers the rest of Kane's things, a warm feeling comes over her.

"I wonder if he's thinking about me," she says to herself. "I can't wait to hear his voice and see his smile again."

She retrieves her purse from the kitchen and checks inside to make sure Travon's number is safe and secure.

"I'm going to call you, baby, just as soon as I get to my mother's house," she whispers.

"Look at how stupid I'm acting," she thinks. "I'm acting like he can take me away from this."

Angel knows that for her to have a chance with Travon or anyone like him, she will have to leave the stripping lifestyle and break away from Desiree.

Angel decides that she will talk to Desiree when she comes home from her mother's house tonight.

* * *

Angel's first month stripping at Illusions was unlike anything she ever imagined. She expected to work at the club for only a few months–just until she made enough money to help her mother to save her house. Being the club's "new bootie," everyone wanted a piece of her, something she had never experienced. She loved how her moves could make men drool, and she felt powerful that anyone would pay her $50 to grind on them during a song.

When one of her best customers, Allen Baker, asked her out a month after she began working at Illusions, she broke house rules by going on a date with him one night after work. She figured he'd spent nearly $2,000 on her, so why not go out to dinner with him. He seemed harmless.

After dinner, when Allen asked Angel to come home with him, she was caught off-guard. Although she knew that the 40-plus-year-old man liked her a lot and was nice, she did not find him physically attractive. His pot-belly, receding hairline, and short stubby fingers turned her off, but she did like his stability. The owner of a small construction company on Chicago's north side, Allen was kindhearted and loving.

He remembered everything Angel said and even helped her get her mother's car started one night when the battery went dead.

Before they arrived at his house, Allen was the perfect gentleman. As Angel entered the house, she noticed all of his décor was either black or dark colored, and his office space was cluttered with piles of papers and old catalogs that should have been tossed out years ago.

Noticing Angel's perplexed expression, Allen sheepishly spoke up.

"As you can see, I could use a woman's touch."

They talked for several hours and Angel grew comfortable around Allen the way a girl would feel around her older brother. Allen, on the other hand, wanted more.

When Angel said she was ready to go home, Allen became agitated.

"I thought you were spending the night," he said. "I can't, Allen, I have to get my son." Angel stood up to get her purse. "I really had a good time though."

"Can I give you some money to stay with me?" Allen asked. "I mean, I know you could use it. How does $500 sound?"

Feeling a bit offended and scared, Angel asked Allen to please take her home.

"OK. I'm sorry. I didn't mean to offend you, but you are a stripper," Allen said. "I mean, look at how you are dressed. You come to my house in a mini-skirt and thigh-high boots. What am I supposed to expect?"

"If you want more money, the best I could do is about $800 and you ain't worth no more than that."

What little respect Angel had for Allen was quickly lost.

"I mean, that thick white girl at Illusions cost me $400 and you are way better than her," he added.

Just when Angel thought she couldn't be offended any further, Allen told her he would throw in an extra hundred if he could fuck her in her tight little ass.

With that comment, Angel stormed out the door, leaving Allen standing in his cluttered living room with nothing but his words to keep him company.

Although she didn't know where she was going and only had $72 dollars in singles in her purse, she figured that she would keep walking until she saw a bus line or cab. After walking for hours and breaking a heel on her Jimmy Choo boots, she was finally able to flag down a taxi.

The fare was $58.75. Repairing the heel on her boot was another $37. The cost of her night from hell? Priceless.

It was the worst date she ever had. Even Dexter had treated her better than that, and the most expensive place he ever took her was Red Lobster.

Times were a lot less complicated when the only thing Angel had to worry about was whether or not Dexter thought she was showing too much skin when they went out.

On her night out with Allen, showing too much skin cost her $95.75 and a blister on her big toe.

Angel knew that she would never go out on a date with another customer again.

The blister on her right foot got infected and kept her from dancing for five days. Although Memphis told her that she should at least come up to the club to show her face and maybe serve a few drinks, none of the other girls seemed to care about her situation—except for Desiree.

Angel will never forget the night Desiree popped up at her mother's house with fried rice and egg rolls from her favorite Chinese restaurant. When the doorbell rang at eleven o'clock, Angel limped to the door to see who it was, and was in awe that the club's premier dancer was standing on her front porch.

"So are you going to let me in or am I going to have to eat this food out on the porch by myself?" Desiree asked.

"Please, come on in," Angel said, opening the door wider.

"Girl, where have you been?" Desiree asked, making herself at home. "I've been worried about you."

"I brought you something from Chin's." Desiree held up the bag. "Why don't you go back and sit down and I will bring you a plate." Desiree pushed Angel toward the couch.

"Where is everyone?" Desiree asked.

"Everyone's sleeping," Angel answered, lowering her voice with each word.

"I'll be quiet," Desiree whispered.

Before Desiree arrived, Angel was curled up in front of the television watching *Set It Off*.

"Oh, girl, that's my movie right there," Desiree said handing Angel a plate piled high with Chinese food and a glass of Diet Coke.

"What part are they on?" Desiree asked peeling out of some of her clothes.

"I'll rewind it to the beginning," Angel said, happy that she was connecting with the most popular girl at Illusions.

When Desiree came back into the room with her plate, she sat down next to Angel and snuggled next to her under the covers.

Desiree's friendly demeanor made Angel feel at ease.

"This is, like, my favorite, how did you know?" Angel asked biting into the still warm pork and veggie egg roll.

"I've been watching you," Desiree said.

"What do you mean?" Angel replied, still munching away at the fat egg roll.

"I think you have a lot of style, and you are really cute."

Angel didn't know what to make of Desiree's newfound interest in her.

Over the next few hours, the women got to chatting about people at the club, especially Stallion, Memphis, and Allen.

"He did what?" Desiree said surprised when Angel told her how crude Allen was to her.

"Girl, he has been through every woman at the club and you were his flavor of the month," Desiree said.

"Are all men dogs?" Angel hoped that Desiree would reassure her that she would one day meet her knight in shining armor.

"I wouldn't say that all of them are," Desiree responded. "But I wouldn't know."

Angel apologized. "I'm not trying to imply that you get around or nothing like that."

"You don't have to apologize," Desiree said. "I have not been with a man in over five years."

"Oh, are you celibate?" Angel asked.

"I guess you can say that," Desiree laughed. "If that's what you want to call it."

"Well, what do you call it?" Angel asked, confused.

"I'm a lesbian," Desiree said. She rose to take the dirty plates to the kitchen.

Angel's mouth was still hanging open when Desiree walked back in to wipe the small table with a cloth.

"You can close your mouth now."

"I'm sorry. I didn't mean it like that," Angel said. "I just thought . . ."

"Let me finish it for you." Desiree sat back down on the couch next to Angel. "You thought that all gay women look like men, and have facial hair."

Embarrassed, Angel covered her face.

"Let me see your foot," Desiree said taking Angel's right leg into her lap and rubbing her foot.

"How are you treating this? You let it get infected. Where is your bathroom?" Desiree got up from the couch and walked into the darkness without even waiting for an answer.

Desiree came back with alcohol, cotton gauze, and tape.

Soon Desiree was doctoring up Angel. She cleaned the blister site and taped it closed. Then she told Angel to lie back and offered to rub her legs.

"You don't have to," Angel said.

"Just lay back, baby." Desiree pushed Angel back on the couch.

Desiree's rubs were deep, with the flat part of her hand. Angel's calves were tight from walking around in heels all the time, and Desiree released that tightness making Angel's legs feel loose.

"Let me get the baby oil," Desiree said.

When she came back into the room, she carried a big towel. She told Angel to take off her shorts so she wouldn't get oil on them.

Reluctantly, Angel removed her red shorts, revealing a red cotton thong.

"You can take that off, too," Desiree said, looking at Angel in the same way Dexter did during their first time.

"I'd rather keep it on," Angel said, hoping that the thin cloth could protect her from something she had never experienced.

Desiree told Angel to lie down on her stomach so that she could massage her legs more thoroughly.

When Angel turned over, her ass sat up like a moon peeking out from its shadow. Desiree rubbed Angel from the bottom of her feet to the middle of her back. It was soooo relaxing.

Then Angel felt Desiree's teeth pulling down her thong.

"What are you doing?" Angel reached back.

"Just relax," Desiree said. She kissed Angel's hands and placed them back at her side.

"I don't know about this," Angel said. "I've never been with a woman before, and . . ."

"I'm not trying to turn you out," Desiree said. "I just want to make you feel good. Let me show you how a woman is supposed to feel."

As Angel tried to find her voice, Desiree continued to remove the red thong.

She rolled Angel over onto her back. Angel felt scared and excited as Desiree kissed her inner thigh.

For the next fifteen minutes, Desiree used her tongue in ways that Angel never knew existed. As Angel squeezed her erect nipples, Desiree licked up and down Angel's private place that had only been touched by Dexter. But Dexter was never this good. Soon Angel's hips betrayed her, moving to the motion of Desiree's tongue and fingers.

Angel didn't know whether to scream in ecstasy from Desiree's touch or scream for her to stop. As the whirlwind of thoughts and sensations flashed through Angel's mind, her body took over and sent her into a powerful orgasm. She placed her hands on Desiree's head as she came, forcing Desiree to taste all of her juices.

As Angel's body shook uncontrollably, Desiree continued sucking on her clitoris, sending Angel into even more spasms.

"Waaaaitttt! Waaaittt!" Angel muttered uncontrollably. "I'm peeing. I'm sorry," Angel said, jumping back.

"It's OK, baby." Desiree says wiping her face with the towel. "It was not pee. Come here and look."

Angel looked down to feel and smell the couch.

"You squirted, baby," Desiree said delighted. "You had a female ejaculation."

"I have to use the bathroom," Angel said tiptoeing on shaky legs to the back.

When she came back into the living room, Desiree was gone and the towel and covers were folded up on the couch.

That night Angel did not want to fall asleep alone. She went upstairs to Kane's room, but he was not there. She peeked into her mother's room, and found Kane curled up into a small ball next to his grandma.

"Hey, ma, are you sleep?" Angel whispered to her mother.

"What is it, baby?" her mother asked groggily.

"You have enough room for one more?" Angel inched closer to the queen-sized bed.

"Come on in," her mother said. "But I've got to tell you, Kane is sleeping wild tonight."

Angel cuddled up to her mother, sandwiching her mother in between her and Kane.

"Now this is what I call love," her mother said jokingly. "I've got cold feet on the back of my legs and a little foot in my chin."

Angel closed her eyes and wondered if she truly understood love for someone outside of her family. All her relationships had been rocky at best.

She wondered what Desiree would say to her when she returned to work at the club.

She hoped they could pretend like nothing had happened.

CHAPTER 15

"*GIRL SHAKE YOUR . . .
Laffy Taffy . . .*"

"Hello."
"So, did I do you right this time?" a guttural voice asks.
"Yeah, Willie, you did right."
"Have I ever let you down, son?" Willie asks.
"No, Willie, you have never let me down," I say in between a long stretch and a yawn. Then I tell Willie how wild the party got.
"Man, Willie, brothers were getting blow jobs, girls were eating each other out, and Darnell ended up sexing this thick, white girl named Stallion."
That draws a big chuckle from Willie.
"Stallion," Willie repeats the name. "I remember that girl when she was a fifteen-year-old. Back in those days, I would say about twenty years ago, she didn't even have to fuck nobody to make money."
"What do you mean, Willie?"
"Strippers didn't have to sleep with you to get theirs back in the day. Dancing was all about the fantasy. Don't get me wrong, Tray, they would grind all up on you and make you feel like you were about to hit that wet spot, but that was just to keep you coming back for more."
"The game started to change when younger girls started coming in, doing whatever. They were constantly pushing the envelope and niggas gladly put the stamp on it," Willie says, pausing to cough in between words.
"You see, these young girls didn't have anybody to teach them the rules of the game and show them that it was all about the presentation."
"Stallion was a classy girl," Willie says, drawing a laugh out of me.

"Now, I haven't seen her in years, so I don't know what she's like now," Willie admits. "But we used to call her White Chocolate because she could move her big, white ass better than some sisters."

Willie says Stallion took a Greyhound bus from St. Paul to Milwaukee to get away from her abusive father.

Willie spotted the runaway sitting in the dark Greyhound station downtown and asked her who she was with and what she was running from.

"She didn't know anything, I took her in and hipped her to the game before somebody put her ass on the streets," Willie says.

"After talkin' to her, I could tell that she wasn't book smart, so I taught her how to use that thick frame of hers."

At fifteen, Willie said Stallion had the body of a twenty-four-year-old.

"I cleaned her up, put some nice clothes on her, and got some of my best girls to show her how to be seductive so she could make some money," Willie says. "I knew niggas would pay good money for a bad-ass white girl, so I brought her in."

"I taught Stallion everything she knew and, within a year, she became my most requested dancer. Customers loved her white skin and her ghetto talk."

"She was bringing in good money until Memphis fucked shit up. That fool was droppin' hundreds on her ass and he couldn't even afford to."

Willie perks up. "That's how you know you got a good bitch, 'cause she will make niggas dig deep into their pockets for their rent money, gas bill money, and baby diaper money, to see them shake they ass. WC had the power to get men to do that shit!"

"When I met Memphis, the nigga was all sprung, telling me that he was in love with her white ass," Willie recalls.

"She had just turned sixteen and he was every bit twenty-seven or twenty-eight. He asked her to marry him and they tied the knot in my club.

"She kept working for a minute but he was gettin' all jealous, makin' it hard for her to make her ends. He was mean mugging customers up and down and stupid shit like that.

"If you deal with a woman in this business, you gotta' have some thick-ass skin!" Willie yells. "Cause the bitches will get you stressed out in a minute. And Memphis ain't never had that cold-hearted mentality it takes to deal with a female like that."

Willie stopped Memphis from coming into the club and eventually Memphis bought White Chocolate out of her contract with Willie.

"To make a long story short," Willie says, "I let him buy her out cause he was cock-blocking her money anyway. So they moved to Chicago and started Illusions. She dances down there, and I heard she even changed her name to some shit. But she's still the same old ghetto-talking bitch I found on the streets."

"How much did he give you to buy her out?" I ask.

Willie chuckles. "True players never talk about finances, Travon. You know that. But I'll tell you this. The headaches that white girl gave him ain't worth what he paid for her."

"She ain't the classy lady you remember," I inform Willie. "She was fucking Darnell and then she gave my other frat Bo Bo some pussy for forty bucks!"

"She fell waaay off then," Willie says.

Curious, Willie asks, "You didn't hit that, did you?"

"No!" I shout.

"Well, where were you when your buddy was all up in it?" Willie asks. "'Cause I know his corny ass didn't plan on fuckin' and he was gettin' married the next morning."

Tongue-tied, I confess that I was in the back with a dancer by the name of Angel.

"Oh, so you were gettin' your groove on, too, huh?" Willie laughs. "How much did you give her?"

"What? I didn't give her shit! I've never paid for pussy."

Upset, Willie clarifies, "That ain't what I'm saying, stupid. Nobody has to pay for pussy. You know that the game don't work like that! If you fucked her and she didn't make no money the whole fuckin' night, then that's just like you fucked Memphis."

"I would've whipped her ass good for that," Willie adds.

"Oh, yeah, I forgot to tell you that I got into it with the Green Goblin," I say, laughing as I flash back to how he fell down and split his pants when he tried to hit me.

Bragging, I tell Willie how I played hero. "He was about to hit her, and I had to step in."

Willie is as quiet as a mouse.

Then suddenly he rushes off the phone.

"Tray, I'm going to have to call you back; I've got to fix this shit," he says.

"Wait a second, Willie," I say, not realizing the storm that is about to brew.

"There's a heavyweight title fight next week on pay-per-view. I think one of those Russian boys is fighting. Why don't you stop by and we can watch the fights like old times."

"I may do that, Tray," Willie says abruptly. "But right now I got to go."

After hanging up, I look in my mirror and see that Janet's phone number is still there.

I get out of bed and brush my teeth, then give Janet a call. We talk on the phone for hours, like we did the night we met.

We agree to go out to dinner Monday night and although I am excited about the possibilities of learning Janet all over again, in the back of my mind I cannot stop thinking about Angel.

Angel and I made a connection that went beyond sex. Although it sounds funny, I think we made a soulful connection, and I want to see if there is anything behind that feeling. Until I can find out, I am not going to lead Janet on.

As I clear out my twenty voice mail messages from Nicole, I have some time to think about relocating to Miami.

In all the wild escapades, I forgot to tell Willie about the job offer. I'll call him later and give him the good news.

I know what my mother's reaction will be. However, trying to persuade my mother to move to hurricane alley would take a lot of effort on my part. Besides, I don't think she could leave her sister right now. My aunt is my mother's best friend, and I know she's not going anywhere.

There's a lot of drama going on in Milwaukee. Maybe it is time for me to move on like my mom said and try to establish new roots elsewhere. Feeling a bit like Superman, I decide to head down to the twenty-four-hour gym to work off some of my anxiety. After all, I joke to myself, I need to stay in shape for my rematch with the Green Goblin.

* * *

"Hey Memphis, what's going on with you?" Willie says to his gold-toothed friend.

"Yeah, Willie," Memphis replies dryly. "What's going on man?"

"I just called to see how the bachelor party went last night," Willie asks.

"Well, you know. It is what it is," Memphis says, not wanting to tip his hat.

"I heard that you had some words with Tray. I was checkin' to see if we were cool," Willie says.

"Me and you cool," Memphis says. "But Tray . . . that nigga needs to be taught a lesson."

"Well, I talked to him, and he doesn't understand the game like us old school. You know. So I was hoping that we could squash this shit now."

"Naw, Willie. I can't let that shit ride. You know that. I'm already havin' a hard enough time keeping the bitches in order, so you know I just can't drop it. Remember, you taught me that."

Willie clears his throat to make sure every word is clear.

"Yeah, I know. But I'm tellin' you, this shit here," Willie pauses. "It's over. You hear me. It's over."

"Is this a threat?" Memphis pipes up. "'Cause you know I ain't scared of you, Willie. I ain't never been scared of you."

"Take it like you want to. But ain't nothin' gonna happen to Tray. You hear me, don't you?"

Willie waits for a response.

"Yeah, I hear you."

Memphis picks up the silver Glock that he keeps in the desk of his office. When he pulls out the clip and slips it back into its interlocking chamber, Willie hears that familiar noise and realizes what he has to do.

"Don't force my hand, Memphis," Willie says. "'Cause you gonna lose."

"Bye, Willie."

Willie's next call is to his funny man, but no jokes are going to be shared in this conversation.

"Hello. Nate," Willie says. "I need you to put in some work for me."

Crazy Nate asks only one question. "Who is it?"

"Memphis," Willie says quietly.

"What? Memphis? Why you want him dead?"

"'Cause if we don't, he's going to hurt Tray."

"Are you serious?" Nate says angrily. "You can keep your money in your pocket for this one. This nigga is all mine."

"But just answer this question," Crazy Nate says. "How do you want this nigga done? You want it to look like an accident? Or you want me to send a message?"

"I just want that nigga dead . . . and fast," Willie says and hangs up.

Nate pulls out an arsenal of semi-automatic weapons out from under his bed.

"That ugly mutherfucka thinks he gone hurt Tray. *Fuck that!*"

"Nobody's gonna miss a nigga in the ghetto."

CHAPTER 16

WHEN ANGEL WALKS into the room to get Kane, he's sitting on Desiree's lap listening to his favorite story *The Very Hungry Caterpillar.*

"Kane, I need you to get ready so we can go see grandma."

The boy hops out of Desiree's lap and runs to give Angel a hug.

"Mommy," he yells as he showers Angel with kisses. "I missed you."

"I missed you too, baby," Angel says. She glances over at Desiree, who is still dressed like a skank.

Desiree folds her arms across her chest. "I was reading him a story," she says, irritated.

"Well, you need to be putting on some clothes," Angel snaps back.

"That ain't never bothered you before," Desiree says.

"Kane, let's get ready to take a bath," Angel says.

She heads into the bathroom and runs water. Desiree waits for Angel in the hallway.

"Mama, can I put my Batman in the water?" Kane asks, passing the women with a bunch of toys in hand.

"Sure, baby," Angel replies.

When Kane is in the water, Desiree tells Angel that she wants to talk before Angel and Kane leave.

"What's going on with you, girl?" Desiree asks. "You act like you don't want me to touch you and you definitely don't touch me anymore."

"That's not true," is Angel's only response.

"OK, Angel, since you wanna play dumb, the last time we had sex was three weeks ago. And god knows when the last time was you initiated anything."

"Can you keep your voice down?" Angel whispers. She peeks in on Kane, who is carrying on a conversation with his toys in the water.

"So, what's going on with you?" Desiree says, quieter. "My feelings for you have not changed. I just wanna know where I stand."

Angel stands with her arms crossed and looks down at her feet. Desiree hugs her, but Angel does not reciprocate.

"Talk to me, baby," Desiree says. "I can't do this alone. You know that there is nothing I wouldn't do for you and Kane. You two are all I have, and I won't let anything tear us apart."

Desiree kisses Angel on her neck and begins to work her way down. Angel gets weak in the knees.

"It's OK, baby," she says as she pushes Angel into the bedroom and closes the door.

"I can't, Angel says as Desiree kneels in front of her, forcing open Angel's muscular thighs.

"I can't do this anymore." Angel moves out of a position that no longer feels comfortable.

"Mommy! I'm done," Kane yells from the bathtub.

Angel gratefully heads to the bathroom.

When she returns to the bedroom to get some more of her things, Desiree just stares at her.

Angel tells her they will talk when she gets home tonight.

"I hope so," Desiree says as she heads to the bathroom to shower.

As Angel packs up the last of Kane's things, Desiree comes out of the bathroom fully dressed.

"Where are you going?" Angel asks.

"I was going to drop you off," Desiree says matter-of-factly.

"You don't have to. We can take the train," Angel mutters.

"What? Now you don't want a ride? I always give you a ride to your mother's, and I pick you up when she doesn't drop you off."

"It's OK, because I really need to clear my head. I just need some time," Angel says.

As she rushes to the door, Desiree grabs her by the arm.

Angel snatches away, and the contents of her purse spill out onto the floor.

"Shit," she says.

As she bends down to pick up her things, Desiree notices a crumpled brown piece of paper and steps on it, hiding it from Angel.

"Come on Kane, let's go," Angel says.

"It's snowing," the excited youngster says as he rushes out the door.

When the door slams shut, Desiree smoothens out the brown piece of paper.

"Travon? Is she trying to trick on me behind my back?"

"I'll just hold on to this paper, Mr. Travon, and see if Angel asks about it."

With both Angel and Kane gone, Desiree decides to go shopping. But first she needs to go over to Illusions and pick up her check.

* * *

When Desiree arrives at Illusions, Stallion greets her with a smirk.

"So you're finally over your cold?" Stallion asks, not the least bit concerned.

"I guess you can say that."

"You're not scheduled to work today are you?" Stallion probes.

"No, I'm just here to pick up my check."

"And to pay your girlfriend's debt," Stallion says under her breath.

"What did you say?" Desiree turns toward Stallion, but the woman she often refers to as "white trash" or "pale donkey" just walks off.

Before she leaves the club, Desiree decides to pick up her costumes so she can take them home to wash them. The only person in the back of the quiet club is Jade, who always seemed to be around.

"Hey, girl, how you doin'?" Desiree says as she takes the clothes out of her locker.

"Hey," a surprised Jade says back.

"So, how was Miltown?" Desiree inquires, hoping to get more than a sentence or two out of the club's newest hot ass.

"It was fine," Jade says. "I mean, those niggas were paying."

"That's good," Desiree says, checking the tattered schedule hanging on a clipboard on the dirty, graffiti-splattered walls.

"Can I ask you something?" Desiree asks Jade, who's sitting in the changing area in a silver shorts and bra set.

"What is it?" Jade says, as she puts oil on her feet and legs.

"Did anything happen to Angel in Milwaukee?"

Jade chuckles nervously before responding.

"She almost got her ass beat by Memphis."

"What are you talking about?"

"Well, she ended up fucking this fine-ass nigga with dreads, and she didn't even get paid for it."

The shock forces the Amazon down on the stool.

"What's wrong with you?" Jade asks. "I would've fucked his fine ass, too. Everybody's just jealous of Angel because she beat us to him."

When Desiree recovers, she walks out of the club leaving her musty outfits by the locker.

"I can't believe that shit," Desiree says sitting in her BMW. She bangs on the steering wheel then speeds out of the parking lot, sliding in the snow, and nearly causing a three-car accident.

Desiree doesn't know whether to hurt herself or Angel.

"I can't believe this bitch fucked somebody else," she says, driving toward Angel's mother's house. "I should beat her ass."

Sitting at a long red light, Desiree's crying suddenly turns to crazy cackling.

"I should have known this bitch would hurt me," she says to herself. "But you know what, that's why I fixed your ass already because I already knew."

Desiree decides to go shopping after all. She turns off the highway to head back to downtown Chicago.

"I wonder if that dress from Nine West is still on sale. If not, too bad, that's what our money is for anyway."

"That'll teach your ass a lesson."

Desiree laughs maniacally.

CHAPTER 17

"MA, YOU MIND if I open up some curtains and let some light in?" Angel asks as her mother plops down on her father's old, brown recliner in front of her television.

"Help yourself, baby."

With the heavy maroon curtains open, Angel sees how dusty the house really is. The sunlight breaking through the dirty glass reveals what looked like months of caked-on dust on the coffee table, television set, and hundreds of knickknacks scattered about the house.

"When was the last time you dusted in here?" Angel asks her mother, who is now flipping through an old TV guide, with her legs propped up in the recliner.

"What did you say?"

"When was the last time you cleaned up?"

"I can't even tell you," her mother says. "I don't have any reason to clean up. Nobody comes to visit except you and Kane. Baby, promise me you won't end up old and alone like me."

"Well, Mom, I can't promise you that I won't get older because that one is sorta out my hands."

"Ah, girl you know what I mean."

"So how is that pretty roommate of yours doing? And when are y'all getting married?"

"What, Mama?"

Angel was hoping her eighteen-month love affair with Desiree wasn't out of the bag.

"Don't act like you scared now," her mother says, leaning toward Angel so every word becomes clearer. "I mean both of y'all are pretty girls. And you have a birthday coming up next month. You'll be twenty-five, right? And she's just a little older? I mean what y'all waiting on?"

Angel stares at her mother as if she's seen a ghost, then ask her how long has she known.

"Known what girl? The only thing I'm saying baby girl, is that Kane needs a father and you need a husband. It's too hard out here to do it all by yourself."

"I'm all for that women's lib and I watch Oprah every day, but everybody out here ain't making Oprah's money, so they can't afford to be by themselves."

"Besides, Angel, you don't want people out there saying you gay—now do you?" she says. "That's what they say about Oprah," she whispers, as if someone from Harpo Productions is in the next room.

Angel burst out laughing in nervous relief that her mother doesn't know about her relationship with Desiree. Despite Desiree's push for the two of them to go public, Angel had kept their relationship secret.

"So when was the last time you got a little bit of, you know?"

"Mom! I don't know!"

"The only thing I'm telling you is that there's nothing wrong with finding you a good man that will take care of you like that every now and then. Now I know that you are all into your career, but women have needs just like men . . . That's all I'm going to say about that, baby. I didn't mean to get all up in your business."

"You are too much, Mama," Angel says as she walks into the kitchen to clean up.

"You know I got a package in the mail from the Dixon Correctional Center," Angel's mother yells out from the front room. "I'll bring it to you."

After she hands Angel the thick envelope, she leaves the kitchen to give Angel some privacy.

"Here we go," Angel say before she sits down to read.

It's better to misgovern ourselves than to be governed by someone else.
  —Kwame Nkrumah.

Angel,

I trust that you and Kane are well and in strong spirits.

Sorry I haven't written you, but being in prison is rough, and thinking about anything outside these walls makes every passing day more difficult.

To be honest, I feel like a caged beast.

There's nothing inside a prison that's rehabilitating. What can be rehabilitating about being around stone-cold killers?

The only thing I've learned from my time here is how to be a better criminal. The system better keep me locked up, because I'm scared of what I would do on the streets.

My cellmate is a lifer. He shot and killed two men during an armed robbery on Chicago's lower east side back in 1998, but he's cool though.

He taught me how to stay alive and how to keep my mind free.

The first year in here was the toughest because you don't know who to trust. I had to learn the hard way, and it almost got me killed.

I read everything that I can get my hands on, but I'm not going to come at you saying the "white man this" and "the white man that" because some of this shit we bring on ourselves. However, you should read the "Isis Papers" by Dr. Frances C. Welsing it will open your eyes to a lot.

I'm not going to blame anyone for me being in here though. I did the crime so I have to do the time, but EIGHTEEN YEARS! I've never killed anyone, but living in here I know that I CAN. Unfortunately, I CAN'T be there to teach my son the things my father didn't teach me.

I didn't write you earlier because I wanted you to move on with your life and find a man that will show my son how to become a man. I never meant to hurt you Angel. I hope you believe me. What you have to do now is do for YOU and OUR son. Get married one day and show our son what a family looks like.

Can you do me one favor though, Angel? Never tell Kane that his daddy was a two-bit drug dealer that cheated on his mama and ended up behind bars. My mother told me that about my dad and look where I ended up. I guess things have a strange way of repeating themselves, and I want to break that cycle.

Always,
Dexter
Dixon Correctional Center

Reading Dexter's letter left Angel feeling numb because after nineteen months, she finally had something her own mother may not ever have–closure.

* * *

The dishes have not been washed in at least a week. The refrigerator only contains three hot dogs, two eggs, and what looked like an old church chicken dinner on a paper plate.

"Mom, what's going on? The house is a mess! You have no food in the kitchen, and when I called you a couple of days ago you told me everything was fine."

"I can't keep depending on you to give me money every time I look around," Angel's mother says. "You're in nursing school and working at Cook County Hospital."

"Yeah, Ma, we're going to have to talk about that at another time," Angel tries to change the topic.

"You done gave me more than $5,000 in the past five months," her mother says. "I just got to get through this, but it's hard, baby. God knows it's so hard." Her mother starts to cry. Angel tells her she will give her another $500 to help her pay her bills.

"Baby, I don't know what to say," her mom says, giving Angel a hug.

"Have you talked to Faith?" Angel asks. "Maybe she can help out too."

"Your sister hates me."

"No, she doesn't, Mama. What makes you say that?"

"Angel, I have something to tell you, and I know that you are not going to like it, but I think it's time that it's said."

Over the next two hours, Angel's mother tells her how she did nothing to stop her father from molesting her sister.

"I saw blood in the front of Faith's underwear," she says, crying. "I knew then what my husband was doing."

Feeling isolated, she went to the church pastor and told him about what she suspected was going on in her home.

"He told me that Faith was the devil. Reverend Daniel's only response was to pray on it and cast the demon out of my house. Putting my daughter out of my house was the hardest thing I ever had to do. When I slapped my firstborn and put her out, I died."

Angel's mother pauses to gather new words.

"Your father didn't touch me anymore after that," she says. "We lived a sexless marriage."

"I take that back. *I* was living a sexless marriage, but I don't know what else your father was doing."

"When Faith moved back in, I tried to protect her, but what could I do? I think she got numb to it, and it was killing me to see her suffer like that."

Angel doesn't know whether to lash out at her mother or hug her.

"Why didn't you do something?" she whispers.

"I tried, baby. I just wanted to keep the family together. I had no friends. Your father didn't let me talk on the phone to my mother when she was on her deathbed. When my mother died, he didn't even want us to go to the funeral.

"Your father was very controlling. I hated him, but I knew he wouldn't let us leave him."

Searching her mother's eyes, Angel asks, "Why are you telling me this now?"

"'Cause you need to know. I talked to your sister yesterday about it. I told her something that I should've told her a long time ago. I told her that I was sorry."

"Sorry, Mama? That's all you could say?

"I've never been close to Faith and now I see why," Angel says.

"I have to go, Mama."

"Angel, don't do this," her mother begs. "Sit down and talk to me. I've been keeping this in for so long, and I can't do it anymore."

"Kane!" Angel yells upstairs. "Come down here. It's time to go."

"Angel, don't do this."

"Kiss your grandmother good-bye."

"Why are we leavin'?" Kane asks, looking at his grandmother.

"'Cause your mother is being pigheaded," her mother blurts out.

Angel turns Kane around abruptly to zip up his coat.

"I know this is hard for you to take, Angel, but I've been keeping this in for more than fifteen years, and the first person I tell this to is walking out of my door."

"I just can't deal with this right now, Mama.

"I will send you a check in the mail."

"Bye, bye, Grandma." Kane waves with one hand as Angel pulls him out the door by the other. "See you tomorrow."

* * *

"Mama, I miss Grandma already," Kane says, the EL train rocking them in their seat.

"I miss her too, baby," Angel says, taking off his Chicago White Sox's hat and running her fingers through his pretty sandy-brown hair.

"Somebody is going to need a haircut soon."

"You sure do, Mommy," Kane says, giggling.

"Why did we leave so early?" he asks.

"Sometimes grown-ups need their space," Angel says. "Sorta like me and Desiree right now."

"Why?" Kane whines.

"You're too young to understand, baby, but you will one day."

"Dexter was right. I do need to move on," she thinks. "Holding on to Desiree is not fair to me, her, or Kane."

She paws through the purse. "Where is it?" she says, turning the purse upside down.

"What's wrong, Mommy?" Kane asks, picking up her MAC lipstick.

"*No!*" she says, scaring Kane.

"Desiree's wrong, baby," Angel says as she puts her stuff back in her purse.

CHAPTER 18

"AMTRAK. CAN I help you?"
"Yeah, I want a round-trip ticket to Chicago."
"OK, sir, what is your name?" the polite woman on the other end of the phone asks.
"Nate. I mean, Nathaniel Briggs."
"And where are you leaving from?"
"Milwaukee."
"And you're going to Chicago," the woman says, hitting buttons.
"Yeah. I'm going down to Chi."
"OK, how long will you be staying?"
"A day or two. Hold on, why don't you make that a week."
"Is this a business trip?" the woman asks. "Business travelers qualify for a reduced fare."
"Naw, this is personal," Nate says, giving a sinister snicker. "But since you askin' so many questions, let me ask you one." Can I get a veteran's discount or something?
"Yes, sir, veterans qualify for the same discount as our Triple A members."
"So you sayin' you give the same discount to a vet that lost a leg or an arm to someone with a towing service card?" Nate is offended.
"Yes, sir, we offer various discount packages such as student, senior citizen, and . . ."
Nate is silent.
"Hello? Hello?"
Nate slams down the phone.

"I'll fuckin' drive instead," Nate says. "I just hope the hooptie gets me there. I ain't cranked that bitch in a week."

Nate makes up his bed, tucking his sheets like he learned during basic training at Fort Bragg. He runs his palm over the sheets, reaches into his pocket for a coin and bounces a quarter off the bed, catching it in his hand.

"Good job, soldier," Nate says, impersonating his drill instructor.

"Thank you, sir! Yes, sir!" he says with a salute.

"Soldier, I want those shoes shined so well that I can see my reflection in them. You hear me, solider?" Nate gives commands to himself.

"Sir, yes, sir!"

He takes a seat on a wooden arrowback chair next to his bed and spit-shines his black loafers.

"Solider, I want those pants ironed so crisp they look like they just came from the dry cleaner! You hear me, solider?" Nate barks.

"Sir, yes, sir!"

Nate pulls out his khaki pants and heats his antique iron on his small, two-burner stove. When the front of the iron turns amber, Nate sprays water on his pants and irons them on a board placed on his bed.

He goes to the bathroom to pack his overnight bag, and glances up in the mirror at a man he hardly recognizes.

"Is that the haircut of a man representing Uncle Sam?" he says to the man in the mirror.

"You better get your ass in gear, soldier."

Back in his room, he grabs a shoebox from under the twin bed. Inside are a pair of thick metal scissors and a brand-new hair clipper.

Over the next hour, Nate takes off twenty years by cutting away his matted mane. When he's done, he takes a bath.

He takes two suits out of his closet, a black one and a chocolate-brown one.

"This will be the suit they bury me in," he says, holding up the black suit and looking it over.

"And you were going to be the suit I wore when Tray won his first professional boxing championship," he says to the brown suit. "Maybe I'll get a chance to wear you to his wedding."

"Shit, who am I fooling? That boy ain't marrying nobody no time soon. He's havin' too much fun sowing his oats." He laughs as he places both suits into a garment bag. He grabs two unopened dress shirts and his belt and then looks around the room to see if he's forgetting anything.

"You're going to need money, soldier," a voice inside him says.

Nate opens the combination safe that is hidden in the back of the closet and takes out $3,000. He folds the money neatly and places it in his overnight bag.

"Can't forget change for the tolls," he says, shaking the coins out of a glass milk bottle and placing them in his pocket.

As Nate walks out the door, a woman who lives down the hall notices him.

"Is he in there?" she asks, not realizing the dark, handsome man is Nate.

"What are you talking about, Cindy?" Nate looks the woman in the eyes.

"Nate, is that you?" Cindy Williams steps closer. "That sounds like you, but that can't be you."

As Nate throws his garment bag over his shoulder, Cindy yells, "*Crazy Nate? Damn you look good!* What happened to you? You look like you got hit with a bar of soap, hot water, and a razor."

Nate shoots back at the plus-sized woman, informing her that she looked like she's been hit with something too.

"If I've been hit with soap and hot water," Nate says, "then your fat ass been hit with Mickey D'zzzz, KFC'zzzz, Wendyszzzz, Chiliszzzz and all the other Z's I can't even think of."

"*Well, I never!*"

"Yes, you have," Nate says. "You didn't get that big for nothing."

Before Cindy can think of a snappy comeback, Nate walks past her and out the door.

Nate throws his bag into the passenger seat of his raggedy 1987 Oldsmobile Tornado.

"Come on, bitch, and crank," he says turning the key and bouncing in the seat.

Surprisingly, she cranks on the second try, and black soot shoots from the tailpipes.

"I'll see your ass in about two hours, Memphis," Nate says as he heads toward the I-94.

Although the car's interior is weathered, his cassette player still works like a charm. As he merges into traffic, Nate is preoccupied with finding the right cassette tape from the box on the floor of his car.

"Where is it?" he says, as he pops tapes in, fast-forwards, rewinds and ejects, all while watching the road. After twenty minutes of searching, he finds the right cassette. Al Green's *A Change Is Gonna Come*.

As Green croons, Nate sings along. He also caresses his gun and bayonet knife.

"Yeah, nigga, killing you is going to be soooo easy," Nate says. He takes a swig of Southern Comfort from the engraved army flask that Willie got him last Christmas. It reads: "To Nathaniel "Nate" Briggs, you are one of America's unsung heroes."

He hits the rewind button to hear Al Green again.

"I waaaaaas born down in the river. In a big ole tent," Nate sings along, saying the words wrong.

* * *

"I wonder where that fool is," Willie says after Nate's cell phone rings ten times. Although Willie considers himself retired from the game, Travon's mistakes are pulling him back in.

Travon always lacked real street knowledge. Luckily, boxing saved him, Willie thinks proudly to himself, because his father sure in hell didn't.

When Travon's father was not running the streets chasing women, he was in some club trying to make it big as a saxophone player. When Willie told him that Travon was headed down the wrong path, Travon's dad asked the pimp what made him an expert on raising kids.

"I'm looking at your situation, and I don't think you can judge me," Travon's father said.

The only thing that kept Willie from killing that coward that night was his love for Travon.

Right after that, Travon's dad packed up his sax and moved out east to try to make it as a musician. But he never hit it big and he never saw Travon again.

Willie did admit that he failed his two boys. Although he made sure his sons had everything they could want financially, he failed to teach them what it took to be a man.

Willie's oldest son, William Jr., stood about six-foot-five and was a high school basketball sensation. As a sophomore, he was already being pursued by colleges both locally and nationally. During his junior year, he led the city conference in points, assists, and steals per game. Then two nights before the state championships, William smoked some coke at a birthday party, saw a kid talking to his girlfriend, and ran him over in the new Ford Mustang that Willie had bought for him.

The tragic tale made national news. Ironically, the kid he killed was his girlfriend's cousin, whom she had not seen in years.

The turn of events devastated Willie, who vowed not to lose his second son, Christopher, who was the spitting image of Willie–overweight, light-skinned, and a loud talker.

Saving Christopher would prove far more difficult. By the time Willie started to pay attention to Chris, his son already had a $500-a-week cocaine habit.

When Willie cut off Chris's allowance, the seventeen-year-old stole Willie's semiautomatic, drove to a liquor store in the heart of the central city, and blasted the pregnant clerk in the stomach. Chris walked away with $25.57 from the register.

Although the fetus and the woman miraculously survived, the judge sentenced Chris to fifty years, no parole.

With his sons locked away, Willie made a pact with god that he would not let Travon fail, and that has not been easy.

But now, Willie feels as though he is left with no choice but to destroy a man who will certainly harm Travon, if he doesn't step in.

"I hope you can appreciate this, Tray, because this may cause a shit storm," Willie says, dialing Nate's number again.

CHAPTER 19

WHEN I ARRIVE at work Tuesday morning, I have messages from Miami Herald recruiter Jonathan Burnett and fifteen messages from Nicole apologizing for "being herself."

I joked to myself on who wants me more-the recruiter or Nicole.

"**Message 20: Monday, 7:45 a.m.**"–"Travon, my man! This is Jonathan giving you a call to see if you are any closer to making a decision. Give me a call so we can clear up any issues you may have. I've also e-mailed you my contact information. Hope to hear from you soon."

"**Message 30: Monday 11:00 a.m.**"–"Travon, yeah, this is Jonathan again. I forgot to tell you that I was looking at the Weather Channel this morning. We're expecting 87 degrees for a high today. I think you guys are digging out from about five inches of snow. Milwaukee is expecting a high of 40. Just thought I would mention that, but hey, there's no pressure on our end. Just give me a call when you get this message. Thanks."

"**Message 38: Monday 1:30 p.m.**"–"Travon, I have some more good news about the position that I think you'll like, so give me a call. Thanks."

"**Message 40: Monday 3:15 p.m.**"–"Hello, Travon, this is Jonathan once again. I left a couple messages on your cell phone and didn't hear back from you, so I'm trying you again. I was hoping we could talk today about the columnist's position to see if you have come to any kind of a decision. Like I explained to you before, we created this position *especially* for you. It's prime; I would like to think of it as a hybrid-like position, columnist/reporter/blogger. But you can make it whatever you want. You have the skills to bring this entire thing together. I sent you my home number as well with my last e-mail, so be sure to get back to me at the earliest. Thanks."

"**Message 46: Tuesday 8:33 a.m.**"–"Travon, it's Jonathan. Hey, I know you're thinking a lot about whether moving to Miami is right for you. Think about this, we are so impressed by you that if by chance you don't like the job, we can tweak it to make it work for you. Bottom line—we want to see you succeed with us. You have my word on it. Now, I need you to at least give me a call and let me know what you're thinking. I just want to get a feel on which way you're leaning. Give me a call. Thanks."

* * *

I already know in the back of my mind that I am taking the position with the Herald, but there is nothing wrong with taking my time to make sure everything is right. The Herald is asking me to pack up, and leave my roots, and everything else I know behind me. That's a big decision for anyone, and I don't take it lightly. I'm comfortable in Milwaukee, but maybe I've have become too comfortable. I need a new challenge, and I'm not getting that in my current beat. Lately, it seems like every story idea I pitch to Marcus is not what *he's* looking for. His standard lines are: "How much does it cost?" and "We don't have enough money in our budget for that right now."

The entire atmosphere in the newsroom is polluted, and I'm not referring to Marcus' breath. His crudeness and bravado make it difficult to work for him. My grandfather used to say, "Someone is starting to smell himself," or in other words, believe his own hype, and Marcus is lost in the blue haze of his own Kool smoke. Unfortunately, many of my coworkers are stuck at the paper, so they have to take Marcus's crap.

As I zip through my 148 e-mails, looking for the six or seven legitimate story tips, I see that my company's spam filter is down again. As I delete the latest X-rated *Pam and Tommy's Uncensored* DVD, I come across a message from Marcus.

"I need to see you IN MY OFFICE FIRST THING TUESDAY," is all it says.

"Oh, shit!" I say out loud, thinking Marcus has found out about my courtship with the Herald. I haven't let anyone around here know about my visit to Miami because the word "secret" does not exist in a newsroom.

Telling a coworker that you're visiting another paper is like making an announcement during halftime at the Super Bowl.

I bet he's going to try and blast me on this, I think, as I grab a notepad and pen.

Before I head into Marcus's office, a nosy coworker leans over his dusty cubicle and warns me that Marcus has been on the war path since my mini vacation.

Although Marcus has everyone in the sports department scared of him, I simply think of him as the toughest guy in an empty telephone booth. He can talk a strong game, but it doesn't go any farther than the newsroom. To me, no loud mouth could do anything to me that hasn't been done to me in the streets or in the boxing ring.

I approach Marcus's office; his door is ajar.

"You wanted to see me?"

"Close the door," Marcus says. His back is turned and he continues typing on his computer. "Move those papers and sit down."

Stacks of old newspapers and magazines sit on both of the other chairs. I clear off the chair with the smallest stack and wonder what he wants to tell me that is so important.

"So, did you enjoy your time off?" Marcus turns in the chair, puts his feet up on his cluttered desk, and knocks over a plastic cup filled with coffee.

"Damn!" He picks up a bunch of coffee-stained papers and tosses them into the wastebasket.

"Yeah, it was cool," I say, wondering what's up with the small talk.

"That was your boy that got married right?" Marcus inquires.

"Yeah, that was my frat, Darnell. I don't think you know him."

"So, how was the bachelor party?"

"Party?"

"You know what I'm talking about." Marcus leans across the desk. "I heard you had some Chi town dancers that were off the chain."

"Who told you that?"

"I ran into your frat Chris at a singles party on North Third Street last night, and he was telling me all about it. He said it got pretty wild."

Not knowing how to respond, I ask, "Am I in trouble or something?"

"Yeah, you're in trouble because you didn't invite me. Come on Tray, I thought I was your boy. And look at how you do me. How are you gonna have ass everywhere and I didn't get a piece?"

Relieved that I'm not in any trouble, I assure Marcus that he will be invited to the next party.

"You just tell me when and where, and I will be there," he says. "Just give me enough time so I can come up with something to tell my wife." He's grinning now, a tobacco-stained smile.

"Was that the only thing you wanted to ask me?" I ask before standing up to leave.

"Yeah, that's it," Marcus says. "What did you think it was?"

"I thought it was work-related."

"Well, this is work-related. The next time you have party with strippers and I'm not invited–consider yourself fired! Now, get out of my office and tell my lazy-ass receptionist to come in here and empty the trash."

If Marcus knew that I was talking to the Herald, he would make my life very difficult, but right now he has only one thing in mind–getting his rocks off.

I'm going to talk to Chris and tell him to keep his crooked mouth shut about the party, before he blabs something to the wrong person.

Right now though, I need to give Willie a call for some much-needed confirmation about my big decision.

CHAPTER 20

ANGEL DOES NOT want to face Desiree, but she knows it is not fair to take it out on Kane.

"Mommy, it's late and I'm getting sleepy," the little boy says, wiping his eyes and yawning. "Can we go home now? Please."

"OK, baby, we'll leave in another hour. Can you hang in there for me?"

"Yeah," Kane says, not really sure of himself.

"Do you want some more ice cream?" Angel bribes her son as the two sit inside an ice cream shop about twenty-five minutes from home.

"No, Mommy." Kane climbs into his mother's lap. "I just wanna go home."

One of the parlor's workers approaches Angel and asks her if she wants anything else, because the store will be closing in fifteen minutes.

"Oh, I'm sorry, what time is it?" Angel asks the acne-faced teenager, who has ice cream spots all over his white tuxedo work shirt.

"It's a quarter to eleven," he says, as he wipes the table and clears away the empty ice cream containers. "But you can sit here longer if you like."

"Thank you," Angel says. "But I guess it's time to get the young one home."

Angel zips up Kane's jacket and they step out into the cold. She knows Desiree will be waiting to talk, and she knows she can't hide any longer.

"What am I going to say to her?" she thinks as she flags down a taxi.

Angel has very little conversation for the chatty, musty-smelling cab driver, as she gazes out the back window at couples walking hand in hand along Michigan Avenue. The people seem so happy and problem-free.

Before she knows it, the driver is pulling up in front of her apartment.

"That will be $23, ma'am," he says. He has turned in his seat and is staring at Angel's breasts and thighs. She moves Kane to shield her breasts while she pulls the cash from her purse.

"A woman like you don't need to be out here like this," the driver says. "If I was your man, you wouldn't be out here this late. I could take good care of you, if you could take care of me." He offers her his business card.

"All I have is $20," Angel says, "but if you wait, I can rush into my apartment right quick and bring you out a five." She does not take his card.

"Sure you will, toots." The driver snatches the $20 from Angel's hand. "You think I was born yesterday? If I'd known you only had $20 I would have dropped your ass off eight blocks back," he says. "Now get out of my taxi before I call the police."

Angel doesn't waste time arguing.

As she turns the key in her door and walks in, she's greeted with the pleasant smell of Chinese food. Desiree is sitting in the kitchen, but Angel walks past quickly without saying a word to put Kane to bed. Desiree has already set out a pair of clean jammies for Kane.

"You need to brush your teeth, Kane, but I'm not going to worry about that tonight," Angel says tenderly as she pulls off his snow bottoms. After another few minutes of stripping a sleepy child who offers no assistance, she manages to get him tucked in. She kisses Kane on the forehead, turns on his nightlight, and closes the door.

Angel slowly makes her way to the kitchen. Desiree has ordered food from their favorite Chinese restaurant and has Angel's plate already made. Desiree is wearing a long, silky, black dress.

"Go wash up," Desiree says, as she lights a candle. "Your food will be getting cold soon."

When Angel steps into the bathroom, she sees that Desiree has prepared a warm lavender bubble bath for her. Angel quickly ditches her clothes and submerges herself up to her neck in the water.

This feels so good, almost too good, she thinks.

Angel closes her eyes for a moment, but her catnap is only interrupted by the song "Still" by The Commodores coming from the next room.

> So many dreams that flew away
> So many words we didn't say
> Two people lost in a storm
> Where did we go?
> Where'd we go? . . .

"Knock, knock." Desiree calls before walking in.

She stands over Angel with a kettle full of boiling water.

Angel jumps. "What are you going to do with that?"

"Now you scared of me? I would never hurt you, like you did me."

"I figured the water was a little cold." Desiree pours the steaming water into the tub and slams the door on her way out.

The next twenty minutes, Angel goes over in her head how she will talk to Desiree. What to say? How to say it? And what will she do next?

Angel is wrapped in a plush, oversized towel, when she walks into the kitchen and sits down in front of her veggie egg rolls and Kung Pao chicken.

"This is nice," Angel says, not letting her guard down.

"I just thought I'd take you back to the first time we were together," Desiree says. "Did you forget that?"

"No." Angel bites into her egg roll.

"Are you sure?"

"I didn't forget, Desiree."

"Do you remember how we met?"

"Yes, you approached me on the El, and I didn't know who you were or what your intentions were, but you seemed to be nice."

"I knew at that time that I wanted to be with you," Desiree says, reminiscing. "You had on this sexy little business skirt and blouse on with some cheap Payless shoes. But you were rocking it with that body."

"I told you that you could use that to make some serious money. Do you remember?"

"Yes, I do."

"When you came to Illusions to see me that Saturday, I gave that performance especially for you, because I saw you when you came in the club," Desiree says. "I made love to you that night before I ever touched you physically. I knew I would have you after that night, but I never knew that I would fall in love with you." Desiree says, pausing to sip some red wine.

"When I did fall for you, it was OK because I fell in love with Kane, too."

Angel picks at her food; her appetite has vanished.

"When I gave myself fully to you, Angel that was the hardest thing I've ever done. I didn't think I could love again." Tears well up in Desiree's eyes.

"I'm going to tell you something that I've never told anyone," she says. "I told you the last time that I was with a man was with my husband, but did I tell you how he cheated on me, physically abused me, and ultimately ended up in prison for trying to rob a bank?"

"Even today, I buy all these expensive clothes, shoes, and makeup because I don't like myself. My husband encouraged me to start stripping, and he didn't care that other men were gawking at me. He was cheating anyway, and his cheating ways left me with something that I can't ever get rid of. But that nasty taste in my mouth was erased when I met you.

"My husband preyed on my weaknesses. When he found me, I was seventeen and he was thirty-five. He was the first man to make love to me, and I was like, 'Wooh, this is what it's like.'

"I was sexually abused by my aunt for seven years, Angel, and I didn't know anything about my body until he came along and showed me how to use it.

"I don't think I've ever loved myself."

Desiree walks to the dining room and picks up a Nine West shoebox.

"Let me show you something," she says. "I've saved mementos from everything that we've done together."

She opens the box. "Look at this. These are tickets from last summer when we went to The Taste of Chicago. Remember how you tried the alligator and got sick?"

"These are tickets from when we went to Atlanta for the hair show last August. And these are ticket stubs from our trip to St. Louis to see your mother's sick aunt."

Desiree holds the ticket subs. "I saved these because it was the first time that you said you loved me."

"That's not true!" Angel interrupts. "I said I loved you before that."

"Let me finish. It's the first time you said you loved me and really meant it. Or I felt you meant it.

"So talk to me. What changed?"

"I don't know," Angel says.

"Well, I can tell you fucking Travon didn't help!"

"It's not even like that," Angel says.

"Well, what is it like? Tell me something." Desiree folds her arms across her chest.

"I think I . . ." Angel pauses.

"You think what? That you love him?" Desiree jumps up from her chair. "You fucked *a man* at a bachelor party, and now you think you love him?"

Desiree looks up into the ceiling.

"That must have been one hell of a fuck!"

"It wasn't about sex," Angel says defensively. "He understands me."

"*No*, Angel, it was about the sex. You met a fine brotha at a bachelor party. The other girls wanted him, but you had to show them that you could have him all to yourself."

"How could you do this to me and to us?" Desiree shouts. "I told you that I could *not* be hurt again."

"I didn't mean to hurt you but I really believe I can love this man." Just saying it, Angel feels stronger.

"What do you know about him, Angel? What does he do for a living? How many kids does he have? Is he married?"

"I bet you don't even know his last name."

Desiree doesn't know that she's batting a hundred with her questions, and Angel isn't about to let on.

"I can tell you that he touched my heart in a way that it has never been touched before," Angel says. "I can tell you he's the most beautiful man that I've ever laid eyes on. And I can tell you that if he would have me and Kane, I would go with him."

"Girrrl, please! It sounds like he just touched your G-spot," Desiree fires back, sorting through the contents of the shoebox.

"Well, I guess you are going to need this to get in contact with him." Desiree holds up the rumpled brown paper Angel was looking for.

Angel rises from the table.

"Give me that." She demands.

Desiree clutches the paper to her chest.

"Oh, do you really expect me to hand you over this piece of paper? You must be crazy!"

In a flash, Angel's hands are around Desiree's throat. Desiree fights back and both women fall to the kitchen floor.

Desiree has an iron grip on the paper. With her free hand she slaps Angel hard in the face and knocks her away. Desiree scrambles to her feet and makes a mad dash for the bedroom. Angel is just getting to her feet when the lock clicks.

"Give me that paper, you crazy bitch," Angel pounds her fists on the door. "You know that's not going to stop me from seeing him!" She's panting now and wiping her face.

"I'm a crazy bitch, but you are on the other side of the door, yelling." Desiree's voice is calm, and soon she begins to laugh. "And your dumb ass didn't even get paid. You fucked that nigga for free. What the fuck is your problem?"

Desiree laughs again, then opens the door. Smoke wafts from the trash can.

"I suggest you use that little Indian in you and read smoke signals, because I burned up Travon's number."

"You bitch!" Angel screams. She runs to Kane with tears streaming down her face.

"I'll be that bitch," Desiree says. "And I'll be the bitch with the last laugh."

CHAPTER 21

"THERE'S THAT SHITTY-ASS-HOLE-IN-THE-WALL club right *there*," Nate says to himself as he drives his rusty car around the block to survey Illusions like a hawk.

"It's 1700 hours and Operation Kill Memphis is in effect." Nate grins as he pulls over across the street from the club, then scoots down in the driver's seat so that he won't be detected. After watching Illusions's employees and clientele for more than an hour, Nate decides he's seen all he needs for the time being.

He makes a U-turn in front of the club and drives around for a while, until he finds a $39.95-a-night motel.

"This should do it," he thinks as he grabs his gear from the trunk. He checks in and then calls Willie.

"Hey, Willie, I'm here," Memphis says as he hangs his suit on the back of a closet door.

Willie is irritated. "Why did it take you so long to call me?"

"'Cause I had some shit to do, you know. I gotta bring this nigga down to his *knees*. You know what I'm talking about."

"What are you talking about?" Willie asks. "You just need to do what you do and get your ass back here."

"Nawwwwh, Willie, Operation Kill Memphis is already in effect," Nate says. "He talking 'bout hurtin' one of *ours*. Now you know what I gotsta do," Nate says as he yanks the sheets off the twin-size bed and remakes it military style with the sheets tucked extra tight.

"Don't be stupid, Nate," Willie warns. "Memphis is crazy, too."

"You ain't even heard the plan yet," Nate says before bouncing a quarter off the sheets and catching it in his hand.

"If it doesn't involve taking care of business before the end of the day tomorrow, I'm not interested."

"Why are you questioning me, Willie?" Nate demands. "I mean, you didn't question me when I killed that white boy for you after he hurt Rose! You didn't question me when I killed that mark for you on Wisconsin Avenue, did you? And what about that crack-fiend Katrina, who was about to rat you out to the police?"

"What's your point?" Willie yells.

"The point is, I'll determine when it's time for that punk-ass nigga to die! It *ain't* up to *you*! It *ain't* up to Memphis! It *ain't* up to god!" Nate says, taking out his boning knife. "I'm going to be the judge and jury on this time. Your money ain't good on this one, Willie."

"Nate, wait!" Willie yells between fits of coughing.

But Nate continues, "I'm going to start out with his white bitch, then his best ho, and then just when he thinks it can't get no worse, I'm going to cut his ass up." Nate makes a slicing noise with his mouth as he waves the sharp knife in the air.

"This ain't got nothing to do with White Chocolate," Willie says.

"Yeah, it do," Nate says. "I always wanted to fuck her white ass, but you kept me away from her. But even Big Bad Willie ain't going to be able to save her ass from my dick and this sharp steel this time. I've been waiting a long time to get a piece of that ass, and when Memphis sees what I did to her . . ." Nate laughs, the rest of his thought hanging in the air.

"I gotta go, Willie."

"Nate . . ." Willie starts to say before he's cut off again.

"There's a war brewing, and a good soldier has got to be well-rested," Nate says. "I'll talk to you in a week."

Nate cranks out hundred sit-ups and three hundred push-ups and then turns out the light. The sheets remain neatly tucked in. He sleeps on the hard floor, with his knife under his pillow.

Willie, on the other hand, is wide awake.

"That fool is about to start a war when all he has to do is cut off the head of the snake," Willie says to himself as he goes into his vault to pull out his .44 Magnum.

"I haven't used you in a long time, bad boy," Willie says as he wipes the gun with a soft cloth. "I guess what my father told me is true–you can only get people to do your dirt for so long, before you have to go and clean up your own shit."

"Looks like I gotta go to Chi to handle some business."

* * *

"These bills never stop!" Memphis says, throwing up his hands at his desk. "Stallion! Stallion! Come in here!"

"What is it, baby? I'm getting ready to go on stage pretty soon." Stallion sucks in her stomach so she can zip up her red sequined miniskirt.

"You may not have a stage to dance on if we don't start bringing more cash in here," Memphis says. "Can you read this letter so I can get the full understanding of it?"

"Let me close the door first, baby."

"It says here that we're five months behind on our mortgage," Stallion reads. "And that if we don't come up with $10,000 by next Friday, the bank is going to start foreclosure procedures!"

"How can this be, baby?" Stallion asks, handing the letter back to Memphis, who tears it up and throws it in the dented gray garbage can next to his desk.

"Business ain't booming like it used to," Memphis says. He looks out of his window at the drug dealers hanging out on the corner. "The girls ain't bringing in the money they used to, and the bills keep going up. You know the gas bill was over $2,000 last month!"

"Shit, if it wasn't for Jade, we would've lost Illusions four months ago," Memphis confesses.

"What about Desiree?" Stallion asks.

"Desiree and Angel bring in a lot of money, but most of it goes directly to them in tips."

"Can't you take more out of their checks?"

"You don't know shit!" Memphis yells. "Desiree already works for tips now. I pay her a couple hundred dollars a week, but if we lose her, Chase Bank will be running this place."

"She could have gone to another club by now," he adds, "but she's here out of loyalty, and I don't know how long that's gonna last."

"Loyalty my ass," Stallion says. "She just wants to keep an eye on her damn girlfriend."

Memphis lashes out at his unfaithful wife, whom he has not slept with in years.

"I remember when you used to make niggas break themselves to see your ass wiggle," Memphis says. "*Now* look at you. You bring in less than country-ass Lexus and lazy-ass Roxie."

"I used to call your ass 'bad habit' because niggas would give up drinking, smoking, and gambling just to see that ass move for one more song." Memphis shakes his head in disappointment.

"And you were one of them," she says.

Memphis glares at her.

"I tell you one thing, I'm not going to lose this club 'cause y'all got lazy and fell off," Memphis declares. "I'm going to hit the streets and find me some hungry bitches willing to put in work!"

"And now I think it's time for you to make me, *us,* some cash," Memphis says, pointing toward the door.

After Stallion has gone, Memphis sits down at his desk and ponders how his club went from bringing in profits of nearly $20,000 a month to faltering in the red zone today. Although it is easy for him to blame the strippers, he knows it's not their fault entirely.

"The game's changed, but it ain't passed me by," he thinks as the thudding beat from Lil Jon vibrates in his chest from the next room. "Now it's time for me to shine."

* * *

The next day, Memphis arrives at Illusions at 7:00 a.m. to organize a game plan. Although he doesn't read, he understands numbers. He looks at his books, and the money that has come in over the past six months, and it's easy to see that Jade, Desiree, and Angel are the only dancers bringing in a significant amount of cash. However, Roxie, Lexus, and some of the girls on the "undercard" all had dramatic drops in the amount of money they brought in although the customer base had increased.

In January, Jade brought in $6,800; Desiree $6,000; Angel about $4,200; Lexus and Roxie combined $4,500; and Stallion $4,000.

Last month the numbers took a strange twist: Jade $5,800; Desiree $6,400; Angel $5,000; Lexus and Roxie combined $2,400; and Stallion $2,100.

Memphis frowns.

"These bitches are skimming off the top."

"It looks like Desiree and Angel were the only real ones." Memphis twirls a toothpick in his mouth.

"I expect this shit out of Roxie and Lexus, but Stallion? I'm going to go high-tech on these bitches."

His next call is to the 411 operator.

"What city please?" the operator asks.

"Chicago."

"The name?"

"I don't know. Give me somebody that installs those little security cameras really fast."

"There are many listings, sir. I can give you two, but you can call back for more."

"OK."

Memphis is soon on the phone with Steven Mills, a security company owner talking about having security cameras installed throughout Illusions.

"How fast can you put them in?" Memphis asks.

"If you tell me this is what you want, we can have them installed in a couple of hours," Mills says.

Memphis explains the situation, and Mills tells him that no one can be trusted, and suggests that he also have a camera installed to watch the doorman to see if he's letting people in for free.

"That's what I'm talking about," Memphis says.

For $7,000 that he really cannot afford right now, Memphis has hidden cameras installed in the girls' dressing rooms, behind the cash registers, behind the stage, at the bar, and somewhere that Memphis hadn't thought about—in his own office.

"You would be surprised at what you find," Mills tells him. "I've been in the security camera business for fifteen years, and some criminals are so bold that they'll steal right from your desk."

"Thank you, Mr. Mills, for doing this on such short notice," Memphis says.

"Not a problem, sir. This is what we do. Let me know if you need anything else in the future. My company would be glad to handle to it for you."

Sixteen mini flat screen monitors, installed right behind Memphis' desk, are hidden by a tarp.

Memphis feels as if he's regaining control over an operation, that's been spinning out of control for months. It didn't help when that punk kid embarrassed the hell out of him in front of his hos in Milwaukee.

"Your ass ain't outta the woods yet," Memphis says, thinking about Travon. "You must be a lucky-ass nigga or have a guardian angel, because if I didn't have to handle this shit, I would have killed your ass by now."

* * *

When the girls start to arrive at Illusions around 5:00 p.m., Memphis carries on as if it were business as usual.

Soon he slips into the back to tune into his new favorite reality show: *Do You Know What Your Strippers Are Up To?*

He locks the office door, puts on his headphones and listens as the girls chat about everything from their broken homes to getting over. It isn't long before Roxie and Lexus start talking about how they were going to steal more money from Memphis.

"That ignorant-ass nigga is so stupid," Lexus says as they slip into their tight-fitting leopard-print outfits for tonight's performances.

"Yeah," Roxie chimes in. "Taking money from him is like taking candy from a baby. We should've started juicing his ass a long time ago."

"I know that's right, girl," Lexus says laughing and putting her hand out to slap Roxie five.

"I hear you bitches," Memphis says to himself.

He clicks over to camera 5, which takes him into the bathroom with Jade, who's sitting on the toilet, crying. Soon, she pulls out a rubber and a syringe. She unzips one of her long patent leather boots, ties the condom around her thigh, taps the needle with her finger, finds a vein and injects herself.

Memphis puts his hand up to his mouth in shock.

"Damn, Jade," he says. "I never knew *that shit* had you."

Memphis knew "*that shit*" all too well.

That shit killed his sister, and caused his cousin to leave her three kids alone in a filthy home for four days, while she sat in a dope house getting high. He also had seen what it did to other girls who worked for him in the past.

It was an unwritten policy at Illusions that no drugs were allowed. Memphis despised them, and if a girl was caught with anything harsher than marijuana, he would terminate her in a heartbeat.

But with one of his best moneymakers obviously getting high, Memphis is caught in a catch-22. Firing Jade would be just like handing the keys to the club over to a new owner.

Clicking over to camera 6, Memphis notices several customers coming in the door. Most of them are regulars, but one clean, dark-skinned man stands out as unfamiliar. The man is wearing a chocolate brown suit and shiny, black wing-tipped Stacey Adams and shades. Memphis trains the camera on the new customer as the man looks all around the club as if it were new to him as well.

When the man parks himself at a table in the middle of the club, Memphis wonders how long it will take before one of his lazy girls takes her ass up to the customer.

One of Memphis's newest booties walks up to the man and smiles, but keeps walking.

"It's been ten minutes and all he got so far is a smile," Memphis says angrily.

Before another second goes by, and an obviously paying customer gets up to leave, Memphis storms out of his office over to the door of the women's dressing room.

He grabs his newest girl, Eva, by the arm as she goes in.

"Do me a favor and tell Roxie and Lexus to bring their asses out here right now!" he demands.

"OK," the intimidated youngster replies.

"She won't last a month," Memphis thinks to himself.

Soon Roxie and Lexus appear at the door.

"What's going on?" Roxie asks.

"Why are ya'll back here when there's paying customers sitting out there waiting and willing to spend some money? One man has been sitting out there for ten minutes and the only thing he's gotten so far is a damn smile!"

"We still gettin' changed," Roxie says.

"I'm getting sick of that backtalk!" Memphis says. "If you bitches don't get out there in two minutes and get this nigga's money, you won't need to come back here anymore."

They rush back into the changing area to put on their shoes, and are surprised when they walk out to find Memphis still standing outside the door, looking at his watch.

"We're going right now," Roxie says as she runs in heels, a true art for a stripper.

Soon Roxie and Lexus are all over the neatly dressed black man and the dollars are literally falling out of his pockets.

After two double lap dances that include Roxie in the man's lap and Lexus rubbing her pierced breast against the back of his neck, they urge the gentleman to join them in the Champagne Room.

"You ever had your dick sucked by two country-fed women?" Lexus asks.

"Or what about seeing two women 69 each other and stroke your hard dick at the same time?" Roxie whispers into his ear.

Minutes later the man is walking behind Lexus and Roxie, trying to conceal his hard-on with his suit coat as the women lead him by the hand to the cashier.

The cashier explains how the Champagne Room works.

"You buy a bottle of champagne for $200 and then you get to go upstairs for thirty minutes," the cashier says, handing the man a bottle that normally sells for $30.

The man hands over the money, the aging heavyset cashier opens the rope, and the customer follows Roxie and Lexus up the steep, dimly lit stairway. They make a right into a glass room furnished with a soft, fake leather couch and matching chair. Three black lights create a glow-in-the-dark effect.

Roxie and Lexus waste little time undressing one another, like they have so many times before. They stand before the customer, and tell him to sit back and get comfortable. Before he can loosen his collar, Roxie is moving her long tongue all over Lexus' breasts. She sucks on her friend's nipples to bring them to attention, and the customer gives them a military salute.

Soon Lexus buries her head between Roxie's meaty thighs and the women begin moving in a rhythmic wave. The wave becomes a turbulent ocean as Roxie starts to lose control. As her hips move faster into Lexus' head, the slurping sound sends her into a hurricane of fury. Roxie screams, sits straight up on her lover's face and rocks, leading the dance with her partner's tongue. As she explodes and her fluid drains down her lover's throat, she continues to satisfy herself with her free hand.

The women get lost in each other and nearly forget that the customer is there until they hear him release himself.

"Oh shoot! Oh shoot! Shit thaaaaat was gooood!" he shouts his hand gripping his still-throbbing member.

"Damn, you musta been holding that for a long time," Lexus says as she hands the man a dry towel.

Soon Lexus is prying more money out of him.

"So, how did you like our performance?" she asks.

"It was good. Ya'll get into it," he says.

"Well, you know we don't get any of that $200 that you gave the cashier for us to come up here," Lexus says, as she helps the man clean himself up. "We live off the tips."

The man reaches into his pocket and gives each woman $100.

Memphis is watching it all on camera 12.

"Thank you," Roxie says, as she stashes the money in her bra. "You know, if you want to see us outside the club, you can."

"I would like that," the man says. "Do I call the club for that?"

"No!" both women say. "You can call us at this number," Roxie says, handing the man a business card that reads: "For the Best 69s call Lex-Rox."

"Thanks," he says.

"We didn't even get your name," Roxie says.

"My name is Mark," the man says.

"Well, we hope to hear from you soon," the girls say as they lead Nate back downstairs.

Although most men leave the club after visiting the Champagne Room, Nate goes right back to his seat and begins to watch the other dancers. His spending does not stop—a fact that quickly catches the eye of Memphis, who has the waitress send the next drink over to Nate's table on the house.

When Stallion dances, Nate appears to be the only patron to show interest in her. As she moves, he inches closer to the edge of his seat. For three songs, Stallion makes $300 off the customer of the year.

When she leaves the stage, Memphis calls her to his office.

"What is it, baby?" she asks.

"I need you to get back on your job and find out what these bitches are up to," Memphis says.

"I think Roxie and Lexus are stealing money from the club and I got a feeling Jade is on drugs," he says.

"I knew that bitch Jade had to be on something, 'cause nobody can go on all day and all night like that and never need a break," Stallion says.

"Did you hear what I said about Roxie and Lexus?" Memphis asks, his voice rising.

"Yeah, I heard you."

"But before you do that, I want you to get out there on that high roller," Memphis says. "Have you seen him before?"

"He looks familiar," Stallion says. "I can't place him, but he's dropping money like a big baller."

"I know I've seen him before, too, but I can't put my finger on it," Memphis says, scratching his head. "I want you to stick to him like glue and get all the money you can out of him. He's all yours."

But before he sends Stallion back out to the customer, Memphis makes his way into the club and pulls up a chair next to the man.

"So, you having a good time?" Memphis asks.

Nate briefly looks at Memphis and then turns his attention back to the performers.

"You ain't no faggot, are you, 'cause I don't swing that way!" Nate says and then takes a sip of his rum and coke.

Offended, but keeping his cool, Memphis clears his throat and replies, "Hell, nawh. I'm Memphis, and I run this club."

"I'm Mark," Nate lies, turning to shake the hand of the man he plans to kill.

"Customers dropping money like you we give special treatment to at Illusions," Memphis says. He's staring at Nate now, running Nate's physical features though his memory Rolodex trying to figure out who this man is.

"Whatever you want, you can have. But everything has a price," Memphis says.

Nate doesn't respond.

"So where are you from, Mark?" Memphis asks.

"I like that white bitch right there," Nate says, ignoring the question.

"How much would it cost to fuck that white bitch?" Nate asks not taking his eyes off Stallion.

Memphis says that all prices can be negotiated.

"Tell me right now how much would it cost to take that bitch home, 'cause it's clear that her man ain't laying the pipe right," Nate says, crudely grabbing his dick under the table.

Memphis rises up from the chair to say something, but instead motions for Stallion to come over when he sees Nate's bankroll.

Nate whispers something to Stallion, then takes $400 from his stash, folds it up, and hands it to Memphis. Stallion races to get her coat.

"Bye, baby," Stallion says to Memphis as Nate pops her hard on her ass.

"I'm going to warm this ass up like your nigga should," Nate says, looking back at Memphis, as he and Stallion leave the club arm in arm.

Memphis returns to his office and just sits in the dark as the music continues to thump. He doesn't want to look at the cameras anymore; he just wants to be alone.

"I know, I know him from somewhere," Memphis says.

Then, like a shotgun blast, it suddenly hit him. Memphis jumps up and screams out the name.

"*Crazy Nate!*"

CHAPTER 22

"GIRL, WHATCHA DOING?" Sandra asks Faith, sneaking in a personal call at work.

"Driving home, girl. I just closed a lucrative deal in Lawrenceville," Faith tells her old college roommate and best friend.

"Go ahead, girl, and get that money!" Sandra says. "I called you to see what you're doing tonight."

"I didn't have any plans," Faith says, a note of self-pity creeping into her voice.

"We need to catch up, because I have some big news."

"I have something to tell you, too. It's about a conversation I had with my mother a couple of days ago." Faith sounds positively glum now.

"Well, where are you now?"

"With this traffic, I'm about ninety minutes from downtown," Faith says, as she smoothly switches lanes in her 330i BMW, riding her brakes before coming to a complete stop on the crowded I-85.

"You want to meet me at that new Mardi Gras restaurant downtown?" Sandra asks. "*The Atlanta Journal Constitution's* food critic gave it three stars last week."

"I *read* that," Faith says, happy that she will get a chance to let her hair down with her best friend over dinner.

"I'll call and make reservations for eight o'clock."

"That's good. That will give us enough time to grab a couple of cocktails."

"Oh, girl, I'm going to have to pass on the drinks," Sandra says.

"What!" Faith jokes. "The white Zinfandel queen is passing up a drink! What are you trying to do, lose weight or something?"

"No, girl," Sandra says. "That was gonna be part of the surprise. I'm eating for two now." Sandra's voice drops to a whisper.

"Girl, you for real?" Faith screeches.

"Yeah, girl, I'm going to be a mother and you're going to be a godmother," Sandra says. "Now, I expect you to spoil this baby."

"I'm going to be a godmother?" Faith is so excited that she almost collides with a semi roaring up on her passenger side.

Hooonk! Hoooonnnnnnnk!

"Is that somebody blowing at you, girl?" Sandra asks. "Let me get off this phone before you cause an accident. I'll tell you more about it at dinner."

"Don't worry about it, girl, these damn semis think they run the road," Faith says, trying to keep her friend on the phone just a wee bit longer. "You've *got* to tell me more, girl! How excited is David?"

"That's what I've got to tell you about tonight," Sandra says. "Now, let me get back to pretending that I'm doing work."

"Girl, you know you ain't gonna do nothing but surf the net for shoes and purses," Faith says, causing her friend to chuckle.

"So, does he want a boy or a girl?"

"Here's my boss now," Sandra says, suddenly businesslike.

"OK, girl, he just dropped a bunch of cases at my desk that I need to get to, before I leave tonight."

"Is that the guy who's always scratching around his privates?"

"Yeah, girl, that's him. He must have crabs or something," Sandra jokes. "That reminds me. Do you remember when we were in college and that girl down the hallway from us got crabs? Remember how we walked with her to Walgreens to buy some Rid at two o'clock in the morning?"

"I do. What was her name?" Faith says, laughing.

"Her name was Karen. Remember, she got crabs from that Jamaican guy from Howard," Faith recalls.

"All three of us were in Walgreens looking for the stuff, and it was behind the counter, and we were all too scared to ask the pharmacist for it."

"Karen was trying to convince us that she would be OK, so we started walking back to the dorms, but halfway back she said those bugs were eating her coochie up." Sandra laughs so loud that she's forgetting that she is at work.

"Then, when we walked back into the store we tried to play it off," Faith says. "How many excuses did we give the pharmacist on why we wanted the crab killer?"

"First, we said we needed it for an experiment in school, and he looked at us crazy," Sandra recalls. "Then we said we needed it for a friend, and he acted like he wasn't going to give it to us. So Karen just busted out and said, 'I need it for me because these crabs are eating my coochie up.'"

"That girl was a fool," Faith says.

"She sure was. You remember? She went back with the dude and got crabs again."

"No, she didn't!"

"I thought you knew that," Sandra says. "He tried to convince her that she got crabs from the toilet seat, and she believed that dumb-shit."

Suddenly Faith stops laughing.

"I guess I can't laugh at her too hard, because I did a lot of stupid stuff with boys when I was in college." Faith is reflecting on the bad times, when she traded her body for false friendship.

"Yeah, but that was not your fault, girl," Sandra says. "You had a rough childhood, but you got through it."

"I could not have done it without you, girl," Faith says, tearing up.

"OK, don't you get all mushy on me now, because you know my hormones are all out of whack. You're going to have me crying," Sandra says. "I will see you later on tonight."

After she's had a little time to digest Sandra's big news, Faith realizes that being a godmother may be the closest she will ever come to being a mother.

Right now, Faith couldn't even get a date. She felt as though black men avoided her like the plague, and she didn't quite understand why. She was a successful businesswoman, owned her own home, had two cars, considered herself an 8-plus on a 10-point scale, but she could not find a black man to even approach her.

She takes one hand off the steering wheel and sniffs up under her arm. "I'm not musty," she says to herself.

Then she takes her hand and blows into it.

"But *my breath* is a little tart," she laughs. "That must be it."

Laughing at herself has always been good therapy.

But as she remains stuck in traffic moving at a snail's pace, Faith begins to think back on her last serious relationship. It started out like a fairy tale and ended up like an episode of the *Jerry Springer Show*.

* * *

It began just as tonight had, with plans to meet Sandra at a restaurant.

"Girl, I don't know if I'm going to be able to meet you up at Justin's. Something came up," was the message Sandra had left Faith on her cell phone that night. When Faith got the message, she was already in the parking lot of the soul food restaurant; it was packed for the monthly First Friday event that always promised to bring out the city's best and brightest black professionals. While First Friday started out that way, it quickly gave way to whoever wanted to pay the $25 cover to get into the club.

"Damn, Sandra, I wish you would've called me earlier," Faith said after listening to the message. "I could have been at home soaking my feet and watching reruns of 'Girlfriends.'"

But as she was already there, Faith decided to go in and grab at least one drink before leaving. After all, she wanted to show off her fitted class act floral dress and Tabasco leather Larny shoes from Nine West.

"That'll be $25, sister," the doorman, who did double-duty as a security guard, said as she gave him the money to squeeze into the overcrowded bar and restaurant.

The longest line of the night was for the finger food in the middle of the club/restaurant. People piled their plates with fried jumbo shrimp, chicken wings, mac and cheese, greens, and cheese, and crackers but just looking at the food was enough for Faith.

"I know I don't need any of that," she thought as she found a place at the bar. "It took me ten months to lose twelve pounds, but I bet I can easily put three 3 pounds in two hours here tonight."

"What will you have, sexy?" asked the rotund bartender with an infectious smile.

"I really don't know. What would you recommend?" Faith said.

The barman grinned like a Cheshire cat.

"Well, that all depends. Do you want something smooth and easy or do you want something hard and strong?"

Although the sexual attention felt good, Faith let the alcohol pimp down easy.

"Well, since I have a man that can give it to me any way I want it, why don't I just have you give me some water to keep me calm, until I make up my mind."

"Water," he responded.

"Yeah, water, but can you put it on the rocks please?"

As she waited for her water, Justin's filled to the point of making the claustrophobic squeamish.

"I see why they call ATL Chocolate City!" said one man who kept annoyingly bumping into Faith, while two-fisting his drinks.

"There's some honeys up in this bitch! I know I can find my baby's mama up in here," the crude man said as he touched the arm of every woman who walked past. Before long, he was trying to get up in Faith's face.

"So whatcha doin' in here?" he asked.

"Excuse me?" Faith replied.

"Whatcha doin' in here, sista? I mean this don't seem like your type of setting. I mean you sitting up here all high and mighty, with your tight dress on, lookin' all fine. I bet you won't even give a brotha like me a chance in hell, huh?" The man sipped on brandy and then his chaser.

"Well, it is First Friday, right?" Faith said. "I'm here to be around black professionals."

"Damn, you don't have to be a bitch about it. I'm just trying to get to know you."

"What did you call me?"

"I'm sorry, baby. I didn't mean to call you a bitch. It's just something I say to women, but I didn't mean no harm," the man said turning his attention to another group of women walking in.

A man who had his back to Faith the entire time turned around in his stool and told the man that his apology was not good enough.

"Who is you, her brother or something?"

"No, but I'm the man that's about to put you out of here unless you apologize properly," said Faith's steel-jawed knight, who was dressed in a cream-colored suit and pumpkin-colored shirt with a matching pocket square.

After a slight hesitation, the drunken man apologized properly and walked away.

"Thank you," Faith said to this six foot three, dark, statuesque man.

"It's all right." The man extended his powerful hand. "By the way my name is LaMar. LaMar Powell."

"I'm Faith. Faith London," the suddenly shy Faith responds.

"You wouldn't happen to be Faith London of Faith London Real Estate that just did a big deal right outside ATL last week, would you?"

"I'm the one."

LaMar reached into his suit coat and handed Faith his business card.

"It looks like we're competition," he said.

"You run Powell Real Estate," Faith said with a flushed face after reading his business card. "Well, how about that."

"It's cool. Now I see why I've been losing business to you, left and right," LaMar said. "You don't back down, and you're very attractive, and that goes a long way in this business."

"Being smart helps, too," Faith said.

"Touché," LaMar replied, slightly embarrassed. "Would you like to go over to the restaurant section and grab a real meal?"

Faith was surprised by the offer, but gladly accepted.

As other single women stared at them, Faith ate up being the center of attention. Even though she had to use the bathroom, she held it until LaMar excused himself to wash his hands, so she would not give any of the hovering vultures the opportunity to swoop down on her clean-shaven king.

Once in the bathroom, Faith could hardly get tissue down on the seat before she began to pee.

"Wooooo," she thought. "I almost didn't make it."

Through the crack in the stall door Faith could see two of the women who had been staring at LaMar come into the smoky bathroom.

"That is one fine-ass nigga in that cream suit," the taller of the two said as she powdered her face in the mirror.

"I've seen him around before, girl," the other woman said. "I think he runs his own business or something like that." She rummaged through her purse for a Black and Mild.

"Well, I wouldn't mind making that nigga my babies' daddy," the tall woman said, slapping five to her friend. "I'm gonna get that nigga before he leaves here tonight."

"I've already seen him with one bitch. How do you plan on getting to him?"

"I'm gonna slip him my number on the side. Tell that nigga that I want to suck his dick, and when I get him good and ready, see if he would wanna hit this. You know when you got a nigga's dick in your mouth, and you act like you don't know what you doing, they'll choose the pussy every time."

Soon the two chickenheads cackled their way back out to the booming music on the other side of the door.

"Tramps like that make it hard on the good women," Faith thought as she flushed the toilet and washed her hands.

Back at the table, LaMar pulled out Faith's chair.

"I thought you got lost," LaMar joked. "Is there something wrong?"

Reluctantly, Faith told LaMar she had just met what she had heard the women talking about in the bathroom.

Before she could finish, LaMar interrupted her.

"Do me a favor, and look in that crumpled napkin," LaMar said, pointing to a napkin put to the side for trash.

"What?"

"I want you to open up the napkin and look in it," he said, with a smile.

Faith opened the napkin. Inside was a crumpled hairstylist's business card. She turned it over. "Hit me up if you want your D-k sucked. You can figure out the rest," it said.

"Do you really think I would want someone like that? I took her card not to offend, but I didn't mention it to you because we were having such a nice time. Now, can we get back to enjoying ourselves?"

Faith knew that LaMar was a keeper.

After dinner, neither of them wanted the date to end. When LaMar walked Faith to her car, he gave her a kiss on the cheek and pulled her closer to him.

"Will you call me so I know you made it home, OK?" LaMar asked, writing his cell phone number on the back of another business card and handing it to her. "I'm just going to get my friend up out of here and take him home."

"Sure," Faith said smiling, as she drove off.

When Faith called LaMar forty-five minutes later, he was on his way home with his friend.

"I really enjoyed spending time with you tonight," Faith told LaMar. "I owe this night to my best friend, Sandra."

"I don't understand," LaMar responded.

"Well, if Sandra had not stood me up tonight, we probably wouldn't have ever met."

"It doesn't have to end here. I would love to see you again."

Like a schoolgirl, Faith responded eagerly, "Tell me when and where and I'm there."

"I will call you tomorrow and we can talk more then. I really want to get my friend home; he's had way too much to drink."

"OK, I'll be waiting."

"Goodnight, Faith."

The next three months were the best of Faith's life. LaMar was with her almost all the time, and when he wasn't with her, she was thinking about him. It was the first time since her college days that she had given her old "Mr. Dependable" vibrator a break.

LaMar was the first man to be patient with Faith. Their lovemaking sessions were never rushed; instead, LaMar was slow and gentle. He never gave her a slam-bam, thank-you ma'am.

When Faith opened up to LaMar and told him that she was the victim of sexual abuse, he held her in his strong arms and let her cry for what seemed like forever. When she woke up, he was still holding her.

Just when things appeared to be reaching their zenith, Faith got the call that suddenly changed her life.

Rinnng! Rinnnng!

"Hello," Faith said.

"Yeah, is this the bitch that's been sleeping with my man?"

"Who is this?" Faith asked. "You must have the wrong number."

"This is Tracey! And I know you've been sleeping with my man, LaMar," the angry woman on the other end said.

Faith's heart sunk deep into her stomach.

"You must have me confused. LaMar told me that he was not with anyone else," Faith said, rolling out of bed and looking directly at a framed picture she took with LaMar three weeks ago at the aquarium. "I can't believe this shit."

"He's my maaannnn, bitch! I've been with him for three long years. We can meet and talk about it, if you don't believe me," the woman said, suddenly sensing that Faith really didn't know that LaMar was a cheater.

"I'm on my way downtown, but I can meet you at the Lenox Square mall in two hours," the woman offered.

Against her better judgment, Faith agreed.

"I have your cell number. I will call you when I get there," Tracey said.

Faith was pulling into the mall's parking lot when her cell phone rang, causing her to jump.

"Where are you?"

"I'm in the parking lot."

"I'm outside the main entrance of the Louis Vuitton store," Tracey said. "You know where that is?"

"OK, I'm walking there now. But how will I know you?"

"Oh, you'll know me," the woman said with a chuckle. "I have on a long red dress."

Faith's heart pounded as she made her way toward the expensive store.

"What am I going to talk to this woman about?" she thought. "Why did I agree to this? She could be setting me up."

But she knew the reason why. She wanted to meet this woman. She needed to know if this woman was really sleeping with her man, and if she was, what did she look like. She needed to know if this woman was prettier than her, sexier than her, or more educated than her.

Faith's pace increased to an assertive trot.

As she got closer she could see a tall figure in a red dress. The woman's back turned to Faith, and she was talking on the phone as she stood in front of the store.

Right before Faith could tap her shoulder, Tracey turned around.

"You're a man!" Faith screeched.

"No, I'm not, bitch, I'm a transsexual, honey," Tracey fired back. "And I'm more woman than you could ever be."

Faith threw up.

As the transsexual continued to berate her, Faith crumpled onto a bench, holding her head and stomach.

"You need to face it, bitch! LaMar is gay, and he's my man. He don't want you, bitch! He loves gurl pussy!" Tracey yelled. "We have been together for three years. He paid for these beautiful breasts." Tracey pushed up her 38-DDs. "LaMar don't want you!" she said again, pointing her long, red fingernails at Faith's face.

Soon mall security was escorting the six-foot-two tranny away.

Faith had no idea that LaMar slept with men. Although Atlanta is known as the black gay capital of the world, LaMar would have been the last man she suspected of such a thing.

She had to face facts; her king was an undercover queen.

When she confronted LaMar about his secret life, he did not deny it. As a matter of fact, he told her he was not gay, because he only did the penetrating.

Faith put all of his stuff out that night, and scheduled an emergency visit to her doctor the next day to take an HIV/AIDS test. She received her negative results three days later. Those were the longest three days of her life.

LaMar tried calling Faith several times after that, but she never talked to him again.

She had never told Sandra about the events, because she was too embarrassed. After all, Sandra had the perfect relationship with David.

Instead, she had to laugh at herself to keep from going crazy.

It could have been worse, though–she could have found out about LaMar on The Jerry Springer Show.

"First, let's introduce LaMar."

"LaMar, it says here you have a secret to tell."

"Yes, Jerry, I'm in love with my girlfriend of three months, but I'm here to tell her today that I've been having sex with a transsexual for three years . . . Jerrrrrrryyy! Jerrrrrryyyyyyy! Jerrrrrryyyyyy!"

* * *

As Faith pulls up in front of the Mardi Gras restaurant, she realizes that she's been crying. "Come on girl," she says to herself. "Get yourself together. You're about to be a godmother."

When Sandra walks in, Faith jumps up from her seat at the bar and rushes over to hug Sandra and touch her belly.

After the waiter seats them, the two chatter like they haven't talked in years.

Faith tells Sandra about her mother finally apologizing to her for the years of abuse, and Sandra gives her a long hug and holds her hand.

"You probably need to go talk to your mother in person," she suggests. "It's been a long time, and it could help you in the healing process."

"I don't think I could ever set foot back in that house," Faith says. "There are just too many bad memories there."

"Now, do you think I would let you do that on your own?" Sandra asks. "I'll go with you. I have to face my parents anyway, to tell them that they are going to be grandparents."

Faith thinks for a minute, then nods.

"I think I can face her with you," she says. "Thank you for being such a wonderful friend."

"So what is the deal, girl?" Faith probes, as the server places red beans, rice, and cornbread on the table.

"This is going to be good," Sandra says, reaching for the Red Dot. "I don't know, but since I've been pregnant, I've just been craving hot food."

"Girl, stop stalling and tell me what's going on."

"OK, girl, here it is: David may not be the father."

"What!" Faith can't believe it.

"I don't know how to explain it. You see, I love David, but I don't think I was ever *in love* with David. We had our problems; he cheated on me and I cheated on him, but I ended up falling in love with the person I slept with."

Faith's jaw drops. She cannot believe that Sandra cheated on her husband. It's like June Cleaver cheating on Ward, on "Leave It to Beaver"–it just can't be.

"Girl, close your mouth," Sandra says.

"I'm sorry. I just can't believe this. Does David know?"

"Yeah, he knows. I told him right after I found out I was pregnant. We went to counseling, but I can't stop seeing my lover."

"Why not? Are you a-*dick*-ted?"

"You can't judge me," Sandra snaps.

"When I told David that I was pregnant, and I knew that he could not be the father, he forgave me and told me that we could just continue on, and not let anyone know and that he will raise my baby as his," Sandra says.

"Well, that's good–ain't it?" Faith is genuinely puzzled.

"Faith, David just wants to save face. He doesn't want his family to look at him any differently. You see, David has always been the pretty, playboy type and everyone knew him as that, but when I messed around on him, his world crumbled. But instead of trying to fix *us*, he was only worried about *his* image."

"So what are you going to do?" Faith asks.

"I want to be with my lover. He loves me, Faith. David and I stopped *loving* each other like that a long time ago. We just went through the motions, because that's what everyone around us expected *us* to do."

"I don't understand," Faith says.

"I guess what I'm trying to say is that we have to make ourselves happy, and stop trying to do the things that make everyone around us happy.

"We got married, because everyone around us was obsessed with us getting married. David and I gave everyone that, but no one was really interested in my life until Mark came along."

"So that's his name?"

"Besides *you*, Faith, Mark was the only person who showed that he cared for *me*. David simply used me as a trophy. I was the cute wife who said all the right things and supported him in his career, while he totally ignored mine."

"This is not where I wanted to be at this time in my life, Faith," an exasperated Sandra says. "I dropped out of law school for him so he could earn his MBA. And when I wanted to go back to school, it was never the right time. Faith, do you realize how much it hurts to know that I know more than my boss but I'm nothing but a glorified clerk?

"I don't want to be getting someone's coffee, picking up their dry-cleaning, and doing their filings the rest of my life, so I've decided that I'm moving back to Chicago. I'm going to stay with my folks until I have my child, and then do everything within my power to get back into school."

Faith interrupts: "Well, what about Mark?"

"He's coming with me," Sandra says. "I have not told David that yet, but I will, soon."

"Who is this guy?"

"That doesn't matter, Faith. What I will tell you about him is that he loves me, and he will love our baby. But trust me on this; I knew he was the one from the moment I laid eyes on him."

"I don't know what to say," Faith admits. "You've always made the right decisions."

"The only thing I need you to say is that you will be *the best* godmother in the world."

"I will," Faith promises. A tear runs down her cheek.

"Now, let's make a toast," Sandra says.

"To love, health, prosperity, and friends," the two say before clinking their lemonade glasses.

Faith's cell phone rings.

"Who is this calling me?" she asks. "It's a Chicago number."

"You'd better answer it," Sandra says, while diving her fork into her friend's bowl of jambalaya.

"Hello."

Faith doesn't know the caller's voice, either.

"Who is this?" she asks.

"This is your sister, Angel."

"Oh my god, Angel! I haven't spoken to you in years. What's going on?"

"I need a favor," Angel says, sniffling.

"What is it?" Faith asks. "And why are you crying?"

"I need to know if I can stay with you for a while until I get my feet on the ground." Angel sobs. "I really need to get out of Chicago."

Faith hesitates and then says, "Yeah, you can. Do you need money to get here?"

"No, I have it," Angel says.

"Do you have Kane?" Faith asks.

"You know I'm not going anywhere without my baby."

"How are you coming?" Faith asks.

"I will leave in a couple of days," Angel says. "I will call you back tomorrow."

Faith hangs up.

"What was that about?" Sandra asks.

"One more toast," Faith says. "To family drama."

CHAPTER 23

"PICK UP THE phone!" Memphis yells frantically into the receiver as Stallion's line rings and rings.

Giving up, Memphis slams the receiver down.

"If that nigga hurts *my* bitch, Willie, your ass is dead."

I see how you wanna play. "You send your top dog to do your dirty work. Now you done made this shit personal."

Memphis picks up the phone again—this time to call Willie.

"Will, this is Memphis," he says. "Don't say shit nigga. I see you sent crazy-ass Nate to do your dirty work. You know you done fucked up."

Willie is calm. "It didn't have to go this far, but you were determined to hurt my boy, and I'm not going to let that happen."

"You act like that muthafucka is your son or somethin'!" Memphis yells. "Tray ain't shit to you. He ain't shit! Ain't shit but a soon-to-be dead-ass nigga!"

Memphis turns quiet and matter-of-fact, "You taught me the game, partna', but you done changed the rules, and now you got your man down here to hurt my woman."

"I didn't have nothin' to do with that," Willie clarifies.

"Too late, muthafucka," Memphis says. "Tray is dead before the week is out, and I'm going to do to Nate what the fucking Vietcong should have done to his crazy ass in 'Nam."

"You sound like you talking war," Willie says. He grins as he slips his gun into his slacks.

"It is what it is, fat boy!" Memphis yells just before he slams the phone down.

A few minutes later, Memphis's phone rings.

"Hello!" he yells.

"Memphis, it's me, Desiree." Her voice cracks. "I need some time off," she says.

"Don't do this to me now, baby girl." Memphis' tone changes to concern. "You know you're the best dancer I got, and I need you to help us keep this raggedy muthafucka going."

"I'm just hurting right now," she says, crying. "I won't be any good to you for a while."

"What's wrong?"

"Angel is gone, and I don't know when or if she's coming back."

"You know I don't mean to be all up in yours, but did ya'll fall out over that punk-ass nigga named Tray?" Memphis asks.

"Yeah," Desiree says, crying even harder. "I hate him with a passion, and I can't believe Angel would let someone come between us. She told me she actually loved him."

"Do you want him dead?" Memphis asks.

The boldness of his words catches Desiree off-guard.

"What? No, I don't want him dead . . . I don't even know him."

"I understand. You want Angel and her son to be happy with this nigga," Memphis says, the words drenched in sarcasm.

"When was the last time you've seen her?" he asks. "Yeah, he's probably serving that pussy up nice and good right now."

"Why are you saying this?" Desiree asks, sobbing.

"'Cause the only way she won't take her ass back to that nigga is if he's dead," Memphis yells. "Now, I don't know about you but I need to get at this nigga for some payback."

"But you don't even know how to find him," Desiree says.

"I'll look all over Milwaukee until I find his ass. He can't be that hard to find."

"I can help you find him," she offers, after thinking about how her lover could be in Travon's arms.

"How can you do that, baby girl?"

"I have his number."

"That's good," Memphis says. "But hold on to the number for now. We have to come up with a plan. I will be over there as soon as I shut the club down."

Two hours later, Memphis pulls his black truck up in front of Desiree's building.

"I have a plan, baby girl," Memphis says, dropping down on the couch where Kane used to sleep.

"Goddamn, ya'll have a lot of shit," he says, observing the overflow of clothing in the living room.

Desiree stands in the doorway, her arms folded.

"So what's the plan?"

* * *

When Nate and Stallion make it back to his motel they are walking arm in arm, like they've been friends and lovers for years.

"You're so sweet," Stallion says.

Inside the small room, Nate quickly takes Stallion's imitation fur.

"Why don't you go wash up a bit?" Nate suggests. "I have a bar of soap in the shower. I left something in the car, so I'll be right back."

When Nate returns, with a large roll of thick plastic, he hears a voice as earthy as a cupped handful of dark, moist sand coming from the shower. Stallion is singing "Portuguese Love."

> You make love forever, baby
> You make love forever . . .

"For poor white trash, she sounds pretty good," Nate notes. "Sounds just like Tina Marie."

When Stallion opens the bathroom door, the steam rolls out like fog. Wrapped in a threadbare, blue motel towel, she pads over to Nate who is sitting on the edge of the bed in only his military green boxers.

"You smell really good," Nate says as he wraps his arms around Stallion's body and squeezes her round tight ass.

"Not bad for an old lady, is it, Daddy?" Stallion whispers. "I have to work extra hard to keep up with the new bootie in the club."

"It's nice," Nate says as he pulls the towel off.

With Stallion's body illuminated only by the bathroom light, Nate notices how perfectly flawed her body is.

"You have moles on your chest," he says.

"Yes, I do, baby," Stallion replies. "My grandmother had lots of them, or so I was told."

As Nate stands up, he forces Stallion down to her knees to service him. She gently begins to suck him, but he grabs her wet hair and forces her to suck him harder.

Stallion's gags soon drown out the sounds of the persistent drip from the rusted showerhead. She tries to push away, but Nate is in charge.

"Suck this dick good, baby, because I'm about to fuck you in all that white juicy ass of yours," he says in a demented voice.

In one swift motion, Nate lifts Stallion up by her shoulders and forces her facedown on the twin-sized bed. He mounts Stallion and plunges deep into her ass with his stiff dick. She tries to fight him off, but she loses the war against her much stronger opponent.

"Owwww, Mark, Please stop." She cries. "You're hurting me."

"Take this shit bitch!" Nate yells. "I've wanted to fuck your ass for a long, long time."

He pulls her arms behind her back and holds them in place with his own weight, raping Stallion for fifteen minutes. Then he explodes on her back and quickly climbs off the white horse.

She is broken, angry, and confused.

Stallion sobs into the soiled pillow that had muffled her cries as Nate raped her. How did she go from being a woman who never had to pull her panties off to make a thousand dollars, to being raped by a man for $100?

Her despair turns to panic as she hears the rustling of plastic in the darkness, along with the whispering and humming of the song "Take me by the Water."

> Take me to the water,
> Take me to the water,
> Take me to the water
> To be baptized.
>
> I'm going back home, going back home,
> Gonna stay here no longer
> I'm going back home, going back home,
> To be baptized.

Stallion switches into survival mode.

"Mark, I'm ready to go home now," she says, wiping her tears and reaching for her purse, which was near the bed but is now gone.

"I know," Nate replies from the blackness. "I will take you home soon."

"Mark," she says, her voice barely above a whisper, "I hope you had a good time. Can you turn on the light for me please? You hurt me a little bit," she says, sitting up on the edge of the small bed, feeling plastic under her feet.

"Mark! Mark! What are you doing?" She pulls the thin sheet up to her chest in a futile effort to protect herself.

Soon she feels a sharp blade next to her jugular.

"Why are you doing this to me?" she pleads through tears. "Please, if you let me go, I won't say anything to Memphis, I promise."

The pleading gives Nate another erection.

"Bitch, you really think I'm worried about that muthafucka?"

"What did I do?" Stallion pleads.

"White Chocolate, this ain't got nothing to do with you," Nate says. "You're just one casualty in this man's war."

"By the way," Nate says turning on a small nightstand light, "They call me Crazy Nate."

"No! Nooooo!" were the last words Stallion could muster before Nate plunged the 7-inch blade deep into her throat.

As he leans her forward onto the plastic, Nate holds her arms and croons, "Shhhhhhhhh. Let it bleed, baby."

White Chocolate's blood runs onto the plastic tarp like paint poured from a can.

"Damn, that's a lot of blood, I musta' hit that vein just right," Nate says, admiring his handiwork.

As the life drains out of her thirty-seven-year-old body and Stallion's struggle to remain here on earth comes to an end, Nate takes his calloused hands and helps her close her eyes for the last time.

"You won't be alone," he whispers into her ear as he lays her down onto the plastic and begins to wrap her up like a cocoon. "I will bring your husband to you soon. Till death do you apart."

CHAPTER 24

A LOT HAS TRANSPIRED during the weeks that Darnell has been in Jamaica with his new wife, and I cannot wait to fill my best friend in on all the details. In the waiting area of Mitchell International Airport, I make small talk with a curvaceous AirTran flight attendant.

When the newlyweds come through the tunnel, they are both three shades darker from the hot Jamaican sun.

"Man, I didn't think ya'll was coming back," I tease, grabbing Taylor's overnight bag. "Damn, girl, what do you have in here—bricks?"

"Stop it, Tray, and give me a hug," Taylor says. "Actually, your gift is in there."

"Tray, did you remember to go over to the house and feed my fish?" she asks.

"Now don't you start, Taylor. You're *supposed* to nag your husband, not his best friend."

After piling all of the luggage and themselves into my car, Darnell and Taylor tell me about walking along Dunns River Falls, snorkeling, walking nude on the resorts of Hedonism I, II, and III, and even deep-sea diving.

"So, Tray, what have you been up to?" Taylor asks. "And who was that *cute* flight attendant you were talking to?"

"Oh her, nobody important." I glance in the rearview mirror to gauge Taylor's reaction.

"Did you get her number?" Taylor asks.

"That's a little personal, don't you think?"

"Oh, I understand, you boys want to talk about that amongst yourselves."

"Man, what have you been telling your wife about me?" I joke to Darnell.

"I just told her that you usually get any woman you want," Darnell says.

"We have to get you married, Tray," Taylor says, flipping through a *People* magazine that she bought in the airport.

"I know what this is. It's called wedded-couple bliss. Just because you got married, you want everyone around you that's single to get married so you don't lose your single friends. I'm hip to that," I respond.

"No, don't take it that way," Taylor says. She puts the magazine down. "You're a good man, Tray, and I know one day you will be able to make *one* woman happy."

"Also, since the wedding, my girlfriend can't stop talking about you," Taylor says.

"What are you talking about?" Travon asks, merging onto I-94 to take the couple to their suburban home.

"She's right, Tray," Darnell says. "Her girlfriend Mya called us on our honeymoon four times asking about you."

"Which one was she?" I flip through my mental Rolodex.

"She's very cute, has cropped hair, about five foot seven. Oh, yeah, and she's a prosecutor," Taylor says.

"Baby, Tray doesn't process like that," Darnell says. "She was the light-skinned honey with an ass that J-Lo wished she could have. She was dancing like a sex kitten with our frat Craig."

"Ohhh, yeah, now I know who you're talking about."

"I knew you would remember," Darnell says, laughing.

"That's a damn shame," Taylor says, laughing in the backseat.

"Well, I guess you can hook me up with her," Travon offers.

"Nooooo way," Taylor says. "You're not ready to settle down, and my friends are not going to be your sleeping buddies."

"What are you talking about, Taylor? You're the one with *your* mind in the gutter, talking about sleeping with the girl, and I don't even know her last name."

"From what I heard, that has not stopped you before." Taylor playfully pushes my shoulder.

"Frat, what have you been telling your woman?"

"OK, we're going to leave you alone, Travon," Taylor says. "We just want you to be in a stable relationship when you become our child's godfather."

"What? Are you pregnant?" I turn around looking at Taylor's stomach.

"Keep your eyes on the road, boy. I ain't pregnant yet."

"But it ain't from a lack of trying," Darnell says, slapping his frat brother five.

That night, Darnell and I meet up at Roots, a posh new club on the city's lower east side.

"Can you believe it? My first night out as a married man," Darnell boasts, while looking around at a group of skimpily dressed blond-haired women walking by and giving us both sexy looks.

"All of this is behind me now, Tray," Darnell says. "I've turned over a new leaf."

"Come on, Darnell, don't come at me like that. I've been knowing you too long. You're married—not dead."

"No, I'm serious this time, man," Darnell explains.

"So did you tell Taylor you were all up in a white girl raw dog hours before you married her?"

"Well, you told me not to tell her that. And besides, this leaf turned after I said, I do."

"OK, I see how it works," I try to look serious at Darnell before we both spit out our drinks laughing.

"You got me, man," Darnell concedes. "I love her with all my heart though, Tray," he says, raising his bottle for a toast.

"You should love her. She makes you a better person."

"May your love last for all eternity, and may your bond grow to more than just husband and wife, but best friends, too."

"Damn, that's pretty deep," Darnell says. "But you know you will always be my ace."

"I know, frat."

"Which brings me to the big news. I decided to take the job in Miami. I start in two weeks."

"What? Congratulations, boy!" Darnell shouts jumping off his stool.

"But wait a minute, frat, that means you're leaving." The pain of losing his best friend starts to set in.

"I know frat," Travon says. "It's a little weird. We've been knowing each other since freshman year in college, and been best friends ever since."

"You're right," Darnell says. "Now I hope this doesn't sound gay, but when I was on my honeymoon that was the longest period of time that we didn't see each other."

"Yep, that sounds gay," I joke, punching Darnell in the arm.

"But seriously, Darnell, I'm moving into a huge market, and I'm ready to blow up. They're giving me free rein to do whatever I want, and the money . . ." I let out a long whistle for emphasis. "Let's just put it this way, my company could not even come within the same stratosphere on the ends."

"I'm going to miss you, frat," Darnell says, giving his best friend a hug.

"I'm going to miss you too, boy." I slap Darnell's back.

"So what did your boss say?" Darnell asks, returning to his happier self so as not to rain on my parade.

"Well, Mark was pissed at first, but when I told him what they were offering me, he just looked at me and said 'You're going to love those beaches.'"

"By the way, he's throwing a going-away party for me at the Hyatt in a week, so it should be cool. But I got to warn you, I think he's going to have strippers."

Darnell laughs so hard beer comes out of his nose.

"I can handle it, frat," he says. "Where is he getting them from?"

"I don't know, man, and don't really care. This will be a party for everyone else to enjoy. The real party for me is when I start my new job."

"Speaking of strippers, Tray did you ever hear back from the stripper that you hooked up with at my bachelor party?"

"Nawh, dude. And I really thought we made a connection. I mean, I really can't stop thinking about her."

"Damn, Tray, did she put it on you that good?"

Nodding my head, I reveal that it really wasn't about the sex. "I saw something in her eyes. She's really a good person."

"Did you tell Nicole that you're leaving?"

"Are you crazy? I'm not telling her, and you'd better not tell her."

"The only other people who need to know are my mother, Willie, and Janet."

"Well, your mother is going to be OK," Darnell says.

"I know, she will. She was never really the same after my father left. I think she lost some of her mind, and she's just now getting some of it back."

"Janet though?" Darnell asks.

"Yeah, frat. I think I'm going to ask her to move to Miami with me."

"No, you're not!"

"I am. When I didn't hear back from Angel, I figured that was a sign to move on."

"Janet and I have both changed for the better. I think we can make it work."

"Well, frat, I wish you luck on that. But I don't think she's going anywhere with you unless you're ready to bust out with a ring," Darnell warns.

"You think so?"

"Not only that, I think Nicole will kill her and then kick your ass if she finds out," Darnell jokes.

"Why do you keep bringing her up?"

"Because, frat, she's crazy–and I mean crazzzzzzzzyy–in love with you and she is not going to let you leave that easily."

"Man, you're starting to freak me out," I say.

"Now, let's be real. Nicole will not let any girl get close to you. I think she would hurt anyone that had enough courage to try. I'm surprised you've been able to get as many women as you have with her around. But I guess she does have to eat and sleep," Darnell jokes.

"She's not my woman, man. She knows this."

"OK," Darnell says. "The problem will be you getting out of town and her not knowing about it. As a betting man, I don't see it happening."

* * *

"You're giving me some of your best stuff before you get outta here for sunny Florida," my boss says to me before my exit interview.

"Tray, I know we didn't always see eye to eye on a lot of things, but I've always respected you as a journalist. Never lose that edge and always continue to push the envelope no matter where your career takes you."

"I will. I'll clean off my desk in the morning and knock off a little early today."

"You do that because you're going to need all your energy for the parrrrrtay I have planned tonight at the Hyatt, and, man, do I have a surprise for you," Mark says.

"You know I don't like surprises, so tell me what it is."

"OK, well, I got these strippers from an ad in one of the alternative weeklies." Marcus hands Travon the advertisement. "So we can do *anything and everything*. They work for themselves," he whispers.

Marcus can hardly contain himself as he rubs his chapped hands together. "Let me show you what one of the girl looks like," he says, going through the bottom drawer of his desk. He throws Tray the January issue of "Black Tail" magazine.

"Turn to page 15, and look at Suga. One of the girls looks just like that. No lie," he says.

"She's tight," I agree, admiring the dark-skinned beauty with 36-28-38 measurements spread across the glossy pages of the skin magazine.

"Tight! That's all you have to say? That's wifey material right there. Now give me my magazine back." He reaches over the desk and snatches the muff mag out of my hands.

"Now, go ahead and get out of my office. I've got a section to get out before we can have some fun tonight."

When I arrive at the Hyatt with Darnell at eight o'clock, there are already more than twenty-five men crowded into Suite 1920. As the guest of honor, I'm quickly greeted by frat, friends, and soon to be former coworkers.

Heavy bass music plays, and the men turn to focus their attention on the seven girls who showed up to perform. The dancers are wearing Mardi Gras masks and pass out masks to the men as they strip to "Back That Thang Up," by Juvenile.

> Got you working with some ass, yeah
> You bad, yeah
> Make a nigga spend his cash, yeah
> His last, yeah . . .

Soon the dancers are entertaining the men in corners, the bathroom, on the bed, and on the floor, and the dollars are flying. "I have a special surprise for you, Travon," Marcus says as he pulls the executive chair to the middle of the suite for the man of the hour to have a seat.

"I picked this thick-ass girl out myself; she goes by the name 'Dark Angel,'" Mark says as he puts on his Mardi Gras mask and hands one to me.

"Let me get my singles ready." Mark pulls out a wad of dollars.

A dancer comes into the room crawling cat-like on her hands and knees toward me. Her muscular thighs and arms remind me of a strong feline. As she gets in front of me, she grabs my penis through my pants and turns around to rub her round ass on it.

"Go ahead, boy, you can touch her," my grinning boss says as he drops dollars over her head.

When she starts to unzip my pants, I grab her wrist gently to stop her. Out the corner of my eye I see more of my boss than he ever wanted to.

"This nigga is standing next to me with his dick in his hand," I mumble under my breath as I slide my chair away from my boss' dick.

When the dancer mounts me for a kiss, I notice something strangely familiar about this "Dark Angel."

I pull off her mask.

"*Nicole*! What the hell!" I shout, pushing her off me and onto the floor.

"Oh my god! Tray!" She scrambles to her feet and runs off to the bathroom.

"What the hell?" Marcus says. "Tray, what did you do?"

I knock on the locked bathroom door as Nicole screams at me "Tray! I'm so sorry!"

Marcus walks up. "Tray, I don't know what's going on with you and that girl, but you're messing up the vibe in here. Can you hurry up and get her outta there, so we can have some fun?"

I roll my eyes at him until he says, "Man, just hurry up!"

"Nicole, I'm not leaving until we talk."

When Darnell comes over to the door to see what's going on, he is in total shock.

"You mean to tell me that's Nicole in there, and she's a stripper?" he says. "I don't believe it."

He grabs me by the arm and pulls me out into the hallway.

"I bet you she's doing this to spy on you," Darnell says. "I read this in a book once. This girl was so obsessed with this guy that she did everything that he did in order to spy on him."

I look at my friend in disbelief at his stupidity.

"Dude, don't you get it? She's a stripper. That's what she does. I'm in shock, because she's been so against anything sexual," I say.

As we continue talking in the hallway, Nicole bolts past us.

At first I figure to just let her go, but Darnell convinces me otherwise.

When the elevator doors open, I hop in with her.

"So you mind telling me what's going on?" I inquire.

Nicole is a tightlipped, high-heeled nightmare.

When we reach the ground floor, she storms off the elevator into the parking lot with me hot on her heels.

"Will you stop for a second and talk to me?"

Nicole reaches her car, opens the door, and hops in without a word.

After cranking up the car, she rolls down her window.

"Do you realize this is the first time you ever chased after me, Travon? I've chased you for five years, and it took this to get you to do it."

"So let me get this straight. You shake your ass for dollars and that's my fault? How long have you been tricking, Nicole?"

"What does it matter, Travon? You don't want me," she screams.

"Fuck it then, Nicole!"

My flip attitude makes her furious.

She climbs out of her car barefoot, stabs her finger into my chest and says, "I did this all for you."

"Get outta here with that shit, Nicole."

"No, I did. Travon you are an expensive-ass man to keep. How do you think you got the closets full of suits, shoes, and shirts?

"I know how tough your profession is, and how tough it is for a black man in your field. To look the part you have to dress the part," she says with tears ruining her mascara.

"I figured one day you would take me with you when you hit it big, that you would never forget me.

"Yes, I danced for the past two years. I stopped sleeping with you because I felt dirty after being pawed at and slobbed over by disgusting men. I did this for us!" she says in a defeated tone before turning away to get into her car.

"One more thing, Travon.

"I found out two days ago that you were leaving. I guess you weren't going to tell me. Why couldn't you at least do that? I thought we were at the very least friends."

"Don't answer that," she says. "I don't think I can take being hurt anymore tonight."

When Nicole pulls off in her well-beaten, 1987 Nissan Maxima, I decide that it is time for me to grow up. I will not ask Janet to come to Miami. I owe at least that much to the woman who loved me in a way that I could not love her.

CHAPTER 25

"I DON'T KNOW IF this is going to work, Memphis," Desiree says as she dials the number that is neatly written on a piece of brown paper.

"It'll work baby, trust me," Memphis whispers into her ear as the phone rings. "For all we know, Angel may be with him right now."

"It's just ringing, he's not picking up," Desiree says.

"Let it ring. He'll pick up."

Just as Memphis predicted, a male's voice answers.

"Hello, hello," I answer the 312 area code number.

Tongue-tied, Desiree garbles her words. "Yes. Ahhh. I'm sorry. May I speak to Tray? I mean Travon."

"Speaking. Who is calling?" I repeat more aggressively.

Memphis nudges Desiree to speak.

"You don't know me, but I'm a friend of Angel. You *do* remember Angel, don't you?"

I'm surprised by the call and somewhat cautious.

"Of course I remember. The question is, does she remember me, since I haven't heard from her."

Caught off guard yet relieved that her lover has not contacted Travon, Desiree feels more at ease talking to the man she blames for ruining her relationship.

"So you haven't *talked to her?*" she asks.

"That's what I said. Do you mind telling me what this is all about?"

"Would you like to see Angel again?"

"I don't know. It's been some time, and I think if Angel really wanted to see me she would have called me by now."

"What do you mean you don't know?" Desiree voice rises. "I mean, from what I heard, you two shared a passionate moment, or are you saying she was just a piece of ass or something?"

I go on the offensive.

"Look, lady, I don't know who you are or what Angel told you, but what *we* shared is really none of your business. But since you're asking, I thought *it would* lead to more. After I didn't hear from her after all this time . . . I just chalked it up as a one-night stand."

Memphis, who's been listening in, motions for Desiree to put her hand over the mouthpiece.

"Tell that mutherfucka that she wants to see him, and that you're planning a surprise party for her."

"Well, Travon, I don't know you, but I know Angel very well," Desiree says, "and she's mentioned you a lot. She's a little shy, and she didn't know how you would look at her after what happened."

"What do you mean?"

"I guess after you two had sex, she didn't know how you would feel about her," Desiree explains.

"It was more than that. I can't really explain it, but it was way more than the way you're portraying it. The only thing that she may be embarrassed about is how I made her flavor flav-looking pimp fall and bust his ass when he was about to hit her."

Cutting her eyes at Memphis, "What happened with that?"

"The only thing I know is the aftermath. Some washed-up white chick was up in Angel's face, and Little Man was acting like he was going to knock Angel out. I wasn't about to let that happen."

"So anyway, how did you end up with my number?"

"Oh, I stole it out of Angel's purse."

"And you are calling me because?"

"A bunch of girls were planning a surprise party for Angel, and I knew that you would be the best gift we could give her," Desiree says, receiving a nod of approval from Memphis.

"That sounds cool. But I don't know if I'm going to be able to do it. You see I'm getting ready to go out of town in a week." I'm not going to share all my business with this strange woman.

"Can you hold on a second, Travon?" Desiree asks, putting her hand over the phone.

"This ain't going to work, Memphis, he's getting ready to go out of town," she whispers.

"Tell that nigga that we can plan the party around him and his schedule, because he's the gift and that we're planning on having the party in Milwaukee anyway," Memphis instructs.

Desiree shakes her head.

"Go ahead and tell him," Memphis whispers forcefully.

"Hello, Travon? Sorry about that," Desiree apologizes. "We can plan the party around your schedule. Since it's a surprise party, we can bring her to Milwaukee. I was wondering if you knew of a not-too-expensive hotel where we could have it."

"I don't know," I hesitate.

"Oh, please, Tray," Desiree begs. "I know she wants to see you."

"Let me check my schedule and get back to you," I finally offer. "What's your number, so I can call you back?"

Thinking on her feet, Desiree quickly says, "Oh, I'm at work right now, so can I call you back in about an hour?"

"Yeah, OK," I'm not sure what I just agreed to.

"OK, I will talk to you soon."

"You think he bought it?" Desiree asks Memphis after she hangs up.

"I don't know," Memphis says, playing with a toothpick in his mouth.

Memphis ponders out loud, "I guess it all depends on how well she put that pussy on him that night."

Desiree storms out of the room and into the kitchen.

Memphis follows her.

"I didn't mean it like that. What I'm trying to say is, if he's as sprung on her as you are, he'll be ready to meet," he says, turning on the stove to heat up some coffee.

Desiree glares at Memphis, with her arms folded, and asks if he really planned on putting his hands on Angel. Memphis answers by not answering.

"So tell me, Memphis, what is this really all about? Is it because he embarrassed you? You want to kill him because of that? I mean, I don't get it," Desiree says, shaking her head in disbelief. "I don't know if I want to be a part of this."

"Let me tell you something, baby girl, we're at war."

"When Angel disrespected me by getting with that punk for free, she basically said: 'Fuck you Memphis, fuck you Desiree, and fuck all you other bitches who wanted to fuck him too'. I seen that pretty-ass nigga. All the bitches probably wanted to fuck him that night, but at least they would have got paid for it. I would've got paid for it."

"When you on the clock, that means yo' shit belongs to me. I don't give a fuck what you do on your own time. You don't know this, but she's been planning on fucking me over for a long time, and this was not the time to do it."

"Then punk-ass wants to play hero, putting his nose in my shit! After what happened, I've been losing respect left and right from these bitches, and you know Rox and Lex are like cancer. Them bitches got foul! Now, they're spreadin' their shit to the other girls."

"We're about to lose this club, *and* we are at war. Now, you either with me or against me, but I need you Desiree, you're one of my best soldiers."

Finally, Desiree speaks up. "How is it a war and nobody's died yet?"

"That's where you're wrong," Memphis says. "Them niggas already made the first move, and they got Stallion."

"What?" Desiree looks at Memphis dumbfounded.

"I let my wife walk out of my club with their best sniper, so I know she ain't coming back."

Clinching a napkin and wiping his face, Memphis proceeds to explain to Desiree what they are dealing with.

"This is an eye for an eye, baby girl," he says. "But you know what, crazy-ass Nate ain't gonna stop there. He's going to come after someone else that's close to me, before he comes after me."

"I'm going to keep you by my side and protect you," Memphis says, taking his .44 Magnum out of his waistband and placing it on the table.

"Are you strapped?" a frightened Desiree eyes the piece.

"No, I don't even know how to shoot a gun, and this shit is really starting to scare me." She pours Memphis's coffee and sits down at the small kitchen table.

"I want you to take this .22 Cal," Memphis says, taking a small semi-automatic out of his boot. He shows her how to load and unload the gun, then hands her the weapon. She takes the magazine out and points the gun toward Memphis.

"Keep this with you at all times," Memphis instructs. "And never point that shit at anyone unless you intend to use it, otherwise they will kill you," he says, snatching the gun out of her hand and showing her that a bullet is still in the chamber.

"I'll pick you up in the morning to take you out to practice using it."

Always the planner, Memphis tells Desiree that he needs her to get focused and act like nothing happened, because he doesn't want the other girls to panic.

"Baby, we still need to bring in the bread or else we won't get fed," he says, nervously playing with his pack of Black and Mild cigars.

"Don't worry, baby." Memphis reaches for Desiree's soft hand. "If you follow my plan, we'll be OK, and you'll get Angel back. I promise you.

"Now I think it's time to call that boy back.

"Remember, make that shit as real as possible," Memphis reminds Desiree as she dials the number.

"Hello, Travon, it's me, Desiree, calling again. What did you decide?"

"You can? Fantastic!" she says, giving Memphis the thumbs-up from the hallway.

"You're free next week, Monday?" she repeats into the phone, seeking a confirmation from Memphis, who nods OK.

"That will work," she says. "I will need one small favor, can you suggest a small hotel that we can have a party at with double rooms? If you can call and hold the room that would be great."

"OK, I know that she will be excited to see you, too. I will call you Saturday to make sure everything is still on."

"Oh, you want me to call you Sunday instead? I will. Thank you so much. We can't wait to see you. Oh yeah, don't mention this to anyone else, because this is a big surprise, OK? Bye-bye."

Desiree feels sick to her stomach after the call.

"You did good, baby girl," Memphis praises. "So, is everything set for Monday? This is what we're going to do . . . Are you listening Desiree?"

As Memphis continues to plot out his plan, Desiree can think only of who she has become and how she got to this point in her life.

* * *

"Desiree London, can you follow me, please?"

"Damn, I hope Lance did not give me something," she thought to herself. "He is such a lying cheat. I don't know why I continue to put up with his shit."

As she paged through the Ladies' Home Journal, she always wondered why they had magazines like this in the doctor's office. "Oh yeah, right after I leave here, I'm going to get started on that Bundt cake," she joked to herself. As she continued to thumb through the pages, she heard talking on the other side of the door. She sat the magazine down in the rack and prayed that the news she was about to receive would be good.

After a knock on the door, Dr. Tillman, who is always a straight shooter, entered the room. He stared at her chart while making small talk with Desiree.

"Three days ago we gave you a series of tests to see what was going on," Dr. Tillman said while putting on latex gloves.

"Let me have a look, please," Dr. Tillman said. Desiree spread her legs for the world to see. After several uncomfortable minutes of poking and prodding, the doctor said, "OK, you can sit up now."

"Well, your results show that you have Chlamydia and Pelvic Inflammatory Disease."

"Excuse me?" Desiree looked at the doctor with a blank expression. "What exactly does that mean?"

Dr. Tillman took Desiree's hand before speaking.

"Well, young lady, there's good news and bad news," he says in a clinical tone. "The good news is that we can clear up the infection with antibiotics. The bad news is that due to the excessive scar tissue buildup from the PID, you will not be able to have children. I'm sorry."

As if on cue, Nurse Williams stepped in and caught Desiree as she began to fall from the exam table. "Doctor, nooooo!" Desiree screamed. "Please take it back! Please!"

As Desiree sobbed into the nurse's shoulder, Dr. Tillman excused himself from the room.

"It's OK dear. It's gonna be OK," the nurse tries to sooth Desiree. "But I've been with the same man for six years. I've never cheated on him."

"OK," Nurse Williams replied sympathetically, "but the same can't be said for him."

She went on to explain the disease to Desiree, and after taking it all in, Desiree made up her mind that her partner had purposely infected her.

"I have one question for you, Ms. Williams, is it possible that my partner infected me on purpose?"

"Chlamydia is known as a 'silent' disease because about three quarters of infected women and about half of infected men have no symptoms. If symptoms do occur, they usually appear within one to three weeks after exposure. So I guess what I'm saying is that only he would know," the nurse explained.

"Is there any way I could have protected myself?"

"You may not want to hear this, but abstinence is the only surefire way to avoid a disease. But since we are beings with desires, the only other way is to be in a monogamous relationship with a person who will remain faithful. An estimated 2.8 million Americans are infected with Chlamydia each year and women are frequently re-infected if their sex partners are not treated so you are not alone.

"Darling, I suggest you have a long talk with your partner," Nurse Williams added before leaving the room.

Desiree left Lance eight phone messages, with no response. The ninth time she called and stressed, "Lance, I need you to come over right after work because we have to talk."

An hour later her doorbell rang.

"Why didn't you return my calls?" Desiree demanded as Lance stood on her front porch.

"'Cause, man, you trippin.' What the fuck is the emergency?"

"You know what the emergency is, Lance."

Looking sincerely dumbfounded, Lance repeated his mantra, "I don't know what you're talkin' bout."

Desiree poked Lance in his chest.

"OK, I will tell you. I went to the doctor today, and he told me that I have Chlamydia, Lance, and now I can't bear children! You infected me, Lance! You robbed me of motherhood, you bastard!"

She reached to slap him.

"Look, baby, I didn't know," he said dodging he strikes. "Are you sure?"

"Stop it, Lance. Stop lying to me. You've lied long enough. Why don't you just leave." She started for the door, to throw him and his things out.

"OK, OK, OK, baby. I'm sorry," Lance grabbed her and begged. "Let me talk to you. I just didn't want you to leave me. I did it because I love you."

Desiree struggled free of Lance's grasp.

"How could you do this to me?" she wailed.

"This way I knew we would be together forever," Lance said, pulling her toward the couch the couple had bought together for their two-year anniversary.

"You're sick, you know that? Get outta here, and I don't ever want to see you again."

After Lance left, Desiree crumbled into a heap on the floor and cried for more than an hour before no more tears would fall. She knew then that she could never trust another *man again. Although she tried to forget about Lance, she was reminded of him every time she looked at a small child. She was also reminded of him every time she met someone new, because when things got to the point of being serious, she had to tell the man that she was barren. After the last man she dated told her that he could never be with anyone who couldn't have children, she decided to exclusively date women; it was easier. Although she knew that was not fair, all is fair in love and war.*

* * *

"Did you hear a thang I said?" Memphis asks, tapping Desiree on the shoulder. "We've got to have this plan on point if it's going to work."

"I will call you later to check on you, OK?"

"Yeah, OK, whatever," a tuned-out Desiree replies.

"Desiree," Memphis repeats. "Baby, you hear me?"

"Yeah, Memphis, I hear you. I just got a lot on my mind."

CHAPTER 26

"MOM, YOU REALLY should think about coming with me," I plead with my mother. "The weather is great. You won't have to worry about snow or the cold."

"But they have hurricanes all the time. Baby, you're moving to Miami. Now you know that you don't need an old woman hanging around cramping your style," she says, as she continues to watch her floor model television as if I haven't said a word.

"Mom, you mind if I turn off the television, because this is very important."

"I hear you, baby," she says, but her attention is diverted by reruns of *Family Feud*.

"I guess what I'm saying, Mom, is that ever since dad left, you have not been the same, and you never want to talk about it. Pops left eighteen years ago, and sometimes I think you think he's coming back. He's not. There is no reason for you to stay here."

I struck a nerve in my mother that I hadn't intended.

"Is that what you believe?" she says, turning off the television with the remote and leaning toward me from her plush burgundy recliner. "Is that really what you believe?"

"There is not a day that doesn't go by when I don't think about your father. As a matter of fact, I don't even know if he's dead or alive. Have you thought about how that makes me feel?" Her voice quivers as she tries to swallow her tears.

"Every time I look at you, Tray, I see your father. You are the spitting image of him."

"There was a time when I tried to move on. I remember your Uncle Willie even wanted to introduce me to a few men, but I just could not go through with it." She reaches for a tissue in a box down by her feet.

"I never thought my life would be like this, Tray. My life is spent waiting for the next talk show to come on and feeling like a prisoner in my own home, because the thugs have taken over the neighborhood."

Great, now I feel like crap for hurting my mother's feelings.

"But you don't have to live like this, Mom. Come with me."

"Tray, that's sweet, and don't think I don't appreciate it, but, baby, you're my son and not my husband," she says with a smile.

"I know, Mom."

"I don't think you do, baby," she says. "It's time for you to establish roots somewhere else, and to do that you should start with clean soil. Stand on your own and be a man–you don't need my old soul to help you in your journey."

"Roots are the foundation of life. When you establish new roots, baby, you need to do it on your own. Then once you get settled, if you really need me to come, I will. But, baby, I know that you're going to be fine. Do you understand me?"

"I do understand you, Mom, but what kind of man would I be to leave you in a situation like this knowing how bad this area has gotten? I mean, when I came by here tonight, I felt like locking the doors on my car while I was stopped at the corner."

"Oh, Tray, you know you can't fear your own people. The media does a good job of that every day in the news by the way they portray us. Never fear a man that looks just like you. Remember that, baby."

"Mom, you know what my biggest fear is? Losing you."

"Baby, I'm going to be fine, I have people to look after me and everything," mom says, wrapping her legs up in her covers while in her favorite chair.

"You do need to tell your Uncle Willie that you're leaving," she reminds me.

"I will," I say lying through my teeth. "I've been so busy."

"You haven't been that busy, Tray," his mother chastises. "Why are you acting like that toward Willie when he has done more for you than your father ever has?"

"I can't really explain it, Mom. I guess when I look out at this neighborhood, I think about how bad it's gotten and how he is partially to blame."

"You really don't believe that he's responsible for all of this, do you? He ain't that powerful."

"Sure, I know he runs girls and he may even dabble in drugs and stuff like that, but as far as I know he's never killed nobody, and he's never put drugs in these people's hands and made them sell it or smoke it," she says.

Just when I think my mother is going on a tangent of how Willie is a product of his environment, her phone rings.

She picks up, and I recognize the loud voice on the other end.

"Hold on a second. You must have ESP or something because we were just talking about you," mom says, tossing the phone over to me on the couch. "Tell your Uncle Willie that you're leaving."

Agitation spreads across my face as I pick up the receiver.

"Hey, Willie," I say in a drab tone.

"How you doing, nappy head?" Willie jokes.

"I'm good. What about you?"

"Well, I'm headed to Chicago to take care of some business. I want to see you when I get back in town. Your mother said you had something to tell me. You want to tell me what it is now?"

"Nawh, I can tell you when you get back."

"You ain't got nobody pregnant now, do you?" Willie asks.

"No, Willie," I respond dryly.

"What is wrong with you boy? You've had a funky little attitude with me over the past month."

"Nothing, Willie."

"Go ahead boy, tell me what it is, because something has you mad at me."

"Honestly, Willie," I pause taking the phone in the bathroom for privacy.

"I guess I'm opening my eyes wider to the things going on in the neighborhood and many of the problems that are a result of the things that you've done."

"What the hell are you talking about, young blood?" Willie says. "You don't even understand the game. The bad shit going on ain't got nothing to do with me. I lost both of my sons to the nonsense in these streets. The shit going on ain't me, it's these new breed of niggas coming in that don't respect the game."

"Son, you've got your eyes open wide, but you don't see the whole picture. You've always been like that boy. Open your eyes and look deeper."

"I don't have to look deeply, Willie, because I know what you and your partners do. How can you justify what you do and say that it's right and that it's not hurting anyone?"

"It affects me because it affects my mother," I feel myself growing angrier.

"Has anything ever happened to you or your mother?" Willie snaps.

"I've had a lot to do with that. Them new-breed niggas on the street know who not to fuck with. I may be older now, but I still got my shit together, boy, and I can't believe after all that I've done for you, that you think I would let anything happen to either one of you."

"You don't understand, Willie," I counter. "Some shit is about to change, and I can't be worrying about my mother, too."

"You don't have to worry about her; you never had to," Willie says. "Now I have some business to take care of. I will talk to you in a couple of days when I get back."

Willie, frustrated, hangs up the phone. He knows he has to act fast in Chicago and get back and check on the kid he raised like a son to find out what is wrong. He also knows he has to kill a man and possibly two, to keep his son alive.

"I'm getting too old for this shit," Willie thinks, "but it's not like I can take my retirement from the pimping game."

He laughs at that thought as he turns up the volume on his "Best of the Isley Brothers" CD.

> Set sail with me
> Misty lady, set my spirit free
> New love to find
> And though I leave another behind
> I'll always Come back to you . . .
> –"Voyage to Atlantis"

CHAPTER 27

"MAMA, HOW LONG do we have to stay here?" Kane whines as he plays in the motel bed with his Marvel comic action figures.

Angel pulls $213 from her purse. "Just two more nights, baby, then we leave for ATL."

"We're going to go back home and pick up some clothes and other things before we leave," Angel says, stroking her son's curly hair, while he makes his toys clash and fight.

"Other than that, we're going to start over fresh and plant new seeds," Angel says.

But before she and her son can board their flight to Atlanta, she knows that she will have to confront Desiree one more time, something that she fears.

"Are you hungry, darling?" Angel asks Kane.

"Yeah. Can we have pizza?"

"Kane, you've had pizza three days in a row. Don't you want to try something else?"

"No."

"OK this is the last time you're going to have pizza in a while, so I'll take you to Giordano's," Angel says, helping Kane into his snowsuit.

As they wait to get on the subway to head to Logan Square, Angel goes over her mental to-do list. She needs to get their belongings and go to the bank to withdraw her half of the more than $70,000 that she and Desiree have saved up from dancing.

She will go to the house when Desiree is at the club and pack up one big suitcase for herself and a smaller one for Kane. She figures she will leave $5,000 with her mother to pay her bills, and she will use the other $30,000, as a safety net while she's back in nursing school.

"Sis, I hope you can deal with me and Kane for a while," she says to herself. "I really need you right now."

Angel realizes that she's been so giving of herself to so many people over the years that she has neglected what she needed to do for herself and her son.

"If I would have stayed in school, I would be graduating right now," she laments.

At Giordano's, Kane gorges himself on double-stuffed cheese pizza and then quickly complains of a bellyache.

"Boy, look at your face," Angel says, smiling as she wipes pizza sauce from his lips and cheeks.

"Kane, I'm going to need you to be a big boy for me right now," Angel says. "We are going to go back to the house now and get a few things, OK."

"To see Desiree?" Kane asks innocently.

"No, baby, Desiree should be at work right now. We're going to go there and pick up a few things. OK?"

"OK, Mama," Kane says, playing with the pizza crust on his plate.

"What I need for you to do, honey, is to get a couple of things and put them in your small suitcase when we get there. We're going to have to move really fast, OK?"

Yawning, Kane just nods, as she places his hat on his head.

He's asleep when they reach the house. She carries him up the stairway slips the key into the lock and enters quietly. Kane is still sleeping when she sets him down on the couch and goes to the closet to get her Gucci luggage. She is walking toward the bedroom when Desiree appears in the doorway.

"Surprise."

Angel drops the suitcase and backs up. "I didn't know you were here," she says.

For a minute, the two women just stare at each other. Then Desiree breaks the awkward silence.

"So this is it, huh? You're just gonna pack your things up and leave me like this?"

Angel doesn't speak.

"What's really funny about this is that you are the one who cheated, but you act like you're mad at me. You are really a trip," Desiree scoffs, still standing in front of the bedroom door, naked except for a pair of hipster panties, with her arms folded.

"After all the stuff I did for your ungrateful ass, you have the nerve to be mad at me. I don't understand you, Angel. You let dick come between me and you."

"I was there for you when Kane was in the hospital. I was there for you when your mother was struggling. And I was there for you when you needed someone to hold you and love you. But now, you're jetting on me for a motherfucker who doesn't even want you."

Finally getting enough courage to talk back, Angel says, "You were there for me Desiree, and I will never forget anything that you did for me, but in all honesty, you held me back."

Angel squeezes past Desiree to get her things out of the bedroom.

"How did I hold you back?" Desiree asks.

"Everything I did, I did for us. I'm the reason Memphis hired your naïve ass in the first place."

"Desiree, you are not that stupid. Memphis has been trying to sleep with me since the day I set foot into his club. And the only reason you wanted me down there was to keep an eye on me."

Sucking her teeth, Desiree walks out of the room. Angel's packing pace picks up speed.

When Desiree strolls back into the bedroom, she is on the phone with Memphis.

"Since you say I didn't do anything for you, I guess you won't mind paying Memphis back what you owe him from your night in Milwaukee," Desiree says, handing the phone to Angel.

Angel snatches the phone from Desiree's hand, rolls her eyes and mutters, "I really don't need this shit from either one of you right now."

"Hello," she says into the receiver.

"So whatcha gonna do about my ends?" Memphis asks.

"You know what, Memphis? I'm not giving you a damn dime for the way you used me and everyone else over the past three and a half years. As far as I'm concerned, you and Desiree can go to hell!"

Angel throws the phone to Desiree, grabs her stuffed suitcase, and stumbles past Desiree, rolling her ankle in the process but not breaking stride to the front room to pack Kane's suitcase.

Hot on her trail, Desiree warns, "Angel, you're on your own. Memphis is going to have his way with your ass now."

The more Angel ignores Desiree, the louder she gets, until she finally wakes Kane.

"ReRe," Kane says, reaching for Desiree, who gladly picks him up, making Angel furious.

"Why don't you put some clothes on your nasty ass?" Angel yells. "I've told you that over and over again."

"You should really be careful about throwing stones," Desiree says. She covers Kane's ears. "I'm not the one who had sex with a man that I knew for less than an hour–oops, or should I say less than fifteen minutes."

Desiree lowers her voice. "Speaking of your fuck fest, did your precious Travon use protection? Or did you let him give it to you raw?"

Angel ignores Desiree's crudeness and zips up Kane's suitcase.

She has just one other thing to say before she leaves.

"I'm taking my half of the money we saved up from dancing, so that should be about $30,000," she says.

"I don't know where you get off talking about $30,000," Desiree says, walking to the back to lay Kane down in her bed.

Angel waits in the living room, standing between the two suitcases until Desiree returns.

"I need my money, Desiree."

The two women face off like fighters before a brawl.

"You can have your half," Desiree says, "but it won't cover a month's rent."

"What?"

"I will let you see for yourself," Desiree says, as she leaves the room and comes back with a savings account book.

"You telling me all we have left is $532.21?"

Angel holds her hand to her mouth and, suddenly feeling light-headed, sits down on the edge of Kane's bed.

"What happened to all the money, Desiree?" she cries.

"What do you mean what happened to it? You're wearing it. Look at all the name brands you wearing. Prada purse, Nine West shoes, Movado watch, Dolce and Gabbana shades, Louis Vuitton bag, Versace dress. Do I need to continue?"

Angel feels like a fool. She never checked the finances, trusting Desiree to put money away for their future.

"You spent $70,000 of our money on bullshit?" she finally says. "I let men rape me with their eyes for three years, and now you telling me that all of that was for nothing?"

"All the shit we have is name-brand shit that we couldn't even get a couple dollars for at a rummage sale."

"I need to go before I kill you," Angel says. "I mean that."

As Angel lunges toward the bedroom to get her son and leave, Desiree reaches for her arm to try to calm her down.

"Don't touch me!" Angel yells. "You will never touch me again!"

Not heading her warnings, Desiree grabs Angel around the waist. The shock of her touch sends Angel into a rage of kicks, screams, and punches. She swings wildly at Desiree, who runs to the bathroom for cover, locking the door.

"You stay your ass in there! Stay your ass in there!" Angel says, breathing hard on the other side of the door.

"Pleassssseee, baby! Don't leave me!" Desiree screams, falling to her knees in the bathroom.

During all the commotion, Kane begins to cry.

"Don't cry, baby," Angel says. "Come to Mama."

The little boy runs to Angel who sweeps him up and almost in the same motion grabs the two suitcases and flees.

She walks as fast as she can from the house, and it isn't long before she is able to flag down a taxi.

Still in the bathroom, Desiree cries on the floor for thirty minutes before she is able to get up.

She walks out to the cluttered living room, alone again.

CHAPTER 28

"THANKS FOR TAKING me to the airport," I say to Darnell, who is focusing intently on the congested highway.

"No problem, Tray," Darnell says, without even glancing over at me.

"So how's Taylor?"

"She's fine," Darnell says bluntly. "Everyone's fine."

After several minutes of riding in silence except for Darnell's occasional sigh, I ask what's bothering him.

"You're leaving, and it doesn't seem to be bothering you," Darnell blurts out. "I mean, you're going along all nonchalant like everything is going to be fine, and you don't seem to care about our friendship."

Surprised that my friend would think that this move has been easy on me, I waste no time telling Darnell how I really feel.

"Look Darnell, this is probably the biggest decision I ever had to make in my life. I'm moving away from everything that I know and love. And you think that's easy for me? I've been second-guessing this move from the time I accepted the offer, but I gotta do me like you gotta do you. I can't let this opportunity pass me by because I'm worried about other people's feelings. I got to do this, man."

Darnell knows what he said was wrong, but he also knows that the dynamics of our friendship will be forever changed.

"I'm sorry Tray. I'm just going to miss you, boy. I'm going to miss our friendship." Darnell extends his right hand in a friendly gesture.

"I'm going to miss you too, boy." I grab Darnell's hand. "But no matter how far I move or where I end up, we will always be best friends. You think distance can break our bond? You know better than that, frat."

"I know, Tray. I guess I'm just trippin'," replies Darnell, finally cracking a smile.

The car pulls up to the drop-off area at the airport. I quickly gather my small bag from the back seat, hoping to avoid an awkward good-bye. And this is just a short trip to find housing. Imagine when I leave for good?

"Now don't forget to pick me up at eight o'clock Thursday," I remind Darnell, as a sheriff's deputy urges drivers to move along.

"I'll be here, Tray," Darnell says, hopping back behind the steering wheel as the heavyset deputy wobbles over to tell him to move his vehicle.

I check in for my flight, and with time to kill, pull out my laptop and write my first column for my new employer.

Hello, Miami

It's not often that a journalist gets an opportunity to write about themselves. The last time I was asked to write anything about myself, the obit writer at my old paper wanted me to write something important about my life, so just in case I died, he would have a good jump on getting the story done and could beat the rush-hour traffic home.

I'm going to be your new sports columnist/sports blogger/podcaster/ sports broadcaster and other slashes that I can't think of right now. To be honest with you, my job has not been completely defined, which is a good thing.

One thing that I can promise is that I will not stop reporting the news.

An old journalism professor once told me that news gathering starts and stops with self-discovery. I will take that a step further, after I learn something new about a subject, I plan on digging even deeper.

You have twenty-four hour access to the news and sports. The Internet has opened up a new world and you also have ESPN, CNBC, CNN, CNN Headline News, MSNBC, FOX News Channel, *and blogs for obtaining information. The news is just a click of a mouse away.*

So what can I do to make you pick up the paper every day, to go to our Web site and to my blog? The answer is simple: I have to be aggressive and do everything I can to earn your trust.

I'm not going to pretend I know everything, because I'll be the first to tell you that I don't. So I'm going to depend a lot on you to help me get through this journey.

In the past, journalists have been hampered by too many bad habits. We tended to use a tone and focus that left millions of common folk feeling like they had been excluded from the conversation. I promise I will not do that to you. I respect this craft too much, and to be honest with you, I am that common folk.

I will work hard to be the essential public source for accurate, analytical information. I will always be the source you can turn to, click on, or download to sort out fact from fiction.

This is the point where I'm supposed to say, "Buy the paper everyday and tune into my blog." But since most of you know that already, I will just say this: Trust me. This will be fun, and I will bring it to you with gusto.

Thanks for your time,
Travon Brown

* * *

Miami is everything I expected it to be, and more: beautiful women, warm weather, fast cars, and expensive as hell. Finding a place to call home in an area surrounded by glitz and tits is going to be a challenge, but with only three days to do it, I don't plan on wasting any time chasing tail.

After checking into a posh art deco-style hotel minutes away from the *Herald*, I hit the pavement looking for a nice place to live. The first two-bedroom condo is $2,500 a month. Next on the list, a one-bedroom in a suburb called Hollywood for $1,800 a month. No matter where I look over the next two days, the prices range between $1,700 and $2,600 a month. And that price only gets you barely to the outskirts of the hood.

On my last full day of searching, I decide to go into the newsroom and meet some of my colleagues and see if they have any leads on places to live.

My immediate supervisor, Chester Gilmore, a brown-skinned man in his mid fifties, with salt-and-pepper hair, looks like he could have played a good friend to Bill Cosby on "The Cosby Show," and he seems to have an answer to everything. "I know a couple looking to sell their condo on the strip at cost."

"I can set it up now, if you would like to see it," Mr. Gilmore says with a smile. "You're young and hip. This place will be right up your alley."

"Sounds good," I reply, admiring all the honors and awards hanging in Mr. Gilmore's neatly kept office. "Maybe I can run through tomorrow morning, before my flight and take a look."

He wears bow-ties, which impresses me. And like most people in Florida, Mr. Gilmore keeps himself in good shape.

"So, Tray, when would you like to write your first column? I was thinking of something along the lines of introducing yourself to the public," he says, pausing briefly to tell his attractive assistant to hold his calls.

"It's funny that you mentioned that, Mr. Gilmore. I just happen to have it right here."

"Let's get one thing straight before we go any further with our relationship. Call me Chester," Mr. Gilmore, says with a smile.

"That'll work if you agree to call me Tray."

Chester makes a few tweaks as he reads my first column, but he is visibly pleased.

"This is good, Tray. We'll run it tomorrow. Now why don't you go out and enjoy the sun, and don't worry about finding a place to stay. That's already taken care of. Now one more thing, are we still on for dinner tonight?"

"Yeah, that will be great."

"I'll pick you up from your hotel about nine o'clock. We can talk about what you would like to do here later."

As I leave the office, the secretary, Maria, takes a long, hard look at the new hire and then gives me a quick wave and a smile.

* * *

"What's up, Darnell?" I ask on the phone, while cruising around South Beach in a rented fire engine red Mustang convertible.

Darnell is upbeat. "Hey, Tray! So tell me about it. Is it like TV?"

"Yeah, it is. I'm cruising along South Beach now and there's '*Booty, booty, booty, booty, booty everywhere,*" I say laughing.

Laughing with a hint of envy in his voice, Darnell replies "Damn, you lucky."

"Nawh, you have what I want," I admit. "You have a beautiful wife to come home to every night."

"I guess you're right. But I wouldn't mind coming home to a different woman, every now and then."

"Well, it ain't what it's cracked up to be, Darnell. Anyway, I think I found a place. My boss told me about a couple trying to get out of their condo. I guess all the hurricanes have spooked them away. It sounds cool from the way he described it."

"That's cool, Tray. When do you get to see it?"

"Tomorrow morning. Which reminds me, don't forget to pick me up."

"I know, I know, eight o'clock. I won't forget."

"Am I missing anything going on up there?"

"Not really, Tray. Just niggas killing niggas. There was a triple shooting off Center Street last night. Two men died, and one is listed in critical."

"Where on Center?" I ask concerned.

As if reading my mind, Darnell responds, "I checked on your mother and she's fine. She didn't even know about it."

"Where was it, Darnell?" my investigative instincts kick in.

"It was about three blocks from your mother's house. The ministers in the surrounding neighborhoods are supposed to be having some sort of community awareness march this weekend to talk about the escalating violence."

"Black people keep fighting over shit they don't own," I shake my head in disgust. "Let me get off this phone, Darnell, so I can check my messages."

* * *

"You have two messages. Message one: 'Travon, this is Chester, I won't be able to do dinner tonight. I have an urgent meeting with the publisher. Anyway, I will call you back with the phone number of my friends. Sorry about that, but we will talk tomorrow before you head back to Milwaukee.'

"Message two: 'Travon, it's me, Chester, calling back. This is my friend's number. He said you can stop by in the morning and look at the condo. I told him to give you a good deal, and he said he would be willing to work with you. Call him and set up a time. Hope this works out.' End of messages.'"

Damn, I thought to myself as my stomach starts to growl.

"Well, so much for dinner," I snap my cell phone shut.

"I'd rather see how quick this pony could reach 0-60 anyway," I laugh as I make a right and turn onto the wide-open expressway.

CHAPTER 29

"Y'ALL NIGGAS GONNA pay for this. That's on everything I love," Memphis says peeking into the monitor that recorded Crazy Nate leading Stallion out of the club.

"This is the last time you get the ups on me. I promise you that," Memphis vows, freezing the frame and drinking Jack Daniels to numb his pain.

"Baby, I'm sorry. You were the best thing to ever happen to me. Baby, if you come home to me, I swear that I will treat you the way you're supposed to be treated. We can do the things that we said we wanted to do years ago."

Memphis takes another swig from the near-empty bottle, and tears pour down his face as reality sets in, and he knows the only thing he can do is prepare for his wife's funeral. He hopes that Nate left enough of her to have an open casket.

"Knowing the lion you are, Nate, I know that you will leave remains behind so I can find her. That is how simple and sick you are, you fuckin' bastard!"

Stumbling aimlessly through the empty club with his bottle in hand, Memphis goes from room to room searching for his white horse.

"Baaaaby!" he howls stumbling over chairs in the dimly lit hallway.

"She didn't have anything to do with this! Nothin,'!" he bellows. "If you wanted me so bad, you should've come after me first, because you know what I'm going to do now. You know."

After searching the club, Memphis makes his way to the wooden stage and plops down with his back against the pole, dropping the empty bottle at his feet.

He looks up at the water stained ceiling in despair.

"So this is how you're going to punish me, huh, god? I mean, you made me feel cursed from the day I was born. Let's look at how you done me wrong," Memphis says, grinning at himself through his drunkenness.

He ticks off the list of betrayals on his fingers. "You took my mother from me two weeks after I was born. Killed off my aunt on Christmas Day when I was five, after her nigga beat her to death with a pipe wrench 'cause he thought she stole his heroin. Had my foster mother rape and beat me for ten years. Ripped my baby out of my wife's womb, and that wasn't enough so you took my second child ten months later. Now you take my wife. *My wife?* What the fuck?"

"What else do you want? Oh yeah, I forgot you want my club, too."

Memphis laughs and slaps his knee. "God, you is a big ole pimp. I can see that now. I told you after you took my aunt that I would never bow down to you. I ain't changed my mind. I guess that's how I managed to get this far without playing by the rules. You can't break me. You can have my wife, she's probably better off with you. But as long as I'm here, I'm going to be hell on earth. Remember, you created a monster."

His ranting at the Lord over, Memphis drifts off to sleep on the very stage where so many women have sold their souls just to make a dollar or two and give it to him.

When sunlight breaks through the window, the self-proclaimed widower stirs, makes a beeline for the bathroom to relieve his bladder.

As he makes his way back to his office, the phone rings.

"Who knows I'm here at seven in the morning?" Memphis says as he reaches for the phone.

"Hello?"

"Turn on your security monitor and rewind it back to 0200 hours. I left you a surprise out back. Oh yeah, nigga, your bitch's ass was pretty good. You should've fucked her more."

Before Memphis can respond, Crazy Nate hangs up.

Memphis begins to fidget with the control panel. "Fuck this," he says and runs outside with his shirt half open. A light snow is falling. He searches the parking lot but sees nothing but his truck. "Fucking mind games!" he yells as he makes a final circle of the parking lot and stomps back inside.

The phone rings again.

"Did you see it?" Nate asks. "I hope you got a strong stomach."

"I'm going to kill you, and Willie, and Tray, mutherfucka!"

Confident in his game of cat and mouse, Nate continues to toy with Memphis.

"I gave you a basic command. Do what I tell you. By the way, your camera layout is sloppy. Good-bye."

Memphis persistently hits the buttons on the monitor until he gets it right.

"This is it," he says as the camera in back of his club picks up movement about two o'clock in the morning.

As he zooms in on the recorded image, it's clear that Nate is putting several small, dark plastic bags into the huge green dumpster on the vacant property next door. Fast-forwarding the video, Memphis notices that Nate steps in his same footprints over and over again.

Memphis knows that the bags encase his wife.

He runs to the dumpster, in his signature green gators, throws open its huge plastic double doors and stacks two milk crates to stand on. Peering in, he sees three bags. He reaches in and pulls them out, one by one, but he cannot bear to open them.

He sits on a wooden crate, lights a cigarette and stares at the bags before muscling up the courage to open the first one.

Taking a knife from his pocket, he slits the double-ply plastic, with a shaky hand. As he peels the plastic down, he sees his wife's bloody head.

Exhaling heavily and not knowing if the man who did this is watching, Memphis holds in his pain as best he can. He places Stallion's head next to the crate along with her torso and an arm, makes a cross in the snow with his fingers and walks back to his club. He closes the door, crumbles to his knees, and pukes his insides out.

When the phone rings, he picks it up and hangs it up.

Then he makes a call to a couple of cops who have frequented his club for free pussy for the past five years. He offers few details as he tells them of the murder.

One of the investigating officers takes Stallion's death personally. He'd been with her several times, and had taken a liking to her. He pulls Memphis aside and asks who could have done this, but Memphis tells him nothing.

"So you're going to handle this yourself?" the officer asks. "You know that's illegal."

Memphis just smirks and walks away.

The Chicago County Medical Examiner is still on the scene as the news of Stallion's death and Memphis's retaliation spread through the 'hood.

Some of the girls at the club feel that it is time for Memphis to redeem himself on the street. Over the next couple of days, customers come out of the woodwork to support Memphis.

Strippers, prostitutes, johns, and customers from all over the city show up at Stallion's funeral.

The one positive to come from Stallion's death is Memphis's stronger bond with Desiree. She is now the top female in the club.

Memphis shares secrets with Desiree that he never shared with his wife, and soon the two use their pain to go full-speed-ahead on plans to kill Travon.

CHAPTER 30

"SO, DO WE need to go over this *again?*" Memphis asks Desiree as he carefully twists the silencer on his 9 mm.

"No, I got it." Desiree is driving Memphis's SUV to Milwaukee.

"This should be easy," she says glancing at Memphis, who's in deep thought with his weapon resting in his lap.

"When I talked to Travon, he seemed excited to see Angel. He told me he was coming back from a business trip, and I got him to hold a room under his name. All you have to do is pay for it, get the key from the front desk, and wait for our star to show up. I'll meet him downstairs and lead him to the room."

"That'll work," Memphis says, looking a bit more energized.

Desiree touches Memphis's rough hand. "You have nothing to worry about Memphis. Everything will go as planned."

"You know what's crazy about this whole thing?" Memphis asks. "I don't blame this kid for everything."

"I blame him," Desiree pipes up. "He's caused both of us a lot of pain. It's because of him I lost Angel, and you lost Stallion."

"You're not listening," Memphis says, his voice raised. "I'm saying some of the shit didn't have nothin' to do with him!"

"I guess when Willie sent that hitman to cut your wife up into chunks, that didn't have anything to do with him either."

Before Desiree can apologize, Memphis backhands her so hard that she briefly loses control of the steering wheel.

"You must've forgot, girl. I'm still running shit! Don't you forget it," Memphis warns.

"I'm sorry, baby," Desiree apologizes through stinging tears. "So what are we going to do?"

When the two arrive at Hotel Metro, Memphis pays for the room, and he and Desiree take the elevator to the fifth floor. Inside the room, Memphis checks the closet and bathroom.

Desiree pulls back the thick gold embroidered curtains, looks out the window, and knocks on the walls to see how thick they are.

"What do you think?" she asks Memphis.

Scratching the nappy hair on his goatee, Memphis plots out exactly how he intends to shoot Travon.

"I'll be standing in the bathroom, with the door cracked. You tell him that the girls will bring Angel up, and you want him to stand right by the bed, so Angel can see him as soon as she opens the door. This way, I can have a clear shot.

"Three pops—one in the chest, two in the head. We roll him up in the bedspread and roll out the back. Being that this nigga is obviously a ladies' man, the police won't know who to point the finger at first. I'm sure there's a bitch out there somewhere who wants this punk dead as bad as we do."

Desiree smiles, thinking that Travon's death will solve all her problems.

"This is going to be easier than I thought, baby," Memphis says in Desiree's ear. "Now I think it's time that you go downstairs and wait."

"I'll call you on your cell when he arrives," Desiree says.

Memphis sits down on the edge of the bed, clicks on the TV, and waits.

Desiree takes her position at a table for two in the hotel bar and drinks a glass of Merlot.

As hard as Desiree has become after her break up with Angel, her heart is still bleeding, and the longer she waits for Travon to arrive, the more anxious she becomes.

As the wine takes effect, she relaxes a little—until Travon pushes through the revolving door. His crimped dreadlocks, tanned skin, and muscular build make him look like a lion, and he immediately commands the attention of the entire room. When he walks up to the bar, Desiree studies him. As he looks around, she smiles and motions him over to her table. As he approaches, she notices how strong he is.

"You must be Desiree," I say pulling off my tan trench coat and extending my hand with a big smile.

"Yes, I am. Pleased to meet you," she says extending her hand.

"I would offer to buy you a drink, but it seems as though the men in here have kept your glass full." I take a seat. "So where is the birthday girl?"

"Huh?"

"Angel, the birthday girl," I say sipping on banana rum and Coke.

"Oh, I'm sorry," Desiree apologizes, blushing. "The girls are bringing her. She should be here shortly."

"This gives us some time to talk," Desiree says, hoping to grill Travon on his fling with Angel.

However, Desiree quickly finds herself in the hot seat, fielding a barrage of probing questions.

"Tell me how long and how well do you know Angel?"

"Well, I've know her for three years or so and we're pretty close," Desiree responds.

"Do you get along with her son?"

"You know about Kane?" Desiree inquires.

"Yeah, she told me all about him and how she eventually wants to give up this lifestyle and go back to nursing school."

"She told you she wanted to stop strippin'!"

"Yeah," I say. "You didn't know that?"

Desiree thought she knew her ex-lover better than anyone, she soon realizes how little she really knows.

During their conversation, Desiree learns that Angel's one-night stand with Travon was more than just sex and although she wanted to hate him, it was difficult.

He is witty, smart, street, handsome, confident, tall, and rough, all rolled up into one.

"So are you so friendly with *all* the women you meet?" Desiree asks. "I see the women checking you out, and the guys in here are jealous, but you don't seem to care."

"Why should I worry about someone else when I'm sitting at the table with someone I'm trying to get to know?"

"Excuse me, I have to take this," Desiree says getting up from the table to answer her phone.

Motioning for her to stay seated, I offer to buy Desiree another drink. As I step away, she takes the call.

"Has the nigga made it yet?" Memphis asks. "Shit, I'm getting hungry. I'm about to order room service."

Desiree lies.

"Just be patient," she says, "I'll let you know when he shows."

I return to the table with Desiree's drink.

"That's not Merlot is it?"

"No, it's a drink I got the bartender to make special for you. I think you'll like it a little better."

Desiree takes a sip. "Oh, this is good."

"I knew you would like it."

Desiree tries to regain her composure. "OK. I have a question to ask you, and I want you to be totally honest," she says.

Always one for a good brain tease, I agree to play the game.

"OK Travon, tell me what a man of your stature would want with a stripper?"

I look into Desiree's eyes. "Is that all you see when you see Angel?"

"No," Desiree says. "She's the best, and I love her."

"I think I do too." The words left my lips before I knew it.

"I can't stop thinking about her no matter how hard I try."

"I know exactly how you feel, Travon."

When Desiree's phone rings again, she steps away to take the call.

"Is the nigga here yet?"

Looking toward Travon, Desiree's ice cold heart begins to thaw. "Memphis, he just called to say that he can't make it tonight."

"What the fuck you talkin' 'bout?" Memphis yells.

"He just called and said something came up."

"Ain't that a bitch," Memphis says, frustrated. "Bring me up some fried chicken and biscuits."

"They don't have that here."

"Well, ho, go to KFC and get me some. And hurry up." Memphis hangs up.

Desiree stomps back over to the table.

"Is everything OK?"

"No," Desiree says. "Angel's not coming. Her mother got sick and she had to turn around and go back."

"Oh, I hope her mother will be OK." I say.

"I'm sure she'll be OK. Don't be too disappointed, Travon."

"Do you have a number where I can reach Angel?"

"Here you go," Desiree scribbles a number on a napkin of Angel's favorite Chinese restaurant.

As she watches Travon leave, Desiree remembers how early on in her relationship with Angel, she sometimes wore a strap on to pound away at her lover, because she knew deep down that Angel really wanted a man.

"When you call looking for Angel at the Chin's, I'm sure there are a couple of women in there that will '*fuck you long time*,'" she says, in her best Asian accent.

"I saved your life, Travon. I just hope I won't regret it."

CHAPTER 31

"PASSENGERS WHO NEED assistance or who have small children may begin boarding Flight 219 to Atlanta. We ask that you have your boarding pass in hand before you get to the gate . . ." "Is it time to go, Mama?" Kane asks easing out of the black chair and onto his feet.

Angel snaps back into reality. "Yeah, I think it is."

The two line up behind a woman with a walker, and soon make their journey down the aisle and into the unknown.

Even though Angel has taken chances as a dancer, she has always been conservative in life. For Angel, dancing never seemed real. It has always been a fantasy. In reality, however, she has been afraid to venture out, and she has never let anyone see her vulnerability except Desiree and her mother, both of whom she is leaving behind. Sleeping with Travon was one of the riskiest things she has ever done. This journey for Angel is not only about the new life she will pursue in Chocolate City, but also a new beginning for her son. At the very moment she hands their tickets to the attendant, Angel knows that she is making the right decision.

Angel walks toward the back of the plane, her eyes gazing intently at the small letters and numbers below the overhead bins and then pauses for a moment to allow Kane to dive into the seat closest to the window.

During the three-hour flight, Angel entertains Kane by pointing out the window at the clouds and playing a game of what the clouds look like.

Kane can hardly contain himself.

"Mama, that looks like a bird, and that one looks like an alligator trying to eat him. Chomp, chomp, chomp." He grins and presses his little oily nose against the window.

As his imagination takes wing, Angel's thoughts turn to a love that she concedes she will never experience again–Travon.

"I wonder if you were worth it, Travon," she says to herself, her eyes closed.

Kane taps her arm.

"Why can't Grandma and ReRe come with us?" he asks.

Angel struggles to give an answer to the inquisitive child, but before she can respond, Kane asks another question.

"Do you miss ReRe, Mommy?"

For a second, Angel doesn't know how to answer that question. She takes a sip of 7-Up.

"Yeah, I miss her," she says. "But she couldn't come with us this time."

"Will she come with us next time?" Kane glances up at his mother's face, waiting for an answer.

Not wanting to lie but ready for the questions to stop, Angel simply says, "Maybe next time."

With his curiosity satisfied, Kane snuggles up to Angel and soon falls asleep. Just as Angel is starting to fall asleep, too, she is startled by a chime, followed by the flight attendant's infomercial-like voice.

"I'm going to ask all passengers at this time to return your seats to the upright position. We will be landing shortly. The weather in Atlanta calls for temps in the mid- to lower 60s. Expect cloudy skies with an occasional shower. We should be touching ground shortly. On behalf of the crew, we would like to thank you for making us your destination carrier."

"Time to wake up, baby." Angel nudges Kane.

Instinctively, Kane looks out the window as the plane's descent starts to make Angel's stomach churn.

"That feels funny, Mommy," Kane says, laughing.

As they wait to exit the plane, Angel goes over what it means to be "a good boy" with Kane again.

"Kane, Auntie Faith isn't used to children, so I expect you to be on your best behavior. No running through the house, no jumping on furniture, and no eating around the house except in the kitchen. I need you to be extra good," Angel says.

"I don't know," Kane says innocently.

"Kane we went over this several times. Do you understand me? Do you?"

"I didn't even do nothing yet," Kane says, which makes Angel smile.

Angel knows that Kane is a beautiful, smart boy who is full of energy, and that will be something that her uppity sister will have to get used to.

As the chime sounds again, there is a unison click as passengers unfasten their seatbelts and jostle for the overhead compartments and the exit. To avoid being crushed by the sea of people wanting to be the first to exit the flying bus, Angel and Kane sit patiently until the first wave of passengers moves through.

As they approach the waiting area, Angel finds herself looking into the face of every black woman, hoping to see her sister. But Faith is nowhere around.

"Where is she, Mama?" Kane asks.

"That's a good question," Angel answers, looking around.

When she checks her cell phone, she sees that she missed a call.

"Faith is caught up in traffic but should be here shortly in a white car," she relays to Kane.

When Faith pulls up curbside, Angel and Kane walk up to the tinted-window Beamer.

"Is that my baby sister and my nephew?" Faith screams, jumping out of the car to hug the sister she has not seen in years. As the two embrace, Kane looks up at the strange woman hugging his mother.

"And you must be Kane," Faith says, kneeling down to his level.

When the boy extends his hand, Faith looks at Angel and jokes, "Are you getting him ready for the corporate world?"

Faith opens her arms, and Kane steps up and musters up the tightest hug he can give.

"How was that?" he asks, smiling at his aunt's playfulness.

"Ohhhhhhhhh. That's a good hug," Faith says, smiling and rocking. "That made me feel very good."

Looking behind Angel, Faith sees only two suitcases. "Is there more luggage?"

"It's all I could bring," Angel says.

"OK. Let's go," Faith says, loading the two suitcases into the trunk.

On the drive to Faith's suburban home, Angel and Kane are amazed at all the greenery and spaces between houses.

"This ain't Chicago," Faith says to Angel, whose eyes are glued to the passing countryside. "You two won't need those winter coats here. I think the coldest it's gotten so far this year is about 40 degrees."

When they arrive at Faith's home, Angel cannot believe how big and beautiful it is. Everything inside is new and looks untouched, especially not by the young hands of a child. Faith tells them to make themselves at home, but Kane does not stray from his mother's reach.

Angel knows that although her sister has said she wants them to feel free, they will still have to abide by her rules. She just doesn't know when the warden will be passing them out.

When Kane can no longer hold his eyes open, the two sisters move to the kitchen to have a heart-to-heart.

"So, Angel, where do we start?" Faith asks while boiling water for tea. "We have so much to catch up on. There's so little that I know about you."

Although Angel knows this discussion is long overdue, she was hoping to put it off until she got some sleep. Judging by Faith's tone, however, the time is now, and Angel comes out with both barrels blazing.

"Well, let's start out about why you left me. I struggled to help Mom keep her house, while you were down here living it up," Angel says, turning to look again at all the beautiful paintings, rugs, and artwork in Faith's home.

Faith knew she had that one coming, and she let it go.

"Why don't you *really* say what's on your mind."

Turning back to face her sister, Angel continues.

"You don't realize what I had to do and what I had to sacrifice for Mama," she says, her arms folded. "I dropped out of nursing school. I had to prostitute myself on a stage for men to help our mother keep the house, and then I come here and see this! I mean, it was like you died, but Mom kept thinking you were coming back, and silly me, I kept believing it too."

"That shit really hurt me." Angel pounds her chest. "It hurts right here." Angel circles her heart.

"That pain that you're feeling right now is the same pain I felt every day for years," Faith says. "It's the pain that I felt when your father touched me, Angel, and I had no one to turn to."

"I had to leave, because every time he touched me, he took a little bit more of my soul. I never wanted you to feel that same pain, but if I didn't escape, I don't know how I would have survived. You know what happened when I told Mama what he did to me? She slapped me! That is the first time Mama ever laid a hand on me, and that's because she knew I was telling the truth.

"She even threw me out of the house for a while, like I was the problem. When I returned home, Mama didn't stop it from happening, so I held a grudge against her, against him and by default against you, too. I don't know why I did, but I was hurting and no one could help me. I know you think I left you, but I did everything in my soul to protect you from him. I felt that if he did what he did to me, then he would not do it to you.

"Angel, you can blame me for leaving, but don't blame me for the bad decisions you've made."

Fuming, Angel moves to walk away, but Faith gently grabs her by the arm.

"Don't walk away, Angel," she pleads.

"You can still do all the things you want to do. Don't be like Mama and give up. She always put men first in her life and ours, because she felt she needed them to keep the family together. And no matter what they did, she forgave them."

Angel, in tears, pulls away from Faith.

"Why didn't you at least visit me?"

"That house was my coffin, Angel. My soul died in that house, and I just could not bear to go back there."

"Try to understand, Angel. I know this was hard on you, but it was just as hard on me. I don't want to lose you again. Allow me to be in your life and in my only nephew's life. Please, we have so much to learn."

"I'm sorry for what you went through, Faith."

Faith opens her arms, and the sisters hold tight to each other. "It's not your fault, Angel."

"I have nowhere else to go," Angel cries.

"You don't have to go anywhere," Faith says, stroking Angel's hair. "This is home as long as you want it to be."

Angel exhales feeling like she finally has her big sister back to protect her.

"I have to get a job," she says.

Faith stops her.

"No. We have to get you back into school. Do you still want to be a nurse?"

"Yes, more than anything."

"Then that's what you should do. I will help you, if that's really what you want to do."

"It's not only what I want to do," Angel says. "It's what I need to do."

* * *

"I can't believe that nigga didn't even show up. I've got to kill that muthafucka," Memphis says on the drive back to Chicago.

"I was never the best husband, I know this. But I owe Stallion for what Nate did to her," he says. "You hear me, Desiree?"

"I hear you, baby."

"I owe it to her. And I need you to help me. Promise me you won't let me down."

Desiree nods.

"You know, baby, we can always tell the girls that we took care of Tray and Nate," Desiree offers.

Memphis rolls his eyes.

"Whatchu talkin' about?"

"I'm just saying. We can tell the girls at the club that we took care of the situation and that way you get your props and respect back to where it should be right away."

"That's what I thought you said," Memphis says, cutting his black SUV across four lanes before abruptly stopping at the side of the highway.

He pulls his Glock and aims it at Desiree's temple. He contemplates pulling the trigger.

"You think I'm some kinda joke? I don't trade war stories, bitch. I make the stories niggas have nightmares about. My shit is legendary. I'll kill who I have to and make that shit as public as possible. The day I make up some old mafia shit is the day I'll take my own life. Don't ever forget that. Do you hear me?!"

Scared of Memphis for really the first time, Desiree nods.

Pulling back into traffic, Memphis warns, "Don't ever question me again."

"The next time you disrespect me will be your last," he says with a sinister smile.

Back at the club, Memphis displays a demeanor that the girls never seen before. When he catches Jade shooting up in the bathroom, he storms the stall, drags her by her hair to the parking lot, beats her with his belt buckle, and takes her money before leaving her sprawled next to some wooden crates, like yesterday's trash.

"My wife never liked your ass anyway," he says walking away. "You come back around here, I'll kill you, and if I catch any of you bitches talking to her I'll kill yo' asses, too. Now get y'all stankin asses back to work!"

Memphis's ironclad, no-nonsense approach even put the fear into Lexus and Roxie. They've cut down on their stealing, and have started turning a larger profit. It isn't enough to keep the club from sinking further into debt, but it is enough to keep the creditors off Memphis for the short run.

Over the next month, Memphis spends most of his time alone, drinking, smoking, and plotting. Like a hungry leopard, he needs his next attack to be lethal, and he will not attack until he knows it is the right time. And the longer he waits, the more his anger and resentment grow.

Meanwhile, Willie's fear grows too. Nate started a war, and Willie knows it will not end until someone he knows and loves feels Memphis's wrath. Memphis's lack of a swift retaliatory attack goes against the strategies of war.

"Calm down," Nate urges Willie, while lying low. "I crippled him. I got him right where I want him. He ain't got the balls to come back on us, because I kill even the shit in his dreams."

Nate laughs. "You should have seen the look on that nigga's face when he pulled his wife's head out of the trash, Willie."

"He's defeated," Nate declares.

"I don't want to hear about it," Willie says. "You did everything I told you not to do."

Willie hasn't seen Nate in weeks.

"I need you to come around now," he says, "because I want to talk to you about something."

"Nawh, Willie. We'll just talk on the phone for now, if you don't mind. Let's just say I'm not trusting much right now," Nate says. "But you don't have to worry, because I've been keeping a lookout over the club and things."

"Nate, you are disobeying a direct order!"

"Who said I was done?" Nate laughs before hanging up.

Willie calls Memphis again.

"Memphis, we need to talk," Willie says leaving a message on his rival's answering machine again. "I know I can't make right on what happened to White Chocolate. But we can work something out. Call me."

Grinning in the dark and staring at the flashing red light on his answering machine, Memphis comes up with his plan.

"I've got you now, Tray. Your pain will be legendary, even in hell."

CHAPTER 32

"SO, HOW ARE you reconnecting with your sister?" Sandra asks Faith as the two catch up over a lunch of Korean barbecue.

Faith rolls her eyes at the mom-to-be and lets out a long sigh before dropping her spoon into her bowl of spicy doenjang soup.

"Damn, girl, is the soup that bad?" Sandra jokes. "I had that soup two weeks ago and I thought it was the bomb. The baby loved it, too." She gently pats her noticeably round belly.

Faith forces a smile.

"Girl, Angel is driving me crazy. I mean, I don't seem to be reaching her."

Sandra slides out of the booth and motions for Faith to scoot over so she can sit next to her.

"Why don't you go ahead and tell Dr. Sandra all about it," Sandra says, pulling a few tissues from her purse in anticipation of some drama. "But you gotta make it quick, girl, because I have to be back at work in thirty minutes. My boss has been riding my ass over my extended lunch breaks."

Faith takes a deep breath and then begins to describe what the past four months have been like living with her sister.

"Well, it started out good. Angel seemed like she was really down with the program. But then something happened, and she just completely shut down. She doesn't talk about school anymore, and she strolls in all times of the morning like a vampire."

Sandra slants her eyes at Faith. "Did you do something to her? Because you know how you can be."

Faith ignores her and continues on.

"For real, girl, she leaves the house as soon as Kane goes to sleep and doesn't come home until three and sometimes four in the morning! She claims she's studying at the library, but I don't believe her because I *never* see her working on any homework or hear any talk about labs."

"Are you sure you ain't jumping to conclusions? Everybody ain't the bookworm you were in college."

"I know she had it rough dealing with our mom by herself all those years, but I'm not going to let her just come down here and go buck wild."

Tears well up in her eyes. "Although Angel and I live in the same house, the wall between us seems greater than when Angel lived in Chicago. I can't talk to her about anything. She just shuts down.

"When I tried to talk to her last night about school, she told me that every time she takes one step forward, something always seems to trip her up or knock her two steps back."

"So what do you think it is?" Sandra asks.

"I don't know. When I asked her if she was missing a boyfriend back home, she just smiled and said, 'Yes, more than you would know.' She didn't go into detail but I don't think she was referring to Kane's daddy."

Sandra shakes her head and interjects, "You know she ain't seeing that jailbird unless they're giving them conjugal visits."

Faith admits, "I even tried to get answers from Kane."

"Girl, look at you trying to get info outta the baby," Sandra teases. She laughs at Faith for a few seconds and then just as abruptly turns serious.

"So, what did the baby say?"

"He didn't say anything about a man, but he did mention that he misses ReRe–that was Angel's roommate."

It's time for Sandra to get back to work. As she scoots out of the booth, her mind is already working in overdrive, trying to put the pieces together like a detective on 'CSI Atlanta.'"

"What are you thinking?" Faith asks, as she leaves $40 on the table.

"I've got it!" Sandra blurts out.

"I bet Angel was fighting with her roommate over a no-good-ass man. They probably liked the same guy. Didn't you say she was stripping? Why do you think she had to get out of Chicago so fast? I bet she seduced the guy when her roommate was out and then got caught."

"I don't know about that, girl," Faith says, defending her sister.

As she drives Sandra back to work, Faith admits what she's been afraid to say out loud. "Being around Angel has stirred up feelings that I thought I had buried years ago–a hatred of Angel's father."

"She has her father's eyes," Faith says. "Sometimes when I look into her eyes, I see him and all the things that he did to me. I know it wasn't her fault, but sometimes I just look into her eyes and I despise her."

At the curb, Sandra hugs her friend.

"Hang in there, Faith. But you've gotta find out what's going on with your sister, because if she's coming and going as she pleases and she's not in school, well, I will just put it to you like this: She may be too old to raise, but she's not too old to check. I'll call you later, girl."

On her way home at the end of the day, Faith drives back to her home office. She calls home to see if Angel is there but, the phone just rings and rings.

"Angel, I can't do this by myself!" Faith declares.

She lets out a deep sigh of frustration.

"Damn, I need a good man," she says. "Maybe if I had a man, I wouldn't have to worry about somebody else's shit."

* * *

"I can't believe I'm four months pregnant," Angel says to herself, checking her body profile in the full-length mirror in her bedroom. "I'm going to have to hide you from Faith." She pats her belly and turns to check if her hips are starting to spread.

Her bed is littered with crumpled tens, twenties, and fifties. She doesn't know how much longer she can conceal her pregnancy, but she knows that she will not be able to dance much longer.

When she walked into Inhibitions two months ago, in an attempt to get a job as a server, she knew that it would just be a matter of time before she'd be up on stage dancing.

Club owners are like used car salesmen; they use every trick of the trade to reel you in. Angel's turn came when several dancers failed to show up and the owner of Inhibitions–Jeff–begged her to do him this one favor.

The rest is history. When times get tough, you always go back to what you know, and Angel knew the stripping game well.

Angel brought home more than $2,100 her first week and nearly $3,200 the second week, when she started getting regulars. Counting the cash on her bed, she is haunted by a familiar refrain.

"I can't believe this is all I am," she says. "I wonder if Travon could ever love me, knowing that I stripped while I was pregnant with his child."

She scoffs.

"I guess I already know the answer to that. He'll hate me."

"I just gotta be strong," Angel says, slipping to her knees to pray. "God, if you ever bring Travon back into my life, please let him know that I did this for our child."

"I just need to do this for another month or two, and I should be straight. I wouldn't be doing this at all if wasn't for Desiree spending all of our money on dumb shit."

Knowing that Faith will probably be home soon, Angel cleans her face and packs her gear in a duffel bag. She puts the biggest medical books from her first semester on the bed–*Staying Healthy with Nutrition, The Duke Encyclopedia of New Medicine* and *Rapid Review Anatomy Reference Guide*. Although she doesn't think Faith believes she is still in school, Angel continues the charade.

She turns on the radio, and comes across a song that takes her back to a time when her life was not so complicated. For a moment, her mind is put at ease by Troop's "All I Do Is Think of You."

> I can't wait to get to schooooool each day,
> And wait for you to paaaasssss my way.
> Then bells start to ring,
> An Angel starts to sing.
> "Hey that's the girl for you.
> So what are you gonna do . . .

She glances at the clock on her dresser, and starts to hustle, realizing that she has only a couple of minutes before her sister arrives. She calls Kane down, to drop him off at daycare before heading out.

"Well, off to the school of hard cocks," she jokes before grabbing some fruit out of the refrigerator and running out the door.

* * *

"*Miami Herald*, can I help you?"

"Yes, my name is Darnell. I was looking for Travon Brown. Is he in?"

"I'm sorry, sir. Travon's filming his weekly television show right now. May I take a message?" Maria asks.

"Yes, I just have some good news to tell him, so can you just tell him to give me a call?"

"I'm going to get on him," she says in a sweet but stern voice. "He's been such a workaholic since he's been here, but I'll make sure he calls you."

Several hours later, after filming the fifth installment of his already popular sports talk show, Travon tirelessly strolls into the office to crank out his daily blog. The young journalist has really turned up the heat on his competition and has quickly become a favorite among athletes because of his straightforward approach. And the fans can't get enough of him.

"Travon, I have a message for you from Darnell," Maria says, handing me the note.

"He says it's important," she says, walking away with a natural switch that has been known to make happily married men take notice. The scent of Red perfume lingers.

"Thanks," I say, reaching for the phone.

"I hope there hasn't been anymore drama near my mom's house," I think as I tap out the number.

"Hey, Darnell. What's up?"

"Well, I see you've been too busy to hit up your best friend, Mr. Miami," Darnell chides.

"I'm sorry, dude. I've just been trying to make a name for myself down here."

I lower my voice to a whisper as Maria approaches with a cup of tea.

"You know, ESPN gave me a call the other day, but I still want to do a few more things down here before I make that leap."

"That's cool," Darnell says. "But I think I have some news bigger than that."

"What is it, Darnell?"

"You wanna guess?"

"Nawh! Just tell me. You know I'm bad at the guessing game."

"Well, I will put it this way: Guess who has a bun in the oven?"

"Ohhhhh, snap! You gonna be a daddy!"

"Yep. I'm gonna be a daddy. You wanna speak to Taylor?"

"Yeah, fool. Put her on the phone."

"Hey, girl."

"Hey, Tray," Taylor says. "We were finally able to do it."

"Well, congratulations to both of you."

Darnell and Taylor are both on the phone now, and they double-team me.

"We wanna ask you something. We want you to be the godfather."

But before I can answer, Taylor adds, "We expect you to be around, Travon, and not just send gifts."

"We want you to be an active godfather. Can you do that?" Taylor asks.

Feeling a little choked up, I manage, "Nothing will make me prouder. I love y'all."

"We love you, too," Taylor says.

* * *

Later, I make my weekly Friday night call home.

"Mama, how you doing?"

"I'm good, Tray, but something has been on my mind that I wanted to talk to you about."

"What is it, Mama?"

"Well, Tray, I've been dreaming about these fish lately. I dreamed about them three months ago, and I've been dreaming about them a lot for the past couple of weeks. Somebody is pregnant."

Travon laughs. "Let me stop you there, Mama. I don't have anyone pregnant, but Darnell's going to be a daddy."

"So that's what it is," she says. "Lord, I was thinking you had one of those Spanish girls down there pregnant. Be careful, baby, because the last thing you wanna do is bring a baby in the world with someone you don't want to be with."

"I know, Mama. I'm not like my father. If I did have someone pregnant, I would be with them—believe me. Anyway, I was just checking on you. I'm getting ready to go out," I attempt to rush off the phone.

"Before you go, baby, Willie says he's been trying to get in touch with you, and you haven't returned his calls. Call him, baby. He's been like a father to you. Don't do him like that. He says it's important."

"Yeah, yeah, Mama."

"You gonna call him?"

"Yeah, Mama. I really don't have much to say to him, though," There's a short silence.

"Mama, I'm sending you a check in the mail. It should come in the next couple of days."

After the call to my mother, I put on a crisp white button-up shirt with charcoal-black Guess jeans and black boots. I let my dreadlocks drop down below my pecs, spray myself with cologne, and head out to the town.

"All work and no play can get boring even to the best of us," I realize, before grabbing my keys off the desk and heading out the door.

CHAPTER 33

"Travon, I've been very impressed with the way your talk show has worked out. The numbers are looking great, and we want to show you how much you mean to us," Chester says before handing me, his star reporter, his six-month evaluation, with a $5,000 raise.

"Thank you, Chester," I say to my boss, whom I deeply respect. "I'm just doing my job.

"But I still want to do bigger things for the paper." This is as good a time as any to tell Chester about the big interview I hope to land.

"I'm listening," Chester says, easing up to the edge of his seat and folding his hands on his neatly organized desk.

"You know the hottest boxer in the Miami area is Brazil "The Executioner" Hill. But much of his life outside the ring remains a mystery. I can get the interview that everyone wants. I will tie it into his clash against Robert "Pretty Boy" Carr in Vegas for the heavyweight championship of the world.

"But this is an investigative piece, and the key to it is his tie to a reputed crime boss in Dade County."

Chester leans back in his worn brown leather executive's chair and clasps his hands behind his head.

"Why do you think Brazil will talk to you?" Chester asks. "He has gangsta ties, we all know that. Some people say he's nothing more than a street-corner thug who can throw a good punch every now and then.

"I don't know what you can tell me about him that's worth putting in print, Tray. He's bad news–that's why it's taken him this long to get a title shot."

"The gangsta ties don't bother me," I defend my story idea. "You may not know this about me, Chester, but I was partly raised by a big-time pimp. A real OG. This man would hurt you if you crossed him, but he helped me get through college and did his best to keep me on the straight and narrow. I've been around that kind of stuff most of my life. If Brazil has gangsta ties and is in really deep, I believe the public, his fans, and the sport of boxing need to know. And I think his story will be an interesting one to tell, regardless."

"I'm listening, Travon, continue."

"Well, he has a tune-up fight in Atlanta in a couple of months. I want to do a cover story on him, using his upcoming fight as the news peg."

Chester trusts my instincts. Everything I've contributed to the paper and its multimedia partners has been stellar thus far.

"I'm going to say OK for now," he says, "but I want you to be careful because this knucklehead has a lot of people from his past who wouldn't mind putting a bullet in him. As a matter of fact, wasn't he shot about a year or two ago?"

I nod in agreement.

"Brazil was shot twice in the leg while leaving a night club. That only added to his thug persona. He gained millions of fans after that."

"Sounds like a publicity stunt to me," Chester says, shaking his head. "But if you want to pursue it, Travon, I will let you do it. I just want you to keep me posted on this one, because like my grandmother used to tell me, 'If it look like shit and smells like shit, it's not roses.'"

"I'll remember that," I say, as he rises to leave. "I'm a journalist first, and if I smell shit on Brazil I'm going to write about it. I don't care who he is. I'll let the public know if he's as crooked as he's rumored to be."

Back at my desk, I skim through my calendar, blocking off two weeks' time to get the scoop on Brazil. If I succeed, it's a profile that will make ESPN salivate.

Over the next month, my attempts to set up an interview with Brazil hit nothing but roadblocks. I even challenged the boxer in one of his blog posts, asking what the fighter has to hide.

I look into the property owned by the boxer and into his earnings. For the past five years, Brazil has grossed about $200,000 a year, but he is living in a $9.5 million estate and owns eight new cars—and he has amassed all of it without a single endorsement.

"This is bullshit. He's getting his money from somewhere, and it ain't boxing. I think its time for me to follow the money."

* * *

"Please be careful, Tray, because I just have a funny feeling about this trip," Maria says as she drops me off at Miami International Airport.

"I really don't trust that boxer or his crew. I just know that they're bad news, and I'm worried about you," she says, as I continue to tap away at my Blackberry, ignoring the potential dangers I could face.

"I'll be fine, Maria, and this is the only way he'll let me interview him. I'm going to spend some time with him before the fight and talk to him after he destroys another handpicked opponent. You don't have anything to worry about."

After nearly a month of cancelled appointments with Brazil, I'm determined not to let this opportunity slip away.

"Maria, everyone knows Brazil is crooked. I'm just going to be the one to bring it to light," I assure her before exiting the car.

Walking through the bustling airport, I assess the risk factor of my trip. First of all, I never got a firm agreement from the no. 1 contender that he would really talk to me. Secondly, getting this boxer to open up the way I envision may be nearly impossible. "He would be a fool to let his guard down all the way, but stranger things have happened."

In Atlanta, I experience culture shock.

Miami's Latin and Cuban influence was everywhere, even to the point of me hiring a Spanish tutor just to communicate.

Atlanta is the complete opposite. It is the melting pot of chocolate and for the first time in months, I feel like I am around family.

I grab some jerk chicken inside Atlanta's Underground and watch as a young couple walks by, hand in hand, like it was them against the world. When the young man leans over and lightly kisses his girlfriend on the nose, she giggles and gently kisses his eyelids.

"This is what I've been missing. I get lost in my work because I've been avoiding commitment."

When I arrive at Brazil's posh training facility just outside Atlanta, I'm approached by a gang of bodyguards and street thugs.

"Where you going partna?" a 300-pound brother in a circulation-cutting T-shirt says, raising his forearm to block my passage.

"I'm Travon Brown, with the *Miami Herald*. I'm here to interview Brazil."

The buff bodyguard, his arms and neck littered with tattoos, growls. "Reporters are not allowed."

"I don't know you," the bodyguard says. "What did you say your name was again? Travon sounds like a bitch name to me, and Brazil ain't talkin' to no bitches," he continues, as street hustlers begin to surround me.

As I reach into my pocket to pull out a business card, I'm shoved from behind into the bodyguard, who uses the opportunity to grab me around the throat. But before the beefy guard can figure out what has hit him, I flip the script and land three stiff blows to the husky man's kidneys, and he drops to the ground in agony.

"Ya'll want some!" I yell, with fists balled up.

More goons rush toward me and their fallen comrade, followed in short order by Brazil, who storms out toward the commotion with a gold robe on.

"What the fuck is you ignorant-ass muthafuckas doing?" Brazil yells, bringing everyone to a stop.

I drop my fists, go back into reporter mode, and introduce myself.

"Nigga, I know who the fuck you is. You, the educated paperboy that just dropped my *fired* bodyguard. I saw the shit on the security camera."

Brazil motions for his street hustlers to remove the fallen guard from the premises.

"And if I see you around here, I'm going to kill your ass myself," Brazil yells at the guard.

He walks up to me.

"I saw what you did, paperboy. You can follow me."

As we walk toward the facility, I notice that I'm being mean-mugged by a dozen of the hardest men I've seen since my younger days when I hung out with Willie.

The climate-controlled gym is nothing like what I'm used to. It's as clean as a hospital, and the floors shine like new money. There are several boxers punching heavy bags as others jump rope, but the only thing that remind me of a real gym is Brazil on the speed bag. The concentrated popping of boxer on bag takes me back to when I practically lived in the moldy boxing gym in Milwaukee.

Brazil lets out a powerful right to end his time on the 100-pound heavy bag, turns toward me and arrogantly says "Now write that down!"

"I'd figured you would show, 'cause you seem pretty persistent," the six-foot-three, chiseled, light heavyweight says as a trainer wipes the sweat off his back. "So what do you think my chances are against this chump?"

"Honestly, I think you should murder the bum," I tell him, drawing a smile from the boxer.

"Yeah, I'll have him seeing the inside of his eyelids by the second round," Brazil says. He whispers something into the trainer's ear, and the older white man scurries away.

Before he agrees to talk to me, Brazil insists that nothing be tape-recorded.

"I still don't trust you," he says, as he uses his teeth to rip the tape from around his fists.

"You won't fuck up anything I have to say, because I speak the realist shit," he says, reaching for a small plastic case the trainer has returned with.

Brazil pulls a diamond-clustered grill from the box and pops it in his mouth. "So, what can a street thug like me do for you?"

"Well, Brazil, quite simply, you are a mystery. What everyone knows about you is only that you have a lot of tattoos, you raised yourself after your mother was killed, you never knew your father, and if you win your next fight, you will be fighting for the heavyweight championship of the world, making you an instant millionaire."

"You already have something wrong," Brazil says. "When I beat this pussy in the Georgia Dome for all my homies and everybody that's locked up, it will be the worst thing that ever happened in this sport. They are going to have a thug fighting for the championship."

"Are you a thug?" I ask. "I mean don't you want people to know more about you? I'm mostly interested in telling your story aside from the boxing."

"So let me get this straight, you don't want to do a story about me knocking this fool out down here, but you looking to tell a story about my life?" Brazil questions.

"Well, yes."

"Nawh, homie, I can't help you with that. I'm in too deep to talk about that. Stuff in my past, shit I did . . . I just can't talk about," Brazil says. "Let's just keep it on the fight. I'll make it exciting for you."

* * *

"Maria, I need to speak to Chester right away."

"Is everything all right, Travon?" Maria asks.

"Maria, can you please put Chester on the phone," I snap.

"OK, I'm putting you through right now," Maria says with an attitude, while at the same time listening in on the conversation.

"Hey Chester, I just got a tip on my phone from someone who claims that the mob owns Brazil and that he's going to throw his Vegas fight, if the odds have him at 7 to 1 or better."

"You know I have to ask you who the tip came from," Chester says.

Pause.

"Chester, I'm not comfortable at this point saying who the tip came from, other than that it's a reliable source."

"Well, right now, Tray, I don't think you can use that. As a matter of fact, how deep is this getting? I mean his fight in the Georgia Dome is tomorrow night, and I don't know what you've got so far."

"I'm going to file something tonight, and I'm going to present my new information to Brazil tonight. I will call you later."

I can't tell Chester just yet that the tip came from the mother of Brazil's daughter. The boxer and his former high school sweetheart have not spoken in over a year and frankly, hate each other.

I worked hard to cultivate Evette as a source but had a hard time believing her until she showed me paperwork that confirmed corrupt bookings, shady contracts, and illegal dealings that helped Brazil maintain his ranking as one of the Top 10 boxers in the world.

Tonight is going to be big. Although I don't expect the boxer to be honest about it, I know something is going on.

Later, when I go to the fighter's room for his interview, the only person there is a half-naked woman.

"Is Brazil around?"

"You must be the reporter," she says. "He told me to tell you that he changed his mind about the interview. He said he gave you enough."

"What?"

"Yeah, he went to The Jungle." she says.

"The Jungle, where's that," I demand.

"Baby, he just pays me to fuck, not to give out his personal information." She makes no attempt to cover her body.

I reach into my pocket and offer the woman $20 for more information.

"Come on now, baby," she says, her arms folded. "I can't buy a Happy Meal with that."

"Well, it's all I've got."

She ungratefully takes the money, and then strolls to the back of the room to find a piece of paper and a pen.

"He left about an hour ago, so I don't even know if he's still there because he likes to club hop," she says as she hands over the directions. "Don't worry, he ain't drinking–he's just chasing pussy."

Coming away from this trip empty-handed is not an option, and Brazil's arrogance makes me even more determined.

"I'm going to find him."

"Damn, baby, I hope you do. And if you don't, take one of my cards and hit me up later," she adds with a smile. "My friends call me Climax."

I take the card and tell her to pass me one of the $20 Kit Kats out of the mini bar.

"Just charge it to Brazil," I say as I walk out the door.

Nearly two hours later, I discover the boxer in a VIP area, surrounded by at least twenty women and men, hunkered down on a couch, with two stallions sitting in his lap.

"I can't believe this shit," I mutter as I approach the group. When I'm stopped at the entrance to the VIP area by two lurking bodyguards, I decide to use my wit instead of my brawn.

"Yeah, fellas, I'm Brazil's handler. I need to get in there to get him ready for his fight tomorrow, so my boss sent me down here to hustle him up."

"Wait here," the larger of the two guards instruct me.

I ignore that and follow the huge messenger into the room. Upon approaching Brazil's table, I immediately join the party.

"What's up, Brazil? I thought we were going to hang out, boy?" I give Brazil a pound.

Brazil waves away the bodyguard, and I take a seat next to the boxer. It is just seconds before an Asian girl hops in my lap.

Brazil looks at me. "Damn paperboy, you just don't give up, do you?"

"I wouldn't be good at my job if I did."

"Is it like this for you every night, Brazil?"

"It's like this every night, paperboy. Every night," Brazil brags.

The bass of the club's music pounds in my chest. I lean into the boxer's ear.

"So, are you avoiding me because you know I know that you're going to throw your Vegas fight?"

The platinum smile disappears, and Brazil turns and administers one of the most intense stare-downs I've ever experienced, but I don't blink.

The boxer stands up, dropping the woman on his lap to the floor.

"Brazil! Where you going?! What's going on?!" a few in the group yell.

I quickly follow suit, trying not to lose the boxer in the crowd of people.

Brazil reaches the door to the alley, kicks it open, and screams, "What the fuck!"

"Stay back! Keep away from me paperboy before I kick your ass!"

"So is it true, Brazil?" I continue to invade his personal space.

"Just talk to me, Brazil! What's going on with you? Who's forcing you to do this?" Brazil plays kick the can with the garbage bins lining the alley.

I finally catch up with Brazil at the end of the alley but realize we are not the only ones there. Out of the shadows, comes an unfamiliar voice.

"OK, muthafuckas, break yourself!" a thug yells as he points a barrel gun at us.

"Now ain't this a bitch!" I stomp my foot in disgust. "You better be glad you got the ups on me, punk, because I would turn your little ass into my bitch!"

The robber steps closer, keeping his weapon on me as he addresses Brazil. "You heard me! Break yourself, fool. I want that watch, your chain, your grill, and your wallet."

"OK, OK, just don't shoot me," Brazil begs, the essence of his manhood crumbling just like the men he has defeated in the ring.

"Yeah, nigga. This ain't no boxing ring. I didn't think you had no real heart," the punk says.

Tears are rolling down Brazil's chiseled face. "Look, man, you got my stuff. Just go. I ain't gonna say nothing. I swear. Please don't shoot."

"Nawh, nigga, I'm running this shit, 'cause I got this big equalizer," the robber says, turning his attention to me.

"All right, nigga, your turn. Give me yo' shit."

"You're gonna have to kill me, fool."

"Aw, man, give him your stuff," Brazil begs, but I'm scoping out an opening to pounce on the robber.

The stickup kid doesn't give me the opportunity. He backs up, knowing he won't get anything from me without a fight.

"I like you, nigga," the robber says. "You're a soldier with a lot of heart. If I was you cuz, I would stop hanging out with this bitch-ass boxer. He's soft as hell."

The robber turns and runs.

I wait until Brazil puts his arms down, and the color returns back to his face. "So, Brazil, you were saying?"

CHAPTER 34

WILLIE FLIPS ON the light as he enters his office.

"Nate, what are you doing here?"

"Did I scare you, Willie?" Nate replies in a slow, somber tone. "You know I ain't got nowhere else to go. I wanna come back home to the family."

Willie's first inclination is to kill his longtime assassin.

"You fucked up, Nate. Your actions turned a simple conflict into a war and now a lot of innocent people are in danger," Willie says, slipping past Nate to take his seat behind his desk.

"On top of that, Nate, you were out of control and, like my grandfather used to say, 'I don't have time to be messin' 'round with somebody who won't listen.'" Slowly, Willie reaches for the Magnum he keeps velcroed under his desktop.

"Do you understand what you did?" Willie asks, his voice rising as he fidgets with his free hand for his piece.

"I know I fucked up, Willie," Nate concedes. He looks defeated, and much older than his age.

"Is this what you're looking for, Willie?"

Nate pulls the gun from his inside coat pocket and points it at Willie.

"I may be crazy, but I'm no fool, Willie. I just wanted to know where I stood with you, and I guess I got my answer to that, huh?"

Willie raises his hands, pausing to smile at the irony of the situation.

"Well, well, look at this. What you gonna do with that gun, Nate? Kill me? You should've done this to Memphis, instead of doing sick shit to White Chocolate. You were supposed to handle that to protect Travon, and you fucked that up!"

"So how do you think this nigga gonna come back on us? He's gonna come back hard. Killing his bitch made a man outta him. You didn't break his spirit. You actually gave him heart. Shit, you gave him something to live for–revenge. That's the only thing that's got him going now! This shit ain't over. It's just beginning."

"I don't know why I did what I did, but sometimes I just wanna do *what the fuck I wanna do!* I think I've earned that right. Shit, I've been putting in work for you for years, and to be honest 'bout it Willie, you ain't never really cared 'bout what happened to me as long as yo' hands stayed clean."

"Tell me, Willie, honestly. How many notches do I have? It's more than twenty. Hell it's more like fifty. Do you even know how many people I off'd for you? Shit, no wonder you and all those funeral directors are tight. My work is making them mutherfuckas rich."

Willie leans back in his chair, reluctant to interrupt as Nate delivers his own eulogy.

"I know this was 'bout Travon and keeping that young nigga straight, but it's 'bout respect, too, Willie. You don't respect me! You've always treated me like a little puppy dog to do your dirt. I always did what you asked–except for this one time–and you wanna kill me?"

"When I had White Chocolate, I had the power. You and I were equals for the first time, Willie, and that felt good.

"So do what you want to do with me, Willie. I'm tired of living anyway. The only thing that's kept me going this long is working for you. I just wanna be free."

Nate pushes the smoke through his nostrils with a sigh of resignation.

When Willie reaches for the gun, Nate closes his eyes and waits for the loud blast of silence.

Nothing.

"Send me to hell, Willie! Send me to hell!" he yells, his arms wide open.

BANG!

Nate opens his eyes, grabs his head and realizes that Willie has fired the bullet right past his ear.

"We're already in hell, Nate," Willie says. "Now we have to figure out how many people we're going to take with us."

Willie yanks Nate up from the chair by his collar.

Nate snaps to attention.

"If you disobey me again, I'll put the next bullet right in the middle of your forehead. No more insubordination out of you, soldier. Do you hear me?" Willie barks.

"Yes, sir!" Nate responds, smiling.

"Welcome back into the family, solider," Willie says, shaking Nate's hand.

Now Willie knows, Nate will both obey him and do anything for him, even if it means putting his life on the line.

"Nate, we've got a lot of work to do, but I've got a plan."

Willie hands Nate some keys, and urges him to go upstairs to one of the VIP rooms to get some rest.

"I'll send one of the girls up there later to bring you some clean clothes, soap, and a razor."

"Thanks, Willie."

"Hey, Nate."

"Yeah, Willie?"

"I just got one question for you. You still getting high?"

"No, Willie, I swear," Nate responds, his eyes red.

"I'm only going to say this once, Nate. I tolerated your drug use for a long time, but if it interferes with what we have to do now, I'll cut you loose for good. Now go get some rest; we have a busy couple of days coming up."

* * *

Memphis has become more of a vampire since Stallion's death with alcohol, and revenge the only things that could quench his thirst.

"An eye for an eye, baby," he says, the words slurred as he drinks vodka alone in his office and stares at the frozen video images of Nate leaving the club with his wife on that fatal night.

"I'm sorry, baby," he says, touching the screen.

Although Memphis never lets his guard down in public, he has no problem crying alone in the dark.

"Killing you, Nate, would be too easy," Memphis says, pointing his semi-automatic weapon at his own shadow on the wall.

He holds up a glass to toast his shadow and clumsily spills the drink on himself.

"Shit," he says, wiping the front of his green, silk shirt.

He stumbles over to a raggedy couch in his office to sleep off his drunkenness. As he begins to doze off, he tells his wife that vengeance will come soon.

When Desiree finds him the next morning still sprawled out on the couch, she tries to lift him out of his own vomit.

"Just let me lay here!" he yells.

"I'm tired, Memphis, and you're not helping me at all," Desiree says. "You know I can make a lot more money at Temptations or doing private shows on my own."

"I've shown you I'm loyal. I've done everything for you, but I'm the one you're always hollin' at. When money comes up short, you always accuse me of stealing it. I'm just tired of it Memphis."

She searches through her purse for a mirror.

"Look at yourself, Memphis," she demands, shoving the mirror in his face.

Even Memphis fails to recognize the person staring back at him. His dry skin and unkempt beard make him look like a weathered corpse.

"This is not the man who came from nothing to become a successful club owner, nor the man who helped rescue me when I was down and out."

Desiree desperately tries to pull Memphis out of his funk.

"You're right," Memphis says, sitting up.

"Look here," he says, his voice dry and cracked. "I don't want to make the same mistakes I made before. I need you to stick around with me to the end, OK. Do what you have to do to get this club in order. I trust you."

"I have to get outta here for a while. Give me a day or two to get my shit right. I have some people I need to see. Then we're going to go to work, all right?"

Memphis gathers up his coat and shoes, and gives Desiree a peck on the cheek on his way out of the room.

"Where you going?" Desiree asks.

"Don't worry about it, bitch! I just got some stuff I have to get together," he barks, tucking his gun into his waistband. "Run this place like a Queen B. You'll see a different Memphis in a few days."

* * *

"You look a lot better, Nate," Willie says, extending a hand to his friend.

"Yeah, it's funny what a razor and clean clothes can do for you," Nate says, sitting down. "So what's the plan?"

"I was thinking that we should just go down there and blast him," Willie says. "Do him in his club. In and out!"

"Willie, you need to leave the killing to me," Nate says. "He has these two dirty cops watching his club and house, day and night."

"So what do you think we should do?" Willie asks.

"I think we need to infiltrate and see what he has going on, because he's too hard to get at right now. If I were you, I would send one of the girls down there, let her get close to the fool, and when she does, we hit him with everything we got."

"It'll work. I know this fool, and I know his kind," Nate says.

"So let me get this straight, Nate. You want me to send a sacrificial lamb to Memphis?"

"Memphis won't even see her coming at him," Nate says. "Plus, this will help us get close to that big-ass girl who's workin' for him, too."

"I bet you, Fancy can pull it off," Willie allows. "I'll talk to her."

* * *

When Memphis comes back to the club three days later, he looks better and his mind is set.

"Is everything OK with you, Memphis?" Desiree asks.

"Yeah, baby. You did good while I was gone."

"I just went back home to visit some of my people and tie up some loose ends. A cousin of mine will be paying us a visit from Memphis this week. He's going to help us take care of our situation in Milwaukee. I will talk to you more about it tonight. Meanwhile, let's go make some money."

The entire night, Memphis is like a man on a mission. He runs the girls hard, like he did when Desiree first started working in the club.

Dancers sitting in the back socializing are hustled out of the dressing rooms, and he fires three girls for being too slow.

"Baby, this was a good night," Desiree says as she and Memphis count the money at the end of the night.

"Yeah, it was. But it shouldn't be this hard," Memphis says. "Girls don't work as hard as they used to. I shouldn't have to work this hard. Back in the days, bitches would just bring you the money with no problems. 'Here you go, daddy.'"

"And the girls who come in here now know we need them, when it used to be the other way around, earlier. The game done changed."

"The game has changed," Desiree declares, "but my appetite has remained the same. You know we always go out to Denny's every Friday, so let's go."

She playfully pulls Memphis by the arm.

"I don't know how you can eat that shit everyday and don't gain a pound," Memphis jokes, checking out Desiree's round bottom.

Desiree doesn't take the credit. "This right here is all on my mom," she says, slapping her ass. "She *still* has a bad body, and she's almost fifty."

Other strippers from the club are sitting in cliques at various tables when Memphis and Desiree arrive.

"Give me the Ultimate Omelet, and he'll have the Grand Slam," Desiree tells the waitress.

As they wait for their food, Desiree notices a beautiful woman sitting alone at a booth not far from them. Although she tries to ignore the woman, Desiree cannot help but make eye contact. The beautiful stranger returns Desiree's flirtatious gaze with her own hazel-eyed stare.

When Memphis leaves the table for a bathroom break, Desiree asks the waitress if the woman is alone or if she came in with someone.

"Who? Her?" the waitress asks, looking over at the woman, who is reading a book. "She's by herself. She's been in here the last few weeks about this time. I thought she was a stripper like the rest of you."

"Maybe I'll go see what this girl is reading," Desiree says to herself, sliding out of the booth.

"Do I know you?" Desiree says as she impulsively sits down at the booth with the woman.

"I just wanted to tell you that you have the most beautiful eyes."

"Thank you," the woman replies. "You do, too."

"So what are you reading?" Desiree reaches to touch the woman's hand on the book. "Oh, your hands are soft."

"I guess I should tell you my name, since I'm coming on to you, huh?"

The woman smiles.

As Desiree moves in for the kill, her flirtation is broken by a yell from Memphis, telling her that their food is on the table.

"You can eat over here!" he calls out sarcastically, and several of the other dancers laugh. "Bring your dessert over to the table while you at it!"

"Would you mind joining us?" Desiree asks the woman.

"Sure, I guess."

Desiree takes her by the hand, leads her to the table and starts to introduce her, but realizes that she doesn't even know her name.

"I'm sorry, what is your name?" Desiree asks.

"I'm Fancy. Nice to meet you," she says, shaking Memphis's hand.

While they eat, Desiree strokes Fancy's leg under the table, and brushes her fingers against her new friend's mound.

They talk about the club, and Fancy asks if she might come by and attempt to dance.

"I've always thought about it," she says, "and since I lost my job, I need to do something."

She and Desiree exchange numbers, and on the way out to her car, Fancy blows a kiss to her new "friend."

Her phone rings almost as soon as she's in the car.

"Can you talk?" Willie says.

"Yes, baby."

"So, how did it go?"

Fancy smiles.

"*Willie*, you didn't tell me the bitch was that fine. I may enjoy her eating me. I'm in. They want me to dance tomorrow."

"Good girl," Willie says. "Call me tomorrow."

CHAPTER 35

"SANDRA, CALL ME back right away, girl, because you will not *believe* where I am."

Faith never thought she would be sitting in the maternity ward waiting for Angel to give birth. She didn't even know her sister was pregnant.

Nervously tapping her pumps on the eggshell white floor, Faith stares at the clock on the wall that seems to be moving at a snail's pace while everyone around her is bristling past like a team of army ants.

"I wonder what she would have done if I hadn't have come home early? Had the baby right in the middle of the living room!" Faith wonders. "How could I have missed the signs? She was eating up everything in the house, and avoiding me like the plague.

"I'm not about to turn my house into a daycare," she says to herself before walking up to a group of chatty women at the nurses' station.

"Excuse me . . . Excuse me! They took my sister to the back two hours ago and nobody has told me anything yet."

Visibly agitated by the interruption, one of the nurses opens a clipboard.

"Name."

"Her name is Angel, Angel Houston. We came in about three o'clock," Faith says before the nurse interrupts her to answer a page.

Holding up a finger for Faith to be patient, the nurse asks the caller about Angel's condition.

"Your sister is doing well," the nurse says. "But we had to perform an emergency C-section. Don't worry, they are both doing fine, and you should be able to see the baby in about twenty minutes. We're still working on Ms. Houston, but you should be able to see her in about a half hour or so. We will call you when she's ready to be seen."

"I'm sorry, but did you say my sister had a baby girl?" Faith asks.

The nurse nods yes, as she takes another call.

Waiting to see the baby, Faith begins to hear the ringing of her own biological clock.

"Here she is having her second baby, and I can't even find a man to have one," Faith thinks as she watches Kane play on the floor with other children in the maternity ward waiting area. Sandwiched in between two men, Faith feels out of place and calls out to her nephew.

"Kane, come here please?

"Yes, Auntie Faith? Kane replies, standing before her in his Atlanta Hawks basketball jersey and matching shorts.

"Can I have a hug?" she asks, with her eyes watering up.

Kane looks over at the other boys in the play area, and leans over to whisper into Faith's ear. "Not now, Auntie Faith. They'll laugh." He motions toward his playmates.

Disappointed, but humored that someone so young could be embarrassed showing affection, Faith tells Kane that she doesn't want him to feel ashamed.

Kane suddenly opens his arms wide and gives his aunt an incredible squeeze and a kiss.

"Thank you, baby," Faith says, surprised. "I needed that. But you thought you were too big to give me a hug in front of your friends?"

"I love you, Auntie Faith," Kane says, slightly releasing his grip.

"I love you too, baby," Faith says, kissing his forehead.

Their embrace is interrupted by the ring of Faith's phone.

"Sandra, guess where I am," Faith says, as Kane reluctantly walks back to the teasing of the other boys.

"I don't know," Sandra says. "If your sister's involved, I would guess jail."

"No!" Faith says, perturbed by Sandra's lack of faith in Angel.

"Well, don't catch an attitude with me. You told me to guess, and that was the first thing that popped into my head."

"Well, guess again."

"I don't know, girl."

"Dr. Towns to ICU, please. Dr. Towns to ICU."

"What you doing in a hospital? Is everything OK?" Sandra asks nervously.

"Angel just had a baby!"

"*WHAT!* Ooooh, girl! Stop lying. Who'd she been fuckin'?"

"Good question."

"I haven't been able to talk to her yet."

"I came home to pick up the Brentwood file that I left on my desktop, and as soon as I walked in the door I heard all this screaming and crying. Kane was traumatized, and Angel was in the middle of the floor, holding her stomach. She just told me not to be mad at her and to please take her to the hospital because she was having a baby."

"I damn near had a heart attack. It still seems like a dream."

"Sounds more like a nightmare to me," Sandra says. "How did you *not* know she was pregnant? I mean, how could you miss it?"

"I thought she was gaining a few pounds, but I didn't know she was pregnant. I ain't never seen her with anybody, and she ain't never mentioned a boyfriend."

"She must have been pregnant before she got here," Sandra says. "But who knows, you let her come and go all times of night, maybe she got knocked up by one of these no-good-ass niggas down here."

"Look girl, I didn't call you so you could tell me how bad my sister is or how stupid I was for not knowing that she was pregnant. I was just calling for your support. Can you just be a friend now without making judgments about me or my sister? Can you just tell me that everything is going to be all right?"

"I'm sorry girl, I didn't mean upset you," Sandra apologizes. "I respect the hell out of you, and you have a big heart. I just don't want anyone to take advantage of you, and that includes your sister. What hospital are you in?"

Holding her hand to her head to hold back an oncoming migraine, Faith tells Sandra that she's at Dekalb Medical.

"OK, girl. I have to go, they're calling my name."

"Wait one second," Sandra says. "What did she have?"

Smiling, Faith tells her friend, "She has a little girl."

"Well, I will see you and your new niece soon."

As Faith and Kane walk toward Angel's room, they're greeted by the sounds of crying babies from both sides of the corridor. Kane grips his aunt's hand tighter.

When the nurse pulls back the curtain around Angel's bed, the two see mother and child together for the first time.

"Mommy!" Kane yells as he runs up to the side of the bed.

"Hey, little man," Angel says in a weak voice. "I'm sorry I scared you."

"You didn't scare me, Mommy," Kane touches his mother's hand.

"Good, baby. You wanna see your little sister?" She pulls back the pink blanket to show the sleeping child, with a full head of black curls and thick eyebrows.

Faith walks up behind Kane to see for herself.

"She's beautiful."

"Take her," Angel says tenderly. "She won't bite you. Not yet, anyway."

Faith reaches into the bed to take the 7-pound, 3-ounce bundle, then makes her way over to the lounger in the corner, with Kane following close behind, clutching the hem of her dress.

When she sits down and starts to hum to the baby, Kane climbs up and snuggles at her side.

"Angel, look," Faith says. "Looks like I've got two babies."

"So what's her name?"

"Tamara" Angel says lightly as she presses the button for the nurse.

"Did you call Momma yet?" Angel asks.

"No, I figured that's something you should do. And Angel, we need to talk, too," Faith says, right before a nurse walks in.

"Yes, Angel?" the nurse says.

"I was wondering if I can have some ice, please, and some more pain medication," Angel says while trying to adjust slightly in the bed.

"You sure can. Does anyone else want anything?"

Faith asks for a Diet Coke and Kane asks for pizza, which makes the sisters laugh.

"We don't have pizza, but I can get you a fruit cup," the nurse says. "You are soooo cute. So what do you think of your new baby sister?"

Confused by the question, Kane just shrugs.

"You can't be like that," the nurse says. "You have to be there for your little sister. She's going to look up to you."

Dr. Towns comes in to check on his patient.

"I don't want to scare you but another hour or so and you could have lost that little girl," he says. "We're going to keep you here for a few days. You've lost a lot of blood, and we want to make sure everything is good before we send you home with that precious little bundle of yours."

"I know I'm lucky," Angel says. "I'm going to do everything in my power to take care of my babies."

With Kane dozing in the lounge chair, Faith decides it's time to get some answers from Angel.

"So, what's going on, Angel?"

"I know you don't want to have two babies running around your house," Angel begins, "so I've saved enough money to get me a little place. Just give me a couple weeks, and I'll be fine."

"You know you can stay with me as long as you want, but you were hiding this from me. What was that about? Were you enrolled in school at all? And who's the father?"

"What difference does it make who the father is?

"It looks like I'm going to be her mother and father anyway.

"I found out I was pregnant my third week here, so I dropped out of school and started working."

"Where were you working, Angel, or do I even want to know?"

"I did what I had to do, Faith. Like I told you, I saved up enough money to get me a place, and I'm not running back to Chicago. Atlanta is my home now, so I'm going to make the best of it—with or without your help."

Faith shakes her head. "I just want to know why you didn't tell me."

"'Cause I know how you are, Faith. You would've been all up in my business, trying to run my life, and I didn't want that. It wouldn't change nothing. You didn't even know I was pregnant, and you already had an attitude with me. Imagine how you would've acted if I told you I was pregnant and working in a strip club."

"Wait, you were what? You were prostituting yourself?"

"No! I was just stripping. That's it."

"Oh, Angel, you know it's the same thing! Ain't no man gonna give you money to take off your clothes and that's it! How could you whore yourself like that–pregnant?

"You should at least have had some kind of decency for your child."

"Is that what you think? I'm a whore? Well, if I'm a whore, what does that make you, Faith? You were fuckin' my father!"

"You little . . ." Faith stops herself. "Your father raped me, and he did it for years. He raped me, Angel, and I know you want to somehow blame your situation on me, but I'm not going to hear it. You did this to yourself. All I've tried to do is help you."

"I'm getting out of here before I say something I'll regret."

"Kane, baby, wake up," Faith says, shaking him gently by the shoulder. "Say good-bye to your mother. We have to go."

"Stop, Faith," Angel calls out. "I didn't mean it. I didn't mean it."

* * *

"She said what?" Sandra says when she hears what Angel had said to Faith at the hospital the night before.

"I can't believe she said that I was fucking her father, after what that rapist did to me! He's the reason that I can't seem to have a normal relationship now," Faith says.

"Well, girl, you were right to tell her that stripping in a club while she was pregnant was nasty. It ain't like she was doing it to stay off the street. She has a roof over her head, and you were giving her money for school. She played you, girl."

"She used my guilt against me. To be honest, if it weren't for Kane, I would throw her ass out and ship her back to Chicago."

"Where is Kane?"

"I just dropped him off at school. I really love that little boy," Faith says.

"I gotta go, girl. I still have to get the Brentwood file back to my office so I can close this deal."

"You go, girl, and make that money," Sandra says. "How much are you going to make off this one?"

"I will put it to you this way: We can go to the Bahamas to celebrate for a week on me."

"Now that's what I'm talking about," Sandra says.

"Anyway, girl, I need to stop off at Starbucks and get some coffee. I didn't get any sleep last night, and I need a caffeine kick to get me through the day."

"OK, well, call me later," Sandra says.

* * *

"Come on now," Faith says impatiently as she waits for her Caramel Macchiato.

Finally, after what feels like an eternity, Faith gets her hot drink. But as she turns to grab a napkin, she runs smack dab into the world's clumsiest man, spilling her drink and his all over her brand-new pinstripe suit.

"You idiot!" Faith shouts.

"Look at what you did! You burned me!"

"I'm sorry," the man exclaims.

"Sorry is not going to pay for this," Faith yells.

"Are you all right?"

"Yes, I'm all right, I think," Faith says, after looking into this man's light-brown eyes. "I'm sorry for yelling. I have to be at a house showing in twenty minutes, and everything in my life is falling apart, and then this."

The man asks Faith to join him at one of the open tables for a few minutes, hoping to calm her down. He hands her his cell phone and urges her to call her appointment and tell them that she's going to be late.

Taking a seat, Faith finally takes full notice of the man before her. He is drop-dead gorgeous.

"I will push back my appointments on two conditions," Faith says.

"And what are they?" the man asks.

"You have to tell me your name and tell me if you're married, gay, on the down low, or have more than three sex partners."

He smiles.

"Well, I'm heterosexual, although I don't have anything against gay people. I don't have a girlfriend or multiple partners, and my name is Travon. Travon Brown."

CHAPTER 36

"I BET THIS NIGGA never thought I would find his ass all the way down here in hot-ass Miami, but revenge can drive you harder than success," Memphis muses as he sits in his black SUV across the street from the Miami Herald.

The sun is starting to set, and within minutes, Travon rushes out of the glass double doors, heading to his car with a gym bag and leather briefcase swung over his shoulders. He turns the music in his car up to full blast as he peels out of the surface lot without a care in the world.

Memphis follows with the precision of a veteran police officer, his 9 mm resting in his lap. His only thought is how close he is to squeezing lead into Travon.

"In the temple is too easy, but if I hit him in the stomach, he can watch me stand over him as his life leaves his body," he thinks, clinching the leather-wrapped steering wheel tighter. "I bet you never saw this coming did you, Willie," Memphis says sarcastically, "but it's OK–you'll be joining Tray soon enough."

Travon heads home, zooming in and out of traffic on I-95 to Carol City, oblivious to the black Cadillac truck trailing him. Memphis follows at a safe distance so as not to tip the reporter and almost loses him several times. When Travon turns the corner and pulls into his driveway, Memphis executes a hard turn right behind him.

Travon looks over his shoulder at the SUV, but can't see the driver behind the tinted windows. But the Illinois license plate, "ILUSON" jogs his memory and bad vibes shoot through his body.

"Now I know this ain't who I think it is," Travon says, as he exits his car and walks up to the truck.

When he knocks on the glass, the window comes down and Memphis points his cold piece right at Travon's heart.

"Back the fuck up, close yo' mouth and let's go inside, 'cause we have some unfinished business partna.'"

Travon steps back, his hands raised, and Memphis is surprised by how easy this mission has become.

"Nigga, put yo' hands down and let's go inside," he says, pressing the gun against Travon's chest.

Travon turns his key in the front door and tries to calm the situation by joking, "Excuse the place. If I knew you were coming, I would have straightened up a bit."

The joke incenses Memphis and he strikes the back of Travon's head with the butt of his chrome 9 mm to show him that he isn't amused. The blow knocks Travon to the ground with tremendous force, and the contact excites Memphis, who delivers a flurry of kicks and punches, unleashing the pent-up rage that has been contained within him for more than nine months. He beats on Travon until blood sprays all over Memphis's light green suit.

"You got anymore jokes, mutherfucka?"

As Travon tries to pull himself up from the floor, Memphis kicks him in the back of the head and knocks him back into the fetal position.

For the first time, Memphis has the ups on the elusive Travon.

"Can you hear me, boy?"

Memphis takes a seat on a soft mahogany leather couch and lights a cigarette.

"Damn, boy, you did good for yourself. This is a hot spot," he says, eyeballing Travon's place.

"I bet you get plenty of ass in here, don't you?"

"Yeah, I know you do. And I almost forgot, you don't even have to pay for pussy, either, 'cause you got it like that. Well, how about that?" He taps the ashes from his cigarette on Travon's forehead.

"Do you even know what all of this is about? You probably don't care anyway, that's why I'm going to remove you from the equation."

Through his daze, Travon mumbles, "Is this over that stripper?"

"Yeah and no," Memphis replies. "Your two minutes of fuckin' caused nine months of hell. The power of the nut is strong, ain't it? It's strong, boy. The power of that nut keeps me in business and makes the world go 'round. It's powerful enough to bring down presidents and strong enough to make people kill for it. You woulda been better jerkin' off that night. And I wouldn't be down here right now to kill you."

"I bet you when you woke up this morning, you didn't think you would see me. And I know you didn't think I woulda bust yo' head wide open, did you?"

Memphis pulls out a handkerchief from his coat pocket and walks over to the door to wipe his fingerprints from the knob and everything else he has touched.

Through his pain and tears, Travon pleads.

"I don't know what you talking about! How is killing me gonna solve your problems? I ain't did shit to you!"

"For every action there is a reaction," Memphis says.

"Travon, you have so much to learn about this game. But I will let you in on a little secret, before you meet your maker. If you keep fuckin' over people, putting your shit first and always think that your people will keep cleaning up yo' shit, you dead wrong, boy."

"When I call Willie and tell him what I did, he won't be surprised."

"You think you the shit! Nigga, right now you ain't nothing but payback. As a matter-of-fact, let me end this now."

"Nite-nite, boy," Memphis says, before shooting Travon twice in the head.

"Travon! Noooooo!" Willie yells, as the phone rings in the background.

"Wake up, baby, you were dreaming!" Cookie says, shaking Willie and then crawling over him to answer the phone.

"Hold on a second, Nate," Cookie says, checking to see if Willie's ready to talk. "It's Nate, baby."

"Hello. Yeah, Nate. No, I can talk," Willie says, sitting on the side of his bed. "I wanna make that move fast, Nate, 'cause I think they got something planned for us. I can just feel it and I can see it in my dreams," Willie explains through his anxiousness.

"Slow down, Willie," Nate says. "How fast do you wanna move, 'cause we got Fancy there doin' her thing. If we change the plans, she may get hurt. What you want me to do?"

"I don't know yet, Nate," Willie says, as Cookie rubs his shoulders to try and relax him.

"You wanna tell me what you dreamed about?"

"I saw Memphis getting Travon. He shot him down in Florida. It just seemed too real to me." Willie wipes beads of sweat from his brow.

"Well, Willie, I don't think he knows where Tray is, so we don't have to worry about that," Nate says.

"I'm not so sure how long that will last. I wouldn't put it past him to make that trip down there. Or did you forget what you did to his wife? Let me get off here, I'm going to call his mama to see if she can tell me the last time she talked to him."

Cookie, a thirty-four-year-old stripper who has managed to maintain her looks and body after thirteen years in the business, has been down with Willie since she first walked into his club.

Although Cookie loves Willie and has been one of his main girls, she knows that his love belongs to someone else—Travon's mother, Thelma.

Dialing Thelma's number, Willie clears his throat and switches his voice from stern to sweet, a side few people ever see.

"Hey, Thelma, I hope I'm not calling you too late. I was just checking on you to see when you last heard from Tray."

"You know it's not too late, Willie," Thelma flirts back. "I was just watching television. He hasn't called you yet? I talked to him earlier. You know he's still in Atlanta. I think he really likes it down there 'cause he was telling me about all the beautiful, black, single women he came across. I told him he should be looking for a wife, so he can bring me a grandbaby one day."

Willie chuckles at the thought. "Thelma you know that boy of ours is not ready. You've got plenty of time for that; besides, he's too much into his career to be playing daddy. But look here, Thelma, tell him to give me a call—it's important."

"I'll do that. Is everything all right?"

"Yeah, everything is good. I just had a bad dream and I wanted to make sure he was doing OK. It was probably nothin'," he says, trying to quash her interest.

"What was the dream about, 'cause I've been having some strange dreams about babies myself. He told me that his friend Darnell and his wife were expecting, but I keep having the same dream. So somebody else must be pregnant, or somebody's about to die."

"Now don't you go getting yourself all worried, Ms. Lady. I'm sure Travon is fine. I just wanted to make sure he wasn't thinking about getting in the ring again, that's all," Willie says. "OK, let me get off here so you can get some rest. Do you need anything?"

"Willie, baby, you got to stop spoiling me and giving me money all the time. I'm doing just fine. You and Travon are sending me money left and right. I just put it up into an account. Why do ya'll think I don't have money?" she jokes. "Now ya'll stop it."

"Oh Willie, before I let you go, if you see Nate, can you tell him that I need my doorbell fixed?"

"I'll send him over first thing in the morning," Willie promises before he hangs up.

He turns back to Cookie, who has her arms folded across her chest, and he attempts to pull her closer, but she doesn't budge.

"What's wrong with you?"

"I don't want to sound jealous, Willie, but the only time you talk that nice to me is when we're intimate or I catch you lying to me. Other than that, there's no love in your voice. I've been down with you from the start, baby. All I'm asking for is just a little respect. That's all."

Willie launches into song.

"R-E-S-P-E-C-T, I know what it means to you."

Cookie cracks a smile, and Willie continues to sing while pulling her closer. His singing turns to whispering sweet things into her ear.

"Baby, come on, you know what you mean to me. I'm under a lot of pressure right now, and you know what I got to do. Travon is like my son, and his mother is like my family. And you know how I treat family—nothing comes before them. Who am I here with right now?" he whispers, kissing her earlobe.

"Me," Cookie whispers back, smiling.

"I want you here with me right now," Willie says.

The few words are comforting enough to make Cookie feel special. She straddles Willie planting long, wet kisses on him from his neck to his navel, occasionally surprising him with a light bite. When she teases him at his pubic bone, Willie guides her head to his spot, and she knows what to do next.

* * *

"Angel, I'm sending you home today, but I want you to take it easy," Dr. Towns warns. "I want to see you in four days, OK?"

"Now you take care of yourself and that beautiful baby of yours. If you need me before Thursday, don't hesitate to call my office."

Angel is a little nervous going home with Faith, because they have not talked about the argument they had in the hospital. They both pretend the harsh words were never said, but the sting was so strong that Angel knew it would only be a matter of time, before it would resurface.

"Angel, you know you have to do what the doctor said and take it easy," Faith reminds her in a motherly tone, as she helps her into her car with the new baby and Kane.

On the drive home, Faith and Angel just listen to the music in quiet. It is only after John Legend's "Ordinary People" comes on that they break their silence.

"You mind if I turn that up?" Angel asks.

"Go ahead," Faith says and by the third verse, they're in sync, singing away.

> We're just ordinary people
> We don't know which way to go
> Cuz we're ordinary people
> Maybe we should take it slow (Take it slow oh oh ohh) . . .

"That was pretty, Mama and Auntie Faith," Kane says from the backseat, clapping his little hands.

"Thank you, Kane," Faith says, smiling in the rearview mirror.

"Girl, where did you learn to hold a note like that?" Faith asks her sister.

"Well, you know Mama knows how to do her little thang," Angel jokes. "But seriously, after what happened with Kane's dad, I just started singing all the time, and it came kinda natural for me."

"Well, you're really good. You ever thought about doing something with it?"

"No, girl. Don't get it twisted. I'm not Fantasia."

Silence.

"Look Faith, I'm sorry about everything, and what I said. That was wrong. I was wrong for keeping this from you, but I didn't know what else to do."

"I know. Don't worry about it. You have a healthy baby girl, and everything worked out. That's the important thing. I, on the other hand, will try to stop playing mother hen to you so much, but I want you to know that you can come to me and talk about anything."

"I really don't want you to keep secrets from me, because if we are going to repair our relationship we need to be open with each other," Faith says.

Angel nods in agreement.

"So what do we do now?" Faith asks.

"Eat," Angel says. "I'm hungry."

"Me too, girl. You want to ask Kane what he has a taste for?"

"You want pizza, Kane?" Angel asks.

"No," he says.

"Well, what do you want?" Faith asks.

"Chick-fil-A!"

"Lord, I'm going to have to write this one down. Kane doesn't want pizza," Faith says, reaching back to tickle the boy.

Inside Chick-fil-A, Angel lets Faith take over baby holding duties while she devours a chicken sandwich, and Kane munches away on chicken nuggets while entertaining himself with his action figures.

"So guess what?" Faith says, excited. "I met this cute guy in Starbucks yesterday."

"Whaaaaaat?" Angel says. "Wait a second. Is he white?"

"No!" Faith says. "Why does everyone assume that I would only date white guys?"

"Well . . ." Angel shrugs her shoulders. "You just carry that vibe about yourself that I think would turn some guys off."

"And what vibe might that be? Because I have my own business, my own car, and earn my own money?"

"That's not what I'm talking about," Angel says. "That's fine and dandy, but most guys want to feel like you desire them, and you don't give that off. Trust me on this one, Sis."

But Angel doesn't want to turn her sister's good news into an argument, so she changes tactics and asks how she met the guy and what he looks like.

"Well, like I was saying, I was in Starbucks, and he spilled coffee all over my navy, pinstripe suit."

"Ohh, girl, I know you went off."

"No," Faith says. "Well, not really, I was in a rush to get to this house showing, and I was running late 'cause the line was long, and they were moving slow, so I turned to get a napkin, and we bumped into each other.

"And get this, girl, after he calmed me down, we talked for hours—about everything. He's really compassionate."

"What does he look like," Angel asks again.

"He's very muscular, has like the prettiest eyes and whitest teeth. He's just hot," Faith says, fanning herself for emphasis. "The only thing, girl, he's not from here, he's from Florida. He was up here for a boxing match."

"And," Angel says looking at her sister confused. "What are you going to do? When does he go back?"

"He's only going to be here another two days. But I don't want to push it too hard, because he'll be down there and I'll be here."

"You like him."

"I do, but like I said, he's hundreds of miles away."

"Girl, if you like him that much, make the most out of your next two days with him and see what happens, 'cause life is too short. Believe me, I know that," Angel says. "If I had the chance to be with my daughter's father over again, I would never leave his side."

Right on cue, Tamara starts to fuss.

"Somebody's hungry," Angel says.

"Let's get going, Lil' Mama, so you can eat," Angel says, getting up from the table.

And to Faith she says, "Remember what I said, girl. Don't let a good man pass you by. You'll regret it."

As they make their way to the car, Faith decides she is going to go out on a limb again and try her hand at love. She just hopes Travon is ready for her.

CHAPTER 37

SINCE THAT FIRST rainy night Fancy showed up at Illusions, a storm has been brewing between Memphis and Desiree for the new dancer's affections.

When she took her 36-28-40 frame on stage that amateur night, with her red, thigh-high, patent-leather boots, she was magical. At five foot three, her body was packed with the energy of an African dance troupe. Then there was the huge spider-web tattoo that covered both butt cheeks. On the web closest to the right side of her crack was a large black widow spider. The venomous web weaver's red underbody shimmered through a veil of baby oil, trapping Fancy's prey, as she matched the thudding rap beats emanating from the speakers.

"We've got a winna' right here!" Memphis yells out from the back after Fancy performed her first song. As customers dropped $10s, $20s, and a few $50s on stage, Memphis glances at Desiree, who is watching intently from the other side of the room.

Fancy wowed the crowd with a second dance, and is getting ready to do a third when Memphis hustles up to the stage to collect the money and take the mic.

"I know ya'll want to see more, but this is amateur night, and my girl Fancy is just one of the new hot girls who will be gracing the stage. But you can see more of her Saturday when she headlines with Desiree!

"Now you niggas keep reaching in yo' pockets 'cause we're gonna bring out some more new bootie," he said as he led Fancy off the stage and to his office.

"Damn, girl! You sure this is your first time on stage?" Memphis asks, as Fancy wiped the sweat and baby oil off her body, while she pulls more money out of her thong.

"Yeah, this is my first time," she lies convincingly. "How did I do?"

Memphis reaches for the money in her hands and began to count it.

"Very well," he says. "Very well... Let's see, we made $400 off two songs. Some of those lazy bitches in the back don't make that in three or four days."

He shakes his head and pockets the money.

"So, if I win tonight, I get $500, right?" Fancy asks.

"Well, let me talk to you about that," Memphis says, wrapping his arm around Fancy's shoulder before telling her the catch. "You have to sign on with me to get the money. That way I know you'll come back. It's like a contract. You understand?"

They are interrupted by a knock at the door.

"Who is it!?" Memphis demands.

"It's Desiree! And why is the door locked?"

"Come back later!" Memphis yells.

"I need to talk to you right now."

Memphis storms to the door and opened it, but only a crack.

"Didn't I tell you to come back? What the fuck you want?"

"You don't have to talk to me like that 'cause you trying to get some pussy! I just wanted you to know that there's a strange man out here looking for you."

The message deflates Memphis's sexual intentions, and he strides to his desk to get his 9 mm.

"What does he look like?" he asks Desiree.

"I'll point him out from upstairs," she says.

Memphis pauses long enough to tell Fancy that he wants to see her before she leaves the club, and then hustles her out of his office.

Fancy doesn't reveal her alarm, but her first thought is that Crazy Nate had come back, and that there had been a change of plans.

When Desiree and Memphis reach the second-floor balcony, Desiree points out a hard-looking man with a chiseled face and an all-about-business attitude. When Memphis lays eyes on the suspect, he laughs.

"Blaaaaaackie! Yo, Black!" Memphis yells out over the booming music.

"That's my cousin, Blackie!" he tells Desiree. "Now shit's about to change for real."

Memphis makes a beeline for the first floor, and the two men embrace like long-lost relatives at a family reunion. Soon, Memphis points up to the rafters at Desiree, who continues to look at Blackie with an eagle-eye. She waves, but Blackie doesn't acknowledge her. The two men head for Memphis's office, and leave the Queen B of the club to ponder what Memphis meant when he said "shit's about to change."

One thing she knew for sure–Blackie was definitely in town for something big.

* * *

"Angel, can you come here please?" Faith yells from her bedroom, flustered.

When Angel enters, sleeping daughter in hand, she sees that Faith has at least ten outfits on her bed, some with the price tags still on them.

"Did you go on a shopping spree or something and didn't tell me?" Angel jokes.

"I don't know what to wear tonight," Faith whines.

"I forgot, you're going out with Mr. Florida," Angel teases. "Let me put Sleeping Beauty to bed, and I will come back and help you pick something out."

Upon Angel's return, Faith has pulled out three more outfits.

Angel giggles; she has never seen her sister so nervous about anything.

"Sis, you're acting like this is your first date or something." Angel raises an eyebrow, considering the choices spread before her like an all-you-can-eat buffet.

"This is my first real date in quite some time," Faith says. "Dating is hard for me, Angel. I don't have the type of carefree personality you do."

"Now what is that supposed to mean?" Angel asks miffed at the implication.

"I don't mean anything bad by it," Faith says. "I guess what I mean to say is that it's been a long time since I went out on a good date with someone . . . Let's just say the last person I dated wasn't who he claimed to be."

Angel holds one of the outfits up to her sister. "It couldn't be that bad. You want to talk about bad dates, now I've got some to tell you."

"Where do I start? . . . Well, there's the guy that I thought was very nice, but when I wouldn't have sex with him he made me walk nearly thirty blocks from his house, until I could get a taxi. And then there's the guy who picked up my favorite food only to jerk off on my leg.

"I don't think you have anything that can top those."

"Well," Faith counters, "the last guy I was dating turned out to be gay—and he was dating a transsexual on the side, who wanted to kick my ass at the mall."

Angel laughs. "Now that is strange," she allows. "That's some old Jerry Springer stuff right there."

"I knew I shouldn't have told you," Faith says.

"Don't get all sensitive on me now. That was funny though. He didn't give you AIDS or anything like that, did he?"

"No!" Faith gasps. "I got checked out."

"Well, that's good. The only thing you can do now is laugh about it," Angel says, handing Faith the black cocktail dress she thinks she should wear.

Faith isn't sure about her sister's taste.

"I never wore this dress out because it shows too much cleavage."

"It ain't gonna hurt to show him what you got," Angel prods. "Now try it on. I think this is a winner."

Faith takes the dress and heads for the shower.

With both her daughter and Kane sleep, Angel decides to take advantage of the rare quiet moment and see what's on television.

As Faith finishes dressing, she hears Angel laughing up a storm in the den.

"Faith, come in here quick, this is funny as hell," Angel calls.

"What are you watching?" Faith asks, putting her earrings in, as she eyes the TV.

"This lady is Alexyss K. Tylor, and she's on Atlanta's public access channel talking about Vagina Power. Sit down and listen to this!"

"Ladies, in order to earn your man, you need to learn your man. A lot of times we get caught up with the wrong man or get caught up in a man's penis power, because it's good if a man has been around–and some of the ones I'm talking about, they been hopping around here, here, and there–and he has a lot of practice and knows a woman's body. He knows the power of his penis, and he knows how to soothe a woman's body, and soothe her vagina. So it's easy to get caught up with that dog kinda man . . . 'Cause the man that's living to ejaculate, he's in the "Predator Mode." And when a man is in the predator mode, he is going to look for the weakness of a woman that's lonely. Her vagina is cold, she's laying in bed at night playing with her toys, or she's got a man beside her and he's a good provider, but he's not hittin' the walls and working the middle like that dog she's having that sneaky sex with."

"This is funny, girl," Faith says as she joins Angel on the couch.

"Remember: Don't let every man hit the bottom of your vagina or the root of your vagina," Alexyss advises.

"No, she didn't!" Faith laughs, slapping her sister's arm.

"Girl, that is the funniest thing I've heard in my life," Angel says, wiping tears from her eyes.

"I've never seen that before, but we've got to watch that again," Faith says. "See if you can program it so we don't miss her."

Angel finally takes a good look at Faith.

"Ohhhhh, sis, look at you," she gushes.

Faith turns around to show off the back of the dress.

"Be honest. How do I look? I mean, do I look too easy?" Faith tugs at the top of her dress in a poor attempt to hide her breasts.

Angel puts on a mock-serious face: "Do you have control of your pussy?"

"Girl, stop," Faith says, laughing. "I'm not giving up anything tonight–even though it has been a long time."

"Well, if he's a pussy 'predator' like our public access sex therapist said, then I would say don't let him know that."

"I must admit, girl, after talking to him, I knew I was in trouble, because he has that thing about him. I don't know how to explain it, but it's that thing."

"I know," Angel says. "I knew a man that had it, too. I know exactly what you're talking about."

"I'll be out late, so don't wait up," Faith says, as she grabs her purse and keys off the hallway table. "If something comes up, I'll give you a call."

"I'll keep the cell by my bed," Angel says. "I'm tired so, I'm going to hit the sack before the little one wakes up for her feeding."

Angel closes the door behind her sister, and as she watches the car back out of the driveway, she whispers, "Good luck."

Outside Travon's hotel, Faith is so nervous that she has to talk herself up just to get out of the car.

"Come on, girl, you can do this. You can do this," Faith gives herself a pep talk as she approaches the lobby.

"Travon Brown's room please," Faith tells the desk attendant.

"Travon, I'm downstairs."

"I'll be right down, beautiful."

When I step off the elevator in black jeans, a white dress shirt and black suit coat, Faith appears pleased.

"Hey, handsome," she says.

"You look gorgeous yourself," I reply, kissing her lightly on the cheek and admiring her attire.

"So where do you wanna go eat?" Faith asks, her eyes locked on my piercing brown eyes.

"You know what? Surprise me. I really don't have a preference, as long as I'm in good company with you."

"Well, well, well, Mr. Brown, I want you to know that flattery will get you everywhere," Faith says.

"Oh, I haven't even started yet."

As we head off hand in hand, I can't help but notice how people stare at us. Although there are millions of black people in Atlanta, the sight of couples holding hands and generally looking like they enjoy each other's company is not as common as you might expect. I can't remember the last time I held a woman's hand in public. It feels nice. People are staring like we are making out in public.

After a wonderful seafood dinner, we walk along Peachtree Street, and Faith points out some of the sights downtown. She's my own personal tour guide.

"Hey Faith, let's sit for a minute."

We find a bench near a beautiful fountain.

"You must have been reading my mind Mr. Brown because my dogs are barking in these not-so-sensible shoes."

"You're not some kind of foot freak, are you?" Faith asks.

"Actually no, I hate feet, but I couldn't stand to see you limp around anymore in those peep-toe pumps."

"Come on put them up here," I pat my lap.

"It's good to know that chivalry isn't dead," Faith teases me as she complies.

"Wow! Where did the time go," Faith asks as we make it back to her car.

"Well, you know what they say when you're having fun."

"What time do you leave tomorrow?" she asks, as we head back to the hotel.

"My plane leaves at 10:00 a.m."

Faith grows quiet.

"I know this sounds crazy, and I know you don't know me that well," she finally says, "but I really don't want this to end."

"I was thinking the same thing." I place my hand on her lap as she accelerates.

With the hotel in sight, I suggest she park in the lot and come up.

Faith nervously sits on the bed, as I pack everything neatly into my suitcase and carry-on bag.

"Can I take you to the airport in the morning?" Faith goes out on a limb to ask.

"I would like that." I look at my watch and smile. "Considering that it's nearly two o'clock now, will that mean that you will be spending the night?"

"Well, you do have two beds," Faith says smartly.

"Oh, well, this bed here, it's broken, and I was watching the health channel one night and it said you should never sleep in the bed closest to the window because that's the bed most people sleep in at hotels, but you are more than welcome to sleep in the bed with me."

Faith sees through my obvious come-on as clear as glass but she smiles anyway. Unsure of what to do next, I head to the bathroom leaving Faith alone with her thoughts. After turning the shower on I return and gently kiss Faith on the lips.

Taking her by the hand, I turn Faith around and slide her dress down, sending goosebumps over her body as she folds her arms to cover her breasts.

"It's OK, you're beautiful," I assure.

Planting kisses along her neck, I unsnap her bra with one hand, while sliding my free hand into the side of her matching black panties to ease them down. When she moves back against my chest, her warmth feels good.

I continue planting kisses on her neck and shoulders, while stealthily peeling out of my clothes.

When Faith turns around to kiss me, I'm naked.

"You are smooth. My sister warned me about men like you."

"You ready to get in the shower?" I ask.

Faith just nods as I take her hand and head to the steam-filled bathroom.

Checking the water, I let Faith get in first and follow after placing down a towel. As I lather up the sponge, I gently take Faith's arm first and rub her entire body, until her nakedness was hidden with foam.

Faith steps beneath the massaging water and as the soap leaves her body, I hand her the sponge for my turn. She starts to hyperventilate.

"Are you OK?" I ask easing the sponge from her grip.

"I'm sorry, Travon."

Faith leaps from the shower and grabs a towel before leaving the bathroom.

I quickly follow, wrapping a towel around my waist. Faith is rushing to put on her clothes over her still damp skin.

"What did I do? I'm so sorry," I respond not really sure of what I have to be sorry for.

"It's not you, it's me, Travon," Faith says, crying. "It's a long story."

"Well, what is it?"

"I don't want to burden you with my issues. I'm just all messed up."

"Who hurt you?" I ask.

She collapses into my arms, sobbing so hard that she shakes both of our bodies. I hold her until her panic subsides.

"I was nine years old when my stepdad first touched me," Faith says.

"You don't have to talk about this if you don't want to."

But Faith keeps going, releasing the memories of the attacks in the safety net of my arms.

We do not sleep. Faith talks until eight in the morning, and I absorb every word. I learn that her sister is living with her now, and when Faith looks into her sister's eyes, she sees the eyes of the man who abused her.

"I know that it must be painful, but you can't harbor those ill feelings against your sister. It's not fair to you or her."

When the alarm goes off, I rise from the bed reluctantly, and Faith finishes getting dressed.

"Well, this is not exactly the way I had in mind to keep you awake all night," Faith says.

"It's fine. Actually, I learned a lot about you."

"What did you learn–that I'm crazy, and you don't ever want to see me again?"

"No. I learned that you are a very strong woman who has overcome a lot to make yourself very successful. And I learned that you are a person I want to spend more time with."

"Do you mean that?" She looks at me suspiciously.

"Yeah, I do, if you would have me. I have to warn you that I have some issues, too."

"Travon, can I just kidnap you?" Faith says, taking a seat on the toilet lid to watch me shave.

"If you don't get me to the airport within the next forty-five minutes, you won't have to kidnap me."

"I would love to have you stay with me a few days, but I have my sister and her two children in the house."

"Well, I'll have to get you down to Florida to visit me."

"You mean that? Because I'll come. I have the time. But I bet you have this bachelor pad with all these women trying to get at you," Faith says testing.

"I have a nice little condo that needs a woman's touch. Maybe I've found the right one to give it that touch."

"Sure, I bet you say that to all the women."

As we embrace, I press my warm hardness against her stomach.

She laughs.

"What's so funny?"

"Nothing, baby. You're just hot, that's all."

* * *

"Willie, this is Fancy." She's calling from her cell phone at her hotel room.

"Well, they are planning on moving on you, but I don't have any details on when or where," she says. "I do know that Memphis's cousin is up here from Tennessee. His name is Blackie, and he's mean as hell."

Willie scratches his chin. He's never heard of Blackie, but he's not surprised that Memphis brought in reinforcements. "That means they have something big planned," he says. "Are you safe, Fancy?"

"Yeah, baby, I'm fine. I've got Memphis and Desiree fighting over me right now, but I may have to let that dyke eat me in order to find out what's really going on. She's the Queen Bitch, but I'm sure once she samples my goodies, she'll get to singing like a bird."

"Just be careful," Willie warns.

"You ain't got nothin' to worry about. After I give her some, I'm gonna flip the script, have Memphis wanting some and turn them on each other. After that, I should know what they have planned. I don't know why you just won't have me pop them while I'm here, baby. You know I'll do it for you."

"I know, baby, but this is something me and Nate gotta do. It's just the code of the street. It wouldn't be right if I had you do it. It ain't got nothing to do with you, but it has everything to do with Memphis and me."

"I love you, Willie."

"I love you too, baby girl. Now be safe."

When Saturday arrives, the crowd at Memphis's spot is over capacity, generated by word of mouth about Fancy and Desiree dancing together.

To capture every dollar, Memphis raises the cover charge from $20 to $35 and men still paid.

"I'm here to see Spiderwoman bootie," one man says to this friend as they wait at the door.

"I'm telling you, boy," his friend adds, "this bitch is thicker than a retarded kid's pencil."

Memphis goes to the back to talk to the girls. His pep talk is short and sweet.

"Look here. There's big money in here tonight, so let's go get it. This is a chance for all of ya'll to make up for slacking off. Some of ya'll are in debt. I've been looking at the books, so don't think I'm not paying attention. It ain't no reason for us not to pull in record numbers tonight. Now get on your jobs, bitches!"

The strippers do all right, but a lot of men are holding out their money for headliners Desiree and Fancy. Although the women have not been intimate yet, Desiree knows that if she plays her cards right, she will have Fancy for dessert tonight.

Before taking the stage, Desiree corners her caramel-colored dance partner. "I can't wait to run my tongue all over that sweet ass of yours."

"You don't have to be bashful. I guarantee you that I'm an experienced pussy-lapping bitch, who won't stop until you cum," Desiree says, as she blows her hot breath down Fancy's neck exciting her.

"I hope that ain't just the alcohol talking," Fancy teases, as she and Desiree prepare for their act.

When the women walk out on the stage to Akon and Snoop Dogg's "I Wanna Fuck You," men crowd the stage. The men, who had held onto their money the entire night, start pulling dollars from their pockets like a circus clown pulling out handkerchiefs.

As Fancy and Desiree double-swirled on the stripper pole, the men rock in their chairs and shower the stage with money. Although the two didn't rehearse, their moves are synchronized.

When Fancy begins to butterfly on the stage, Desiree takes the opportunity to straddle her in a 69 position.

"Oh shit!" one man yells.

Another man walks up to the stage and tells Desiree he wants to change positions with her.

"Can I get that big ass to smother me to death?" he yells out.

Desiree roughly flips Fancy into a doggy-style position and grinds her ass from behind, pulling Fancy's hair as she rams her. And when Desiree uses her teeth to pull down Fancy's panties from behind, one suited-up man walks up and throws his wallet on the stage, drawing laughter and high fives from other men in the crowd.

Not to be outdone, Fancy shows Desiree that she isn't just a bottom, and flips the stronger woman on her back, then stands over Desiree and pops her pussy over the Queen B's face.

This sends the men into a frenzy of high fives and zombie-like trances of excitement. When the extended version of the song ends, the men continue to clap and holler as the women gather their money and leave the stage.

Later, when Memphis and a few of the strippers go out to eat, Desiree's meal plan is Fancy. Although Desiree has bedded several women since Angel left her, Fancy will be the first woman that she will have sex with in her own bed.

When Fancy pulls up behind Desiree and parks in front of her apartment, Desiree wastes little time, feeling out the woman that she hopes will take Angel's place.

"I'm going to turn your ass out," Desiree promises Fancy as the two stumble in the darkness.

Desiree thinks Fancy might be a virgin to lesbian sex—until she feels her experienced tongue. Then she knows that Fancy has been playing her in the same way she has been playing Fancy.

The women are in 69, licking and sucking, and making lots of noise, and Fancy's pussy soaks Desiree's face when she explodes. Desiree can't believe how much cream Fancy oozes, but before she can wipe her face clean with a towel, Fancy stops her and licks her face clean for her.

Desiree feels like she's starring in a porno movie—and Fancy is not done. She mounts Desiree's tongue again and again until Desiree's face is flushed.

Desiree loses count of the number of times Fancy cums.

Spent and happy, Desiree falls asleep, with Fancy by her side. But when Desiree awakens, the lady with the black widow tattooed on her ass is gone. Desiree might have thought it a dream, except for the sweet scent of sex on the sheets and the tart taste still on her tongue and lips.

She rolls over onto the spot where Fancy had lain, inhaling and playing with herself until she cums.

"This bitch is turning me into a cum freak," she says to herself before falling back asleep.

CHAPTER 38

DARNELL'S CELL PHONE rings. He glances at the caller ID and lets out a whoop.

"Hey, Darnell," I greet my best friend. "I'm in Milwaukee, at the airport. I just stopped in to see my Mama. I'm only going to be here overnight, then I've got to get back."

"You can't stay any longer than that?" Darnell asks. "They can't be working you that hard, because I know you won't let them."

"Well, it's a long story–I ended up spending a couple extra days in Atlanta."

"Now that sounds like the Tray I know. Who is she?"

Trying to explain Faith to my friend won't be easy. Darnell has a one-track mind when it comes to me and my relationships.

"Her name is Faith. She has her own real estate firm in Atlanta, and she's really cute. But you know what I like the most about her?"

"Ahhh, yeah, I can think of a few things," Darnell jokes.

"No, seriously, I feel like I've met her before. I can't explain it. I just have this level of comfort with her that I can't put my finger on."

"Well, let's see. You slept with an *Angel*, and now you getting *Faith*. What's next Tray? You gonna deflower a Virgin Mary?"

"Let me stop talking to you, fool." I laugh at his poor attempt at word play. "Are you going to come scoop me up, or am I going to have to grab a taxi?"

"I'm on my way now. I'll be there in about twenty minutes. Which airline did you come in on?"

"Pick me up at United."

"See you soon," Darnell says.

"All right, peace."

I decide against the surprise approach and give Mama a call to see if she is home.

"Hey, baby, I was just thinking about you," she says.

"Hey, Mama, I just wanted to see if you were there."

"Who is that in the background, Mama?"

"Don't you worry about who I'm talking to."

"OK, Mama, I guess you don't want to see your only child, you talking smart like that."

Thelma nearly drops the phone.

"Where are you, Tray?"

"I should be there in about an hour. Darnell is picking me up from the airport. Now who is that making all that noise in the background?"

"It ain't nobody but Crazy Nate. He's fixing my doorbell," she explains, piquing Nate's curiosity.

Hearing his name, Nate sticks his head around the doorway.

"Nate, it's Tray. He's come home to see his Mama!"

Nate wipes his hand on his pants and reaches for the phone.

"Hold on, Tray, Nate wants to talk to you."

"Hey, boy," Nate says. "Where are you?"

"I'm at the airport, but I will be there soon. How you been, Nate?"

"Good, Tray. Say, you need me to come get you?"

"Not in your rust bucket, Nate," I joke. "Darnell is picking me up, so I should be at the house in about an hour. Say, do you know why Big Willie has been blowing up my phone?"

"Yeah, but you should talk to him," Nate says. "I will see if I can get him to stop by and talk to you."

Nate passes the phone back to Thelma. He hopes she doesn't notice his anxiety and tells her he has to get some wire at the hardware store and that he'll be back soon. On his way out the door, he glances down the block at the small-time corner drug dealers and makes a quick call on his cell phone.

"Willie? Yeah. This is Nate. You won't believe who's in town."

"Oh, shit," Willie says, the music in his club pulsating in the background. "Where's Tray now?"

"He's at the airport, waiting for his ride over to the house. But I think he's only going to be here overnight."

"That's good," Willie says. "Why don't we do this—let's get some of those dope boys over on Nineteenth Street to watch the house and him until he leaves. I'm sure we can drop three bills on them and they'll take care of the rest.

"But I don't want Tray to know what's going on. He doesn't need to worry about his mother or anything like that. You hear me, Nate?"

"Yeah, I got it."

"Where are you right now?"

"I'm just going to the apartment to get some more protection, just in case. Don't worry, Willie. We'll keep Tray protected better than the president. But I think you're right—we may have to move on Memphis quicker than we thought."

"I know. I'll talk to Fancy today," Willie says. "You know I'm counting on you, Nate. Don't let me down."

"I won't, boss."

When Darnell arrives at baggage claim, I'm so engrossed in my music that I don't notice his arrival until he honks his horn.

"You startled me, boy!" I say, walking up to embrace him.

"Hey man, long time. How long has it been now? Over a year?" Darnell says as he grabs my overnight duffel bag and tosses it into the backseat. "So I see you got darker. What do you do, lie in the sun all day? And damn, man, your locks are long."

"It's the good weather and the humidity." I reach back into my bag and fish out a sterling silver Man in the Moon rattle by Tiffany & Co.

"My godchild is going to have the best," I announce as I hand the gift to Darnell.

"Look at you, spoiling her already," Darnell says.

"So you know it's a girl?"

"Oh, shoot. Yeah, I know, but Taylor doesn't know. She didn't want to know," Darnell says.

I laugh and slap my knee.

"And the doctor told you? He must not know your history."

"I can keep a secret," Darnell says.

"You can't keep shit, Darnell. Are you forgetting that you wanted to tell your wife that you had sex with a stripper at your bachelor party? Or how about the time we were online and we . . ."

Darnell cuts me off.

"OK, so my track record is not that good. But this is one secret that I promised to keep. I haven't even told her parents, and you know how hard her father can be."

"Yeah, he's pretty tough." I whistle at the thought of the run-in at Darnell's wedding.

"One thing about marriage, Tray, a man learns how to keep secrets. It keeps the peace."

"So why don't you take me to see your wife real quick before you take me to my mom's." I suggest. "How is Taylor doing?"

"Aw, man, she's getting big. We're going to be having that baby in less than a month." Darnell looks over at me. "Now you know you have to come up when she delivers."

"I wouldn't miss it, boy. Look at you all married and about to be a father of a little girl. You making me feel old."

Darnell shrugs. "You know, marriage is not that hard. It's just about give and take. And you know what? Taylor is really good for me.

"It was hard after the newness wore off, and we really started to figure out each other's flaws and stuff like that. But we came to accept each other in spite of them. I really love her, and I couldn't imagine life without her."

"I must admit, boy, I was a little worried when you first took the leap, but now you sound like the Darnell I know and love!"

"Anyway, enough out of me, Tray. Tell me about you and your new romance."

"What can I tell you?"

"Well, skip to the good part because we're almost to my house," Darnell says.

"Everything about Faith is the good parts," I say, gushing over my new lady.

"Let me tell you this first. I haven't slept with her. Well, we did sleep together, but she didn't really sleep."

Darnell is confused so he cuts to the chase. "Was there penetration of any kind?"

"No and yes. We penetrated each other's minds."

"Man, get outta here with that old-school pimp shit," Darnell says.

"Seriously, man, I learned a lot about her before I learned her body, and that's different for me."

"So let me get this right–you learned her favorite food instead of her favorite position?"

"Nawh, dude, I learned a deeper level of her, and some of the things that she's been through. I think I'm going to move this forward and see what happens."

"Wait a second," Darnell interrupts. "What about Maria back at your office? Ain't you feeling her?"

"Actually, I don't think that will be a good idea. Maria and I will be better off as friends."

"Speaking of friends, did you know Nicole and my wife have become good friends?"

"Come on, man, crazy-ass Nicole? What has she been doing hanging with Taylor?"

"You know, just hanging out doing girl stuff like shopping and stuff like that. She has really latched on to Taylor, sorta like she latched on to you."

"Well, be careful, dude, or did you forget all those voice mails she left for me, and how she was stripping undercover at my going-away party?"

"I remember, dude, but I didn't tell my wife about that. I mean, I couldn't. Nicole's really a good girl, and I know she still loves you," Darnell says. "Every time your name comes up, she always has something good to say about you."

"Man, are you crazy? Don't mention my name around her! You know my first month in Miami, I kept thinking that she would just show up at my job or some crazy shit like that."

"OK, home sweet home, Tray," Darnell says, as they pull up to his house. "The only reason I'm telling you about Nicole is because she's supposed to be showing up for lunch."

"I'm not staying that long, but if she shows up while I'm here, I'm kicking your ass," I warn with a smile.

* * *

"So how did you do the other night, Memphis?" Blackie asks his cousin over drinks in Memphis's office.

"We did all right. It wasn't a record night, but it was pretty good. Desiree and my new girl, Fancy, packed them in."

"I think, personally, that you let these bitches get away with too much," Blackie says.

"For instance, I've been down here for about a week now, and I see how the girls pretty much come and go as they please. And a lot of them spend way too much time socializing and smoking out front."

Memphis shakes his head.

"I think you got it all wrong Cuz."

"OK, Cuz, I know you don't want to hear this, but when was the last time you slapped one of these bitches around or showed them who's runnin' thangs?" Blackie asks. "I hate to say this, Cuz but, it looks like you slacking on your pimp game probably got Stallion killed, you can best believe that."

"Blackie, I think you better keep your mouth closed before that alcohol gets you in trouble," Memphis warns. "You startin' to talk out the side of your neck."

"I know you don't believe this, Cuz, but those bitches are playing you. I know you wanna be all nice to them, but this ain't the nice business, this is the ho business or have you forgot?"

Blackie fills his glass again.

"I see that big, tall bitch walking around here like she running shit," he says. "You need to check her tall ass."

"She's been down with me from the start. Seen me at my best and worst," Memphis says. "She's earned her status."

"And how has she done that?" Blackie asks. "'Cause she ain't left? You know they get comfortable and don't want to go nowhere else anyhow. I bet you if you let the bitch leave, she'll be back in a month because it'll be hos at the next club better than her, and at her age, she ain't trying to work her way up. Ain't no bitch that old willing to do that in this business. You know that."

"What you need to do is put your trust in that new bitch with the spider web on her ass," Blackie says.

"I don't know nothin' about Fancy," Memphis says.

"What do you need to know? You know she's got a big ass and that she can make that money. That's all you need to know. Shit, I would have her ass out there on the stroll making me money 24/7.

"Have you even fucked her yet?"

Memphis takes another sip of warm vodka, and just shakes his head.

"I fuck every bitch come through my door–hard, too. Let her know what the business is about."

"Look, Blackie, if all you want to talk about is my business then you can take yo' ass back to Tennessee. You forgot nigga, I'm the one that helped get your ass outta trouble when them niggas were after you about five years ago," Memphis says. "Did you forget how I had to give 'em $150,000 to keep them from killing you?"

"Now you gonna come up in my business, my establishment, and tell me that I ain't running shit right. I've been running my club for more than twenty years and started with nothin'. Nobody gave me shit! It was just me and Stallion."

"How did you get your shit started? Oh yeah, when your mama died, you used her insurance money to start your club. So don't come up here acting like you the shit now, 'cause I know the truth. And another thang, you keep beating them bitches up, they gonna kill your ass one day. The game has changed, cousin. Women don't play that shit no more. They will kill your ass!"

Blackie slams his drink down on the table, and jumps to his feet like he wants to try Memphis.

"Nigga, what you about to do?" Memphis asks. "I know you didn't come all the way to Chi to get killed."

Blackie spies the 9 mm tucked in Memphis's waistband, sits back down and raises his hands in supplication.

"What are we fighting for?" Blackie asks.

"I don't know, nigga. You ready to die?"

"Not yet."

Memphis tosses a handkerchief to Blackie.

"Well, clean up that alcohol before it leaves a stain on my table, and let's talk about why I asked you to come down here. You help me with this and your debt to me is forgiven."

Memphis motions Blackie over to the desk.

"This is what I had in mind," Memphis says as he maps out his plan on a piece of paper.

While Memphis is busy with Blackie, Desiree shows up at the club, hoping that Fancy is there.

She asks the other dancers in the dressing room if they have seen Fancy, but no one has. Lexus, who is sitting in front of the huge makeup mirror, says she hopes Fancy never shows.

"What is that supposed to mean?" Desiree asks.

"That bitch is making niggas be stingy with their money," Lexus says. "I'm tired of all these tricks asking about her."

"Fancy should make you want to work harder." Before she turns to leave, Desiree adds, "Maybe if you lost a little weight and took care of yourself better, you'd have men fawning over you like she does."

Under her breath, Lexus says, "That big-bootie bitch got her sprung already."

Desiree walks out to her car to make a call in private. Fancy doesn't answer, but Desiree leaves a voice mail.

"Hey, Fancy. I just wanted to let you know I had a good time with you last night, and I wanted to know why you were gone when I woke up. I wanted to feel you some more. Anyway, baby, I was thinking about you and was wondering where you were or if you're even coming in today. Call me, baby, you have my number."

Fancy doesn't show up at the club until nearly midnight. Desiree is up on stage when Fancy arrives, and although Desiree is surrounded by men thrusting cash at her, she only has eyes for Fancy, who's in a sexy stretch denim halter dress with a thigh-high split in the front.

The men don't know it, but Desiree is dancing for Fancy now.

Fancy doesn't seem to notice, though. Her attention is on someone else–Memphis. She passes men who grab at her hands to slow her down, but she does not stop until she is in the arms of Memphis. After a quick embrace and kiss, the two walk off hand in hand to the back.

Desiree cuts her performance short to find out what Fancy and Memphis are up to. She picks up the money men have left at her feet on the stage but turns a deaf ear to their pleas for private lap dances.

Desiree doesn't knock on Memphis' door but merely stands outside and waits until Fancy comes out.

"Why didn't you call me back?" Desiree asks, praying for an honest answer.

"I'm sorry," Fancy says. "I was just busy."

"Too busy to call?"

"You're not getting jealous now are you, Desiree? If you are, we can just pretend like what we did never happened."

Although Desiree desperately wants to just walk away from Fancy, she can't.

"We're just friends, right?" Desiree asks, hoping that Fancy will want more.

Fancy doesn't answer. She just turns and walks toward the exits.

"Fancy!" Desiree calls.

Fancy stops but doesn't turn around as Desiree approaches.

"Look, I'm sorry, Fancy," Desiree explains. "I just want to . . ."

Before Desiree can finish her sentence, Fancy asks her to walk her out to her car.

"But I'm not dressed, and it's cold out there."

"I'll keep you warm. Come on." Fancy pushes through the door, with Desiree right behind, wearing only a fitted purple skirt two sizes too small and a matching purple bra.

When they get to the car Fancy tells Desiree to hop in on the passenger side.

"Wait a minute, where you going?" Desiree asks as Fancy starts the car. "I can't go anywhere. I don't have any of my stuff."

Fancy turns to Desiree and kisses her on the lips.

"I love those lips," she says as she pulls out of the crowded parking lot.

Desiree ceases worrying about her state of undress or the stuff she left behind. As long as she can be with Fancy, she's happy. Fancy seductively rubs her legs together as she drives and takes Desiree's left hand and places it under her jean dress.

Fancy's mound is wet, and Desiree easily slips two fingers inside her. Fancy takes Desiree's fingers out of her and licks them as she drives. Desiree can only stare at that wonderful sight, and she is eager to put her hands back inside Fancy so she can taste as well.

Desiree doesn't notice when Fancy turns into a motel parking lot and pulls up between two cars.

As Desiree looks around to get her bearings, Fancy reaches over her and pulls the lever to recline the seat.

"Pull your headrest up," Fancy orders.

Fancy unfastens three of her bottom buttons and starts to unzip her black knee-high boots. "You think you deserve me?"

Her body hot with passion, Desiree pants out, "Yes."

Before Desiree can say anything else, Fancy is straddling her mouth and tongue. With her head and back hitting the roof of the car, she manages to maneuver her hips in such a way that she tries to suffocate Desiree.

Desiree fights for air but doesn't miss a lick, sending Fancy into a body-altering orgasm. When Fancy tries to hop off her lover's face, Desiree won't let her, seizing the moment of having Fancy at her weakest.

"Baby, stop! Baby, stop," Fancy yells as her body convulses.

"Baby, please!" Fancy yelled, until her begging seemed to turn into a small fight in the car. "I'm cumin, ah, again."

After the second orgasm, Desiree releases her grip, and the women lie back, each in her own seat, and enjoy the confined smell of sex and vanilla from Fancy's air freshener.

"That was good," Fancy says finally. "Where am I taking you now?"

"Back to Illusions," Desiree answers.

On the drive back, Desiree smells her fingers and prays that this will not be the last time that she has Fancy.

"When will I see you again?" Desiree asks when they pull up in front of the club.

"I'm supposed to work tomorrow, so I'll see you then."

When Desiree walks back into the club, many of the dancers are packing up their things to head home. She gathers up her things and leaves before Memphis finds her.

"I know he's going to be all up in my face tomorrow," she thinks, "but, damn, it was worth it."

She's tired when she climbs the stairs to her apartment, and she collapses on the bed. Just as she is about to doze off, her doorbell rings.

"Ohhh, shit," she thinks. "Memphis, why can't you just let this shit slide until tomorrow?"

"Yes, Memphis," she says as she unlocks the door.

"No, it's not mean, old Memphis. It's sweet-ass, Fancy."

"Are you ready for round three?"

CHAPTER 39

"FAITH, I CAN'T believe you're going all the way to Florida to see that guy," Angel says with concern for her sister showing through her furrowed brow.

Faith continues packing her things for what may be the biggest trip of her life.

"You spent the night with him, and didn't do anything but talk all night, and he didn't try to make a move?" Angel shakes her head in disbelief. "Are you *sure* he's not gay?"

Faith stuffs her things into her suitcase, smiling at her sister's insistent prodding. Why should she tell Angel anything? The way Faith looks at it, she's grown-up and can do whatever she wants. Besides, she thinks Angel has a lot of nerve questioning her morals, considering that she hid her pregnancy and still has not revealed who her daughter's father is.

"You know you still haven't told me Mr. Florida's name," Angel continues, standing in the bedroom doorway with her hands on her hips. "What if he's crazy and something happens to you? I don't know anything about him. The only thing I know is that my sister taking off to Miami to see *some* guy. He could be connected to the mob."

"Can you at least tell me what he does for a living?" Angel begs as she continues with her solo game of 100 questions.

"Look, Angel, I told you all that you need to know about him. I'll be the first to admit that my choice in men has not been the best, but I'm in a good place now, so I don't need you or anyone else all up in my business trying to throw salt."

"Well, how long are you planning to stay?" Angel whines in a baby tone, hoping that strategy will wear down her tight-lipped sister.

When it doesn't, Angel goes back on the offensive. "I don't know of any man who's going to ask you to travel that far to spend time with him after just knowing him a couple of weeks. That's crazy." She stomps out the room like a brat who has failed to get her way.

"I know this is a little crazy, but *he* asked *me* to come see *him*," Faith says to her own reflection in the dresser mirror. "I didn't ask him–he asked *me*," she says softly, while gripping her hands together to calm her nerves. "Well, Travon Brown, I hope you are as real as you claim to be."

When Angel comes back into the room with her crying baby on her hip, Faith knows one thing for sure–she needs a mental break from her expanding household.

"Oh yeah, I forgot to tell you, Angel," she says, rolling her over-packed suitcase to the car. "It's not going to be a free-for-all while I'm gone."

"What are you talking about?"

"Sandra's going to be staying with you," Faith says matter-of-factly, as she drops the suitcase into her trunk. "So you can close your mouth now and give me a hug."

"Damn, sis," Angel replies, pouting. "At damn-near 26, I don't need a babysitter."

"Well, Angel, don't look at Sandra as a babysitter, consider her more like a friend," Faith says, pinching her sister's cheek and kissing her niece.

"Play nice," Faith warns, cutting her eyes at her rebellious baby sister. "I'm serious, Angel."

Faith gets in her car and closes her door, but before she can pull out of the driveway, Kane rushes out the front door at top speed.

"Wait, Auntie!" Kane barrels toward her, catching himself right before running into the driver side door.

"I thought you were asleep," Faith says kindly to the little boy.

"I was," Kane says, wiping the sleep from his eyes. "Can I go with you, Auntie Faith?"

"Not this time, Kane." Faith reaches her head out the driver-side door to give Kane a kiss.

"Come here, Angel," Faith says, motioning to her sister, who is still standing in the driveway with her lip poked out.

"Be happy for me," Faith says. "Just be happy for me. I mean, I'm taking your advice. It wasn't too long ago that you told me to go after him. Now you're acting like I'm making the biggest mistake of my life. I'm not trying to fall in love with him; it's just happening and I can't help it. I just need to go to see if it's real."

Angel kisses Faith's cheek and hugs her through the window.

"I am happy for you, sis. I just don't want you to be hurt again. That's all," she says grasping her sister's hand as Faith slowly begins to back out of the driveway.

On her way to the airport, Faith calls Sandra.

"Don't be too hard on Angel, OK."

"Angel needs a good dose of tough love," Sandra replies. "I'm just going to find out what her motivation is. She needs to figure out what she's going to do with her life, unless you plan to take care of her and her kids forever."

"Angel has always been a fighter," Faith reminds Sandra. "Now I don't want to come home and find my house all torn up because y'all can't get along."

"You ain't got nothing to worry about. You just go out to Miami and have a good time with Mr. Brown."

"I can handle your sister and her brood. The question is can you handle Mr. Brown?"

Laughing, Faith replies, "Get your mind outta the gutter, girl, I will be just fine."

"Oh, yeah, Sandra, I forgot to tell you," Faith says. "I really didn't tell Angel much about Travon, so if you can keep him a mystery, I'll appreciate it."

Sandra laughs. "What are you scared of girl? You think she's going to steal your boyfriend all the way down in Florida?"

"It's not that," Faith tries to explain. "It's just that I want him all to myself, and I don't want to share anything with her about him just yet."

"Don't worry, girl, your secret is safe with me. Now go and have a good time. Oh, don't forget to bring me back a souvenir for my house-sitting services."

"I'll see what I can do." Faith promises.

* * *

"Fancy, we need to talk," Nate says. "Is this a good time?"

"Yeah, I've got a couple of minutes," Fancy says. "I'm just on my way to the club."

"We haven't heard from you in a couple days. What's going on?"

"Everything is fine. I was just going to call you tonight with an update." That last part is a lie, but Fancy hopes Nate will settle for a call later.

"I'm free now, so update me," Nate says.

Fancy hesitates.

"I really don't know any more than I did before," she finally admits.

"Whatcha doin'? I thought you would've had that dyke talking by now, Fancy. Last time we talked, you said you would have something, and now you telling me the same old shit,'" agitation swells in Nate's tone.

"You don't talk to me like that! My boss is Willie, and he's your boss, too, Nate, so don't get it twisted. Now, when I get *something*, I'll tell Willie! You understand that?"

"Let's get one thang straight," he says. "I'll talk to you *any way* I want to. And if you fuckin' up, I'm going to kill you. You know that, don't you? I'll make you feel pain you have never dreamed in your worst nightmare."

"When I call you back, you better have some info. And I don't want to hear any more stories about how you made some dyke eat you out, because that ain't shit.

You better have times, names, dates, and places. 'Cause if you don't," Nate pauses for a beat, then squeezes out each word like a slow pull on a trigger, "Nobody's gonna miss a nigga in the ghetto."

"Now, do you *hear* me?"

"Yeah, I hear you."

Fancy tries hard to swallow the dry lump in her throat.

Later, at the club, Fancy can't get Crazy Nate's threat out of her head. She imagines she sees him among the customers in the smoked-filled club, and she doesn't know how she'll figure out what Memphis and his cousin have in store, before Nate makes good on his promise.

"What's wrong with you tonight?" Desiree asks, when she notices that Fancy is as jumpy as a crack addict in need of a fix.

"Nothing," Fancy replies, with a fake smile. "I just have a lot on my mind, that's all."

"Well, you better snap out of it, because Memphis is in one of his ornery moods," Desiree warns Fancy softly before turning to the other dancers in the dressing room.

"All right, bitches, it's the end of the month and Memphis wants to see what these niggas are working with, so you know what that means," she tells the assembly line of women milling about in the communal dressing room that reeks of cheap perfume.

When she sits back down with Fancy, hoping to make plans for later, Fancy says she needs to talk to Memphis about money.

"I don't know if this is a good time, girl," Desiree says, rolling her eyes. "He's going to tell you that y'all can talk about it later, but that's as far as that's going to go tonight."

"My rent is due in two days, so he is going to have to talk about it now," Fancy snaps, as she storms out the door and down the hall toward Memphis' office, leaving nothing but the click of her heels behind her.

At his door, Fancy twice raises her hand as if to knock, but something holds her back. She hears voices on the other side, coming closer.

"Fancy," Memphis says, pleasantly surprised when he opens the door, with his cousin by his side. "What are you doing out here? You need something?" He looks her up and down like a bear would a honey hive.

Fancy rubs her hands on her thighs in nervousness.

"Can I speak to you?" she asks. "In private?"

She glances at Blackie, who doesn't move.

"Yeah, come on in," Memphis says. "Blackie, I'll catch up with you later."

Blackie gives his cousin dap, looks at Memphis and then at Fancy's ass when she walks past him and says, "Remember what I said, Cuz! You need to handle that business."

Alone with Memphis, Fancy is willing to do whatever it takes to find out something–anything–about Memphis' plan.

"Have a seat, sexy," Memphis offers, pouring his star dancer a drink. "What can I do for you?"

He passes her a glass of vodka before taking his seat behind the desk.

"Thank you so much," Fancy says. "I just wanted to let you know that I will do whatever to be the best dancer in this club."

"It's been a little under two or three weeks, right?" Memphis asks, looking around his cluttered desk for his calendar.

"I know," Fancy says, moving to the edge of her seat. "But I never thought I would like it this much. The women are cool, and I know I can make a lot more money here than I could on my last job."

Memphis assures her that she has time to decide if she wants to turn her dancing into a career.

"To be honest with you, baby, I'm not even sure how much longer I want to do this," he admits, pouring himself a drink. "These young pimps and young tricks done changed the game. It's not as profitable."

He downs his vodka in one swallow. "Is there anything else? I need to take care of some other business."

"Well, there is one thing," she says, coyly rising and walking around the desk to Memphis.

She kisses his lips and works her way down to his chest. Before she gets down to his bulge in his pants, she turns around and gives him a slow lap dance, letting him run his hands all over her soft, ample, dimple-free ass. When he lifts her tight skirt and pops her ass, the sting makes her nipples hard, but she is not done yet.

As she straddles him in his executive chair, his bulge stabs at her opening through her silk underwear.

"You gonna let me fuck or what?" Memphis grunts.

"Is that what you want?" Fancy breathes, looking deep into his eyes.

"Yeah," Memphis says, inhaling the cologne Fancy has strategically placed between her breasts.

"You sure your woman won't get mad?" Fancy asks, as she rocks in a seductive manner.

Memphis immediately thinks of Stallion.

"Get up," he says, agitated. "You heard me, get up! I've got shit to do."

He shoves Fancy from his lap and almost knocks her to her knees.

"OK, OK," Fancy says, confused. She stands before Memphis in her wrinkled white top, looking down at her feet.

"Is there something else?" he asks, scooting his chair up to his desk.

"Yeah," she says softly. "I was wondering when you were going to pay me. My landlord is on my ass for the rent. I'm three months behind."

"You'll get paid with the rest of the girls, tomorrow."

Fancy turns on her heels defeated.

As Fancy walks out, Memphis reminds her "make that money."

With time running out faster than sand in an hourglass, Fancy hatches a new plan to get to Memphis.

"I guess I'm going to have to use Desiree," she thinks, with a smile that sends a tingle right to her clitoris. "Well, that ain't too bad a consolation."

* * *

Faith flies first-class. It's her way of showing the dozens of people walking past her to coach that she does have some status, although in her heart she lacks confidence especially when it comes to romance.

The repeated rapes by her stepfather reverberated through the years, stealing not just her childhood, but her chances at solid, positive relationships with men as she got older, too.

Her reluctance to examine those attacks gave those demons more power in her life than they deserved. It was only after Sandra convinced her to seek help that Faith faced her fears and acknowledged the anxieties that arose from them. Before she entered counseling, she let the men in her life use her body for their own personal experimentation and pleasure.

She never loved herself enough to say no or consider her own needs.

When Travon accepted her initial "no," it freed her to say "yes".

As the male flight attendant helps Faith take her Louis Vuitton carry-on bag from the storage area, he can't contain his admiration for Faith's style.

"Excuse me for saying this," he whispers, "but you are one sexy bitch." He gives her a snap of the finger, with a twist, and looks her up and down.

The compliment draws giggles from Faith, which just encourages him to continue.

"A lot of these women that sit up here don't take care of themselves like you do, and all I have to say is if you want a man to want your ass, you can't let that ass turn into cottage cheese." He motions with his eyes at a large woman who fills the aisle in front of them.

The flight attendant may be flaming, but his compliments are a boost to Faith's fragile self-esteem. As she steps off the plane, she can't wait to lay eyes on Travon again, and feel his warm touch and his heartbeat pounding against her back. The walk through the gate terminal makes her heart race quicker, and her palms grow damp from excitement and Miami's humidity.

As families are reunited with their loved ones, she searches for her man among the hundreds of people buzzing around her. Her smile starts to fade and panic sets in. She grabs her cell phone to call him. "Please, Travon, be here," she says as she keys in his number. "Where are you?"

"*Girl shake your Laffy Taffy . . . Your Laffy Taffy . . .*" is the song she hears right behind her. She spins around, her phone to her ear, and I hand her a bouquet of red and white roses.

"Is that your phone?" she says, a wave of relief surging through her body.

"You didn't think I would be late now, did you? I've been counting down the moments. Now come here and let me taste those lips." I open my arms, and Faith delivers a Hollywood kiss the likes of which I've only seen in the movies.

I lift her off the ground and swing her around, embracing her as if we haven't seen each other in years.

I grab her by the hand and head down to baggage claim–on what I hope will be the time of our lives.

Faith pauses for a moment. "Can I tell you something, Tray?"

"Sure, baby, what is it?"

She takes me by the hand and motions for us to take a seat.

She looks into my eyes before speaking.

"I just want you to know that you are everything I want in a man. This may sound silly but I've always had this simple list. I wanted someone with a career that they loved, good teeth, handsome, educated, black and with a good body."

I smile, and to break the ice I tell her that I can stand to get in a better shape.

She just touches my face.

"I'm serious, Tray," Faith says with a smile.

"Really, Tray, just to have someone to walk in the park with on summer nights and go to church with on Sundays means a lot to me."

"Church?" I say sarcastically.

"Yeah, we have to work on the church part," she smiles.

"But most of all, I just want a man who would love me for who I am and wants to see me smile. Someone who would protect me, I've never had a man to protect me. Every man that I believed loved me really didn't."

"I feel the same way Faith, now can we get to dinner, I have reservations at this really nice restaurant for us."

When Faith stands up, I plant a big kiss on her soft, full lips.

"Thank you, baby," she says.

"No, thank you."

During dinner, several men approach me and a few women to as well to compliment me on my blogs and sport videos.

"See, I knew you were a social magnet," Faith says. "I should be jealous."

I assure her that there is nothing to be jealous of. "You're more important to me than this, baby," I assure her before we leave the restaurant for the short drive to my home.

"Home sweet home," I announce unlocking the door.

"And what a nice home it is," Faith compliments. "It's cozy. This isn't what I expected."

"What did you expect? A typical black and gray bachelor pad?"

"No."

"Stop lying."

"Well, I didn't expect these colors. I love burnt orange and you mixed it with a red couch too. I wouldn't have ever thought about that combo. It's cool, and it's you."

"Make yourself at home. I want you to feel like you belong here."

I leave her alone for a few moments in the living room, while I take her bags to the bedroom.

Upon returning, I start the tour.

First, start the kitchen where I show her the contents of the refrigerator as if I'm hosting MTV's "Cribs."

"And over here is one of my very first boxing trophies . . . so don't try me," I tease, handing her my three-foot-high trophy. In my bedroom, there's a mural tribute to boxing legends.

"This is a beautiful mural," Faith says, touching the painted wall.

"You like it?"

"Yes, who painted it?"

"I spoke at one of the local high schools during a career day, and during a tour of the art room, I saw these young men painting this huge mural of Malcolm X that they were hoping to sell. So I asked them how they would feel painting a mural in my house and they went for it." I'm proud of how the weeklong project turned out.

"Don't worry, I paid them," I add, pleased that Faith is admiring the details of the mural.

"This is really good," she says, touching her chest. "I recognize him—that's Muhammad Ali. And that's Joe . . ." She cups her chin, trying to remember the last name.

"Louis," I fill in, surprised that she knows something about boxing.

"Who are those two?" she asks, sitting on the edge of my bed to take it all in.

"That one is the "Dark Destroyer" Nigel Benn, and he's trading punches with one of the greatest middleweights of all time who people know very little about—Gerald "The G-Man" McClellan. Gerald was hurt in that bout in London in 1995 and suffered brain damage. I interviewed him in 2002 at his home in Freeport, Illinois. It was one of the hardest things I ever had to do."

Remembering that moment, I take a seat on the bed next to Faith.

She puts her arm around me, rubbing my lower back as she puts her head on my shoulder. We sit quietly for a moment, until Faith springs off the bed.

"I know who that is," she says, pointing at a section of the mural on the far wall. "That's Sugar Ray Leonard after he knocked out the Hitman."

A woman who knows something about a sport I love. This one is a keeper. I can't help but smile at the thought.

"And . . . Oh my god, Travon, is that . . . that you right there?"

"Yeah, that's me."

At the head of the bed, the mural captures the moment when I won my first Golden Gloves championship.

"You're so handsome! Look at you with the belt wrapped over your shoulders." Faith claps with excitement, and crawls across the bed to get a better look.

"Who are the two men with their arms around you?"

"That heavy-set guy on the right is like my stepfather. He helped mold me into who I am today. His name is Willie. And the guy on the left, smiling in the suit, is Willie's best friend, Nate. Folks around my way call him Crazy Nate."

"That may have been the biggest moment of my life."

"I was fighting this kid from Lubbock, Texas, and he was as strong as an ox." I pull Faith off the bed for an impromptu boxing lesson. I raise her dukes to better demonstrate in slow motion.

"He was winning on all the scorecards going into the final round, and I needed to stop him to win."

"He could have coasted to a victory, but he came at me going for the knockout by throwing big looping hooks." Standing behind Faith, I work her arms like a puppeteer to mimic my opponent's blows.

"And when my back touched the ropes, I heard this bellowing voice scream, 'Uppercut, Tray!'"

I spin Faith around to face me.

"And that's when I threw the best right uppercut of my life, catching him right on the chin."

"I stopped a three-time Golden Glove winner that night, and that's when Willie and Nate stormed the ring to hug me and put me on their shoulders."

I pause to relive the moment.

"It was Willie who yelled out, 'uppercut Tray!'"

"He's always been there for me, and when he wasn't taking care of things for me he guided me to show me how."

"Like a real father," Faith says.

"What's really funny about this picture, too, is that Nate, who was like the neighborhood druggie, got cleaned up for me that night and put on a suit. I didn't know who he was when he hopped in the ring. I couldn't believe how such a handsome guy was hidden behind those dirty clothes, matted hair, and beard."

"That fight showed me that I could do anything that I wanted to, because I have never met an obstacle as tough as my opponent was that night."

"Do you still see Willie and Nate," Faith asks.

"It's funny that you ask me that, because I saw them both about three weeks ago, after I left Atlanta. They were both acting kinda funny."

"What do you mean?"

"I don't know how to describe it, but they were both overly protective of me for some reason. I didn't quite understand it, so I was like, 'Whatever,'" I say, shrugging my shoulders.

"They probably just missed you. I know I did. You are magnetic, Tray."

"Let me ask you something," she says turning back to the mural. "Did you ever tell them that this moment was the biggest of your life?"

"I don't know if I ever did," I think back on it trying to remember. "You see, there are a few things you don't understand about Willie and Nate."

"One thing I didn't tell you about them is that Willie is a pimp who runs a lot of women, and Nate is his right-hand man."

Faith's jaw drops.

"Seriously? *You* were raised by a pimp?"

"Yeah, I'm serious. He's a hero to a lot of people in the area I grew up in. They look to him as a guy who made it with 100 percent street sense. And he never moved out of the 'hood."

"Is he your hero?" Faith pries.

"I'm not going to say he's my hero, but there are aspects of his life I admire. Like how he protects the people around him, and his generosity—*hell*, he paid my way through school."

"Wow, that was very generous," Faith says.

"He's not a bad person, at least not to the people he knows. He got me interested in boxing to keep me from knocking little old ladies in the head—so he can't be all bad. I really do owe most of my success to him, because without him, I know I wouldn't be here in the company of you today."

I moved closer to Faith to steal another kiss, which she gladly gives.

* * *

Later, after seeing the sights of Miami and having a grouper at a trendy little restaurant in South Beach, we take a walking tour along the eclectic buildings in the art deco district.

In the car on the way home, we enjoy each other's company without even talking, but our nonverbal cues come through loud and clear. We can't keep our hands off each other.

The windows are down and the sunroof is back, and Faith revels in the breeze as it plants kisses along her face. She holds my arm and smiles.

"What are you cheesing about over there?"

"Nothing," Faith says, holding my arm even tighter. "I don't think you would understand. I'm just enjoying myself with you. This is just so outside of my box of who I am, and I like it.

"I feel like I know so much about you, even though we've only known each other four weeks. Up until this point, this has been a difficult year for me, Tray," Faith says, gazing at my hand, which now holds hers. "I just don't want to mess this up, and in the back of my mind, I guess I believe something has to go wrong."

"I think I know what you're talking about, Faith. It's like things are going so good that there has to be a catch, or why hasn't one of us been snatched up by someone else by now?"

"You do understand," Faith says. "It's like, if something is too good to be true, then it usually is."

"I think I know what will make you feel better." I pull over and park in front of a lemonade stand.

"If life gives you lemons, make lemonade?" Faith jokes.

"Nah. But I want you to tell me about all of your bad habits, and I will tell you mine. Let's just get them out there right now. And don't hold back."

I nod for her to go.

"OK, let me see . . . My sister says I snore sometimes when I'm really tired . . . I know I'm a workaholic . . . I buy waaaaay too many clothes, and I have a shoe fetish. Oh, yeah, I've been accused of playing mother hen sometimes." She searches my expression for any signs of dismay.

"My turn. I leave the toilet seat up . . . I sleep with my socks on no matter how hot it is. I'm a workaholic, and I have a secret love for gangsta rap . . . I used to be a dog, but I'm reformed now . . . And I've been told that I can be arrogant."

"OK," Faith says. "I don't know if I should tell you this, but I have a porn collection." This elicits an eyebrow raise from me, but she carries on. "And although I wouldn't participate in anything like this, I do like seeing gangbang scenes."

Laughing and teasing at the same time, I reply, "Oh you're an undercover freak. Well, based on that information, I would have to say that I don't think I can see you anymore."

"Stop teasing me," she says, playfully shoving me. "Now it's your turn again."

"I guess I can tell you that I'm out of balance. It's always been all about me—Travon—and never about anyone else, and I'm trying to change that. I know I need someone special in my life to even me out. I need someone who can help me shine but also humble me."

"I understand that," Faith says. She clears her throat. "So, Travon, tell me about your last relationship."

"How about I tell you about the last time I think I connected with someone instead?" "OK," Faith nods.

"I met this woman and we talked for what seemed like hours at my best friend's party." I leave out some of the sordid details—like the woman was a stripper and that it was at a bachelor party. "I thought we connected. I mean, we talked for hours, and she seemed very sweet.

"You actually remind me of her in a lot of ways.

"Anyway, we ended up becoming romantically involved that night, and I thought that we had a real connection, but she never called me after that, and I didn't get her number. I felt used, like damn, I thought I would at least get a call back."

"I can sympathize," Faith says. "I know what it's like to be lied to and used."

Faith sits there for a moment before perking up.

"I think god was saving you for me," Faith says.

"Yeah, I think you're right."

I don't ask Faith about her past relationships, and she appears OK with that. After all, I don't have anything to worry about. I'm sure I'll blow those losers out of the water. It's time to start establishing new roots, and if Faith is game, I think we can grow together.

Back at the condo, Faith inadvertently dozes off. I wake her and invite her to join me in the bathroom.

Jasmine-scented candles line the hallway, and inside the bathroom, more candles glow.

"I know we got off to a bad start with the shower back in Atlanta. So would you care to join me in the tub?"

"I would love to."

I pull down my steel-black Calvin Klein briefs and get into the bubble-filled bathtub. As she undressed, she tried to hide her possessions until she stepped into the warm rose-petal-filled water.

Facing me in the jacuzzi tub, she drapes her thighs over mine, and exhales deeply as she welcomes the warmth of the water.

"How does it feel?" I ask rubbing her thighs.

"This feels wonderful, Travon."

Faith reaches for the loofah sponge hanging near her side.

"Can I bathe you, Travon?"

"Of course you can." I comply by pulling myself closer to my beauty. We bathe each other, exploring each and every erogenous zone. I step out of the tub first and place a towel over the toilet seat to sit down. When Faith steps out, I kiss her navel. Faith allows a soft moan to escape her lips. She rubs my head in encouragement. As I pat her dry with a soft, plush towel, I tease her with light kisses. I continue foreplay by rubbing her down with baby oil, in a massaging manner that melts her body and makes her knees buckle.

"I want you so bad," I whisper squeezing her around the waist and back, in slow, deliberate strokes that stokes Faith's fire.

"I want you, too, baby, but I'm scared," Faith says, pulling my head upward until I'm looking into her eyes.

"I made a vow to myself that the next man I give myself to would be the man that I marry," Faith says, caressing my face. "I used to give myself away to men that I thought cared for me, but I found out later that they didn't. I don't want to repeat those mistakes."

I pull Faith down into my lap.

"I didn't want you to come all the way down here just to sleep with you. I feel a connection," I reveal, continuing to rub her back, sending her into a state of surrender.

"I want you, Faith. Now I'm not going to say that we're going to run off and get married tomorrow or next month or next year, but I do know that I want you. I knew that from the time I spilled my coffee all over you and we talked for hours. I knew that from our many conversations on the phone, before you decided to come down here to be with me. I know you feel it, too."

I place my head on her breast to catch her scent.

"Travon, can we go lie down?" Without a word I lead her to the bedroom.

She gets in bed first.

I snuggle up to her and feel the heat emanating from her body. Interlocked like snakes, Faith moans as I lightly brush her torso with my fingertips, sliding seductively down to her thighs. I gently brush against her neatly groomed pubic hairs, which raises goose bumps across her body. I press my chest deep into her back, trying to melt into her body. Faith presses back and caresses my thigh. I turn her over and touch her nipples lightly with my tongue and Faith whispers for more. I move my mouth to her inner thigh, lightly biting until she grabs my head and pushes against it. Even as her body moves with more urgency, I keep my rhythm slow, teasing her body into a wave of sensations.

My teases are the perfect aphrodisiac to make Faith surrender.

"Make love to me, Tray."

"You sure?"

Faith rolls on top of me, lightly pinning my arms, and kisses my chest. I moan with pleasure as she rubs her moist mound against my thigh, causing my penis to jump wildly.

"I need to feel you," I whisper.

She mounts me slowly, taking only enough to tease before backing off.

Faith comes down on me again, and I break free from Faith's grasps, grabbing her hips and plunging deep within her tightened walls, hard and fast. She meets my tempo with her own moves, rocking back and forth on my shaft until we both erupt in unison, never losing each other's gaze as we climax.

Satiated she sighs, but does not move, laying her head on my chest. The rhythmic beating of my heart is strong and fast.

"I don't want to be anywhere else but in your arms," she whispers.

I stoke her hair as a tear falls on my chest.

She takes her finger and writes I love you over my heart.

"I love you more, Faith."

CHAPTER 40

FAITH HAS BEEN in Miami for five days before she thinks to give Sandra a call.

"So how are you two getting along so far?" she asks. "Please tell me you didn't tear *up* my house."

"Girrrrrl, I'm surprised to hear from you. I figured Mr. Miami would have had you all worn-out by now," Sandra teases before going into her living situation with Angel and the two little ones.

"Angel has pretty much kept outta my way. Kane is a prankster who never runs out of energy, and the little one cries all the time." Sandra sighs and then adds sarcastically, "The joys of motherhood sound so sweet."

"But that's enough about me," Sandra stops herself, wanting to hear juicy details about sex, romance, and more sex.

"Let me sit down for this, because this should be good," she says, adjusting herself on the couch. "Now don't spare any details, because this is the closest I'll get to getting some for a long time."

"Well, I'm going to have to disappoint you on that, because you know I still have a hard time talking about stuff like that," Faith says, bashfully.

"You owe me something," Sandra whines. "Where is he anyway?"

"He had to go to work today, and I'm just getting up–if you can believe that," Faith says, yawning and stretching.

"Ahhhhh! That is soooo sweet," Faith gushes.

"What is it? What happened?" Sandra asks.

Faith swings her legs on the side of the bed and sits up.

"Travon fixed me breakfast by the bed with a cute little note."

Sandra can hear the glow in her voice.

"*Wellllll?*" Sandra asks, not liking to be left in suspense. "What does it say?"

Faith clears her throat, eyeing the beautiful stationery and Travon's neat handwriting. "Well, it's kind of long."

"Girl, stop playing and read the dang gone letter to me please," Sandra snaps.

"OK, OK."

> *"Faith, you are wonderful in so many ways. When you were sleeping last night, I just watched your chest go up and down as you slept like an angel. I know that you're leaving to go home today, but I don't want you to go. You will be taking a part of me with you. It's going to be hard for me at work today not being able to hold you and touch you and kiss you . . . You complete me. Remember when I told you I needed balance in my life? You provide that balance for me, and I don't want that balance to be so far away. I guess what I'm saying is that I don't just want you to be my lover, Faith; you mean so much more to me than that. I just wanted to put this seed in your head.*
>
> *When we originally planned for you to stay with me five days, at first I didn't know what to expect. To be honest with you, I was a little scared, as I'm sure you were as well, but after the first five minutes with you, I knew that five days would not be enough.*
>
> *I should be home a little after three. Be waiting for me when I get home.*

Love,
Travon Brown
P.S. I wanted to leave you with this poem inspired by the "Song of Songs."

> The shade of
> your apricot tree
> comforts me from
> the midday sun
>
> The redness of the
> pomegranate seed
> the nectar of the grape
> slip from your lips
> to mine
>
> Your lily's fragrance
> lifts me to a realm
> where midday and
> midnight are one

I am lost in your garden.

"Damn, girl, that's deep right there," Sandra says, contemplating the meaning of the poem.

Faith smiles wide.

"I know. I've never had a man write or dedicate a poem to me." A tear escapes her eye but she doesn't wipe it away–these are good tears for a change.

"Is it possible that he's this good?" Faith asks, as she tries to calm down from a fantasy.

"You tell me, girl. He damn sure seems like it," Sandra says, while still fishing for more dirt.

"I know he done sexed up your mind, but how is he in the bedroom? Is he passionate? Was it at least good?"

"I will say this. First of all, he has complete control in the bedroom, and he is very attentive to all of my needs," Faith says, touching her own breast softly, while squeezing Travon's pillow. "But it just wasn't about sex because, to be honest with you, I haven't had sex in so long that I was afraid to go there with him. But it was the way he touched and talked to me. I mean it was like he knew my body better than me."

"*Oh, no, you didn't!*" Sandra yells. "I *knew* he was too good to be true!"

"What are you jaw-jacking about?" Faith asks, confused.

"You said he knew your body better than you–it's like he's been doing this all his life," Sandra says, raising her voice.

"What are you talking about?" Faith says, trying to figure out what her friend is implying.

"I hate to say it, girl, but your man is a professional pussy hound," Sandra says confidently. "He's probably well-rehearsed in the art of pleasing women."

"What! Are you crazy?" Faith asks, now rising up in the bed. "He is not a hound doggie, or whatever you call it."

"Did he ever mention any other women, or tell you about his last girlfriend, or anything like that?" Sandra asks, playing the role of devil's advocate.

"As a matter-of-fact, he did," Faith says in defense of Travon. "Well, his last girlfriend." She pauses for a second. "Actually, he didn't tell me about his last girlfriend, but he told me about the last–how did he put it–girl he was with where he thought it would lead to something. It sounded like he had a one-night stand with a girl at a party, and then she didn't call him."

Shaking her head and eating Ben and Jerry's Strawberry Cheesecake ice cream out of the container, "Girl, be careful, he sounds sneaky to me."

"If he's all that, plus the bomb in the bedroom like you claim, then ain't no woman just gonna want to have a one-night stand with him."

"What if she was married?" Faith asks innocently.

"Faith, you must have forgot, my one-night stand led to what I've got right now." Sandra pats her round belly. "I thought it would be a one-night stand, but it was good and I kept going back, and I had a good husband–on paper at least."

Not wanting to hear any pessimistic remarks, "Sandra I gotta go, girl."

"I'm sorry, Faith," Sandra apologizes, knowing that she probably overstepped the line. "I could be wrong on the whole thing."

"I know you are about Travon," Faith says.

"Well, there's only one way to find out," Sandra says. "He's at work right? Why don't you look through his stuff? You've got time."

"I'm not going to do that," Faith says. "I trust him."

"I trusted my husband, too, until I was cleaning out his closet one day and found some panties in his suit coat pocket–and I knew he wasn't a cross-dresser."

"How can you be so sure?" Faith asks, sheepishly. "Were they *too* small?"

"No, but that fuchsia G-string was not his color." Sandra's wisecrack sends both women into fits of laughter.

"I'm just so happy that I can laugh about it now," Sandra says, wiping tears from her eyes, while reflecting back on her relationship. "The best part about it is that we both agreed not to keep up the lies to make everyone around us happy."

"Faith, be careful with this guy. I know you have a history of jumping the gun and I don't want to see you hurt anymore."

"The difference in me *then* and me *now* is that I allowed boys to take advantage of the emotionally and mentally wounded girl I was back then. But now, I have a man who seems like he wants to cater to my needs."

"All right now, girl!" Sandra shoots back. "I see you're getting all deep on me, so I'll leave you alone."

"OK, silly, let me get off here so I can take a shower to be ready for *my man* when he gets home."

"OK, I'll see you tonight, Sandra."

*   *   *

"So, Nate, what's the latest from Fancy?" Willie asks, as he sits at his desk and smokes a vintage Cuban cigar given to him by one of his many paying customers.

"I meant to tell you about that, Willie," Nate says, annoyed. "I talked to her three days ago and we had a few words. To be honest with you, Willie, I don't trust her."

Willie raises an eyebrow and takes a long pull from his cigar, making the end light up in bright orange.

"Talk to me," he says, "I'm all ears."

"Your girl is foul," Nate says, taking a toothpick from Willie's desk to pick his teeth, while he talks.

"She keeps giving me the same tired-ass story, and for all we know the bitch ain't even trying. I bet you any money that dyke done blown her mind. We put her in there as a plant and the only thing she's got to show for it is a wet ass. It can't be that hard, because Memphis is transparent as can be. I walked right up in the beehive and took out the queen 'cause he didn't think I could do it. She could have did the same thing by now, 'cause you know he wouldn't think we could do it twice. He ain't that smart," Nate says, tapping his temple. "He don't think like that."

"I'm telling you, Willie, she's foul, and it's going to cost your *boy* his life if we don't hit this bitch."

Nate shakes his head at how the situation is spinning out of control.

Willie pushes back from his desk and turns to look out of his window. He knows what Nate is asking for, and he wants a minute to think.

"What do you think we should do?" he asks finally, still peering out the window.

"We need to strike," Nate says, pounding a fist on the desk.

Willie hesitates.

He knows the consequences of an all-out strike. He turns back to Nate. "Let's give her another week. If she doesn't give us something by then, we'll do whatever we have to do."

Before Nate can say another word, "I need a minute Nate, see yourself out."

"Fancy, we're on the clock," Willie says to himself. "If you don't produce, Big Willie won't be able to save you." He flips over the hourglass paperweight that sits on his desk. "When the week is up, your time is, too."

* * *

"Let's go over this plan one more time," Memphis tells Blackie. But his cousin is caught up in the hidden cameras, spying on the dancers' every move.

"Cuz, this high-tech shit is the bomb," Blackie says, unaware that Memphis is seriously close to slapping him.

"Blackie, you need to listen because this shit has to go down right," Memphis repeats.

"Cuz, whatcha' worried about? I've got this. We just gonna hit these fools early Friday, because he always has Nate to open up. Those crooked pigs of yours did a good job of watchin' his place, so we know how it's going to go down. We bum rush that nigga Nate, hit him, and just wait 'til that fat mutherfucka show up and pop him, too. I say we stack them bitches up on the stage and leave 'em there 'til the hos come in and find them. Either way, we'll be back here by evening and nobody gotta know shit," Blackie says, rubbing his hands together.

He turns his attention back to the security cameras. "Memphis, how can I find Fancy on these cameras."

"I want to check that bitch out," Blackie says, as Memphis searches for the dancer using the remote control. When he spots Fancy, she's heading into the bathroom while taking out her cell phone.

"Do these have sound, too?" Blackie asks.

The question annoys Memphis, who already has the volume control in his grasp.

"That's what I'm talking about," Blackie says. "Shit, all I need is a $6 box of popcorn, a large Coke and a few Slim Jims, and I'll feel like I'm at the movies."

"This shit makes me feel like a peeping Tom." He laughs, "Better yet, a peeping Blackie. You hear me, Cuz?"

But his schoolboy banter stops when he hears who Fancy is whispering to on her cell phone.

"I think she said something about Nate," he tells Memphis.

Memphis slams his drink down and turns the volume all the way up so both men can hear what Fancy has to say.

"Nate, I'm close, I promise," she says. "Please don't say that. I promise you on everything that I'm close to finding out . . . No, I talked to Desiree and she doesn't know shit. I'm working on Memphis, but his cousin is always around, and they don't talk business around the dancers . . . I tried that but he got mad and told me to get up. I don't know, but you've got to get me more time. Please."

There's a knock at the bathroom door. "Somebody is at the door. I have to go, but I will call you back later." She puts the phone away, yells "just a minute!" to the strippers waiting to get in, then opens the door, and rushes past them.

Blackie reaches into his holster and pulls out his 9 mm, but Memphis grabs his arm.

"Hold up a second, let's think this out," Memphis says. "We can use this to our advantage."

He takes a seat on the edge of the desk to plot out his next move. "I knew there was something about her that just didn't feel right," Blackie says.

Memphis remains calm and calculating, but Blackie is agitated.

"Why don't you let me go blast this bitch, Memphis?"

"Nah, man, trust me on this. Let's sit on this for a minute. If we do this right, everybody will get what's coming to them," Memphis says with a cracked smile. "Now I want you to act like your same old self and don't say shit."

Blackie frowns as he slowly returns his gun to its holster, and mumbles, "I still want to fuck that bitch, before I kill her."

Memphis and Blackie keep their cool throughout the night, watching Fancy provide one strong stage performance after another. As Memphis watches the vixen move seductively on the stage, he wonders how much Desiree knows, and if she is in on the deal.

Memphis is torn. For the first time, he feels he can't trust Desiree, and anyone that close to him who cannot be trusted has to go. Her judgment is obviously cloudy, and she can't see past Fancy's big ass.

He watches from the balcony as the customers flock to Fancy, and he can't ignore how Desiree appears to be the dancer's no. 1 fan. Desiree is often the first person to put money in Fancy's G-string. Desiree has not been this caught up in a woman, since she dated Angel.

Memphis may be illiterate, but he's a Harvard professor at game. After everyone has left the club, he sits on the stage thinking about his life. He never thought that a street kid like himself would end up running a strip club. Secretly, he always wanted to be a pilot, but those dreams crashed early in life as he was bounced from house to house, where nobody seemed to care if he went to school or not.

As a child, he would sometimes look up and see the trail of white coming from an airplane and wonder where the pilot was taking his passengers. He often dreamed of traveling to foreign countries–anywhere that was far away from Tennessee. When he followed a friend up north seeking work at Pabst Brewery in Milwaukee, he thought he had it made until coworkers discovered that he couldn't read. He lost that job not long after.

By chance, he stumbled across Willie outside a tavern one night. Willie had pulled up in one of the nicest cars he had ever seen, a yellow Cadillac convertible. Willie had two thick black girls with him and one young, white girl. Willie had come to get some money the tavern owner owed him. The women flirted with the guys and told them to come over to the strip club for some action.

Memphis had just $4 in his pocket, and he used that to go see the young white girl, who he eventually fell in love with. That girl was White Chocolate.

Memphis hated the fact that he had to beg Willie for work around the club. He did odds and ends for Willie, and ran errands for him like a little boy. Willie had Memphis doing everything from running to grab his food, to cleaning out his cars, to sweeping up the club. At the time, Memphis didn't sweat it too much because he used that opportunity to see White Chocolate.

He was finally able to work his way up and earn Willie's trust and put in work, even hurt people for this man. As he rose up the ranks, his love for White Chocolate, who later became Stallion, also grew. When he told Willie that he wanted to marry White Chocolate and start his own club, Willie forced him to buy her, like a slave. It took Memphis two years of putting in work for Willie until he could afford to buy the woman he would later make his wife.

While Memphis saved up money to buy White Chocolate, he had to watch her sell her body and do things for men and women that broke his heart.

"You a funny bastard," Memphis calls out now from the stage of his own club, as if Willie was standing before him. "You felt that I didn't have the heart for this shit, and you had the nerve to tell me that you turned my woman out to make *me* into a man! Well, guess what? This self-made man is going to be the one to kill you."

Memphis rises from the stage and heads to the bar.

He stumbles back to his office with a six-pack of Pabst Blue Ribbon and tortures himself with the video images of Nate walking out of the club with his wife.

Through his drunkenness, his wife appears before him, looking as beautiful and innocent as the day he first laid eyes on her.

"I wish I would've told you how much I loved you."

He reaches out to try to touch her, but his dried out hands cannot touch her soul.

"Baaaby. Baaaaby. I never knew how to love you."

Standing and gripping his can of beer even tighter, Memphis sheds a tear as he again tries to touch his own shadow that he sees as his wife.

"I hear you," he says, with a broken smile. "I never learned how to love anyone. I could not let anyone get close to me because when I do . . . it hurts. If I could take back *anything* out of all the shit I put you through, I would take back losing our baby.

"When I forced you to, you know, get an abortion. I think you died that night. You thought I didn't know, but I knew you mourned April 18th every year after that."

"I knew, baby," Memphis says, wiping his eyes, as the image in front of him fades away. "I know this will haunt me until I die. Baby, you never looked at me the same way again after that. I went from being *your man* to being *a man*. That shit hurt; I guess that's why I let you do what you did with other men. It was like my own hell."

Memphis looks around his office, to see what he has to show for his wife's sacrifice.

He vows revenge.

"You didn't die a second time in vain," he says, shaking his head. He crumples his beer can and lets it fall to the floor.

"That should've been me to die like that. I swear a minute will not pass without me thinking about it."

Hours later, he is dead asleep next to her picture on his computer screen.

When Blackie arrives at Memphis's office early in the morning, he finds his cousin still sleeping.

"Damn, Memphis, you slept here all night?"

Blackie shakes his cousin.

"You need to wake up, Cuz. You told me last night that you had a plan, so let me hear it."

Memphis clears his cracking throat, and moves on to business.

"This shit got me buggin', but I thought about it and I got it. When Fancy gets here this is what we're going to do."

* * *

"I enjoyed myself, too, Travon," Faith says, back at work in her office in Atlanta. "I can't stop thinking about you. You're the best," she seductively whispers into the phone.

Feeling naughty used to be hard for Faith, but Travon has made it easy for her to come out of her shell.

"What are you wearing?" I ask Faith from my office phone.

"Why do you want to know that?"

"Come on, baby, play along with me. Now tell me what you have on," I encourage.

"Hold on, boy, and let me close my door," she says.

She sticks her head outside her office door.

"Shelly, can you hold my calls? I'm on an important conference call right now," she tells the receptionist.

"OK, baby, I'm back."

Faith sits comfortably in her ergonomically correct arm chair.

"Tell me what you have on," I repeat.

"OK. I have on a fitted black skirt. I think you would like it. It has a split on the side and a pink top that's fitted, with a wide, black belt. I thought about you when I picked it out."

"What kind of panties do you have on?" I turn the conversation up a notch.

"Travon!" she says shyly.

"Tell me, baby."

"I have on a pink thong," she whispers.

"Are you at your desk?"

"Yes."

"Pull your panties down to your ankles and hike up your skirt."

"OK," Faith says, practically panting.

"Why are you breathing so hard?"

"Because of what you do to me. You have me so wet."

"I know. Now take your fingers and wet them with your tongue and rub them on the outside of your pussy until . . ."

"Until I cum," she says, breathing heavier.

"Yes, baby," I say. "Rub faster."

"Mmm, Travon this feels so good. I wish you were inside me right now."

Within minutes, Faith is screeching into the phone and crossing her legs tightly. "Baby, I love you, Tray! Why do you do this to me?"

"I want you to remember that feeling," I say. "That feeling right now is how you have me feeling all the time. I can't wait until I can hold, taste, and smell you again."

"Baby, me too," Faith says, biting her bottom lip and trying to regain her composure.

"Call me later, OK?" I send my smile through the phone.

"I will, Love."

"Tray you know when you talk to me like that, it's like you're touching me through the phone with your soft hands," Faith says. "Can I tell you a secret?"

"Yeah, what is it?"

"I keep an extra pair of panties in my purse in anticipation of your calls."

Although Faith and I are hundreds of miles away from each other, erotic phone sex has kept us connected.

* * *

The next night at Illusions, after Fancy performs, Memphis can't wait to approach her.

"Hey, girl, I want to see you in my office later, so we can continue where we left off the other day," he whispers to her. "My cousin and I want a little private lap dance."

"OK, let me freshen up a bit. I'll be right there," Fancy says.

Fancy fears she has been found out, but her fear of Nate is far greater.

"You wanted to see me?" she says, when she arrives at Memphis' office between dances.

"Yeah, why don't you pour yourself a drink and relax a bit. We'll be right with you," Memphis says.

He turns back to Blackie, and they talk about their plan to move on Willie as if Fancy weren't in the room.

They discuss having four armed men storm Travon's mother's house to kidnap her Friday night.

"You sure you want to do that to the old bitch?" Blackie asks in character.

"Yeah, I'm sure, because they would never think about us doing that. We'll hold her ass hostage until we can smoke her son out of hiding–and then you know what we'll do to him."

"In the meantime, I want you to create a diversion at the club around the same time, lets say about 10, and while they worry about the club, they won't even think about her," Memphis continues.

"I know that Willie loves that boy's mother, and he'll never want to see anything bad to happen to her. He'll die for her. I know he will."

"Now we've got to keep this shit on the low. Nobody can know about this. We hit 'em late, we hit 'em hard, and we'll be home within a couple of hours."

Fancy absorbs every word.

"That sounds good, nigga, 'cause it's about time that I head home," Blackie says. "But nothing against Chi; ya'll sure know how to grow 'em," he adds, eyeballing Fancy.

"So, Cuz, can I have a little private time witcha girl here?" Blackie asks.

Memphis gathers a few things before leaving and says, "Shit, nigga, you know I don't care as long as ya' paying."

Memphis closes the door behind him.

As Memphis strolls around the club, he stumbles upon Desiree.

"Have you seen Fancy?" she asks.

"Yeah, she's giving a private show to my cousin right now. What's your rush?" Memphis says, trying to find out where Desiree's head is. "You not letting that girl blow your mind, are you?"

Desiree refuses to answer, and folds her arms like a schoolgirl who's not getting her way.

"She didn't tell me she was dancing for him." Her face sinks in disappointment.

Memphis grabs Desiree by the arm, hard. "She ain't got to tell you shit, but as long as she's in *my* club she's got to bring in the money. And if that means sucking a couple of dicks, I don't give a fuck."

"I'm trying to make her mine, and I want you and everyone else to respect that," Desiree says, defiantly.

"You need to watch yourself," Memphis warns. "I suggest you go out there and get your ass on stage before I . . ." Memphis leaves the words hanging.

Desiree storms away. She wants to first prove to herself that she is committed to Fancy, and for her that starts with breaking away all ties with her former lover, Angel. She thought Angel would one day come back to her, but now Desiree wants nothing more than total closure from her. As a matter-of-fact, she wants to hurt Angel as bad as Angel hurt her, when she chose a trick over their relationship. And she thinks she has figured out the perfect revenge.

"It's not over between us yet," she thinks to herself. "I just hope your mother doesn't have a heart attack in the process."

* * *

After leaving Blackie extremely satisfied, and walking out with $100 for her efforts, Fancy needs privacy to stop her own doomsday clock, but Desiree is not about to give her a precious minute to herself.

"What were you doing in there?" Desiree asks in an accusatory tone as she and Fancy stare each other down in the hallway.

"Gettin' paid," Fancy says, slowly wiping her smeared lipstick.

"Fancy, you know you don't have to do nothing you don't want to," Desiree pleads. "They can't make you do nothing," she says, tenderly putting both hands on her lover's shoulders.

Although Fancy wants to break away, there is something about Desiree that keeps her there. The two women embrace, until the moment is shattered by Memphis' voice on the microphone.

"Next to the stage is one of our premiere performers. Ya'll know who I'm talking about. But before I bring her out, I just want to say this. Today is her anniversary with Illusions. She joined my club exactly seven years ago today. Now everybody show some love for the club's Queen B, Desiree! Desiree, come on out!"

* * *

"You won't believe this, Willie!" Nate says, all in a rush after getting off the phone with Fancy.

Willie motions with his hand for Nate to calm down take a seat, before he calmly takes a seat himself.

"Them fools plan on hittin' Ms. Brown's house," Nate says, bracing for Willie's rage.

But Willie remains stone-faced.

"Did you hear me?" Nate repeats, as Willie lights a cigar and begins to cough uncontrollably.

Willie forces his cough down.

"Are you sure?" he asks Nate.

"Yeah, it's what Fancy told me. They suppose to hit her spot at ten o'clock Friday. They think this is a way for them to force Travon out into the open. They also plan on causing some problems over at the club to keep us busy here, so we wouldn't know what was going on."

Coughing more violently, Willie pounds on his chest before paging Cookie to bring him some water and pills.

"You OK, Willie?" Nate asks. "You don't look so good."

Cookie rushes in and quickly hands Willie two large white pills and a glass of water.

"When was the last time you took your medicine?" she asks, looking as worried as Nate, who is standing over his boss, patting him on the back.

"I'm all right y'all. It's OK. Cookie, baby, would you excuse us a minute?"

Cookie is reluctant to leave. "I'll be back in half an hour to check up on you."

"What's wrong, Willie?" Nate inquires. "You know you can tell me if something is wrong."

"You know what's funny, Nate? I've been stabbed, shot, hit by a car when I was a kid, and nothing could stop me. But I think, I finally found something that may beat me."

Willie's eyes are red, but Nate can't tell if it's from pain, fear, or anger.

"Who is it, Willie?" Nate asks, taking his gun out. "You ain't got nothing to worry about. I'll kill anybody who fucks with you."

Willie smiles. It's an oddly peaceful smile, Nate thinks.

"A bullet can't stop this enemy," Willie says.

"Well, what is it, Will?"

"What I'm trying to tell you, Nate, is that I don't have much longer on this earth. I have cancer, Nate. The doctor told me about a year ago that I had about eighteen months to live."

Nate grabs his mouth and lets out a screech the likes of which Willie has never heard.

"Can you fight it, Willie?" Nate is crying.

"They can't fix lung cancer, Nate. And nobody wants to put good lungs into an old pimp like me."

"I don't want to do nothing without you," Nate says. "I ain't nothing without Big Willie."

Willie has never shown any emotion toward another man that was physical, but he knows the main thing his killer needs right now is a hug.

"Come here, soldier," Willie orders. "Now you need to stiffen your upper lip. Ain't no time for crying. You hear me!"

"Yes, sir," a broken-hearted Nate replies.

"Nate, you will be taken care of when I lose this battle. I just want you to know that. I never thought I would be the one to write a will, but when it started to sink in, I knew I had to do it."

Willie sits back down behind his desk. He doesn't want to talk about the things he can't control. He only wants to talk about Memphis and Blackie's plan.

"So you say they want to hit her Friday night?" he says, scratching his chin. "I think I'll be waiting for them, and I'll have something with me."

The two men debate alternative plans for hours, until one comes to mind that seems perfect. The plan allowed for Willie, not Nate, to be in the house waiting for the kidnappers to show up.

"I'm going to send her to Florida to see the boy. I'll just tell her something like he needs to see her or something like that, and I will call him and tell him that I put her on the plane," Willie says. "I want you to make sure she gets to the airport."

"Gotcha, boss."

"We'll get her outta here by Wednesday, so we'll have plenty of time to set up like we need to," Willie says, coughing again.

As Nate leaves his boss's office, he tries to remain strong, but he feels weak inside. He closes the door, but he can hear Willie coughing inside. The violent coughing forces Nate up against the wall, and he looks up to god for help.

"Why didn't he tell me?" Nate asks, before collapsing in a heap in the hallway.

* * *

"So now that she gave away our plan, what are we going to do?" Blackie asks, confused.

"We change the plan," Memphis says, cutting his eyes at his cousin. "Man, sometimes it's hard for me to believe we're related."

"All right, nigga, don't get smart," Blackie says, angry that Memphis doesn't seem to respect him.

"One thing that you need to know is that Willie loves Travon's mom more than he loves himself. If I know him like I think, he's trying to get her as far away from her home as possible."

Confused, Blackie yells out, "Well, shit, nigga, didn't we want to get that bitch?"

"Nawh, fool!" Memphis says. "This ain't got nothing to do with her. She don't need to die because she brought a selfish-ass fool into the world. We're after big fish anyway."

"Oh, I see," Blackie says, still confused.

So Memphis makes it clearer.

"We're leaving tonight. Willie's gonna wanna do me himself. Nate fucked up his chance so, Willie being the G he is, he will try to take me out himself. He'll have Nate do some lackey shit like protect the boy's mom or some shit like that."

"Now I get it," Blackie says, his eyes lighting up.

"Willie is going to move Tray's mom, and if Nate's doing it, guess what that leaves us?"

Smiling, Blackie says, "That leaves us Willie all alone."

"Bingo, Nigga!" Memphis says with a smile. "There may be hope for you yet."

"Damn," Blackie says, shaking his head. "Nigga, how'd you get so gangsta?"

"'Cause I live this shit, Blackie, and I learned from a good teacher."

"Who, nigga? Me?"

"You wish, fool. I learned from the biggest hustler of them all, Willie."

"Now it's time for the student to school the teacher."

CHAPTER 41

"HELLO, MAY I speak to Tray?" a woman asks, trying to disguise her voice over the phone.
"This is Tray. Who's speaking?"
"You don't recognize my voice?"
"Faith?"
Nicole drops the fake voice.
"Who is Faith?" she demands.
"Nicole! What's up? Why are you stalking me?"
"Who is Faith?" she repeats, warming to the role of crazy ex-girlfriend.
I refuse to go down that road.
"What do you want, Nicole?" I ask, irritated.
"I want to know who Faith is."
"She's a friend. A close friend," I respond, hoping she would take the hint.
Under her breath, Nicole mutters, "Yeah, I bet."
"Anyway I was just calling because as you probably know, Taylor asked me to be the godmother of her child, and I know you're going to be the godfather.
"Yeah, and your point?"
"Well, I was calling to bury the hatchet with us. I'm not mad at you anymore, and I've moved on. I have a boyfriend who's all the man I need. He caters to my needs, and he is just the best . . ."
I cut her off.
"Look, Nicole, I'm happy for you. I really am. But what does that have to do with me? I've moved on as well, and to be quite honest with you, I've never been mad at you, only disappointed."

My words still have a way of stinging Nicole, who seems like she's looking for fight.

"That's right. How can you be mad at someone you never loved anyway, right?" she responds.

"Look, Nicole, I think you're crazy. You really need to seek professional help, and don't think I don't know that you befriended Taylor just to get next to me."

Nicole laughs hysterically and tries her best to deflate my ego.

"It's fine that you think so highly of yourself, Travon. Like I told you, I'm *engaged* to a wealthy man who worships the ground I walk on, unlike you. You had a good thing with me, and you messed that up. I wouldn't come back to you if you begged me."

"Fine, Nicole. I'll send you a wedding gift in the mail," was my snappy reply.

"I don't want your sympathy, Travon," Nicole says. "I just want an apology."

"An apology?" I burst out, laughing, "For what? *You* lied to me! You were the one stripping and whoring around. What's funny is that you flipped and got all religious on me, and you were the one out there sinning worse than me!"

"Excuse me, but don't act like you don't like strippers and whores. Don't think I didn't hear about what went down at Darnell's bachelor party. Oh, yeah, I heard about it, Tray. So you wanna talk about lying, right? I think her name was Angel or something like that. Oh, yeah, I heard about it. Your frat Chris has got a big mouth."

Before I could interject, Nicole continued to throw darts.

"You wanna hear something really funny? Chris sold you out to get with Janet. Yeah, you didn't think I knew about her either, did you? After Chris told Janet that you were fucking a stripper at Darnell's bachelor party, she didn't want anything else to do with you. What's really funny is that run-over-shoes Chris is with Janet right now."

Nicole's words silence me.

Even though I was happy with Faith, I was furious that bucktoothed Chris told Janet about what I did with Angel. But that explained why Janet never called me again.

"What's the matter, Tray? The great reporter is without words? You were out there doing worse than me. I just hoped that you used protection, because you are not invincible."

"Look, I've gotta go, crazy lady."

"You owe me an apology, Tray, and I'm not going anywhere until I—"

Click.

"That mutherfucka was throwing salt like that?" I think back on my relationship with Chris trying to remember any missteps.

I don't sweat it that much, though. The way I figure it, if Chris needed to put me down or put my business on blast to get a piece of ass, then more power to him. After all, I'm happy with Faith and want our relationship to move forward. But one thing Nicole said does bother me: the fact that I didn't use protection when I was with Angel.

That was a form of risk-taking that I usually don't engage in.

"I must have been a damn fool to run up in that girl raw. Well, at least my dick didn't break out with a case of the mumps."

I shake off my conversation with Nicole, and return my focus back to work.

RINNNNNNNNGGG!

"I know this is that crazy-ass girl again."

I snatch up the phone.

"What now, Nicole!"

"Tray. It's me, Faith," my girlfriend responds. "Who is Nicole?"

"Nobody, she's just a crazy woman from Milwaukee who's going to be my best friend's baby's godmother. I'm going to be the godfather. It's a long story . . . but anyway, how are you?"

"I'm fine. I wanted to give you some good news. I closed a couple of deals and I want to come see you."

"That'll be great, baby. When are you talking about?"

I take inventory of my desk calendar to view my upcoming schedule.

"Well, I'm online right now and I can get a one-way ticket there for $39 and be there tonight."

"Do it, baby! I already filed my blog so I should be done by nine o'clock."

"I can just take a taxi to your house," she says, "so you won't have to drive all the way to the airport to pick me up."

"Great, baby. I will see you tonight."

"Tray, I have to tell you something," Faith says, gaining my full attention. "You are a thirst that's never quenched. There's never enough of you. I need to see you more and be with you more."

"I miss you too, Faith."

"You don't get it. I mean, I sleep in your shirt every night. I didn't want to wash it because I didn't want to wash your smell, our smell, out of it."

"Baby, we'll talk more tonight when you get in."

"I know you have to get to work, baby. I will see you tonight. I love you."

Warmed by the words, I say, "I love you, too."

* * *

"Memphis, why did you recognize Desiree with that anniversary bullshit the other night?" Blackie asks, while strapping up for the battle.

"It wasn't bullshit, it was real," Memphis says.

"OK, but why did you do it? I mean the flowers and shit," Blackie says. "That shit seemed a little soft to me."

"Listen Blackie, we're about to do some serious shit, and I needed to know if my main girl has my back."

Memphis explains that Desiree has never been one to lie to him, and her actions showed him that she has no idea that Fancy is a plant.

"How do you know?" Blackie asks.

"Because I can see it in her eyes–she's in love. Fancy done got to her. You would see shit like that, if you weren't so busy beating up on your women all the time."

"Of course," Memphis adds, "once we take care of our business, I'm going to deal with Fancy in my own special way." He stuffs some things in a black duffel bag before the two men leave his office.

On the way out, Memphis reminds Desiree to keep an eye on things, and that he is going to take care of a few things on the south side of town with Blackie.

"OK, baby, I got it," Desiree says. She pauses for a moment, "Can you do me a favor, Memphis, since you're heading that way?"

"What is it?"

"Can you drop a package off for me?" she rushes to grab a thick package from her purse. "I was going to mail it to Angel's mom, but if you wouldn't mind dropping it off, I would appreciate it," Desiree flashes her smile.

Before Memphis can answer, Blackie speaks up: "We ain't got time for that shit bitch. We've got business to take care of."

As Blackie heads for the door, Memphis quietly takes the package from Desiree.

Memphis tells his cousin that the package is their alibi.

"Nigga, you really should think sometimes before you open your mouth," he says, before hopping into his truck. "Now we're going to drop this package off and keep on to Milwaukee."

Blackie shakes the overstuffed envelope like a child would a gift under the Christmas tree. "You don't even want to know what's in it?" he asks.

"To be honest with you, I don't care," Memphis says, snatching the package from Blackie and throwing it on the backseat.

* * *

"How you going to leave a sister like this when I'm due any day now?" Sandra pouts.

"You are not due for nine days. I'll be back in two," Faith says, as she packs her carry-on bag.

"I can't tell," Sandra says. "You're packing like you're going for weeks."

Faith ignores her friend's complaints.

"Where is Angel?" she asks Sandra.

She left with that white girlfriend of hers. By the way, did you see the pictures she got back from Wal-Mart the other day? I think they're in her room; I'll go get you one."

"That is so cute," Faith says when Sandra returns with the family photo of Angel and her two babies. "I'm going to take one of these wallet sizes right now."

"So with your relationship with Mr. Miami getting serious, what are you planning to do?" Sandra asks.

"What are you talking about?"

"I mean, I haven't heard you talk about a man this much in a while. Shoot, girl, I've never heard you talk about a man this much ever. Is your biological clock ticking?"

"No, it's more like my heart is ticking. And it ticks harder and harder every time I'm around him," she says, tucking the picture into her wallet. "I can't explain it. I've never thought about a man this much. He really means a lot to me."

Faith is packed and ready—more than ready—to go.

"OK, girl, give me a hug, and I'll be back before you have that baby," she says, gathering her things for the airport.

"You'd better be back in time," Sandra says, "because I got a feeling she's going to come and not wait for anyone."

Faith knows her best friend is scared of having her first child. Sandra took a huge chance picking her lover over her husband, and although this man said he was going to stay by her side, he changed his mind and decided instead to be with another woman.

* * *

"Throw the package on the porch and let's go," Memphis instructs his cousin.

"I still think we should open it. For all we know, this can be something that'll come back on you."

"Nah, Blackie, what we're about to do will come back on us soon enough."

On Interstate 94 north to Milwaukee, very little is said in the truck, and Memphis insists on listening to Bill Withers' "Ain't No Sunshine" on repeat.

"Damn, Cuz, I know you thinking about your wife over there, but do we have to hear this song one more time? I mean, damn, Cuz, I've heard it twenty fuckin' times. It's depressing. Let me put something else in," Blackie ventures as he reaches for the radio dial.

"Touch that dial and I'll kill you first," Memphis says without taking his eyes off the highway.

"Look at you, Cuz, got that game face on," Blackie jokes. "I guess it's Bill Withers then, huh?"

"Ain't nooooo sunshine when she's gone. Onnllllly darkness everyday. Ain't no sunshine when she's gonnne. This house just ain't no home, every time sssshe goes awayyyyyy," Blackie sings along, while looking at the passing cars.

Soon the only thing he hears is Memphis hitting the eject button.

"What are you about to put in now, Cuz? The instrumental?"

Memphis surprises him and puts in James Brown's "It's a Man's World."

Blackie's applaud. "That's what I'm talking about. My daddy used to listen to that."

Soon Memphis is exiting the highway in Racine, the midway point between Milwaukee and Chicago.

"Are we stopping for gas?" Blackie asks, "'cause it looks like you're sitting on half a tank."

"You don't think we're going to drive this truck right up in there and do what we got to do, do you? I called in a favor and we're switching vehicles," Memphis says, parking behind a '80s Oldsmobile.

"The keys should already be in it," he tells Blackie as the two men get out of the truck.

"Damn, is there nothing that you didn't plan out?" Blackie asks.

"I haven't decided how I'm going to kill Willie yet," Memphis says before speeding off.

* * *

Meanwhile, the package that they dropped off on the porch is whipping up a whirlwind that stretches from Chicago to Atlanta—and beyond.

When Faith's plane touches down in Miami, she turns on her cell phone and quickly notices seven messages from her mother.

"Oh my god, what's going on?" she wonders as people rush past her to exit the plane.

"Mama?" she says, when it rings through. "Mama, what's going on?"

"Did you get my messages?" Faith's mother, Mary Houston, asks.

"I just saw you called, and I called back. What is it?"

"I don't know how to tell you this, Faith, but I got a package on my doorstep, and it has a bunch of pictures of Angel in it and, oh my god." Mary is hysterical.

"What is it, Mama?"

"She's doing all kinds of things . . . with her roommate."

"All kinds of things like what?"

"Sex things, Faith. Freaky sex things!"

"What! Are you sure?" Faith believes her mother is mistaken, or has been pranked.

"They not fake. She has her head where it shouldn't be, and that Desiree's head and mouth is in places where it doesn't belong. I didn't know she was like that," Mary cries.

Her mother's conviction convinces Faith that the photos might be real, but she still doesn't want to believe it.

"Well, Mom, I'm in Miami on business. Can you mail the pictures out to me in a day or so, when I'll be back at home? I'll talk to her, but maybe those photos are fake."

On the taxi ride to Travon's condo, she can't get those images out of her head–that her sister may be gay or other.

"I need to bounce this off Sandra," she thinks as she phones home.

"Sandra, is Angel there?" Faith asks.

"No, she left with her friend. I don't know if you've met this white girl. They were going to pick up something to eat, but Kane and the baby are here.

"Hold on a minute, he wants to talk to you," Sandra says, handing the phone to Kane.

"Hey, Auntie Faith, I love you."

"I love you, too, Kane. Can you put Sandra back on the phone? I have something important to ask her."

"OK. Auntie Faith, can you bring me back a Transformer toy?" he asks politely.

"I'll try, Kane, but I don't know if I'm going to have time. Now put Sandra on the phone, OK?"

"What is it, girl? All this boy has been talking about is Transformer this and Transformer that," Sandra says.

"Sandra!" Faith screams. "I need you to pay attention because I have to ask you something really quick–I'm almost at Travon's house."

"What is it?"

"I just go off the phone with my mother, and she told me somebody dropped off a package of pictures with Angel in them doing all kinds of sexual stuff."

"Well, you know she ain't nothing but a little freak anyway," Sandra says, lowering her voice so Kane doesn't hear.

"I know, girl, but these pictures are with her *female* roommate." Faith is so embarrassed, she's shaking.

"You're kidding!" Sandra gasps. Kane mutters the same thing in the background.

"Hold on, girl, let me go into another room because that boy is repeating everything that I'm saying."

"I think the pictures are fake," Faith says taking up for her sister without even seeing the evidence.

"How do you know? I bet you they're real. You know what? That white girl she's friends with seems like she would get down like that," Sandra says, peeking out the window to see Angel and her friend on their way back with two bags of Chick-fil-A.

"Look, girl, I'll call you back. I'm going to do some snooping," Sandra says, rushing back to the couch in the front room.

"Wait, Sandra, don't do . . ."

Click.

"Sandra? Sandra! Shoot, why did I tell her anything? Well, I can't worry about it now," Faith thought. "I'm going to see my man. I just hope he's ready for me."

"That will be $45," the cabbie says.

"That's about the same as the plane fare here," Faith thinks as she pulls bills from her purse.

As she walks up to the condo, she sees only faint light coming from Travon's window, but it's enough to let her know that he's waiting for her.

His front door is ajar, and Jodeci's song "Freek'N You" is coming from one of the back rooms.

"Travon? It's me, Faith," she says, poking her head in. "Where are you?" she calls out as she walks toward the bedroom.

When she opens the door, she sees an inviting bed with rose petals spread over the sheets. She removes her coat and starts to peel out of her formfitting brown wrap dress.

"So you don't want to see me in my dress? I picked it out just for you," she says, smiling and breathless with excitement.

As she slips into the bed, she notices a note on the pillow.

"Turn off the radio, listen to the iPod next to the pillow, and close your eyes," it reads.

"But how do you want me, baby?" she says in the candlelit, romantic atmosphere.

She places the earphone in her ear, slips off her silk underwear and hits play.

The song is Jodeci's "Love You 4 Life."

Lying on her back, Faith begins to sing the chorus lightly. She closes her eyes, relaxes, and lets the song wash over her.

Soon, she feels the warm touch of my nakedness against her body.

I place my shirt over her face so she can smell my pheromones, and she squeezes it and inhales, while I part her legs.

Deep, wet, controlled kisses along her inner thighs are the perfect aphrodisiac to bring Faith close to screaming. As I feel her losing herself, I quickly move my attention to her breasts and clavicle bone with light kisses and licks.

"I want you so bad, love," I confess as I remove her earpiece.

"Baby, take me now," Faith says, grabbing my hip bones to force me on her.

"Please don't tease me," she whimpers.

I turn her over on her stomach and slide inside her wet opening effortlessly from behind.

"Oh my god, Tray," Faith moans with pleasure. "I don't ever want to leave you."

Faith twines her legs around mine, locking me in position.

With one arm wrapped around Faith's waist I clasp my free hand over hers. We move in beautiful unison, and my breathing becomes heavy on the back of Faith's neck.

"You don't have to hold it, baby. Let it go inside me. Please," she says, thrusting her bottom against me, until I scream out and plunge her hips deeper into me.

"I'm coming, baby," I announce biting the side of Faith's neck and sending her into a wild, wake-up-the-neighbors orgasm.

I fall asleep inside my woman.

* * *

"Where are we going to hit this fool up at?" Blackie asks as Memphis parks in an alley about three blocks away from Willie's club.

"I'm glad you asked, Cuz, because this is where you come in," Memphis says, smiling at how his plan seems to be falling right into place.

"I need you to go into that bar right there and dial this number," Memphis says, handing Blackie a business card with a local number on it.

"Who is it to?" he asks.

"It's the boy's mom," Memphis says. "Tell her that the boy is in trouble and that he will be dead in twenty-four hours. Tell her that Willie is behind it, and if she wants to see the boy alive to have Willie do what he needs to."

"You sure this is going to work?" Blackie mistakenly doubts his cousin.

"Don't question me, boy." Memphis spews the words at Blackie.

After ten minutes, Willie and Nate storm out of the club and head to Thelma's house, but they're stopped short when they're pulled over five blocks later by an undercover squad.

Memphis and Blackie are parked a block away, and they watch the situation unfold from a safe distance.

"Why are you pulling me over, officer?" Willie asks, agitated.

"Sir, step out of the car."

The cops rattle off a bunch of trumped-up charges against Willie and handcuff him to take him in for booking.

"You know this is bullshit," Willie yells as he's placed in the backseat of the unmarked car.

"We'll let your partner go, if he has a valid driver's license," one of the cops says.

"Don't worry Willie, I'll be right behind you to get you out," Nate says.

"Where are ya'll taking me?" Willie asks.

"Downtown," one of the officers says.

"Keep on to Thelma's house," Willie tells Nate, "and call Cookie and have her come downtown and get me out. But get to Thelma's first."

As one of the officers escorts Nate back to Willie's car, he warns Nate to be careful, or they will take him downtown as well.

Nate speeds off to Thelma's wondering if anything else can go wrong tonight, as the squad makes off with Willie.

"That's our cue," Memphis says, following the squad.

"Where are they taking him?" Blackie asks.

"Be patient, Cuz. You'll see soon enough."

As soon as Nate pulls up in front of Thelma's house, she runs out.

"Where is Willie?" Thelma demands. "What did he do to endanger my son?"

Before Nate can try to explain anything to Thelma, he has to call Cookie to get Willie out of jail.

"Let me use your phone right quick, Thelma, and you don't have to worry about nothing–that's just some fools playing with you," he says, rushing to the phone.

"Cookie, this is Nate. We got pulled over about twenty minutes ago. You have to do downtown and get Willie outta jail."

Cookie goes straight to the safe and takes out what she is sure will be more than enough money to cover Willie's bail. Cookie is the only other person that Willie trusts with the combination to the safe. When she rushes downtown to get Willie, she is told that no one by that name has been brought in or picked up.

"He's gotta be here," she insists, and makes both the sergeant and captain check the police blotter.

"No one like that has been picked up or brought in tonight," the captain assures Cookie.

Fear grows in the pit of her stomach. "Oh my god," she says as she runs out of the station to the car and races over to Thelma's house, tears streaming down her face.

When she arrives, she is on the horn until Nate emerges from the house.

"Nate! Nate!" she screams. "Somebody's got Willie. The cops said nobody like that was picked up tonight."

"What's going on?" both women scream at Nate.

"I don't know, but it don't look good. Look here, take this, Cookie," Nate says, handing her his gun. "I want you both to stay here until I call you."

* * *

"Where do you want him?" the cops ask before dropping a beaten Willie off at an abandoned apartment about three miles north of his club.

"Y'all did good," Memphis says, handing the two dirty Chicago cops an envelope full of money.

"Put his fat ass in that chair right there," Memphis motions with his hand.

Blackie soon comes out of the darkness. "Damn, nigga, you did it," he says, surprised.

"Sometimes in order to kill something small, you have to take out the biggest fish. And this right here is the biggest of them all," Memphis says, slapping Willie's bloodied face.

"Wake up, Willie. Wake your ass up 'cause I'm not finished with you yet," taunts Memphis.

"Yo, Cuz, get this nigga up," Memphis says to Blackie.

"How you expect me to get him up? Shit, they damn near killed him. It's ain't much left of him. What did they beat him with? A bag of bricks?"

"Move outta the way," Memphis yells before slapping Willie out of the chair and onto the dirty, crumbling linoleum floor.

Despite the blood, Willie is able to regain some level of consciousness.

"What tha fuck is this," Willie slurs, trying to pull himself up.

When he sees Memphis's face, he suddenly realizes the danger he is in.

"You know where you are, Willie?" Memphis asks. "Of course you don't. This here is where I used to live when I lived here. In this small-ass apartment with three other people," he says, looking around. "This place has a lot of memories. This right here is where my wife was raped. I think you had something to do with that."

"And this will be the place where they find your body."

Willie raises himself up enough to lean his back against the wall.

"Do you feel like a big man now?" he asks Memphis.

"You know you're a dead man walking, and your cousin and his entire family are dead, too," Willie warns.

"What the fuck is he talking about?" Blackie yells.

"Don't worry about it, Blackie, this is what you call a dead man's last wish," Memphis says.

"I just want to know one thing, Willie. Why did you have to go after my wife?"

"She was already dead. I sold you a lemon, nigga." Willie spits blood. "I knew with a bitch like that you would never amount to shit, so I wanted to fuck you twice. I fucked her when I sold her to you, and I knew she would fuck you over and over again and keep you small-time. You ain't shit, Memphis and you will never be shit," Willie manages a laugh.

Memphis wails on Willie, kicking and punching him until there is no more breath and very little blood left in him. The dirty walls and floor run red.

"Let's go, Memphis," Blackie pleads. "We really got to go."

"Not yet, go to the car, and bring me the gas can in the trunk. I want these memories burned to the ground."

Memphis pours a gallon of gas on Willie, and with the flick of a lit match sets his rival and his old apartment on fire.

"Burn in hell, you bastard," he says, before he turns and walks out.

Memphis and Blackie drive in silence, first back to Racine to get Memphis's truck, and then the rest of the way home to Chicago.

So what about Fancy, Blackie asks, breaking the silence.

"After what I did, I think Nate will handle that for us," Memphis says. "But I think I may be leaving Chi soon. And you gotta get outta here now, Cuz, because it's about to get wild."

* * *

"What do you want for breakfast, baby?" I patiently wait to take Faith's order.

"Can I have you?" she asks, joking as she hugs me in the bed. "But before I do that, can I use your phone to call my mother? I forgot to charge my cell last night."

"Go ahead."

Faith walks over to the phone and notices the flash.

"Tray, do you know you have twenty messages on here?"

"Yeah, it's a long story, but I have this stalker from back home who keeps calling. She's crazy, so I turned my ringer off."

"A stalker?"

"Yeah, hold on a second, I'll let you hear a couple of them," he says, reaching for the play button.

"You have twenty-one messages. Message one:"

"Travon, this is your mother. I'm calling to see if you're safe. I got a call saying that someone was going to kill you, and I'm worried to death. Oh god, please call me as soon as you hear this."

"Message two: Travon, I'm going crazy! Call me right away. I tried you at work, and they said you were not there."

"What the hell is this?" I wonder aloud without listening to the other messages. "Somebody is out to kill me? Let me see what's going on."

I speed dial my mother's number. She picks up on the first ring.

"Mom, what's going on?"

"Oh my god, Travon, are you OK?"

"Yes, I'm OK. What's going on?"

"Someone called here saying they were going to kill you over a debt Willie owed them, and now we can't find Willie. We think something crazy has happened to him. Nate is out looking for him. Come home, baby! I'm scared."

"I'm on my way, Mama. I promise you I'll be safe. I love you, too."

I turn to Faith, who sits wide-eyed and silent.

"Tray what on earth is going on and who is trying to kill you?"

"I have to go to Milwaukee," I manage.

"Something bad has happened, but I don't know what yet."

I jump off the bed, grab a small suitcase from the closet, and start packing.

"I'm coming with you," Faith says.

"You sure?" I say with a blank stare, as I pull my things together at a frantic pace.

Faith dresses quickly and repacks her bag.

"Baby, I'm sure everything is going to be fine," she says, hoping to calm me, but it's clear I don't believe it.

When we get to the airport, we split up to try to find the first available flight to Milwaukee. My cell rings, "Faith, any luck?"

"I found one that leaves in an hour," she tells me. "How about you?"

"Nothing yet. Just book it, and I will meet you in a few minutes."

Faith has always been good in a crisis—especially when it's someone else who needs help. And she has long dreamed of meeting Travon's mother, but she never imagined that it would be under these circumstances. She prays that everything will be OK, but the look on Travon's face worries her. There is something that he is not telling her, and she needs to know why he is being so secretive.

On the flight, we barely speak. I am tense and vigilant as I stare out the small window. Faith caresses my hand.

"Oh, shit, one detail I forgot," I pause. "I didn't even call work."

"Don't worry, baby, I took care of that, I called from the airport and said that you wouldn't be in due to a family emergency."

I'm surprised and grateful that Faith met my need before I even realized I needed it.

"Thank you, baby," I kiss her forehead.

"I spoke with a woman named Maria. She seemed nice," Faith adds, "but really nosy."

"Yeah, she's like my little sister. I'm sure she's worried. The entire office is probably wondering what's going on."

"She wants you to call her as soon as you hear something. And she said she would be praying for you."

When we land in Milwaukee, I zip to the nearest rental car desk. I try to reach my mother and Willie by phone as we drive to the old neighborhood. No luck.

When we pull up in front of his mother's house, two boys approach the car and tell me that everyone is at the club.

"Hey, little man, what's going on?" I ask the youngest boy. "Have they found Willie yet?"

The boy is about to tell him, but the older boy shakes his head.

"Come here," I call out to the oldest boy, who's standing on my mother's porch with a .45 caliber visible in his waistband.

The boy strolls over to the car, his jeans sagging, leans in the passenger-side window, and says simply that he was told not to say anything else.

"How bad is it?" I ask, not sure that I really want to know.

"It's bad, dude," was the only clue the boy gave. "But we got your back, Tray."

Faith's eyes water up.

"I'm sorry, Tray," Faith says.

"Don't cry, we really don't know anything yet," I say, screeching off to the club. "It's going to be all right."

When I pull up outside the club, I count six squad cars and two detective cars. Police tape is strung around the perimeter, but I storm through it as Faith struggles to keep up.

Two officers stationed at the door restrain me, and I emphatically state, "I'm Travon Brown! I'm a relative! Let me in!"

The commotion brings out Nate, Cookie, and my mother.

"He's dead, Travon!" his mother wails as she grabs hold of me.

"No! No! No!" I crumple to the sidewalk. "Mama, no! What happened? Who did it? Whooooo?"

Nate lifts me to my feet and pulls me inside the club, past the dancers crying beside the door, past the clutches of men vowing revenge for Willie's killing.

"What happened?" I keep asking Nate, who is oddly mute.

"What did you do?" I demand as I grab Nate by the shoulders.

Faith is aghast as the tussle threatens to become an all-out fight.

"Tray, pleasssseeee," she yells.

It's enough of a distraction that Nate gains the advantage and pins me to the floor.

"Do you really want to know?" Nate asks, leaning nose-to-nose with me. "Well, calm your ass down, son, and I'll tell you."

I take a deep breath, exhale slowly, and nod. Nate rises and helps me up.

"Come with me," Nate says, putting his arm around my shoulder as we walk outside to the back of the club.

Faith follows them until Nate spins around and asks, "Who's that?"

"Travon's my boyfriend," she answers timidly.

"You need to move on 'cause this is family business," Nate says, rolling his eyes and taking inventory of this intruder.

"It's all right, Nate," motioning for Faith to come back. "She can stay."

"All right," Nate says, but he eyes Faith warily.

"So, Tray, somebody called your mama and told her there was a hit out on you, and she called Willie and told him, and we tried to come over to the house. But on our way we got stopped by some supposed-to-be cops who took Willie away."

"When Cookie went to bail him out, MPD said they never stopped anybody like that."

"They found Willie dead in a burned-out apartment house this morning."

"Who did it, Nate?"

"Memphis."

"But why, why did he do it?"

"'Cause of you."

"What the fuck are you talking about?"

"You fucked that bitch at the bachelor party, remember? You embarrassed him in front of his hos! You crossed the line of disrespect, Tray."

"You mean all of this is over that stripper, Angel?"

"Yeah," Nate says. And then, almost nonchalantly, "and because I killed his wife."

"What? This can't be serious." I sink to the ground, my back against a wall.

"All of this is over Angel?" I repeat. "All over Angel."

Faith walks slowly to me and kneels.

"Tray, you keep mentioning the name Angel. This sounds crazy," she says, trembling. "But is this . . ." she hands me a wallet-sized photo of her sister, Kane, and the baby.

My face tells the entire story.

"Where did you get this?" I say shoving the photo in her face.

Nate snatches the picture out of my hand and stares at me and Faith.

"What is it, Tray?" he yells. He jerks his head at Faith. "Who is this? Don't tell me this is the bitch that's at the bottom of all of this."

Nate pulls his pistol from his waistband and points it at Faith's chest.

"You want me to blast this bitch, Tray? Give me the word, boy, and I'll do it."

He cocks the hammer.

"Pleaseeeee, no," Faith cries, before Travon steps between her and Nate's gun.

"Put the gun down, Nate!" I bark. "Put it down now!"

Nate slowly lowers the gun, and shoves the photo into my chest before turning away cursing.

I take time now to really look at the image of Angel, Kane, and her daughter, and I'm overcome with emotion.

"I thought she only had one child?"

I look at Faith for answers.

"She has two. When she moved in with me, she was already pregnant."

"Did you know all along?" I finally ask Faith.

"No. I swear, Tray, I swear I didn't. Why would you think I would know?"

"How could you not know, Faith?" I search deep into Faith's eyes for the truth.

"She's a liar!" Nate yells. "A fuckin' liar!"

"I can't deal with this shit right now, Faith."

I turn toward Nate and walk away from Faith.

"It's time for you and me to ride," Nate says. "You ready for war?"

He hands me a gun.

"We need to do this right and do it tonight."

"I know."

I follow Nate to Willie's car, as Faith begs me not to go.

Before getting in, I turn toward Faith and tell her, "Nate's right, this is war."

Nate and I drive off.

Faith gets in the rental car and slams the door. She puts her head down on the steering wheel when her phone rings.

"Hello,"

"So how's the trip going, sis?"

CPSIA information can be obtained
at www.ICGtesting.com
Printed in the USA
LVHW011007120722
723235LV00001B/41